Matt Beaumont has never work...
he has never met anyone who d...
a single advert in his life. Not o...

He has a vaguely informative w...

Praise for Ma... ......

'A page-turner and a triumph . . . makes Beaumont's position as
one of Britain's best comedy writers more permanent'
Daily Express

'Lively, viciously funny and about as switched
on as a novel can be'
Mirror

'A brilliantly plotted comic novel . . . It gave me more
sense that literature is alive and kicking than anything
else I've read in these twelve months'
Sunday Times

'Depicts the Machiavellian scheming and summary
sackings of the ad world in withering detail and with
no shortage of dead-eye wit'
The Times

'One of the most enjoyable reads of my life! I was enchanted
within seconds . . . clever and extremely funny'
Marian Keyes (in *The Independent*)

Also by Matt Beaumont:

e
The e Before Christmas
The Book, the Film, the T-Shirt
Staying Alive
Where There's a Will
Small World

Matt Beaumont

Illustration by Holly Beaumont

BLACK SWAN

TRANSWORLD PUBLISHERS
61-63 Uxbridge Road, London W5 5SA
A Random House Group Company
www.rbooks.co.uk

E SQUARED
A BLACK SWAN BOOK: 9780552775656

First published in Great Britain
in 2009 by Bantam Press
an imprint of Transworld Publishers
Black Swan edition published 2010

Addresses for Random House Group Ltd companies outside the UK
can be found at: www.randomhouse.co.uk
The Random House Group Ltd Reg. No. 954009

MIX
Paper from
responsible sources
FSC® C016897

Typeset in 11/14pt Sabon by Falcon Oast Graphic Art Ltd
Printed and bound in Great Britain by Clays Ltd, St Ives PLC

2 4 6 8 10 9 7 5 3 1

The Random House Group Limited supports The Forest Stewardship
Council® (FSC®), the leading international forest-certification organisation.
Our books carrying the FSC label are printed on FSC®-certified paper.
FSC is the only forest-certification scheme supported by the leading
environmental organisations, including Greenpeace. Our
paper procurement policy can be found at
www.randomhouse.co.uk/environment

This story is dedicated to the memories of
Adam Theokritoff and Mick Devito.

Saturday
Mood: optimistic

From: **Janice Crutton**
To: Beverly Crutton, Sarah Franks, Geraldine Crutton and 17 others . . .
Sent: 20 December 2008, 14.18
Subject: The Crutton Chronicles, Volume 8

Well, here we are again. Another year, another catalogue of ups, downs and in-betweens. Mostly ups, it has to be said. It's been a good year chez Crutton. As is the custom in these circular missives, I'll take you through the highlights, though contrary to the norm, I'll try not to make my children sound too amazing.

Let's start with the head of the household. David has thrown himself into his new job with abandon. In fact, he's at the office now – he's slowing down a little these days, but he's still of the opinion that God was a slacker for taking Sunday off. As most of you know, he started as The Man (MD in old speak) at Meerkat360 four months ago and he's enjoying himself immensely, though he's still uncomfortable referring to himself as The Man. And, if truth be told, he still chokes a little when he has to say Meerkat360 out loud. He's from an age when advertising agencies were named like accountancy firms rather than pop groups. And to conclude this subject, I think he'd really like to be allowed to call it an advertising agency (which it is! It does adverts) rather than a Thought Collective. But, bless him, he's adjusting to the new orthodoxy, the gist of which seems to be that there is no longer any orthodoxy.

He's thrilled that he managed to mark his first few weeks with a big assignment from Esmée Éloge to launch a raft of celeb perfumes. He led the pitch with all the gusto of old and, as a result, next Christmas you can expect in your festive hampers the alluring scents of Vanessa Mae, Sienna Miller and Margaret Thatcher. No, I made that last one up!

One final note on David – lest you fear this is turning into the DC Annual Report – he has managed to find the time to take up meditation. It really has transformed his outlook and he is sweetness and light personified.

[saved as draft]

From: **Janice Crutton**
To: David Crutton
Sent: 20 December 2008, 14.27
Subject: It would be nice to know . . .

. . . that you're going to leave the office for long enough to put in an appearance this weekend. If you hadn't left at dawn this morning, I would have reminded you that we're supposed to be going to Kath and Graeme's tonight. Would you like to come and at least make a pretence of being a functioning couple?

By the way, I'm writing the annual circular. Anything in particular you want me to include?

From: **David Crutton**
To: Janice Crutton
Sent: 20 December 2008, 14.30
Subject: Re: It would be nice to know . . .

I'll be there. Though if I have to listen once again to Graeme run through each and every one of the 3,452 stations on his digital radio ('which, with splendid irony, Dave, has been designed to look precisely like a fifties valve set!'), I will ball up his ironic fucking tank top and shove it down his ironic fucking throat.

Maybe you could have a word with Kath.

The family circular: nothing I want you to mention; plenty I don't. Meditation for one.

    David Crutton
    T⊢E ΜΛN

Jesus, I cannot go on like this.

From: **David Crutton**
To: Alex Sofroniou
Sent: 20 December 2008, 14.32
Subject: email issues

As head of IT, your first job on Monday morning is to explain to me why every time I type my name at the foot of an email, 'The Man' appears in a typeface that wouldn't have been out of place in *Space 1999*.

Your second job is to make it stop.

The alternative is that I will have to stop signing emails. Which will make me seem rude. Which demonstrably I am not.

Thank you for your cooperation in this matter :-)

See?

David Crutton
THE MAN

Oh, for fuck's sake.

From: **Janice Crutton**
To: Beverly Crutton, Sarah Franks, Geraldine Crutton and 17 others . . .
Sent: 20 December 2008, 15.06
Subject: The Crutton Chronicles, Volume 8 [continued]

On to Noah. I'm delighted to report that number-one child is flying. I must say that David and I were a little baffled by his A-level choices (drama, chemistry and Polish), but he wants to leave the actor/quantum chemist option open for as long as possible. And I suppose, if nothing else, he'll always be able to communicate with his plumber. To his credit, he's really making it work. As I write he's in his room, revising for his mocks.

He's maturing into a wonderful young man. He really looks out for Tamara and it's lovely to behold the growing sibling bond. We have every confidence in Noah. This is going to be his year: stellar A-level results and then on to RADA. Or Quantum Chemistry at the University of Lodz!

[saved as draft]

From: **Janice Crutton**
To: Noah Crutton
Sent: 20 December 2008, 15.12
Subject: List

Since you are intent on recreating last summer's Glastonbury behind a locked and barricaded bedroom door, this is the only way I have of communicating with you. A to-do list:

1   Please turn your music down.
2   If you have dirty laundry in there, chuck it on to the landing. Or are you planning to leave it until it's ripe enough to make its way to the washing machine under its own steam?
3   Please tidy your desk.
4   And while you're at it, look for the stuff I Googled for your biochemical thermodynamics assignment.
5   Which you have to hand in on Monday.
6   Dad and I are out tonight. Can you keep an eye on your sister? I don't want to come home and find a WPC babysitting her again.
7   You are working up there, aren't you? (Remember: biochemical thermodynamics, MONDAY.) I don't know how you can concentrate with that racket. I know that I can't.
8   So *please* turn the music down.
9   I'm making a sandwich. Interested? Or do you have a stash of food?
10 TURN THE BLOODY MUSIC DOWN!

Mum x

	MSN:
NoahsDark:	jus got e from mum
Rialto:	woss her want??
NoahsDark:	sez turn muzik down
Rialto:	she sad. u listening 2 dethrush?
NoahsDark:	track 3. nuns with cocks
Rialto:	wkd guitar @ 4:23. turn it up!
NoahsDark:	trak jus started. mum sez she goin out 2nite. wanna cum over?
Rialto:	kool
NoahsDark:	txt karl madz lulu benny stevo kell seb freddy dev jono chris f. chris b. kriss kyle kevo sash deb dazza an tarkz
Rialto:	party? dubble kool

NoahsDark:	tell em iz byob. dad went mentalist last time coz we drunk hiz wisky
Rialto:	doin im a fava. it woz rank
NoahsDark:	sed it woz malted or 50 yrs old or sumfink
Rialto:	must hav bin off then. u got 2 guitar yet?
NoahsDark:	almost. 4:15. kranking up vol . . .
NoahsDark:	wo! dat kikz muthafukin ass! way2go geeza!!

From: **Janice Crutton**
To: Noah Crutton
Sent: 20 December 2008, 15.17
Subject: TURN IT DOWN!

For God's sake, I asked you to turn it down, not up. I now have plaster dust in my coffee. Thanks for that.

From: **Janice Crutton**
To: Beverly Crutton, Sarah Franks, Geraldine Crutton and 17 others . . .
Sent: 20 December 2008, 15.18
Subject: The Crutton Chronicles, Volume 8 [continued]

Tamara, too, is blossoming into a lovely young woman. Kind, sensitive and, though I say it myself, very pretty. It's a big year for her as well. GCSEs in June and I'm pleased to say that, like her brother, her nose is to the grindstone.

And, like her brother, she's no stranger to drama. She made an exceptional Cecily in the school production of *Earnest*. She looked a picture in crinoline and was a proper Edwardian lady. According to the review in the local paper, she was 'the epitome of modesty and decorum'! I'm tempted to scan it in and attach it to this, but that would be sad, wouldn't it?

[saved as draft]

	SMS:
Mum:	Where are you?
Tam:	Shopping 4 your krissy prezzy Why?
Mum:	Dad and I are going out. Need you home by 6
Tam:	Cool – xxx

	SMS:
Tam:	Where da fuk are you bex???
Bex:	Still in thresher. Fukker wants id
Tam:	Flash your nix. Usually works
Bex:	Worked! Wearing my pink ag provs!
Tam:	Hurry! Tongue hurts like fuk. Need to kill pain. Whose lame idea was stud??
Bex:	Yours???
Tam:	Yeah yeah. Get something good Pinot grigio. Not chavdonnay
Bex:	OK!
Tam:	Mum txtd. She's out 2nite
Bex:	Party?
Tam:	Party! Txt jess helz hollz gaz billy max em elly ali jem hatty bella si kirst kitty s. kitty d. maz girl-sam yaz boy-sam saffy

From: **Janice Crutton**
To: Beverly Crutton, Sarah Franks, Geraldine Crutton and 17 others. . .
Sent: 20 December 2008, 15.24
Subject: The Crutton Chronicles, Volume 8 [continued]

Last and most definitely least, me! I'm still making a decent fist of juggling corporate law and parenthood, though I must say it gets easier as the kids grow older and more responsible. We had a busy year at Bancroft Brooks. Redundancies last March doubled the workload for those of us that remained. Nothing terribly exciting to report. I was mentioned in despatches for my handling of RTZ's acquisition of . . .

As I said, nothing exciting to report.

But I'm happy and I have my health, and doesn't that become increasingly important year on year?

A brief round-up of the other Cruttons:
> Courtney was 17 last week (about 1,000 in cat years).
> Henry Hamster sadly passed away. Tamara's eighth Henry and, though she buried him with the usual tears, her last. She is definitely growing up.
> The fish are well. They send their regards.

I've attached a pic of the four of us in Sardinia last summer. Please try to ignore the tum! I've lost 9lbs since then. And yes, that glint in Tamara's nose is a stud. After not a little pressure, we finally gave in. We've drawn the line though. Definitely no tongue stud!

That's all from us. I hope you're all well. And I hope you all have fantastic Christmases and wonderful New Years.

All our love,

Janice, David, Noah & Tamara
xxxx

Sunday
Mood: **sober**

From: **Janice Crutton**
To: Jon Parkin, Sita Brahmachari, Blair Krempel, Aneil
          Bedi, David Glass, Pippa Reedy, Justine Rogers, Kuo
          Lee Chien-Fu, Ron Hanlon, Hazel Park
Sent: 21 December 2008, 09.12
Subject: Apology

I will be round later to apologize to each of you in person, but since I have you in my contacts as the Neighbourhood Watch group, I thought I'd rattle off an early e to register our sincere regret at what took place last night.

Firstly, I want to assure you that neither David nor I sanctioned the party. Certainly if we had, we would have stayed home to keep a discreet eye on things and we would not have allowed our children to invite the 250+ that the police claimed turned up.

(Personally, I feel it was definitely no more than 200, but that is splitting hairs.)

However, David's and my obvious horror does not absolve us of our responsibilities. We should not have allowed it to happen and we are deeply, deeply sorry for the horrendous noise and also for the unforgivable abuse that some of you endured. I don't suppose it's any consolation at all, but our house now resembles Ground Zero.

Sita, I promise that Noah will be round later to clean the graffiti from your wall. And, Blair, please let me know what the vet charged for stomach-pumping your beautiful Burmese.

Once again, I am sincerely sorry and I hope that, in time, you can find a way to forgive us.

Janice Crutton

From: **Janice Crutton**
To: Kath Hunter-Firth
Sent: 21 December 2008, 09.23
Subject: Thanks

Hi Kath,

First of all, thank you so much for last night. The meal was truly wonderful. You are such an adventurous cook. Honestly, I wouldn't have a clue where to buy goat's tongue, let alone what to do with it.

I must apologize for David though. In mitigation, he has been terribly overworked, but that doesn't excuse his grouchiness. Please assure Graeme that he wasn't casting aspersions at his digital radio. He loves anything digital. It was the stress talking, as well as, I suspect, a certain amount of male gadget envy!

I'll get you guys over here soon. I will attempt to do something thrilling with chicken breast and my husband will prove what an utter charmer he really is.

Thanks again and Christmas hugs,

Janice x

From: **Janice Crutton**
To: David Crutton
Sent: 21 December 2008, 09.31
Subject: Question

So, while I am cleaning vomit off the floors, the walls and (incredible but true) the half-landing skylight, while I am trying to figure out how to get fluorescent pizza grease out of an ivory sofa, while I'd rather not figure out the provenance of the stains on our duvet, while I am grovelling on my knees to our neighbours because of our children and to my best friend because of you, where the hell are you?

Oh, that's right, work.

Honestly, what can be so important that it keeps you away from your imploding family? Happy bloody Christmas, David.

From: **David Crutton**
To: Dotty Podidra
Sent: 21 December 2008, 09.35
Subject: Still in bed?

As my longest-serving PA (is it really seven years?) you should be fully conversant with my views on sleep. Get up, eat your croissant/Coco Pops and get your arse in here. I need you to show me how you do frog accents on Word. Can't do the angled thing on the second e of Esmee and the first of Eloge, which, in a letter to the CEO of Esmee Eloge, is not good form.

And I need coffee. Not bloody decaf. I can tell the difference.

	SMS:
Bex:	You awake tam?? Has your mum killed you?? Does she know about tongue stud?? Txt me asap!!

Tam: Tamara won't be texting you because her mother has confiscated her phone. And no she didn't know about the tongue stud. But she does now. Thanks

Thursday
Mood: **turkey**

From: **David Crutton**
To: Ted Berry, Caroline Zitter
Sent: 25 December 2008, 14.44
Subject: 2009

I trust you're both having excellent Christmas days. I know I am.
There's nothing better for one's concentration than a deserted
office in a deserted West End. That being the case, I decided to
come in to gather my thoughts on the year ahead.

There is no doubt that Meerkat360 is an exciting young company.
The two of you have pooled your considerable talents to found a
visionary agency, fully tooled up to provide highly creative, web
2.0-enabled marketing services.

I sense your continued resistance to my appointment, but as owners
of 75% of your venture, Aspire Invest has a right to protect its
stake in any way it sees fit. In their wisdom, they see me as that
protection. Boring as it must seem, we need to focus on the bottom
line. If we don't, come Christmas '09, Meerkat360 will be but an
entry on our respective CVs. It *is* that serious. Dazzled as your
backers are by your creativity, Aspire is in the business of profit,
not arts subsidy, and they *will* pull the plug. We are in the worst
recession in living memory and they will not suffer financial runts.

There is genuine hope. We have a solid base upon which to build. Our existing clients signed up because of your credentials as box-free thinkers. Unfortunately, to date, not one of these accounts has been run at a profit. We must turn this situation around.

To this end, the winning of Esmée Éloge marks a new dawn. This is an A-list cosmetics brand and I intend to take a hands-on approach with this client, thus demonstrating the meaning of profit-oriented account management.

Also, early in the New Year, I hope to be able to reveal the identity of another new client, one with a marketing budget that closely resembles a bottomless pit. If I succeed in signing them up, our problems will ease considerably.

In the meantime, may I suggest that you consider some simple New Year's resolutions that will assist the move into credit?

Caroline, as the partner responsible for strategic thinking, perhaps you can illuminate me on the stratagem behind Primordial Ooze Therapy. Call me old-fashioned, but I question the wisdom of taking ten key employees to Iceland to wallow in mud during a period of global financial meltdown.

And, Ted, far be it from me to fathom the creative mind, but I do wonder at some of your appointments. Does the Creative Department really need a hairdresser? Since I see no legal way of passing on the cost of highlights and pageboy bobs to our clients, I recommend you stick to hiring designers, art directors and writers who can produce billable items of work.

Finally, I must put my foot down. The completion of the office refurb (which, I feel obliged to remind you, was commissioned before my arrival) will mark the start of a moratorium on cap ex. Until we have turned the financial corner, such items as pinball tables and sensory-deprivation think tanks are luxuries we can ill afford.

I apologize for my bluntness, but I would be doing both you and

Aspire Invest a disservice if I failed to speak as I found. And if we're honest with one another, we *can* turn this around: 2009 is a new year – Year Zero, in fact.

For now, a happy Christmas to you both.

David Crutton
THE MAN

PS: One other change I would like to institute in January is a transition to more conventional job titles.

From: **Caroline Zitter**
To: David Crutton
Sent: 25 December 2008, 14.45
Subject: Out of Office AutoReply

I am attending the Jesus: The Original Sales Wiz seminar in Bethlehem. I will return on Monday 5th January.

Caroline Zitter
THE SEER

From: **Ted Berry**
To: David Crutton
Sent: 25 December 2008, 14.59
Subject: Re: 2009

I'm having a smashing Christmas, thanks, big dude. Testing the reach of my iPhone on the foothills of Aconcagua! Christmas dinner here means a can of chickpeas and a few gasps on the oxygen cylinder.

I take exception to the hairdresser jibe. Kirsten has made a significant contribution to my department's output. The human brain is an amazing organ and there's strong anecdotal evidence that if you wrap it in a cutting-edge barnet, its left-side performance is enhanced significantly. It's no coincidence that during his most fertile period, Bowie sported some of the wackiest hairdos in pop history. As soon as he got the bank-clerk cut in the 80s he went right off the boil.

Fair play on the other thing though. Caroline's solution to every problem is a self-awareness awayday.

So who's this new super-rich client? Do tell. Don't worry about me blabbing. I've only got a monosyllabic Argie Sherpa and some stray llamas for company.

Gotta go. Paco tells me Trevor Beattie has broken camp at 4000 metres. If that cunt beats me to the top of this motherfucker, I'll never be able to show my face in Shoreditch House again.

Ted Berry
MC IDEΛZ

Sent from my iPhone

From: **Janice Crutton**
To: David Crutton
Sent: 25 December 2008, 15.17
Subject: Christmas dinner

Tamara, Noah and I have gone to your sister's. Your turkey's on the ceiling.

Monday
Mood: resolute

From: **David Crutton**
To: Dotty Podidra
Sent: 5 January 2009, 08.58
Subject:

Switch that fucking iPod off, get your arse in here and push down the plunger on my cafetiere. Every time I try, it sends up a scalding jet of coffee. And would you mind disposing of the tinsel vomit around your workstation? In case you haven't got there yet, it's January.

From: **Róisín O'Hooligan**
To: All Staff
Sent: 5 January 2009, 09.00
Subject: It's not bloody Christmas any more . . .

. . . so is anyone going to take down the tree in reception? It's dropping needles like a bastard, and isn't it bad luck for it still to be up?

Róisín
Reception

From: **Ted Berry**
To: Susi Judge-Davis-Gaultier
Sent: 5 January 2009, 09.04
Subject: help

yo sooz get in here do me e cant type frostbite a fucker

From: **Susi Judge-Davis-Gaultier**
To: Ted Berry
Sent: 5 January 2009, 09.05
Subject: Re: help

Be right in, sweetz. Just preparing your hot poultice. (Is llama poo microwavable?!)

From: **Ted Berry**
To: All Staff
Sent: 5 January 2009, 09.15
Subject: New Face

Welcome back to the glamour factory, guys. And now you're here, say hello to a new boy. He's called Yossi and he joins us as our in-house musician. He's a lovely bloke, full of energy, enthusiasm and top tunes. I'm sure he'll be a massive asset to the Creative Department.

Click below to see his online CV.

Ted Berry
ΜC IDEΛZ

<u>yossiriffs.com/biog</u>
Yossi Mendoza
A Life in F#

BORN TO AN ISRAELI MOTHER AND A PERUVIAN
FATHER, YOSSI'S MUSICAL TRAINING BEGAN IN

THE WOMB, WHERE HIS MOTHER PLAYED HIM BLUES, NORTHERN SOUL AND BAROQUE MADRIGALS.

He owns a large collection of instruments, including violin, harp, glockenspiel, banjo, Fender Stratocaster, nose flute and the actual harmonica used by Larry Adler to pleasure Princess Margaret aboard the Royal Yacht Britannia.

Yossi can turn his hand to compositions in any genre from light opera to hip-hop. He has created epic symphonies and mood-drenched soundscapes for exhibitions, corporate videos and weddings. He also finds the time to work with educationally challenged teenagers, running the acclaimed Bavarian Oompah Workshop in Brixton.

Yossi's ultimate ambition? To create an epiphanic fusion of Schönbergian twelve-tone composition and Scandinavian death metal.

From: **Liam O'Keefe**
To: Bill Geddes
Sent: 5 January 2009, 09.18
Subject: what's that stench?

You let one off again?

From: **Bill Geddes**
To: Liam O'Keefe
Sent: 5 January 2009, 09.22
Subject: Re: what's that stench?

It's llama cack. Just caught Susi in the kitchen heating it up on the new Aga. She says Ted's come back from the Andes with both frostbite and a traditional Argentinian remedy. But she assured me it's 100% organic, so that's OK, then. We can safely warm up our spaghetti hoops at lunchtime.

You seen Ted's all-staffer?

From: **Liam O'Keefe**
To: Bill Geddes
Sent: 5 January 2009, 09.24
Subject: Re: what's that stench?

Just read it. Exactly what we need, eh? A strolling minstrel, wandering the corridors, soothing our creative birthing pains with song . . .

Oh, hang on, can I hear the fucker? Is that a fucking nose flute?

From: **Ted Berry**
To: Creative Department
Sent: 5 January 2009, 09.30
Subject: New Facilities

As you'll have noticed, a bunch of hairy-arsed Poles have spent their Christmases getting scabby knees and calloused hands on your behalf. I hope you appreciate their efforts and think of them as you enjoy your fully reconfigured and radicalized Creative Department.

The three beach huts (bought for a song from Herne Bay Council) are intended as creative retreats. Enter and tell the world to fuck off.

The new basement Romper Room is solely for your use. I give you Wii, PS3 and good old-fashioned Lego. And give the ball pit a whirl. It's wicked – you can see why pre-schoolers are hooked. I promise you, an hour in there will give you an excellent cardiovascular workout as well as inspire some boundary-free thinking.

Ted Berry
MC IDEAZ

PS (mostly for Harvey): the 'grass' on the floor of the creative conference room ISN'T REAL. It's plastic. So please don't bring your rabbit in to graze. It'll fucking die.

From: **Sally Wilton**
To: All Staff
Sent: 5 January 2009, 09.31
Subject: New Facilities

I am pleased to announce that the office refurbishment is now complete. To ensure the smooth and efficient operation of the new facilities, the following guidelines should be noted.

1   Kitchen: wet clothing should not be placed on the new Aga for the purposes of drying as this represents a fire hazard and will invalidate any insurance claim. Also, various health and safety directives prohibit the proving and baking of bread and other yeast-based foodstuffs.
2   Sessions in the SenzDep Think Tanks™ situated beside the post room must be booked with reception. Swimwear must be worn. Strictly no 'skinny dipping'.

Thank you for your cooperation.

Sally Wilton
PRINCESS
PAPERCLIP

Q   What smells like Diego Maradona's septic tank and
     sounds like a Radio 3 history of Balkan funeral music?
A   Meerkat360 on the first day of term.

Ted has returned from the Andes, pissed that Beattie jammed his
pole in the summit first and he's taking it out on us with a potent
mix of world music and the stench of the pampas.

Times have changed. In the olden days, Simon Horne would
make do with shouting at us in poor French. (I wonder what he's
up to. Any sightings?) Mind you, this is getting more like the
olden days in some respects. I told you Crutton is now at the
helm, flailing about like a dad trying to body pop at the school
disco. He carries a permanent look of incomprehension and a
small leather cosh to beat off street hawkers and the weirder
creatives. Actually, I haven't seen him resort to violence once
since he got here. He does seem a lot calmer. Maybe he's discovered God. Or Ritalin.

Continuing the theme of Twats Reunited, another Miller Shanks
refugee joined in December. Tell Vince to brace himself: Susi is
Ted's new PA. She hasn't changed much except that now she's
triple-barrelled – Susi Judge-Davis-*Gaultier*. She married a
Frenchy, a very distant relative of the fashion queen himself.
She's predictably vocal about the connection, though I don't suppose Jean Paul has registered that he now has a total fuckwit
dangling from the family tree like a label-dressed gibbon. Her
skirts are shorter than ever. Her gynae needn't bother getting
her in for an exam any more. He just has to sit opposite her on
the tube.

Final Miller Shanks link: remember Nigel Godley? Speccy God-
botherer in accounts, used email as a prototype eBay. No,
he's not here. But Neil his identical twin is. The two of them are

indistinguishable. Exactly like Mary-Kate and Ashley. Only you wouldn't want to fuck them. No, really you wouldn't.

So how am I, you ask? How am I doing in the agency that's so cutting-edge you slice your finger on the lift button? So love-struck with postmodernism that several meeting rooms have been laid with turf? I hate it, if you must know. I have no idea what the job is any more. We're not allowed to just do ads these days. Everything has to be viral-guerrilla-left-field-pushing-the-envelope-out-of-the-box-and-up-the-shitter-of-convention *different*.

A for instance: just before Christmas we brainstormed a list of celebs for some new perfumes. We flicked through *Nuts* and *heat* and came up with the usual suspects, plus Helen Mirren and Kirsty Wark to add a bit of class. Ted took a look and said, 'Bollocks. Too fucking predictable. Gimme something different . . . Gimme Margaret Thatcher.'

Margaret Thatcher? She wasn't hot when she was twenty-one. These days she dribbles out of the side of her mouth, for fuck's sake. What's she going to smell of? Piss and meals on wheels? What next? Eva Braun and *Eau de Zyklon B*?

But as I write, Maggie's stroke-skewed mug adorns an A1 board and is on its way to Rotterdam for presentation.

I should be happier, really I should. The office was done up over the break with the design brief of taking it as far away from Dilbert-style cubes as possible. A Good Thing, you'll agree. But coming in this morning was like the big reveal at the end of *Changing Rooms*. You walk in to see your front room transformed into an MDF Persian whorehouse when all you wanted was a bit of beige and a nice tartan throw for the sofa.

There's barely any room in my office now that the company-issue pinball machine is in here. I hate pinball. I put in for a one-armed bandit (making the sound business argument that, given my luck on the wheels of fruit, it would turn a handsome profit), but I was told we'd need a gambling licence. Their point being . . .?

I'm only thirty-seven, but I'm too old for this. I've come to realize that, actually, I just want a Dilbert-style cube. And a brief I can get my head round. And some workmates from the same planet – or at least from one in the same solar system. Weary of convention, Ted no longer hires on the strength of portfolios of fresh and original ideas. No, he's wowed by offbeat haircuts and interesting psychiatric reports (on which topic, some day I'll tell you about Harvey Harvey). And the average age of this lot must be fifteen. They look at me funny because I can actually draw a layout – you know, with a pen, like it's a fucking goose quill. The next time one of the spotty gobshites asks me if I remember the days when Whitney Houston wasn't a crack whore I'll floor him. Or her. I don't care.

You know it's come to something when your only mate is a suit. He's called Bill. He's thirty-six and we reminisce about Eternal, Mis-teeq and smoking in pubs. Give us rocking chairs and pipes, I say. Though obviously you'd have to put the rockers in a field fifty miles from the nearest human settlement on account of the FUCKING SMOKING BAN.

Jesus, I'm ranting now.

How are you? I still can't believe you shipped out. I know we've got the congestion charge and Harpo Marx for mayor while you've got 24/7 sunshine and Gary Neville for a neighbour, but Miller Shanks Dubai? What were you thinking? Anyway, give me news. Has Vince had a fatwa declared on him yet? Write soon. If there's any consolation to being thirty-seven, it's that I'm now mature enough to admit I miss you.

Liam

From: **Susi Judge-Davis-Gaultier**
To: Ted Berry
Sent: 5 January 2009, 09.39
Subject: Fwd: Please tell Ted I'm very, very sorry but I won't be able to come in

Hi Ted. I just got this email from Harvey. Should I call his care worker?

Begin forwarded message:

> From: **Harvey Harvey**
> To: Susi Judge-Davis-Gaultier
> Sent: 5 January 2009, 09.38
> Subject: Please tell Ted I'm very, very sorry but I won't be able to come in
>
> As I was leaving my flat this morning I was abducted by the Swampies of the Third Moon of the planet Delta Magna who plan to sacrifice me to their god, Kroll. Don't worry because I know what to do. This is exactly what happened to the Doctor (Season 16, 1978). Assuming I manage to find the Fifth Segment (which is most likely disguised as an ancient Swampy relic), I will be able to get Kroll to ingest it when he emerges from the marsh. Then he will be disabled and the inhabitants of Delta Magna will once again live in peace.
>
> All being well I should be in tomorrow. Please give my apologies to Ted and tell him that even though I'm quite busy with the threat of Kroll and everything, I'm still thinking about the Murray Mints brief and I've had quite a few ideas already.
>
> Harvey Harvey

From: **Neil Godley**
To: Kirsten Richardson
Sent: 5 January 2009, 09.43
Re: hair appointment

Hi Kirsten. I was wondering if you could fit me in for a quick trim at lunchtime. I'd normally nip out, but I'm up to my neck in reconciliations.

From: **Kirsten Richardson**
To: Neil Godley
Sent: 5 January 2009, 09.47
Subject: Re: hair appointment

I'm strictly a Creative Department resource. Ted's orders. Even if I wasn't I've got a perm, three highlights and a mega backcomb to do over lunch. Soz – Kx

From: **Bill Geddes**
To: Kazu Makino
Sent: 5 January 2009, 10.12
Subject: Donald

What time is his flight to Rotterdam?

From: **Kazu Makino**
To: Bill Geddes
Sent: 5 January 2009, 10.14
Subject: Re: Donald

11.30

From: **Bill Geddes**
To: Kazu Makino
Sent: 5 January 2009, 10.15
Subject: Re: Donald

So he's not coming in to pick up the presentation boards?

From: **Kazu Makino**
To: Bill Geddes
Sent: 5 January 2009, 10.16
Subject: Re: Donald

He'd have to move like Billy Whizz, so I doubt it.

From: **Bill Geddes**
To: Kazu Makino
Sent: 5 January 2009, 10.18
Subject: Re: Donald

Since the purpose of the meeting is to present the boards, not much point in him going at all. DC will go ape if he finds out. I'd better get in touch with him.

	MSN:
Bilge:	Where are you?
Dong:	Stansted.
Bilge:	Know why you're going to Rotterdam?
Dong:	To present the celebrity long list to Esmée Éloge.
Bilge:	So why are the boards still by your desk?
Dong:	Forgot them. Also forgot toothbrush and concertina thingy of photos of my nieces. Totally stressed out.

Bilge: What have you got to be stressed about?

Dong: Stansted.

Bilge: It's just an airport terminal.

Dong: Yes, an airport terminal that connects to a potentially lethal aeroplane.

Bilge: Ah.

Dong: And when it crashes, I won't even have my concertina thingy of photos to comfort me.

Bilge: You need to relax. What are you doing?

Dong: YouTube.

Bilge: Perfect distraction. What are you looking at?

Dong: Did search for plane crashes. 8,534 matches.

Bilge: Stop it! Stop it right now!

Dong: But planes are crashing ALL THE TIME.

Bilge: Repeat after me: flying is statistically safer than driving, crossing road and brushing teeth.

Dong: Bollocks.

Bilge: OK, not brushing your teeth. Unless the bathroom light bulb goes and you unwittingly squeeze Maxoderm on to your toothbrush.

Dong: Maxoderm?

Bilge: Erectile enhancement cream. Probably wouldn't kill you. It would give you a very stiff tongue though, which could lead to asphyxiation.

Dong: Are you trying to distract me?

Bilge: Yes.

Dong: It isn't working. Do you know that if you look carefully at 9/11

	footage, you can see Satan's face in the smoke?
Bilge:	Now you're being ridiculous. Pull yourself together and type 'chill out' into search box. You'll get soothing videos of tropical fish, lava lamps and Enya.
Dong:	Can't chat. Situation worsening. Thick fog. Going to talk to Kazu re options. Over and out.

From: **Milton Keane**
To: All Staff
Sent: 5 January 2009, 10.27
Subject: Workies?

Are there any work-experience bods free to do some vox pops in Soho Sq? Free pastries for the successful applicant. Caroline's out and I'm on my New Year diet,* so they'll only go stale!

Milton Keane
Assistant to Caroline Zitter

*Diet sponsorship form on my desk for anyone that hasn't yet signed up. It's for PETA – Caroline's favourite charity, so a v.v. worthy cause!

From: **Donald Gold**
To: Kazu Makino
Sent: 5 January 2009, 10.29
Subject: travel arrangements

Kaz – look into the possibility of me getting on a boat to Rotterdam ASAP.

From: **Kazu Makino**
To: Donald Gold
Sent: 5 January 2009, 10.31
Subject: Re: travel arrangements

Your meeting is at 2.00. Think a boat might be on the slow side. And aren't you at Stansted? No boats. Just big shiny planes.

From: **Donald Gold**
To: Kazu Makino
Sent: 5 January 2009, 10.33
Subject: Re: travel arrangements

FYI, there's a pea souper engulfing the entire airport. Just trying to be proactive here. Ferry timetable, please.

From: **Kazu Makino**
To: Donald Gold
Sent: 5 January 2009, 10.36
Subject: Re: travel arrangements

I'll look into it. Not a cloud in the sky in the West End, by the way. Also by the way, you left the boards by your desk. Don't you need them?

From: **Donald Gold**
To: Kazu Makino
Sent: 5 January 2009, 10.37
Subject: Re: travel arrangements

I'll busk the presentation. The boards are crap, anyway.

From: **Kazu Makino**
To: Donald Gold
Sent: 5 January 2009, 10.39
Subject: Re: travel arrangements

You're going to mime perfumes? That I'd love to see. Especially when you get to *DDaring* by Jodie Marsh.

From: **Donald Gold**
To: Kazu Makino
Sent: 5 January 2009, 10.40
Subject: Re: travel arrangements

Very funny. Hold ferry search! Sirens going off. Jesus, it's 9/11 all over again.

	MSN:
Dong:	Bollocks, bollocks, bollocks. Not fog, after all.
Bilge:	Sounded like wishful thinking. What was it?
Dong:	Smoke. Catering supply truck went up outside. 120 airline dinners burning like the Springfield Tyre Dump. What the hell do they put in those meals? Firemen pouring foam on it now. Still, all the shenanigans mean flight's been delayed.
Bilge:	A silver lining in every cloud (of smoke).

From: **Dotty Podidra**
To: All Staff
Sent: 5 January 2009, 10.48
Subject: Workies?

Are there any workies free to dust the leaves on David's kentia palm?

Dotty Podidra
Assistant to David Crutton

From: **Susi Judge-Davis-Gaultier**
To: All Staff
Sent: 5 January 2009, 10.49
Subject: Workies?

Any workies free to apply Savlon to Ted's frostbite?

Susi Judge-Davis-Gaultier
Assistant to Ted Berry

From: **Róisín O'Hooligan**
To: All Staff
Sent: 5 January 2009, 10.50
Subject: Workies?

And when the workies are done palm polishing and ointment applying maybe they can take down the bloody tree, which is still bloody here and on top of everything else it bloody well smells of cat wee.

Róisín
Reception

From: **Darren Bates**
To: Asif Mohammed
Sent: 5 January 2009, 10.59
Subject: emergency!

In-flight meals for BJ404 to Plovdiv up in smoke! Some sort of spontaneous combustion. My guess is too much saturated fat in the new-recipe lasagne. Flight booked with Bulgarian weight-lifting team. Anticipate they'll be v. hungry and/or popped up on steroids. Not a good combination. Any chance you could get down to the Bishop's Stortford Subway and buy 120 jumbo turkey-breast subs?

Darren Bates
Ground Operations Manager, Stansted

BizzyJet™
The Best Way is a BJ

From: **Neil Godley**
To: David Crutton
Sent: 5 January 2009, 11.10
Subject: hairdressing privileges

Hi David

I must bring a serious matter to your attention. I have been told that access to the company hairdresser is restricted to the Creative Department. In my opinion, this policy is not in the egalitarian spirit of a so-called 'Thought Collective'.

All I wanted was a trim.

I look forward to your views on this matter.

Neil Godley (Accounts)

From: **Janice Crutton**
To: David Crutton
Sent: 5 January 2009, 11.11
Subject: Tam

What time will you get off tonight? I'll be stuck in a partners' meeting until seven. One of us needs to be home early-ish to have a word with Tamara. I've had a call from school. She's been excluded from PE on account of her tattoo. Did you know anything about this? Apparently it's on her thigh and it's of a skull with a dagger through the eye socket. It only shows because the gym shorts she insists on wearing are so small they're practically a thong.

What is it with her fetishes for exhibitionism and self-mutilation? Please get home and talk to her because I'm at a total loss.

And you and I need to talk. About something else. Entirely.

    Janice x

From: **Ted Berry**
To: Susi Judge-Davis-Gaultier
Sent: 5 January 2009, 11.12
Subject:

agony get in here do e 4 me

From: **Ted Berry**
To: David Crutton
Sent: 5 January 2009, 11.15
Subject: Esmée Éloge

I just walked past Gold's office and saw Maggie T. She's supposed to be in Rotterdam getting the arse presented off her. Why has the stupid cunt left the boards here? I thought you were going to be hands-on with this account, David.

From: **Susi Judge-Davis-Gaultier**
To: Milton Keane
Sent: 5 January 2009, 11.17
Subject: need love and latte!

Ted's fingers look like big fat sausages and he's been making me do his emails for him all morning. I don't mind, honestly, but he just literally forced me to type the C word! I feel sick now and my hands are still shaking. I'm trying so hard to get on with him, but he makes it impossible. What am I going to do? Starbucks in 5?

From: **Milton Keane**
To: Susi Judge-Davis-Gaultier
Sent: 5 January 2009, 11.18
Subject: Re: need love and latte!

Cazza's out so I'm free! (God, that makes me sound sooooo gay.) Starbucks in 2.

From: **David Crutton**
To: Janice Crutton
Sent: 5 January 2009, 11.19
Subject: Re: Tam

Not sure what time I'll make it out of here. Should we think about a boarding school for Tam? Didn't do me any harm.

From: **David Crutton**
To: Janice Crutton
Sent: 5 January 2009, 11.20
Subject: PS

What's the other thing you want to talk about?

From: **Janice Crutton**
To: David Crutton
Sent: 5 January 2009, 11.21
Subject: Re: PS

Not something for email. Later. Please get home at a reasonable hour.

From: **David Crutton**
To: Ted Berry
Sent: 5 January 2009, 11.23
Subject: Re: Esmée Éloge

Gold's a useless pillock. I'll get on it. I must say, though, that I have misgivings about presenting deliberately whacky celebrity names to a company as essentially conservative as Esmée Éloge. Aren't they looking for the likes of Keira Knightley and that woman who used to stand in the middle in Destiny's Child?

Incidentally, is the new office troubadour an example of the new fit-for-purpose hiring policy? I'm intrigued.

From: **David Crutton**
To: Kazu Makino
Sent: 5 January 2009, 11.24
Subject: Esmée Éloge

Tell me, how is your boss planning to present the Esmée Éloge work without the actual work? He's either a genius or a complete twat. Let him know I want a full debrief the second he returns.

From: **Ted Berry**
To: Susi Judge-Davis-Gaultier
Sent: 5 January 2009, 11.25
Subject:

if back from coffee run need you do e

44

From: **Ted Berry**
To: David Crutton
Sent: 5 January 2009, 11.29
Subject: Re: Esmée Éloge

If Esmée Éloge had wanted 'conservative', they'd have gone to Miller Shanks. They came here because they wanted outer-rim thinking and I'm fucked if I'm going to disappoint them.

On your second point, Yossi is here because I intend to restore the jingle to its rightful position in British advertising. Some cunt is going to produce the next Shake 'n' Vac and I intend that cunt to be working at Meerkat360.

Capisce?

From: **Susi Judge-Davis-Gaultier**
To: Milton Keane
Sent: 5 January 2009, 11.31
Subject: C word again!

Twice in one e!!! Feel so tainted.

From: **Milton Keane**
To: Susi Judge-Davis-Gaultier
Sent: 5 January 2009, 11.33
Subject: Re: C word again!

Remember what I told you. Ted is just a naughty potty mouth and he gets a kick out of upsetting you. The best way to beat him is to rise above it. Be strong, Sooz. And maybe book a soothing sesh in the Think Tank.

From: **David Crutton**
To: Neil Godley
Sent: 5 January 2009, 11.34
Subject: Re: hairdressing privileges

Discussions on the status of the office hairdresser are ongoing. In the meantime, I suggest you forgo the trim. By the way, if you bother me with this crap again I will come down to the basement and cut your hair myself. Nicky Clarke I'm not.

David Crutton
THE MAN

From: **David Crutton**
To: Alex Sofroniou
Sent: 5 January 2009, 11.35
Subject: why isn't this bollocks sorted out yet?

David Crutton
THE MAN

From: **David Crutton**
To: Caroline Zitter
Sent: 5 January 2009, 11.36
Subject:

I sent you an email on Christmas Day. A response this month would be nice.

From: **Caroline Zitter**
To: David Crutton
Sent: 5 January 2009, 11.37
Subject: Out of Office AutoReply

I am out of the office attending Business Goals Through Buddhism III. I will return on Wednesday 7th January. If you have an urgent request please contact my assistant, Milton Keane, on milton@meerkat360.co.uk

Caroline Zitter
THE SEER

From: **Kazu Makino**
To: David Crutton
Sent: 5 January 2009, 11.38
Subject: Re: Esmée Éloge

Hi David. Donald had the boards redone over the Christmas break. He made a call to check out the lighting in the Rotterdam meeting room and felt a matt finish would work better than gloss for presentation purposes. Hope this is OK.

Kazu Makino
Assistant to Donald Gold & Bill Geddes

	MSN:
Kazoo:	DC knows you forgot the boards. Gave him some plausible BS. You owe me.
Dong:	I'll bring you clogs. If I make it back alive.
Kazoo:	Man, you're so melodramatic.
Dong:	No, I'm not. Waiting to board and can see my plane through the window. There's a man with a spanner tightening something on the engine. He can't be more than seventeen. He has spots. How can he possibly know what he's doing?
Kazoo:	I'm only twenty-three and I know exactly what I'm doing. Relax.
Dong:	You've got a first in geophysics, but you wouldn't know how to fix

Kazoo:	a jet engine. See my point?
	But I would know to trust the man with the spanner and probably several diplomas in jet-engine maintenance.
Dong:	Looks like a spanner you'd get in a cheap 72-piece set from B&Q. Fine for bikes and lawnmowers. Wholly unfit for making adjustments to something as finely tuned as a jet engine.
Kazoo:	FYI, a modern turbofan generates over 100,000 lbs of thrust and heats up to around 700 degrees centigrade. I think it can take a whack from a cheap spanner.
Dong:	700 degrees? Jesus, that's . . . That's really hot. *Dangerously* hot. You seriously expect me to get on something where the engine could burst into flames at any moment?
Kazoo:	If you don't shut up I'm going to copy this conversation into an all-staffer so everyone can see how ridiculous you are.
Dong:	Buggeration. Spanner Man's getting an instruction manual from his back pocket. He hasn't a clue! Got to talk to someone in charge.
Kazoo:	Just get on the plane. The only thing you should worry about is meeting the Marketing Director of Esmée Éloge without any presentation materials.

From: **Kazu Makino**
To: Bill Geddes
Sent: 5 January 2009, 11.55
Subject: Don

He's hysterical. Has he always been like this about flying?

From: **Bill Geddes**
To: Kazu Makino
Sent: 5 January 2009, 11.59
Subject: Re: Don

His fear of flying is matched only by his terror of spiders. He has a recurring nightmare about flying long haul and being served chicken/beef by a tarantula dressed as a stewardess.

From: **Alex Sofroniou**
To: David Crutton
Sent: 5 January 2009, 12.11
Subject: Re: why isn't this bollocks sorted out yet?

Hi David. Sorry for the delay in replying – several server issues to resolve. Changing the signature protocol for department heads requires agreement from the partners. In the meantime, I can change the typeface. Some suggestions:

David Crutton
The Man

David Crutton
THE MAN

David Crutton
the man

David Crutton
The Man

Personally, I like Lewinsky (second from bottom). It has a certain cool modernity and the italic suggests restless dynamism. Let me know what you want to do.

Alex Sofroniou
ZORBA THE GEEK

From: **David Crutton**
To: Alex Sofroniou
Sent: 5 January 2009, 12.18
Subject: Re: why isn't this bollocks sorted out yet?

What is it with this collective decision-making? It worked for about ten minutes in post-revolutionary Russia before common sense prevailed in the shape of Stalin. It doesn't work at all here. I'll have to do something about it, won't I? For now, I'll go with the bottom one. There's something pleasingly despotic about it.

From: **Alex Sofroniou**
To: David Crutton
Sent: 5 January 2009, 12.23
Subject: Re: why isn't this bollocks sorted out yet?

It's called Blackmoor. I'll action it ASAP.

From: **Neil Godley**
To: All Staff
Sent: 5 January 2009, 12.31
Subject: FYI

I will not be at my workstation between 1.00 and 2.00, since I am obliged to leave the building to obtain a haircut. I apologize for any inconvenience caused by my unscheduled absence.

Neil Godley (Accounts)

From: **Janice Crutton**
To: David Crutton
Sent: 5 January 2009, 12.38
Subject: Noah

Just had a call from him. He's in casualty. He didn't make much sense but it seems there was some sort of explosion in the science lab. He said he has no eyebrows. Can you go and pick him up? I'd go, but I'm due in court at two.

From: **David Crutton**
To: Janice Crutton
Sent: 5 January 2009, 12.44
Subject: Re: Noah

It's only his eyebrows. Can't he catch a bus?

David Crutton
The Man

From: **Janice Crutton**
To: David Crutton
Sent: 5 January 2009, 12.50
Subject: Re: Noah

I was thinking he might need some emotional support. You know how sensitive he is about his appearance. I'll call him and tell him to get a cab. But please be home early for him. And to talk to Tamara. And to me.

By the way, what's with the new sign-off? Makes you look a bit Cap'n Barbossa.

From: **David Crutton**
To: Janice Crutton
Sent: 5 January 2009, 12.57
Subject: Re: Noah

Barbossa?

From: **Janice Crutton**
To: David Crutton
Sent: 5 January 2009, 13.01
Subject: Re: Noah

Pirates of the Caribbean.

From: **David Crutton**
To: Janice Crutton
Sent: 5 January 2009, 13.04
Subject: Re: Noah

Geoffrey Rush? Thanks a lot.

From: **Janice Crutton**
To: David Crutton
Sent: 5 January 2009, 13.07
Subject: Re: Noah

You were Cap'n Jack Sparrow once. Don't worry. I always preferred my pirates grizzled.

From: **David Crutton**
To: Janice Crutton
Sent: 5 January 2009, 13.08
Subject: Re: Noah

You flirting?

From: **Janice Crutton**
To: David Crutton
Sent: 5 January 2009, 13.10
Subject: Re: Noah

Get home at a decent hour and find out. Got to go. Court: HMRC vs. Echelon Holdings plc. God, have you any idea how un-sexy typing that makes me feel?

Janice xx

From: **Kazu Makino**
To: Bill Geddes
Sent: 5 January 2009, 13.35
Subject: yikes!

Click the link quick.

---

bbc.co.uk/news
Stansted disaster averted

62 passengers and six crew safely evacuated from budget airline jet after engine fire.

The pilot of a BizzyJet Boeing 737 successfully aborted take-off at Stansted Airport after an engine burst into flames. The Rotterdam-bound jet was evacuated and five passengers were taken to hospital. There are no reports of serious injuries. The Civil Aviation Authority has begun an investigation and is considering all possible causes.

Eyewitnesses reported hearing a loud bang immediately before seeing flames and smoke pour from the plane's starboard engine. One passenger, who declined to give his name, said: 'It was a sharp metallic clank, exactly as if a cheap B&Q spanner had become caught up in the works. It was absolutely terrifying. I'm telling you, the sooner all air travel is banned and our airports are grassed over and turned into nature reserves the better.'

From: **Bill Geddes**
To: Kazu Makino
Sent: 5 January 2009, 13.38
Subject: Re: yikes!

I'm in shock. I was really taking the piss out of him earlier. Feel terrible now. Should I go to Stansted and see how he is?

From: **Kazu Makino**
To: Bill Geddes
Sent: 5 January 2009, 13.40
Subject: Re: yikes!

Stay put. He'll be up to his neck in trauma counsellors. Call him though.

From: **Neil Godley**
To: All Staff
Sent: 5 January 2009, 14.01
Subject: normal service is resumed!

I am now back at my desk. Anyone who would like to inspect my 'trim' can visit me in my basement cubby!

From: **David Crutton**
To: Kazu Makino
Sent: 5 January 2009, 14.14
Subject:

I've just had a call from our Esmée Éloge client. They're waiting for the meeting to start. Where the hell is your boss?

From: **Kazu Makino**
To: David Crutton
Sent: 5 January 2009, 14.15
Subject: Re:

He was on the plane that caught fire at Stansted. Sorry, I should have told you, but things went slightly headless-chicken when we found out. Bill talked to him. He's pretty shaken up but physically fine.

From: **David Crutton**
To: Kazu Makino
Sent: 5 January 2009, 14.16
Subject: Re:

That's good news. So which flight is he on? I'll call the client and let him know.

From: **Kazu Makino**
To: David Crutton
Sent: 5 January 2009, 14.18
Subject: Re:

I think he's gone home. According to Bill, he's too shocked to fly anywhere.

From: **David Crutton**
To: Kazu Makino
Sent: 5 January 2009, 14.19
Subject: Re:

Best piece of advice I ever got: when you fall off your bike, get straight back on. Tell him I'll be writing 'sissy boy' at the top of his next appraisal.

From: **David Crutton**
To: Dotty Podidra
Sent: 5 January 2009, 14.24
Subject:

Book me on earliest flight to Rotterdam.

From: **Dotty Podidra**
To: David Crutton
Sent: 5 January 2009, 14.25
Subject: Re:

You've got your anger-management session with Fabio at 3.30. You said before Christmas that whatever happened not to cancel it.

From: **David Crutton**
To: Dotty Podidra
Sent: 5 January 2009, 14.26
Subject: Re:

Cancel it. Book ticket. Unless you want to see me very fucking angry.

From: **David Crutton**
To: Janice Crutton
Sent: 5 January 2009, 14.28
Subject: sorry

Won't be home tonight. Got to fly to Rotterdam to present the most ridiculous list of celebrity names I have ever seen. If it's any consolation, the meeting will almost certainly be the end of my career. I'll call you.

From: **Róisín O'Hooligan**
To: All Staff
Sent: 5 January 2009, 14.37
Subject: delivery

Got a guy in a helmet standing in front of me. He's got a package for Tony Blair. Is he working here now (honestly, nothing surprises me about this place any more) or has bike man screwed up?

Róisín
Reception

PS: Bloody tree. Still bloody here.

Tuesday
Mood: slurpy

blogass.co.uk
Posted by **Veiko Van Helden**
06/01/09, 02:31 GMT

Dethrush take Jisalmi by storms!

The greatest gig ever! Yes, reader, we conquer Jisalmi making day when Dethrush crown Finland biker-cheesy-power-metal kings soon come. This were the highlightings:

- Aadolf break 24 drum stick. New world records!
- Bass Bastard Alpo drink too many Bud before show and pee himself! His trouser plastic so it not show.
- My solo in 'Nuns with Cocks' making nosebleed in fan stage right. He spurt like bleugh-agghhh decapitate zombie in snuff slasher movie!
- Chick stage left with boob tattoo. Sweet, baby! Make comfy chair on my face any time you want!!

- Wow, too many other fantastic highlightings I have no time to mention cause I have to post and go make slurpy noise with leather groupie chick. (Not boob tattoo chick but another chick different completely. I lining them up tonight, guys!)

Till the next time. Homantsi on 15th. Rokk till your spleen go splat!

Views: 1,692
Comments: 93

Comment posted by **jesus666**:
I was there, man! You guys rock! Necrophobic, Autopsy Torment, Hatesphere? You shit on them big time!!!

Comment posted by **Necrophobicluv**:
Jisalmi? Anyone notice it sound like jism? Dethrush suck. Dethrush = jism!

Comment posted by **jesus666**:
Necrophobicluv = jism + shit

Comment posted by **Necrophobicluv**:
jesus666 = jism + shit + piss x knob cheese^2

Comment posted by **MaryMary**:
Confused! I'm looking for a blog that gives info on fungal infections (of a personal nature). I really got my hopes up because I thought de-thrush might be it. Can anyone help?

Comment posted by **jesus666**:
Let me explain cuz you're obviously

completely lame-oid. Death put together with Rush makes Dethrush. I thought people this dumb wasn't allowed on the internet.

Comment posted by **Necrophobicluv**: You got that right. MaryMary = total flid

blogass.co.uk
Posted by **Tiga**
06/01/09, 18:44 GMT

Laser Torture

Today my human rights were violated. I was forced to have a tiny (like almost **invisible**) tattoo removed. By my mother! With the support of my **fascist** school, she dragged me to a sadist on Harley Street who attacked my leg with a laser gun. He said it would be painless, but it was **agony**. I could actually smell **burning flesh**.

The scar will be a permanent symbol of the emotional damage I now have to live with for **the rest of my life**. Doesn't anyone care that the tattoo (which, by the way, was **not** a skull. It was supposed to be Hello Kitty. It wasn't my fault that the tattoo guy couldn't draw) was an expression of **my individuality**?
Not my so-called mother, obviously. The most unbelievable thing is that she is a lawyer and is therefore supposed to understand the rights of the individual. The other most unbelievable thing is that she is also a member of Amnesty

International. Yes, she gives money to **stop** torture! Doesn't she realize that what she did to me was **exactly the same** as what the secret police do to people in countries like Burma, Belgium and Guantanamo?

I haven't been defeated though. Mum and my **Nazi teachers** don't know about the tattoo on the back of my neck and as long as I keep my hair down they never will!!

Views:	175
Comments:	17

Comment posted by **littlepinkpony**:
100% empathy, Tiga. My mom has kept me locked in my room for five days just coz I dyed my hair blue. What's she gonna do? Keep me in here till it grows out? That so wouldn't surprise me coz she's a total bitch. I'm like that Australian girl in the cellar. Except I've got a window. And Mom isn't making me have babies. Not yet anyway. My only contact with the outside world is my PC. Anyone in the Saginaw, MI area, call Child Services. Please! I'm at 1215 Jeffers St. Look out for the sign in my window. A pic of Lindsay Lohan. She's totally persecuted too, you know.

Crépuscule dans le Périgord
Partie 79: Fenêtres Givrées

'Froid vif, esprit vif,' as they are wont to say in these parts. *Mots justes*, indeed, because I awoke at dawn to both Jacques Frost's delightful filigree upon my windows and a distinct sense of a sharpened mind.

And in that intellectual limpidity one certainty was clear: I have made the right decision. Leaving the narcotic-fuelled and vanity-powered Soho media fest for *la simplicité rustique* of le Dordogne was *une bonne idée*.

'Tu traines encore en pyjama, mon couillon d'Anglais?' remarked dear old M. Papin when he arrived on his rusting bicycle to re-point the wall around the plum orchard. Papin and his forebears have worked this land since Neolithic times. His craggy and leathered visage is as much a part of the Périgordian landscape as Les Caves de Lascaux. I poured him his *tasse de café* and he set match to Gitanes, settling down for our customary rumination on *la vie du pays*.

'Elle est où ta salope?' he asked.

Ah, Celine. I explained that she hasn't yet returned from her yuletide visit to her parents.

'Elle revient quand?' he went on.

She hasn't called, I told him, but the mobile reception in these far-flung parts is *sporadique* at best.

Papin nodded sagely at that, though the frustrations of *le mobile* are as alien to him as warm English ale would be to *un Chinois*. 'Elle était bonne. Ses gros nichons vont me manquer,' he said finally.

I'll miss her too, I agreed. But if Celine has chosen the dubious comforts of SW6 over *la pureté* of our new home, then so be it. I have made my choice and it is assuredly the right one.

Or as the inimitable Papin put it, 'Tu es un vieux connard, seul et pathétique. Vas-te faire enculer.'

Wednesday
Mood: positive

From: **Róisín O'Hooligan**
To: All Staff
Sent: 7 January 2009, 09.00
Subject: It's me or the tree

If it hasn't gone by lunchtime, I'm out of here. And believe me, the tree won't be as good as I am at keeping clients plied with coffee until you lot are ready to get off your lazy arses to collect them. Do I make my point?

Róisín
Reception

From: **Harry Frisby**
To: All Staff
Sent: 7 January 2009, 09.01
Subject: Workies for hire

I have five excellent workies available. They're fast learners, adaptable and used to getting hands dirty. Available singly or as job lot.

Harry Frisby
Senior Account Director

From: **Bill Geddes**
To: Kazu Makino
Sent: 7 January 2009, 09.03
Subject: Fat Harry

Has he brought his kids in again?

From: **Kazu Makino**
To: Bill Geddes
Sent: 7 January 2009, 09.05
Subject: Re: Fat Harry

Looks like it. Heard he sent them to summer camp in China. What was that all about?

From: **Bill Geddes**
To: Kazu Makino
Sent: 7 January 2009, 09.06
Subject: Re: Fat Harry

Had them working in an iPod sweatshop in Guangzhou. Their small hands were much prized on the nano production line.

From: **Brett Topolski**
To: Liam O'Keefe
Sent: 7 January 2009, 09.16
Subject: Re: Happy New Year, Rag Head

Sorry about the delay in replying. Been shooting a swimwear ad in Bahrain. If you're picturing *Penthouse* Pets in next to nowt, don't. It was impossible to tell if the model was fit because she was wearing a burkini – a cross between a deep-sea diver's wetsuit and a Tesco carrier bag. It offers no advantages whatsoever to either wearer or voyeur, but it does keep Allah sweet and that's the main thing, isn't it? Vince nearly caused a diplomatic incident. His 'Can't we get some ice cubes on those nips, Abdul?' didn't go down at all well with the Arab crew.

I haven't told him about the Marriage of Susi yet. I'm going to have to pick my moment with that one. Not that he still holds a torch for her, but he won't be pleased that his baby Bubbles has a new *Papa*. You know what he's like about the French.

And the Arabs. When we joined, we got the standard Miller Shanks letter about the need to show 'cultural sensitivity'. Vince reckons that cuts both ways and when the Dubai police start showing sensitivity towards his need to throw up outside the Grand Hyatt after half a dozen banana daiquiris, he'll return the favour. It's a full-time job keeping him out of mischief. I'm afraid that I'll nod off for a moment and wake up to find him with his head on a block and some swarthy fucker poised over him with a scimitar.

Sorry to hear things aren't too bright in Blighty. Vince and I had an interview with Berry when he was at Fallon. He spent the time taking us through a laptop slide show of his assault on K2. Vince reminded him that Beattie had scaled it via the trickier North Ridge the year before. That might have been why we never got the job. Alternatively, Berry might just have thought we were crap.

I'll say ta-ta now. We've got a junk-food campaign to knock on the head. Hot dogs. They love them out here. And I thought it was all sheep's eyeballs. Later we're going for a dip in Ashley Cole's pool. No, Ashley's not there, obviously – it's mid-season, isn't it? But we made friends with his gardener and he lets us in through the back gate. Vince is under orders: however much he lusts after Cheryl Cole, he's not allowed to jiz in the jacuzzi.

Go with Allah

Brett

PS: How's Lorraine? You didn't mention her.

From: **Liam O'Keefe**
To: Brett Topolski
Sent: 7 January 2009, 09.35
Subject: Re: Happy New Year, Rag Head

You're right, I didn't mention her.

From: **David Crutton**
To: Janice Crutton
Sent: 7 January 2009, 09.36
Subject: Sorry. Again

Are you talking to me yet?

From: **Janice Crutton**
To: David Crutton
Sent: 7 January 2009, 09.39
Subject: Re: Sorry. Again

I'm emailing you. Not quite same as talking, but as close as we get these days.

From: **David Crutton**
To: Janice Crutton
Sent: 7 January 2009, 09.43
Subject: Re: Sorry. Again

Jan, if I could have done anything to avoid Rotterdam, I would have – you know my feelings on the Dutch. But account management here is such a shambles that I had no choice. I'm sorry.

From: **Janice Crutton**
To: David Crutton
Sent: 7 January 2009, 09.46
Subject: Re: Sorry. Again

You never have a choice, do you? With every family crisis you magically have an 'urgent appointment' to flog a rickety concept to a gullible client. Yesterday I had to deal with Noah's eyebrow trauma, declare war on Tam over her tattoo and delegate a court appearance to Corinne Tate Tait, who'll only use it to make me look slack at the next partners' meeting. What do I get for my troubles? A bottle of Coco from duty-free. Very nice, except it was half empty. A sampler you snatched from the spray monkey's hand on the dash through departures?

From: **Brett Topolski**
To: Liam O'Keefe
Sent: 7 January 2009, 09.49
Subject: Re: Happy New Year, Rag Head

Have I touched a raw nerve? Mind if I poke at it some more with a salted cocktail stick by asking what's going on?

From: **Liam O'Keefe**
To: Brett Topolski
Sent: 7 January 2009, 09.53
Subject: Re: Happy New Year, Rag Head

I'd sooner not talk about it.

From: **David Crutton**
To: Janice Crutton
Sent: 7 January 2009, 09.54
Subject: Re: Sorry. Again

I will make it up to you, I promise. I'll start by leaving tonight at

5.25. We do have to talk. About us, of course, but about Tam as well. I found something in the bathroom wastebasket when I was shaving this morning.

From: **Janice Crutton**
To: David Crutton
Sent: 7 January 2009, 09.56
Subject: Re: Sorry. Again

What was it? A home-piercing kit?

From: **Brett Topolski**
To: Liam O'Keefe
Sent: 7 January 2009, 09.57
Subject: Re: Happy New Year, Rag Head

Soz, mate. Know when to leave well alone. I'll shut the fuck up now.

From: **Liam O'Keefe**
To: Brett Topolski
Sent: 7 January 2009, 10.00
Subject: Re: Happy New Year, Rag Head

God, you don't half go on. I'll tell you, but after this not another word. OK?

From: **Brett Topolski**
To: Liam O'Keefe
Sent: 7 January 2009, 10.01
Subject: Re: Happy New Year, Rag Head

OK.

From: **Liam O'Keefe**
To: Brett Topolski
Sent: 7 January 2009, 10.08
Subject: Re: Happy New Year, Rag Head

She left me. On Christmas Eve. With a 10lb turkey half defrosted. She went up to Manchester to see her folks, but I know she's back in London now because she started her new job on Monday. Most of her gear is still at mine. Don't know what to do with it. Stuff it in bin bags and leave it on the pavement? Heap it up in the living room and weep over it?

Yeah, yeah, I know what you're thinking: *what the fuck has he gone and done now?*

From: **David Crutton**
To: Janice Crutton
Sent: 7 January 2009, 10.09
Subject: Re: Sorry. Again

Not something I particularly want to discuss in an email.

From: **Janice Crutton**
To: David Crutton
Sent: 7 January 2009, 10.10
Subject: Re: Sorry. Again

Why not? It's never stopped you before.

From: **David Crutton**
To: Janice Crutton
Sent: 7 January 2009, 10.13
Subject: Re: Sorry. Again

OK, I'll tell you. It was a pregnancy tester and it was positive.

From: **Brett Topolski**
To: Liam O'Keefe
Sent: 7 January 2009, 10.14
Subject: Re: Happy New Year, Rag Head

You're right. What the fuck have you gone and done now?

From: **Liam O'Keefe**
To: Brett Topolski
Sent: 7 January 2009, 10.19
Subject: Re: Happy New Year, Rag Head

Nothing, I swear. I'd been completely good since the thing with the thing. I didn't even go to the office party this year because she had tonsillitis and I stayed home to look after her. OK, I also didn't go because I'd reached the conclusion that, unless you're twenty-three and are therefore stupid, office parties are crap (especially since the smoking ban). But it was mostly because of her tonsils.

Why did she do it? I've grown up, settled down, matured, done all the things you're supposed to do. Why, why, why?

From: **Brett Topolski**
To: Liam O'Keefe
Sent: 7 January 2009, 10.21
Subject: Re: Happy New Year, Rag Head

Have you tried asking her?

From: **Liam O'Keefe**
To: Brett Topolski
Sent: 7 January 2009, 10.22
Subject: Re: Happy New Year, Rag Head

Her mobile's dead. Must have a new one. Obviously doesn't want to talk to me.

From: **Brett Topolski**
To: Liam O'Keefe
Sent: 7 January 2009, 10.26
Subject: Re: Happy New Year, Rag Head

Vince thinks you should go to where she works and tip a bucket of sheep's blood on her workstation (something he saw on the Al Jazeera version of *Springer*). There might be something in it. Not the blood. The going-to-where-she-works bit. You know, just to talk to her.

From: **Liam O'Keefe**
To: Brett Topolski
Sent: 7 January 2009, 10.29
Subject: Re: Happy New Year, Rag Head

That'd make me look desperate.

From: **Brett Topolski**
To: Liam O'Keefe
Sent: 7 January 2009, 10.31
Subject: Re: Happy New Year, Rag Head

Hate to be the one to point this out, but you are desperate.

From: **Liam O'Keefe**
To: Brett Topolski
Sent: 7 January 2009, 10.35
Subject: Re: Happy New Year, Rag Head

Confession: I went yesterday morning. She works at Endemol so I had to schlep to Shepherd's Bush. Couldn't bring myself to go in. I just lurked on the pavement. Eventually a receptionist came out and said if I was there to audition for *BB10*, I should pop a video in the post. See? I obviously looked desperate.

Don't want to talk about this any more. What's the weather like with you?

From: **David Crutton**
To: Janice Crutton
Sent: 7 January 2009, 10.36
Subject: Re: Sorry. Again

Is that it? Our fifteen-year-old daughter is pregnant and you've got nothing to say?

From: **Brett Topolski**
To: Liam O'Keefe
Sent: 7 January 2009, 10.38
Subject: Re: Happy New Year, Rag Head

What the fuck do you think it's like? It's fucking hot and fucking sunny. Look, you have to do something. I won't mention it again, I promise, but you and Lorraine have been together eight years and you've been through a lot (well, she's been through a lot) and you can't leave it without an explanation. Vince agrees. He says you need to achieve closure. Something else he picked up on *Springer* Al Jazeera-style. I suspect his and Jamal Springer's take on closure involves a public stoning, but I trust you to take a less confrontational approach.

From: **Liam O'Keefe**
To: Brett Topolski
Sent: 7 January 2009, 10.43
Subject: Re: Happy New Year, Rag Head

I'm taking relationship advice from a diagnosed psychotic? Think I'll leave it be.

By the way, if/when you decide to tell Vince about Susi, don't mention she brought Bubbles in before Christmas. She was

73

dressed in head-to-toe Gaultier. Poor kid looked like a prostitute from *Moulin Rouge Junior*. Susi had also doused her in Allure, which sent out a clear scent signal to anyone within a half-mile radius on the sex offenders' register. Made me feel distinctly uncomfortable. But what the fuck do I know about parenting? Maybe Tiny Ho is the new look from Gap Kids.

Enough. You've got your hot dogs and I've got a particularly tricky product-recall ad to do for Winter Sun instant tan. We did the packaging for it. The instructions read 'leave on for 3 hours' instead of '3 minutes'. There are roaming packs of angry women out there with complexions like pickled walnuts. God knows what Ted wants. A viral? A pavement poster? The world's first ad delivered via ESP? Certainly won't be a nice old-fashioned quarter-page in the *Mail*. That would be boring, wouldn't it?

From: **David Crutton**
To: Janice Crutton
Sent: 7 January 2009, 10.47
Subject: Re: Sorry. Again

Are you even there, Janice?

From: **Janice Crutton**
To: David Crutton
Sent: 7 January 2009, 10.52
Subject: Re: Sorry. Again

I'm here. It wasn't Tam's pregnancy test.

From: **David Crutton**
To: Janice Crutton
Sent: 7 January 2009, 10.53
Subject: Re: Sorry. Again

Whose was it, then?

From: **Janice Crutton**
To: David Crutton
Sent: 7 January 2009, 10.55
Subject: Re: Sorry. Again

Well, it wasn't Noah's.

From: **Accounts@SafeBet.com**
To: Liam O'Keefe
Sent: 7 January 2009, 11.01
Subject: Your account

We regret to inform you that we have been obliged to terminate your account due to the failure of your credit card. We advise you to contact your bank as a matter of urgency to discuss the situation. We must also inform you that we cannot review this decision until you have cleared your outstanding debt, which now stands at:

£26,745.02

This is an automatically generated email. Please do not reply.

SafeBet.com
Go on, have a punt

From: **Susi Judge-Davis-Gaultier**
To: All Staff
Sent: 7 January 2009, 11.03
Subject: Workies?

Any workies free to clean Ted's car?

Susi Judge-Davis-Gaultier
Assistant to Ted Berry

From: **Offers@SafeBet.com**
To: Liam O'Keefe
Sent: 7 January 2009, 11.05
Subject: SPECIAL OFFER!

Why not take advantage **today** of our special offer on **online debt counselling**? Talk in **complete confidence** to our **professional** team of financial **experts** for just £49.99 per hour.*

Click SafeBet.com/debt-hell **now** for full details.

SafeBet.com
Go on, have a punt
Just a little one

*Terms and conditions apply. Offer not available to customers outside UK and those currently serving prison terms.

From: **Liam O'Keefe**
To: All Staff
Sent: 7 January 2009, 11.10
Subject: Workies?

Any workies free to kiss my arse? My self-esteem has taken a bit of a battering.

From: **Susi Judge-Davis-Gaultier**
To: Liam O'Keefe
Sent: 7 January 2009, 11.17
Subject: Re: Workies?

FYI, Ted's Cayenne is covered in mud after his orienteering trip yesterday. He has to drive to a client meeting this afternoon and it needs to be clean. Therefore the job of washing it is *work*-related and is a perfectly reasonable thing to ask a *work*-experience person to do.

Also FYI, I didn't like your attitude when we worked together at Miller Shanks and I don't like it any more now. I'll thank you not to continue sending snide all-staffers.

Susi Judge-Davis-Gaultier
Assistant to Ted Berry

From: **Liam O'Keefe**
To: Susi Judge-Davis-Gaultier
Sent: 7 January 2009, 11.23
Subject: Re: Workies?

Don't think my email mentioned Ted's car, but since you have, why does a certified midget need one big enough to carry the entire Serbian basketball squad? Have you ever seen the Serbian basketball squad? They're like a copse of extremely lanky elms.

Anyway, I think car-washing makes an excellent entry on any undergrad's CV. Bound to land him/her that top job at McKinsey/Goldman Sachs/NASA. Shit, I'd do it myself if I didn't have an important Esmée Éloge product-recall ad to do. Do you reckon Ted will be happy with a few ideas for guerrilla street happenings or is he looking for something more left field?

From: **Liam O'Keefe**
To: Kirsten Richardson
Sent: 7 January 2009, 11.25
Subject: feeling shite

You available to pick me up with a therapeutic tease? I'm thinking quick wash 'n' trim, but I'm happy to be your plaything.

From: **Kirsten Richardson**
To: Liam O'Keefe
Sent: 7 January 2009, 11.28
Subject: Re: feeling shite

I'm about to do some remedial work on Ted's split ends, but I'm free after that. About 1.00? You haven't got much to play with, have you? No. 2 again?

From: **Susi Judge-Davis-Gaultier**
To: Milton Keane
Sent: 7 January 2009, 11.33
Subject: Help!

Just had a really unsettling email from Liam in creative. I think he was being ironic, but it's so hard to tell. Need to discuss. Starbucks in 5?

From: **Milton Keane**
To: Susi Judge-Davis-Gaultier
Sent: 7 January 2009, 11.34
Subject: Re: Help!

Cazza's out so I'm free right now. Starbucks in 2!

From: **Sally Wilton**
To: David Crutton
Sent: 7 January 2009, 11.38
Subject: Office Audit
Att: inventory_jan09.xls

Dear David

I have completed the audit of office furniture and equipment that you actioned prior to Christmas. Everything is pretty much in order. We appear to be slightly over-inventorized on copiers and scanners, but otherwise OK. Stationery stocks are running at adequate levels, assuming current levels of staffing are maintained. You can view a full breakdown on the attached spreadsheet.

I did come across a couple of anomalies. A Wii console and remote, three Wii games and two leather-upholstered beanbags appear to be missing from the new Creative Romper Room. Let me know if you wish me to investigate further.

Best wishes,

Sally Wilton
PRINCESS
PAPERCLIP

PS: Is there anything we can do to amend our job titles? Personally, I'd be more comfortable with Office Administrator.

From:	**Janice Crutton**
To:	David Crutton
Sent:	7 January 2009, 11.40
Subject:	Re: Sorry. Again

Well?

From:	**David Crutton**
To:	Janice Crutton
Sent:	7 January 2009, 11.41
Subject:	Re: Sorry. Again

Well what?

From: **Janice Crutton**
To: David Crutton
Sent: 7 January 2009, 11.43
Subject: Re: Sorry. Again

Over half an hour ago I told you I'm pregnant. No response. What the hell have you been doing? I'm going out of my mind here.

From: **David Crutton**
To: Janice Crutton
Sent: 7 January 2009, 11.45
Subject: Re: Sorry. Again

I'm staggered, to be honest. How long have you known? When were you planning to tell me? And how did it happen?

From: **Janice Crutton**
To: David Crutton
Sent: 7 January 2009, 11.48
Subject: Re: Sorry. Again

I've known for a few days. That's what I wanted to talk to you about on Monday but you buggered off to Rotterdam. How did it happen? We had sex. Remember? Or are you so self-absorbed that you didn't notice I was with you when we were doing it?

---

eBay.co.uk

Wii console plus 3 games

Item specifics: slightly used Nintendo Wii console, including remote and Nunchuk. Three games included: Mario Olympics, Big Brain Game and Guitar Hero IV.*

*A personal thought on the Guitar Hero phenomenon: have any of you sad twats playing air guitar to a second-rate graphic rendering of a Guns 'n' Roses tribute band ever thought of buying, you know, an actual fucking guitar and, you know, actually learning to fucking play it?

Current bid: **£2.99**
End time: 9d 12h 06m

---

eBay.co.uk

2 leather beanbags

Item specifics: two large beanbags upholstered in tan leather. Supremely comfortable. Would suit family that enjoys casual lounging. Or person with piles.

Current bid: **£5.00**
End time: 9d 12h 05m

From: **David Crutton**
To: Janice Crutton
Sent: 7 January 2009, 11.59
Subject: Re: Sorry. Again

I thought you were on the pill.

From: **Janice Crutton**
To: David Crutton
Sent: 7 January 2009, 12.03
Subject: Re: Sorry. Again

I stopped taking the pill when our sex life withered to virtually nothing in 2005. Jesus, David, a bit of concern wouldn't go amiss right now.

From: **David Crutton**
To: Janice Crutton
Sent: 7 January 2009, 12.05
Subject: Re: Sorry. Again

Don't you think I'm concerned? Very bloody concerned. Have you thought about your options?

From: **Janice Crutton**
To: David Crutton
Sent: 7 January 2009, 12.07
Subject: Re: Sorry. Again

I've thought about nothing else. Why do you think I'm going out of my mind?

From: **David Crutton**
To: Janice Crutton
Sent: 7 January 2009, 12.08
Subject: Re: Sorry. Again

And?

From: **Janice Crutton**
To: David Crutton
Sent: 7 January 2009, 12.10
Subject: Re: Sorry. Again

Oh, you want me to decide this all by myself? What do you think I should do, David?

From: **David Crutton**
To: Janice Crutton
Sent: 7 January 2009, 12.12
Subject: Re: Sorry. Again

Well, you are forty-five.

From: **Janice Crutton**
To: David Crutton
Sent: 7 January 2009, 12.13
Subject: Re: Sorry. Again

Excuse me, but what the fuck is that supposed to mean?

From: **David Crutton**
To: Janice Crutton
Sent: 7 January 2009, 12.17
Subject: Re: Sorry. Again

Nothing. Can't talk about this now. Client hovering outside.

From: **Janice Crutton**
To: David Crutton
Sent: 7 January 2009, 12.19
Subject: Re: Sorry. Again

Isn't there always? You deal with business and I'll just go mad by myself. I'm sure I can manage.

From: **David Crutton**
To: Dotty Podidra
Sent: 7 January 2009, 12.20
Subject:

No calls.

From: **Dotty Podidra**
To: David Crutton
Sent: 7 January 2009, 12.21
Subject: Re:

No calls at all?

From: **David Crutton**
To: Dotty Podidra
Sent: 7 January 2009, 12.22
Subject: Re:

Do I have to spell everything out? No calls from Janice.

From: **Dotty Podidra**
To: David Crutton
Sent: 7 January 2009, 12.23
Subject: Re:

With you. But you'll take calls from other people?

From: **David Crutton**
To: Dotty Podidra
Sent: 7 January 2009, 12.24
Subject: Re:

Use your judgement. You have that, don't you?

From: **Liam O'Keefe**
To: Kazu Makino
Sent: 7 January 2009, 12.26
Subject: loose end . . .

. . . I'm at one tonight. Are you? We could go for a drink and I could show you that we Brits are completely over the whole River Kwai thing.

Yours slightly pantingly – Liam

From: **Milton Keane**
To: Susi Judge-Davis-Gaultier
Sent: 7 January 2009, 12.27
Subject: let me take you away from all this

You mustn't let Liam upset you so much. He's just an unreconstructed 'lad'. He's virtually bald too. And sooo *paunchy*! Looks at least forty-five – way too elderly for this place. Let's make it a long lunch – I'm sure TB can type his own emails for a couple of hours. Something carb-free (my diet!) and Carnaby St?

From: **Susi Judge-Davis-Gaultier**
To: Milton Keane
Sent: 7 January 2009, 12.29
Subject: Re: let me take you away from all this

You're a lifesaver. Reception at one.

From: **Kazu Makino**
To: Liam O'Keefe
Sent: 7 January 2009, 12.33
Subject: Re: loose end . . .

Some things you should know about me, Liam. I was born in Godalming and I hate sushi. My English is impeccable, my Japanese patchy. In short, I'm as British as you are, Paddy, and I get as patriotic as you probably do when I watch *Merry Christmas Mr Lawrence* (though I can't help going gooey when Ryuichi Sakamoto whips out his sword – it's the uniform plus the hint of mascara).

By the way, have you fallen out with your girlfriend? You only ever email me when you've rowed.

From: **Liam O'Keefe**
To: Kazu Makino
Sent: 7 January 2009, 12.35
Subject: Re: loose end . . .

What girlfriend?

From: **Kazu Makino**
To: Liam O'Keefe
Sent: 7 January 2009, 12.39
Subject: Re: loose end . . .

I'm sorry and everything, but there's something else you should know about me: I don't do sympathy shags.

From: **Liam O'Keefe**
To: Brett Topolski
Sent: 7 January 2009, 13.07
Subject: runners 'n' riders

Two possible punts for the discerning better:

1   The Snipper
    Comely, flirty, probably easy
    (she's a fucking hairdresser)
    7–4
2   Ninja Babe
    Slanty little Jap, super-intelligent, nigh-on impossible
    (she has *standards*)
    30–1

Your guidance, please.

From: **Kirsten Richardson**
To: Liam O'Keefe
Sent: 7 January 2009, 13.08
Subject:

Hi Liam. You're late for your cut. Do you still want it? Only I could be down the gym working on my thighs.

From: **Liam O'Keefe**
To: Kirsten Richardson
Sent: 7 January 2009, 13.09
Subject: Re:

Don't move a (thigh) muscle. On my way.

From: **Brett Topolski**
To: Liam O'Keefe
Sent: 7 January 2009, 13.15
Subject: Re: runners 'n' riders

Another possibility:

3   Talk to Lorraine.

From: **Ted Berry**
To: David Crutton
Sent: 7 January 2009, 13.16
Subject: Esmée Éloge

When were you going to debrief us on your triumph in Rotterdam?

From: **David Crutton**
To: Ted Berry
Sent: 7 January 2009, 13.17
Subject: Re: Esmée Éloge

I think triumph is the right word. Still can't believe it myself. I doubt Gold would have had as much success with a list as bizarre as the one you gave me. I'm writing the contact report now.

From: **David Crutton**
To: Caroline Zitter, Ted Berry, Donald Gold, Kazu Makino, Camille Brunel, Maurice Wéber, Betina Tofting
Sent: 7 January 2009, 13.28
Subject: Esmée Éloge Contact Report

Date:	5th January 2009
Venue:	Hilton Rotterdam
Present for client:	Camille Brunel, Maurice Wéber, Betina Tofting
Present for agency:	David Crutton

David Crutton apologized for the late start of the meeting. The Esmée Éloge group extended their best wishes to Donald Gold after his unfortunate experience at Stansted.

David Crutton went on to present the long list of celebrities for Project Red Carpet. Initially Camille Brunel expressed surprise, having briefed the agency to come up with names from the worlds of film and popular music – she cited Keira Knightley and the girl who used to stand in the middle in Destiny's Child as examples. David Crutton explained that consumers are tiring of the conventional take on the celebrity as brand and are ready for a post-modern approach.

After much discussion, Camille Brunel expressed approval of the list's boldness and audacity. She said that she would be prepared to commission qualitative research to gauge the limits of consumer acceptance. Betina Tofting asked who Chantelle was.

David Crutton thought she might be a Sugababe, but he wasn't certain. The meeting adjourned while Betina Tofting Googled her.

A shortlist of eight celebrities was agreed:

Margaret Thatcher (*Dame Bleue*)
Monica Lewinsky (*Robe Bleue*)
Myra Hindley (*Blonde Dangereuse*)
Beth Ditto (*Gigantique*)
George Michael (*Eau de Toilette*)
Kelly Osbourne (*Révulsion pour Femme*)
Jack Osbourne (*Révulsion pour Homme*)
Ron Jeremy (*Lucky Bâtard pour Homme*)

It was further agreed that Meerkat360 would carry out additional creative refinement with a view to putting the shortlisted perfumes to focus groups at the beginning of March (action: Ted Berry).

The client remains committed to launching three new scents in time for Christmas 2009 and requested that steps be taken to sound out the shortlisted celebrities (action: David Crutton and Donald Gold).

The client thanked Meerkat360 for the work carried out to date. It was agreed to schedule a meeting in two weeks' time to review progress (action: Donald Gold). The meeting will take place in Rio de Janeiro, due to the client's attendance at Expo OLAD 09.

David Crutton
𝕿𝖍𝖊 𝕸𝖆𝖓

From: **Caroline Zitter**
To: David Crutton
Sent: 7 January 2009, 13.29
Subject: Out of Office AutoReply

I am out of the office attending Professor Derek Blundford's discussion of his book, *The Lemming Theory: Sales Techniques for the Countdown to Apocalypse*. I will return on Friday 9th January. If you have an urgent request please contact my assistant, Milton Keane, on milton@meerkat360.co.uk

Caroline Zitter
THE SEER

From: **David Crutton**
To: Milton Keane
Sent: 7 January 2009, 13.32
Subject: your boss

As per the instruction in Caroline's AutoReply, I am contacting you, her no doubt thoroughly clued-up assistant. My urgent request: WHY THE SHITTING FUCK IS SHE OUT OF THE FUCKING BASTARD OFFICE AGAIN?

From: **Milton Keane**
To: David Crutton
Sent: 7 January 2009, 13.33
Subject: Out of Office AutoReply

I am out of the office introducing Mr Tum to Ms Lunch. I will be back at 3.30 pm. Apologies for any inconvenience.

Milton Keane
Assistant to Caroline Zitter

From: **Dotty Podidra**
To: Sally Wilton
Sent: 7 January 2009, 13.36
Subject: slight emergency

Could you get someone with a mop and bucket to come up to David's office please? There's been an accident with the cafetière. Not as bad as last time. Managed to save the kentia palm!

From: **Dotty Podidra**
To: David Crutton
Sent: 7 January 2009, 13.42
Subject: afternoon schedule

Just a thought, but do you want me to see if Fabio can fit you in for a quick anger-management session later this afternoon? Or perhaps half an hour in the sensory-deprivation tank – it's supposed to be really soothing! If you don't reply, I'll take it as a no to both suggestions.

From: **Donald Gold**
To: Kazu Makino
Sent: 7 January 2009, 14.09
Subject: the nightmare continues

Does David really expect me to fly to Rio? Does he know how many disasters there've been at Brazilian airports? It's like the Battle of Britain over there. I'm going to have to resign, aren't I?

From: **Kazu Makino**
To: Donald Gold
Sent: 7 January 2009, 14.16
Subject: Re: the nightmare continues

No you're not. Just Googled 'fear of flying'. There are dozens of courses that cure it. You can sign up for one this weekend and be looping the loop on Monday. Want me to check out times and prices?

By the way, what's Expo OLAD 09?

From: **Donald Gold**
To: Kazu Makino
Sent: 7 January 2009, 14.19
Subject: Re: the nightmare continues

OLAD is the Organization of Laboratory Animal Distributors. Esmée Éloge goes to the Expo to bulk-buy critters for mascara tests. It was held in Shanghai last year. They came back with a container ship of kittens.

Yes, book me on to a course. I've got to do something because the way I feel right now I'd rather be one of those kittens.

From: **Dotty Podidra**
To: David Crutton
Sent: 7 January 2009, 14.21
Subject: afternoon schedule

That's a no, then?

From: **Liam O'Keefe**
To: Brett Topolski
Sent: 7 January 2009, 15.08
Subject: Re: runners 'n' riders

Why talk to Lorraine when I have both a youthful new haircut (actually, the usual no. 2) and a date with the provider of said do? As well as being a gifted stylist, she's a fully qualified beauty therapist. She's going to give me a lower back massage. Shall I get her to wax my bum crack while she's down there?

From: **Milton Keane**
To: Susi Judge-Davis-Gaultier
Sent: 7 January 2009, 15.31
Subject: unreal!

Just got back to an absolutely hideous email from DC. Does he have Tourette's? And I bumped into Dotty in the kitchen. She said he chucked his cafetière at the wall. The man is totally insane. Was he this bad at Miller Shanks?

From: **Susi Judge-Davis-Gaultier**
To: Milton Keane
Sent: 7 January 2009, 15.36
Subject: Re: unreal!

OMG, he was ten times worse. I think he must have been in therapy because he used to fire people for fun. Rumour was that when he found out he couldn't fire a workie because she was going back to uni the next day, he chucked her down the lift shaft. Don't know if it was true, but there was a dreadful smell for weeks.

BTW, thanks for taking me out. Retail therapy so works! I love my Daphne from *Scooby-Doo* dress. And those white loafers are so you!! Sx

From: **Milton Keane**
To: Susi Judge-Davis-Gaultier
Sent: 7 January 2009, 15.38
Subject: Re: unreal!

Don't you think they make me look a bit gay?

From: **Susi Judge-Davis-Gaultier**
To: Milton Keane
Sent: 7 January 2009, 15.39
Subject: Re: unreal!

Don't be a sausage. Only a real man could carry off white shoes with Prince of Wales check trousers and a salmon-pink cardie. Trust me, I'm a Gaultier!

From: **Brett Topolski**
To: Liam O'Keefe
Sent: 7 January 2009, 15.48
Subject: Re: runners 'n' riders

Great idea. I'm sure the reason Lorraine dumped you was your anal hirsuteness. In case you're completely stupid, I'M BEING IRONIC. Cancel the hairdresser, go see Lorraine. She was the best thing that ever happened to you and if you let her walk away, you're more insane than Vince (who as I write is turning a hot dog pack shot into a big spurty cock. He's been a terror since he mastered Photoshop. Life was much safer when he just had his colouring-in book). I'll check in tomorrow, by which time you will have talked to Lorraine. DO NOT LET ME DOWN.

From: **Ted Berry**
To: David Crutton
Sent: 7 January 2009, 15.53
Subject: Re: Esmée Éloge Contact Report

Already got some great ideas for the Maggie bottle. We're looking into casting it in pig iron. Might be a weight issue, but I'm sure we can overcome it with a premium price. And how about getting Armitage Shanks to produce a limited-edition porcelain bottle for George Michael?

Any news on this Big Client you cock-teased me with over Christmas?

From: **David Crutton**
To: Ted Berry
Sent: 7 January 2009, 15.59
Subject: Re: Esmée Éloge Contact Report

Might have something before the end of the week. I'd love to tell your partner too, but is she ever here? It's just one bullshit seminar after another with her.

From: **Ted Berry**
To: David Crutton
Sent: 7 January 2009, 16.07
Subject: Re: Esmée Éloge Contact Report

Caz does love her courses. Frustrating at times, but she gets some serious networking done at them. Kwik Fit and Trebor both signed up with us after they met her at Sex Sells: What Lap Dancers Can Teach Us About Marketing.

From: **Róisín O'Hooligan**
To: All Staff
Sent: 7 January 2009, 16.12
Subject: Can't believe I'm still here . . .

. . . because the tree hasn't moved a fucking inch. I swear that if someone doesn't do something soon, the next client that walks in here will get it up his backside.

    Róisín
    Reception

From: **David Crutton**
To: Sally Wilton
Sent: 7 January 2009, 16.15
Subject: reception

Am I right in thinking that the foul-mouthed navvy on reception reports to you? Do you think she's the ideal face of Meerkat360? I suggest you begin the process of finding someone a little more decorous. And pretty.

She does have a point about the Christmas tree though. It's a fucking eyesore. Please see that it's removed.

	MSN:
Bilge:	You there, Irish?
Keef:	I'm here. Supposed to be doing your Winter Sun recall ad, but frankly can't be arsed. What's up?
Bilge:	Got shock of my life when I walked out of the lift and saw Daphne from *Scooby-Doo*. Turned out to be Susi in a lookalike outfit. V unsettling. I had a major crush on Daphne when I was 8. The idea of fancying Susi makes me nauseous. You need to buy me a remedial beer after work.
Keef:	Can't. Hot date. She has straightening irons and she knows how to use them.
Bilge:	The hairdresser?!
Keef:	Affirmative.
Bilge:	What about Lorraine?
Keef:	What about her?
Bilge:	What aren't you telling me?
Keef:	Plenty. Go for a beer with Yossi the Minstrel. Take him karaoke.
Bilge:	Might just go home, thanks. BTW, you seen Milton's white shoes?
Keef:	Gay twat. Incoming from Daphne. TTFN.

From: **Susi Judge-Davis-Gaultier**
To: Liam O'Keefe
Sent: 7 January 2009, 16.19
Subject: Esmée Éloge

Ted would like to know if there's any chance of you showing him the Winter Sun recall ad before end of play. You have had the brief since Monday.

From: **Susi Judge-Davis-Gaultier**
To: All Staff
Sent: 7 January 2009, 16.20
Subject: If anyone can see . . .

. . . Harvey Harvey, tell him Ted wants to brief him on Kwik Fit. And it's time for his tablet.

From: **Sally Wilton**
To: David Crutton
Sent: 7 January 2009, 16.21
Subject: Re: reception

Hi David. Although Róisín does report to me, she was interviewed by Caroline and Ted and was very much their choice – Ted felt that she would 'spunkify' the front-of-house area. The way things are normally done here, you would have to have Caroline and Ted's agreement if you want to replace her.

My apologies for the delayed removal of the tree. Caroline gave me instructions that, since it still has its roots, it shouldn't be disposed of in the usual fashion, but should be replanted. It has taken me a few days to locate a suitable plot.

A team of qualified arboriculturists will arrive shortly to transport it to the Christmas Tree Sanctuary in Abergavenny.

Sally Wilton
**PRINCESS
PAPERCLIP**

From: **David Crutton**
To: Sally Wilton
Sent: 7 January 2009, 16.23
Subject: Re: reception

Tell me, Sally, how the hell did Caroline manage to a) interview
the navvy and b) give you instructions on tree removal, since she
is never fucking here? Is there some kind of telepathic technique
you people use, to which I, as a relative newcomer, am not party?

From: **Liam O'Keefe**
To: Susi Judge-Davis-Gaultier
Sent: 7 January 2009, 16.25
Subject: Re: Esmée Éloge

I'd say there's roughly no chance. It's an especially tricky brief. I
know how Ted likes to challenge us and I don't want to fail him.
BTW, Harvey's in the Romper Room. You'll find him in the ball pit.
You might need an excavator to get him out – he's been there all
day and I think he's sunk. Also BTW, Bill thinks you look like
Daphne from *Scooby-Doo*. Reckon you're in there, girl.

From: **David Crutton**
To: Donald Gold
Cc: Ted Berry, Kazu Makino
Sent: 7 January 2009, 16.39
Subject: Fwd: Project Red Carpet

This just in from Maurice at Esmée Éloge. I expect you to take
suitable action. No flying involved.

Begin forwarded message:

From: **Maurice Wéber**
To: David Crutton
Cc: Camille Brunel, Betina Tofting
Sent: 7 January 2009, 16.29
Subject: Project Red Carpet

Hi David

We had excellent meeting on Monday. Thanks you for making the journey. Your presentation has stimulated many more discussion.

We are particular excited about *Dame Bleue* (Margaret Thatcher). Camille especial feels that there is big market opportunity in political celebrity. She believes there is something highly sexual about the strong, independent political woman that may work on international stage. We would like you to consider other names: Angela Merkel, Carla Bruni, Michelle Obama, Hillary Clinton and Cristina Fernández de Kirchner of Argentina all exude powerful musk. We understand that your own Harriet Harman also arouses passions of the same flavour.

Men also must be consider. Nicolas Sarkozy, Barack Obama and Vladimir Putin press strong buttons of homoeroticism, which is the big factor in male scent selection at purchase point. We put these names in the hat. In your creativity you can certainly think of more.

We look forward to meet in Rio.

Best wishes,

Maurice Wéber
Director, New Brand Development (Europe)
Esmée Éloge

From: **Kazu Makino**
To: Donald Gold
Sent: 7 January 2009, 16.40
Subject: Re: Fwd: Project Red Carpet

I give you John Prescott, *Eau My God*. Am I pressing your strong buttons of homoeroticism, big boy?

From: **Donald Gold**
To: Kazu Makino
Sent: 7 January 2009, 16.41
Subject: Re: Fwd: Project Red Carpet

Can't think straight. Thoughts of Harriet Harman have sent blood rushing from brain to groin. It's enough to make me hetero.

	MSN:
Bilge:	Just walked past Romper Room and saw TB trying to talk Harvey Harvey out of ball pit. Remind me, why does he work here?
Keef:	Because he and Zitter spotted 'a chasm-like gap in the market for an agency with a wanton disregard for conventional definitions and boundaries' (TB quoted in Campaign, Oct 2007) and together they decided to set up Meerkat360.
Bilge:	Not TB, you prat. HH.
Keef:	Soz. Thought you liked it when I'm obtuse. TB hired Double H on the basis that anyone so utterly whacked must be hiding at least one genius idea about his person.
Bilge:	Isn't it a bit cruel? The poor guy clearly can't cope. Wouldn't he be better off basket weaving?

Keef:	He's fine as long as your Daphne remembers to medicate him. Anyway, there's no appreciable difference between this place and Broadmoor.
Bilge:	Can't argue with that. Oh, shit. Daphne just walked by, winked and said, 'Hi, Fred' in the voice she thinks makes her sound sexy but actually makes her sound like Fearne Cotton on helium. You've been blabbing, haven't you?
Keef:	Yes.
Bilge:	Arse.
Keef:	Can't argue with that.

From: **Ted Berry**
To: Creative Department
Sent: 7 January 2009, 16.44
Subject: Fucking result!

The guys at Esmée Éloge are officially blown away by our slebs. Maggie, having got them seriously hard, has the green light. They've asked for more names from the political arena. Ideas, please. Don't hold back. Let's have some out-there thinking. My starter for ten: Eva Braun.

Ted Berry
ＭＣ ＩＤＥＡＺ

From: **Sally Wilton**
To: All Staff
Sent: 7 January 2009, 17.10
Subject: Mugs

Luisa in the kitchen has informed me that eight mugs are missing. Can all those who have not returned them please do so or we will be obliged to revert to the days of environmentally unsound Styrofoam beverage receptacles.

Sally Wilton
PRINCESS PAPERCLIP

From: **Kirsten Richardson**
To: Liam O'Keefe
Sent: 7 January 2009, 17.29
Subject: Ready?

I'm starving!

From: **Liam O'Keefe**
To: Kirsten Richardson
Sent: 7 January 2009, 17.30
Subject: Re: Ready?

Couple of things to do. See you in reception in five.

_____ eBay.co.uk

8 mugs

Item specifics: sturdy yet elegant white china mugs. Genuine Conran logo. Equally suitable for coffee and tea. Would suit large family of coffee/tea drinkers. Or single coffee/tea drinker who can't be arsed to wash up.

Current bid: **£0.00**
End time: 9d 23h 59m

Thursday
Mood: litigious

	MSN:
MiltShake:	Why aren't you at work, Sooz? Need you!
sjdG:	Waiting in for my new lime-green Smeg ☺☺☺ Plz don't say anything! Phoned in sick. Told TB I've got flu. Everything OK?
MiltShake:	So not OK.
sjdG:	What's up, sweetz?
MiltShake:	Outraged!!!!!
sjdG:	☹ Is it DC again?
MiltShake:	Much worse!!!
sjdG:	OMG! What??
MiltShake:	Went to my mum's last night. She got out shoebox of piccies I did when I was little. Found one that was on Blue Peter.
sjdG:	Wow!! Used to love BP. Did you get a badge?
MiltShake:	Not the point! You have to see pic. Going to scan it. Check your email in 10.
sjdG:	Can't wait!

Liam:	Feel terrible about last night
Kirsten:	Don't worry. It happens – x
Liam:	Not to me. Let me make it up to you
Kirsten:	Last night was fun but not good time for relationship. Soz. Friends?
Liam:	Cool. Trust you not to say anything tho
Kirsten:	Who do you think I am?!

SMS:

Kirsten:	Sneak off reception and meet me by Aga. Wicked goss on L
Róisín:	That streak of Irish piss? See you in 5

From:	**Milton Keane**
To:	Susi Judge-Davis-Gaultier
Sent:	8 January 2009, 09.39
Subject:	piccy
Att:	blue_peter.jpg

Attachment:

sjdG:	Aw, that's so sweet! Didn't know you were so artistic ☺☺ Lovely handwriting too. Wish Bubbles was as neat!
MiltShake:	Don't you get it????
sjdG:	Of course I do. It's a pic of a Stone Age man and it was on TV. You're famous!!
MiltShake:	You're so dense sometimes. Look at his feet!!!
sjdG:	Cute little booties. Hey, they look a bit like UGGs.
MiltShake:	At last! EXACTLY like UGGs!!!!!!! It even says 'Ugg' in the speech bubble. With two Gs!
sjdG:	Amazing! What a coincidence!!
MiltShake:	So NOT a coincidence. Pic was on telly when I was eight. How long have UGGs been around? Work it out!
sjdG:	Is this a maths question? I'm rubbish at sums.
MiltShake:	It was on TV in 1989!! UGG designer must have seen it.
sjdG:	OMG!!!!!!!!! You've been totally ripped off!!!
MiltShake:	I'm devastated. Feel as if I've been raped.
sjdG:	You poor, poor thing. You have to sue!
MiltShake:	Really??
sjdG:	Absolutely!! Oncle Jean Paul sues rip-off merchants in Thailand and Topshop all the time.
MiltShake:	Know any lawyers?
sjdG:	The guy I got to sue Bubbles' school over her SATs results.
MiltShake:	Any good?

sjdG: Rubbish. Judge said case was 'wholly frivolous' and threw it out. I'll talk to Pierre tonight. He can ask Oncle JP for name of his lawyer.

MiltShake: Thanks, sweetie.

sjdG: Aagh! Smeg's arrived. It's PASTEL green. Total disaster!! Gotta go.

From: **Bill Geddes**
To: Liam O'Keefe
Sent: 8 January 2009, 10.05
Subject:

How did it go with the hairdresser?

From: **Liam O'Keefe**
To: Bill Geddes
Sent: 8 January 2009, 10.06
Subject: Re:

Piss off.

SMS:

Róisín: Want to know why Liam looks like a pricked party balloon? Meet me by Aga to find out

Dotty: On my way

From: **Bill Geddes**
To: Liam O'Keefe
Sent: 8 January 2009, 10.08
Subject: Re:

That well? You probably don't want to hear this then, but I'm getting grief from Betina at Esmée Éloge. The Winter Sun problem isn't going away. Negative PR is piling up and the client has seven lawsuits pending already. When's the recall ad going to be ready?

From: **Liam O'Keefe**
To: Bill Geddes
Sent: 8 January 2009, 10.10
Subject: Re:

Like I said, piss off.

	MSN:
DottyPod:	Aga in 5 if you want to hear latest on Liam.
MiltShake:	Really not in the mood for girly gossip about his massive willy or whatever.
DottyPod:	You're so wide of the mark! You'll definitely want to hear this.
MiltShake:	Make me a latte and I'm there. BTW, you know a good lawyer?
DottyPod:	DC's wife? She's a partner or something.
MiltShake:	Is she insane like him?
DottyPod:	Seems fairly normal. Has a twitch in her eye. Probably just stress. I'll bring her number.
MiltShake:	On my way.

From: **Maritza Person**
To: Liam O'Keefe
Sent: 8 January 2009, 10.11
Subject: eat yourself stiffer

Stay up all night long and take your ladylove to Planet Orgasma. Go http://www.cheapmeds.com

From: **Bruno Strong**
To: Liam O'Keefe
Sent: 8 January 2009, 10.12
Subject: iron rod

Hey, guy, want giant love wand you can use on submarine like a periscope? Click now http://www.bestviagra.com

From: **Shabbir Gokulam**
To: Liam O'Keefe
Sent: 8 January 2009, 10.13
Subject: weapon of mass ecstasy

Have stiffest cum stick in city!! Go http://www.viagrabonanza.com right now!!

From: **Liam O'Keefe**
To: Alex Sofroniou
Sent: 8 January 2009, 10.15
Subject: spam

What's happened to the spam filter? I'm getting inundated and it's fucking me right off.

From: **Alex Sofroniou**
To: Liam O'Keefe
Sent: 8 January 2009, 10.18
Subject: Re: spam

Sorry, Liam. Filter's down. Working on it now. Please bear with us.

Alex Sofroniou
ZORBA THE GEEK

Racist attack

A Cleveland man was badly beaten outside a Middlesbrough nightclub.

William Maddren, a 27-year-old man from Stockton-on-Tees, is in hospital with severe facial injuries after what the police believe was a racially motivated attack. The apparently unprovoked assault by a gang of up to six youths took place in the early hours of this morning outside the Shampers nightclub in Middlesbrough. Before the attack, Maddren was allegedly taunted with racist insults.

The incident was witnessed by Joanne Craggs, Maddren's girlfriend. She said: 'It was absolutely terrifying. These vicious skinheads were shouting the N word and everything. I was screaming at them to stop, telling them that William is white. He's a ginger and his skin is like magnolia emulsion. But he got a can of that Winter Sun and he came out looking like Samuel bloody Jackson.'

From: **Róisín O'Hooligan**
To: All Staff
Sent: 8 January 2009, 10.25
Subject: Someone get their arse down here NOW

I've got a very angry woman who wants to speak to whoever's in charge of Winter Sun. She's the colour of my nan's mahogany dresser and she's freaking the sweet shit out of me. Is it asking too much that some fucker deals with her?

Róisín
Reception

From: **Bill Geddes**
To: Liam O'Keefe
Sent: 8 January 2009, 10.26
Subject: Winter Sun

Hate to be a nag, but I really need that recall ad.

From: **applications@E-zimoney.com**
To: Liam O'Keefe
Sent: 8 January 2009, 10.28
Subject: Your Loan Application

Dear Mr O'Keefe

We regret to inform you that your application for a loan of

£40,000

cannot be approved at this time. We are unable to accept

caravan held in name of Mrs S. O'Keefe (applicant's grandmother)

as security. Please feel free to reapply for a **hassle-free E-zimoney** loan in the future.

E-zimoney.com
The sub-subprime people

From: **consultations@cro-magnon.com**
To: Liam O'Keefe
Sent: 8 January 2009, 10.29
Subject: Your Free Consultation

Dear Mr O'Keefe

Thank you for submitting your photograph for a **free** online consultation. Unfortunately we are unable to help you at this time. For the **Cro-Magnon**® Miracle Transplant Technique to work, the client must have sufficient pre-existing hair to transplant. Regrettably your picture shows this not to be the case.

However, all is not lost! We are pioneering **Cro-Magnon Canine**®, a revolutionary technique that utilizes the hair of specially bred transgenic dogs. If you would like to take part in clinical trials, go to cro-magon.com/woof today.

Cro-Magnon® Clinic
Gone today, hair tomorrow!

From: **Liam O'Keefe**
To: Bill Geddes
Sent: 8 January 2009, 10.31
Subject: Re: Winter Sun

This morning's correspondence has established that I couldn't give a tuppenny fuck about a poxy recall ad for a product aimed at those who believe their pathetic lives will be transformed if only they were the colour of oiled teak. Speaking personally, I believe Esmée Éloge should tell the whinging sods to get lost. Let their unwanted deep-cocoa complexions shine as a very public symbol of the vacuous cunts they are. For once, we'd be doing society a favour.

Now fuck off and leave me alone.

From: **David Crutton**
To: Ted Berry, Caroline Zitter
Sent: 8 January 2009, 10.33
Subject: new business

Good news to report. My office at 11?

From: **Ted Berry**
To: David Crutton
Sent: 8 January 2009, 10.34
Subject: Re: new business

This the big one? Looking forward to it, geezer.

From: **Caroline Zitter**
To: David Crutton
Sent: 8 January 2009, 10.35
Subject: Out of Office AutoReply

I am in Finland attending Dr P. Van Helden's workshop, Ice Fishing: The Path to Environmentally Sound Management. I will return on Monday 12th January. If you have an urgent request, don't hesitate to contact my assistant, Milton Keane, on milton@meerkat360.co.uk

> Caroline Zitter
> **THE SEER**

From: **Paula Sterling**
To: Milton Keane
Sent: 8 January 2009, 10.39
Subject: Meeting

Dear Mr Keane

I am writing to confirm your meeting with Janice Crutton here at Bancroft Brooks at 10.00 a.m. on Monday 12th January 2009. If you have any questions in advance, please do not hesitate to contact me.

Yours sincerely,

> Paula Sterling
> Assistant to Janice Crutton
> Bancroft Brooks & Partners

From: **Bill Geddes**
To: Donald Gold
Sent: 8 January 2009, 10.44
Subject: straightjackets all round

What is it with the Creative Department in this place? Liam – the only one with any sense – has turned evil and the rest of them are plain unfathomable. I went to see Zlatan and Adrijana (with my handy Serbian phrasebook) to check how they're getting on with my Kwik Fit brief. 'We nearly finish,' Zlatan grunts and points at a heap of junk on the floor. Turns out they're working on an 'installation' involving 5,000 teaspoons, 200 breeze blocks and lots of sticky-backed plastic (at least I think that's what Adrijana meant by 'lodsa stiggybagplaztig'). And as they're telling me this I have to listen to Yossi down the corridor refashion 'Yes We Have No Bananas' as a trance anthem.

All I want is a half-page black-and-white for a tyre and exhaust sale. I give up.

From: **Donald Gold**
To: Bill Geddes
Sent: 8 January 2009, 10.51
Subject: Re: straightjackets all round

You and me both. Harvey Harvey just told me he can't look at Bassetts Allsorts before Wednesday at the earliest because he has 962 emails to answer. Why does TB hire these people? Does he have to fulfil some freak quota?

From: **Bill Geddes**
To: Donald Gold
Sent: 8 January 2009, 10.55
Subject: Re: straightjackets all round

TB told me Double H is the finest lateral thinker he's ever met. Which is just a fancy term for fucked up.

From: **Daniela**
To: Harvey Harvey
Sent: 8 January 2009, 10.57
Subject: hiya!

Hello. My name is Daniela. I'm 19, blonde and I'm bored. Let's chat and have some fun. daniela@gotmail.com. My firm breasts ache for you.

From: **Harvey Harvey**
To: Daniela
Sent: 8 January 2009, 10.59
Subject: Re: hiya!

Hi Daniela

Nice to hear from you. I'm at work, so I'm a bit too busy to chat at the moment, but if you're bored, there's usually something good on TV now. I like to watch *Cash in the Attic* (BBC1, 11.30) when I'm not at the office.

I'm concerned to hear about your breasts. Could it be hormonal? I don't want to be presumptuous, but my sister often gets discomfort in her boobs when it's 'that time'. She says Feminax helps, so maybe give it a try. If it continues, though, I'd definitely see a doctor.

Thanks for writing. Usually I'm free in the evenings if you still fancy a chat.

Harvey Harvey

From: **Marlon Norbert**
To: Harvey Harvey
Sent: 8 January 2009, 11.00
Subject: hey, little man

My buddy couldn't give his girl big satisfaction until he add extra two inch to his frankfurter of love. Now he is the bedroom hero. Get extra steel for your rod if you are man enough. http://www.natural-herbal-gain.com

From: **Harvey Harvey**
To: Marlon Norbert
Sent: 8 January 2009, 11.01
Subject: Re: hey, little man

Hi Marlon

Great news about your buddy! Thanks for the info. Sounds interesting. I am currently single, so it's of no immediate use to me. However, I'll file your email for possible future reference.

All the best,

   Harvey Harvey

From: **Britney**
To: Harvey Harvey
Sent: 8 January 2009, 11.04
Subject: let's get it on

I am lonely sexual teen who need friendly chat. Reply me and we make fun. britney@gotmail.com. My breasts are on fire.

From: **Harvey Harvey**
To: Britney
Sent: 8 January 2009, 11.06
Subject: Re: let's get it on

Hi Britney

Amazing that you should write because I've only just had an email from another girl who was bored and wanted to chat. She's called Daniela and she seems very nice. Remarkably, she also complained of inflammation in the breasts. Maybe it's a winter virus thing. I really think you should get in touch with her. I'm sure you'd cheer each other up. Her email is daniela@gotmail.com

Thanks for writing. And do get in touch with Daniela. I bet it helps chase away the January blues.

Harvey Harvey

From: **Alex Sofroniou**
To: All Staff
Sent: 8 January 2009, 11.17
Subject: spam filter

Just to let you know that the spam filter is up and running again. Apologies for the inconvenience.

Alex Sofroniou
ZORBA THE GEEK

From: **Harvey Harvey**
To: Alex Sofroniou
Sent: 8 January 2009, 11.19
Subject: Re: spam filter

What's spam?

From: **Liam O'Keefe**
To: Lorraine Pallister
Sent: 8 January 2009, 11.32
Subject:

Hi Lorraine

I know you don't want to hear from me, but please don't hit delete now . . .

Please, please, please don't . . .

You still there?

You haven't trashed this yet?

Thanks.

OK, where to begin? I honestly don't know why you left (it's not because of the thing with the thing, is it? That was ages ago). All I want is an explanation. I think you owe me that much. Fair dos, I owe you a lot more, but one tiny-weeny explanation isn't a lot to ask, is it? OK, it might be a big explanation, a humungous one the size of a house or a truck or Keith Richards' smack bill circa 1971. I can take it. I have both the time and a cast-iron emotional constitution . . .

You still haven't trashed this? Amazing, but thanks.

We could do it over a drink. I'll buy. And I promise I won't plead with you to come home. Well, only a little bit.

Please say yes (you'll meet me, not yes you'll come home – though you can if you want. I'd really like that).

Liam x

From: **Liam O'Keefe**
To: Lorraine Pallister
Sent: 8 January 2009, 11.33
Subject: PS

I got your email address from your receptionist. I didn't do any-thing stalker-ish. I just asked nicely. It was really easy. Endemol security seems a bit slack. You might want to have a word.

From: **Liam O'Keefe**
To: Lorraine Pallister
Sent: 8 January 2009, 11.35
Subject: PPS

You left some bits and bobs in the laundry basket. I washed them for you.

From: **Liam O'Keefe**
To: Lorraine Pallister
Sent: 8 January 2009, 11.36
Subject: PPPS

I ironed them too.

From: **Bill Geddes**
To: Liam O'Keefe
Sent: 8 January 2009, 11.37
Subject: possible jumper

I'm really sorry to do this to you, Liam, but I have Betina from Esmée Éloge on hold. She's crying, literally hysterical. I'm gen-uinely afraid that if I don't give her a Winter Sun recall ad soon, she may do something crazy, possibly involving self-harm. What do you say, old pal?

From: **Liam O'Keefe**
To: Bill Geddes
Sent: 8 January 2009, 11.38
Subject: Re: possible jumper

Clients, suicidal or otherwise, are your job. Why are you bothering me with it? I'm in the middle of something VERY IMPORTANT here.

From: **Liam O'Keefe**
To: Lorraine Pallister
Sent: 8 January 2009, 11.39
Subject: PPPPS

You've got a lot of post. I haven't opened any of it, but you haven't given me a forwarding address. So we have to meet up, don't we? You know, so I can give it to you.

From: **Liam O'Keefe**
To: Lorraine Pallister
Sent: 8 January 2009, 11.40
Subject: PPPPPS

I love you.

From: **Bill Geddes**
To: Liam O'Keefe
Sent: 8 January 2009, 11.41
Subject: Re: possible jumper

I'd call the fucking Samaritans, Liam, but they won't be able to do me a FUCKING RECALL AD. That's YOUR job. I could jeopardize our friendship by taking this to Ted. Do you really want me to do that?

From: **Liam O'Keefe**
To: Bill Geddes
Sent: 8 January 2009, 11.47
Subject: Re: possible jumper

Doing your ad now, you cock.

From: **Ted Berry**
To: David Crutton
Sent: 8 January 2009, 12.09
Subject: new biz

Did you know Caroline has a Warhol pastiche hanging in her bedroom? It's a screen print of that famous shot of the smoking lab beagle. Every time she goes to sleep, it reminds her that humanity's two worst sins are cruelty to animals and the invention of fags.

Don't get me wrong. I'm a total fucking whore and I think your new biz win is fantastic – a terrific creative challenge and a very nice earner. Just to warn you, though, that Caroline probably won't feel the same.

From: **David Crutton**
To: Ted Berry
Sent: 8 January 2009, 12.12
Subject: Re: new biz

But Caroline isn't here, is she? If at some distant point she does show up, you can comfort her with the fact that no animals were harmed in the signing of the contract.

From: **David Crutton**
To: Dotty Podidra
Sent: 8 January 2009, 12.13
Subject:

Book me in for a lunchtime session with my trainer. I'm feeling manly.

David Crutton
The Man

From: **Dotty Podidra**
To: David Crutton
Sent: 8 January 2009, 12.15
Subject: Re:

You've got anger management with Fabio at lunchtime.

From: **David Crutton**
To: Dotty Podidra
Sent: 8 January 2009, 12.16
Subject: Re:

Tell him to go screw himself. But tell him nicely.

From: **David Crutton**
To: All Staff
Sent: 8 January 2009, 12.22
Subject: New Business Announcement

I am delighted to announce that Galax International Tobacco has appointed us as its lead agency in Europe and the Middle East. We will have custody of GIT's entire roster of brands, including Lucky Seven, Ambassador, Montana and Old Scrote hand-rolling tobacco.

As you must know, GIT has a magnificent heritage that includes some of the most famous advertisements of any age. There's the iconic Montana Man, of course, and I'm certainly old enough to remember when the Lucky Seven poster featuring all three Charlie's Angels adorned every schoolboy's bedroom wall. And despite the fact that it is over fifty years old, the now legendary 'Those Smoking Moments' campaign for Ambassador remains an object lesson in single-minded communication. Who could forget the terrifically moving image of doctor and patient sharing their love of a harmless puff over the respirator?

Indeed, we have a great deal to live up to and our challenge is made that much tougher in these times of repressive legislation that infringes upon the legitimate commercial rights of tobacco manufacturers. It is, however, a challenge that we at Meerkat360 are more than equipped to rise to.

There will be champagne in reception at five.

David Crutton
The Man

From: **Dotty Podidra**
To: David Crutton
Sent: 8 January 2009, 12.23
Subject:

So do you want me to organize the champagne?

From: **David Crutton**
To: Dotty Podidra
Sent: 8 January 2009, 12.24
Subject: Re:

Er, what do you think?

From: **Dotty Podidra**
To: David Crutton
Sent: 8 January 2009, 12.25
Subject: Re:

Yes?

From: **David Crutton**
To: Dotty Podidra
Sent: 8 January 2009, 12.27
Subject: Re:

I knew there was a reason I hired you.

And when you get a minute, nip out and buy me a pack of Montana Red.

From: **Dotty Podidra**
To: David Crutton
Sent: 8 January 2009, 12.28
Subject: Re:

I thought you'd given up?!

From: **David Crutton**
To: Dotty Podidra
Sent: 8 January 2009, 12.30
Subject: Re:

Did you read my all-staffer? Make it two packs.

From: **Róisín O'Hooligan**
To: All Staff
Sent: 8 January 2009, 12.42
Subject:

If you lot are going to tramp through my nice clean reception at five, make sure you wipe your feet. After the last new biz celebration, the place looked like fucking Glastonbury at chucking-out time.

Róisín
Reception

From: **David Crutton**
To: Janice Crutton
Sent: 8 January 2009, 12.52
Subject: tonight

Hi Jan

I know it's been a fraught few days, but how about you let me make it up to you over dinner tonight? I've just signed up Galax International and I'm feeling celebratory. We'll celebrate the pregnancy too, of course. Fantastic news! I'm going to be a dad again! Hooray!

I'll get Dotty to book something spectacular – David x

From: **Neil Godley**
To: David Crutton
Sent: 8 January 2009, 12.57
Subject: Re: New Business Announcement

Hi David

I must inform you that, as a matter of conscience, I will be unable to work on the accounts of Galax International Tobacco.

Although I support the principles of the free market, I cannot condone the sale of an addictive poison.

Also, Jesus was a non-smoker.

I'm sorry if this creates a problem.

    Neil Godley (Accounts)

From: **Liam O'Keefe**
To: Bill Geddes
Sent: 8 January 2009, 12.59
Subject: Winter Sun

Left an idea with Ted. So long as he's not having one of his contrary days, you should have something to present after lunch.

From: **David Crutton**
To: Neil Godley
Sent: 8 January 2009, 13.02
Subject: Re: New Business Announcement

The only problem we'll have with GIT will be finding a truck big enough to transport our fees to the bank. I think we'll manage without you. Oh, and praise Jesus that I'm in a charitable mood and not asking the collective committee to fire your collective butt cheeks.

    David Crutton
    𝕿𝖍𝖊 𝖒𝖆𝖓

From: **Bill Geddes**
To: Liam O'Keefe
Sent: 8 January 2009, 13.03
Subject: Re: Winter Sun

Thanks, Liam. You're a lifesaver. Possibly literally. I'll call Betina and tell her she can stop trying to figure out how to slash her wrists with a Ladyshave.

From: **Paula Sterling**
To: David Crutton
Sent: 8 January 2009, 14.04
Subject: Re: tonight

Dear Mr Crutton

I am writing on behalf of Ms Janice Crutton in response to your email of 12.52 today. Ms Crutton thanks you for the offer of dinner this evening, but she will be unable to accompany you. Being in the early stages of pregnancy, she feels it would be inappropriate to celebrate your acquisition of the advertising account of a tobacco company. She does, however, ask me to pass on her congratulations to you for your part in said acquisition.

Yours sincerely,

    Paula Sterling
    Assistant to Janice Crutton
    Bancroft Brooks & Partners

From: **David Crutton**
To: Dotty Podidra
Sent: 8 January 2009, 14.06
Subject:

Get your arse in here and take an email.

From: **Dotty Podidra**
To: Paula Sterling
Sent: 8 January 2009, 14.13
Subject: Re: tonight

Dear Ms Sterling

I am writing on behalf of Mr David Crutton in response to your email on behalf of Ms Janice Crutton. Mr Crutton thanks you for informing him of Ms Crutton's unavailability this evening. This being the case, he asks that you tell her that he has decided to travel to Galax, Virginia for his meeting with the President of GIT a day earlier than scheduled, and he will therefore not be home tonight.

He asks that you wish Ms Crutton a pleasant weekend in his absence.

Yours sincerely,

Dotty Podidra
Assistant to David Crutton

From: **Paula Sterling**
To: Dotty Podidra
Sent: 8 January 2009, 14.22
Subject: Re: tonight

Dear Ms Podidra

Ms Crutton asks that you wish Mr Crutton a productive trip and suggests that, while he is with the President of Galax International Tobacco, he takes the opportunity to remind him that he is scheduled for a court appearance in February in the case of the State of California vs. GIT Inc., where the Los Angeles office of Bancroft Brooks will be representing the State of California.

She also asks you to assure him that, despite the extreme fatigue she is experiencing as a result of the aforementioned pregnancy, she will have no trouble coordinating his children's weekend activity programmes (which will include busy study schedules, transportation to and from an inter-school hockey match, shopping for school-uniform items, the distinct possibility of having to peel his son from the pavement outside The Clef & Crotchet at closing time and the inevitable journey to collect his daughter from an inappropriate West End nightclub when she calls for a lift at 2.30 on Sunday morning).

Yours sincerely,

Paula Sterling
Assistant to Janice Crutton
Bancroft Brooks & Partners

From: **Dotty Podidra**
To: Sally Wilton
Sent: 8 January 2009, 14.24
Subject: small emergency

Hi Sal – can you get the bucket and mop up here again? There's been another slight accident with the cafetière.

From: **Ted Berry**
To: Liam O'Keefe
Sent: 8 January 2009, 14.39
Subject: Winter Sun

What's this bollocks you've left on my desk? Who briefed you to do a humorous viral? Have you any idea what a product-recall ad is? In case you're unsure, it's a simple press announcement in a sober typeface that a product is faulty or unsafe and should be returned to the manufacturer ASAP. Who the fuck told you to get creative with this? You're the most experienced member of my team and I should be able to count on you to knock off pony briefs like this in your sleep. What the fuck's got into you? I'll level with you, geezer. You've been making a habit of fucking up lately. Sort yourself out or find alternative employment.

From: **Bill Geddes**
To: Liam O'Keefe
Sent: 8 January 2009, 14.40
Subject: Re: Winter Sun

Any word from Ted yet on the recall ad? Betina is calmer but still a loose cannon.

BTW, caught the fag end of some secretarial bitchery in the kitchen. You won't like it, but I think the hairdresser's been talking about you.

From: **Liam O'Keefe**
To: Lorraine Pallister
Sent: 8 January 2009, 14.42
Subject: help!

I'm falling apart here, Lorraine. Don't know what the hell I'm supposed to be doing any more. We've got to talk. Please!

	MSN:
DottyPod:	You there?
Paula86:	I'm here.
DottyPod:	JC looking over your shoulder?
Paula86:	Safe.
DottyPod:	Have our bosses flipped again?
Paula86:	Looks like it. Hasn't been this bad since the Spearmint Rhino 'misunderstanding' of 07.
DottyPod:	Aagh! Don't want to think about that one. What's with JC? She's normally the sane one.

Paula86:	Pregnancy is what's with her.
DottyPod:	She is 45.
Paula86:	That's *exactly* what Colin Jelf said to her. She replied, 'What the f*** does that mean?' I have never *ever* heard her use the F word before.
DottyPod:	Who's Colin Jelf?
Paula86:	Only the senior partner. I reckon she's carrying the spawn of the devil.
DottyPod:	Well, if DC's the dad!!!
Paula86:	LOL! Gotta go. She's screaming for Peperami.
DottyPod:	Definitely eating for 1 + devil child.

From: **Lorraine Pallister**
To: Liam O'Keefe
Sent: 8 January 2009, 16.16
Subject: Re: help!

<< I'm falling apart here >>

What do you think *I've* been doing for the last eighteen months, Liam?

<< I honestly don't know why you left (it's not because of the thing with the thing, is it? That was ages ago) >>

No, it's not because of 'the thing with the thing' (though, ages ago or not, I'll be holding that one against you for a while yet. You will burn in hell for 'the thing with the thing' alone). It's because you're a lowlife thief. Did you seriously think I wouldn't notice you'd nicked my ruby brooch? It was the only valuable piece of jewellery I had (or was ever likely to have because, let's be honest, you were never going to buy me a ring, were you?). It was given to me by my mother and given to her by my nan. It was priceless to me. If you'd cared about me at all you'd have a) known that and b) wouldn't have stolen it to pay off some twat-faced bookie.

<< All I want is an explanation. I think you owe me that much. Fair dos, I owe you a lot more >>

Too fucking right you do. You want a list? I haven't got the time right now, but when I do get round to it (and I will) the total will be several thousand quid, the nine years of my life I wasted with you and Christ knows how much in emotional damage. Have you given any thought at all to what it's like to live with a lying, thieving addict? Of course not. You've been far too busy lying, thieving and gambling your life away.

<< I can take it. I have both the time and a cast-iron emotional constitution >>

You can't take it. You may have the time, but you don't have the guts. We've been here before, haven't we? Several times. Whenever I've tried to talk to you about the problem, you've blubbed like a baby and promised you'll change, but it's all meaningless. Lies like everything else.

<< We could do it over a drink. I'll buy >>

What with? You're bankrupt, financially and morally.

<< I love you >>

No you don't. If you did, you wouldn't have stolen my brooch, would you?

I used to love you, but now I despise you. I don't want to see you again. Ever. I'll come and collect my stuff when you're at work. It might not be for a while because I've got a very nice boss and I don't want to take the piss by bunking off while I'm still new. But when I do show up, I expect all my stuff to be there and not on eBay. And that includes my brooch. I don't care if it literally costs you an arm and a leg, get it back.

Lorraine Pallister
Assistant to Philip Edgar-Jones
Endemol

From: **Milton Keane**
To: All Staff
Sent: 8 January 2009, 16.25
Subject: Workies?

Any workies of Chinese descent free to feng shui Caroline's office before she returns on Monday?

Milton Keane
Assistant to Caroline Zitter

From: **Brett Topolski**
To: Liam O'Keefe
Sent: 8 January 2009, 16.27
Subject: Lorraine

I don't know why I'm emailing you. I'm sure you've talked to her (because you know your Uncle Brett is ALWAYS right) and I bet you feel a whole heap better.

Vince and I are lying low today. Bit of a kerfuffle last night. You know that complex of artificial islands they're building in the shape of the world? Vince got a bit ADHD on whisky sours and emptied a very large dumper truck of rocks into the sea. Now the toe of Italy is sporting an outcrop that looks like a severely inflamed bunion. I've Google-Earthed it and you can see it from space. Dubai's Finest are out in force.

Allah G

From: **Liam O'Keefe**
To: Brett Topolski
Sent: 8 January 2009, 16.38
Subject: Re: Lorraine

Your advice sucked. I will never take advice from you again. If I were standing on a cliff edge and you advised me not to jump, the jagged rocks at the bottom would suddenly seem as inviting as a feather-stuffed mattress. You are the steaming turd of advice-giving and *my* advice to *you* is to keep your fat fucking beak out of my business.

_____ eBay.co.uk

Antique ruby brooch

This item has been withdrawn and is no longer offered for sale.

From: **Liam O'Keefe**
To: Bill Geddes
Sent: 8 January 2009, 16.42
Subject: Re: Winter Sun

Review with Little Ted didn't go as well as hoped. We need to thrash out this recall ad. Clearly the best way to do this is by getting drunk in a major way. Aperitifs at the GIT party and on to the House. You're buying.

From: **Dotty Podidra**
To: All Staff
Sent: 8 January 2009, 16.51
Subject: EMERGENCY!

I seem to have mislaid some champagne. I'm sure I put six cases in reception, but now there are only three. The party kicks off in a few minutes and if I can't find it, we're all going to have to make do with extra-orangey bucks fizz! Help!!!

---

eBay.co.uk

Joseph Perrier Brut Royale

Item specifics: 3 cases (18 bottles) of this most excellent champagne. Would suit small wedding party. Or wino who has recently won on the dogs and has wearied of Special Brew.

Current bid:	**£00.00**
End time:	9d 23h 19m

Sunday Mood: confessional

blogass.co.uk
Posted by **Hornblower**
11/01/09, 14.25 GMT

Crépuscule dans le Périgord
Partie 80: Je Suis Français

As a wine takes on *le caractère* of its
cask, so have I acquired the personality of
mon milieu de choix. I came to le Périgord
determined to assimilate (or as *les
Françaises* would have it, *assimilate*). I
was not going to be like those expatriates
held in contempt by *les natifs*. You know
the type: huddled in their cagoules,
chuntering about the late arrival of the
Daily Mail and the refusal of Monsieur
l'Épicier to stock McVitie's Digestives,
Cheezy Wotstits or some other miserable
British titbit.

By contrast, I threw myself into *la vie*. *La
chemise paysanne* became my default
wardrobe and French my *langue*

maternelle, even at home with Celine. In fact, my decision to respond to her twitterings only in French infuriated her until the day she left.

(By the way, you will be pleased to learn that *ma femme* has been in touch. She has delayed her return to be with her mother. She promises to come back as soon as the new hip has bedded in, and no later than August.)

Yesterday *à le fromagerie* I was vindicated in my resolution to blend. As I entered this wondrous grotto of cheese, old Mme Poincare affectionately introduced me to her new *l'employée du samedi* as her 'tarlouse anglaise', and commanded the callow poppet to sell me 'ce qu'on a de plus merdique.'

And when I returned to the homestead, Papin immediately picked up the heady bouquet of my near liquid *Carré de l'Est*. 'Je vois qu'elle t'a vendu celui qui pue comme un branleur de bougnoules,' he murmured approvingly.

Yes, I told him, only the very best for me, *un vrai Français*.

Posted by **Veiko Van Helden**
11/01/09, 15.44 GMT

The pants or not the pants?? The big question for the crazy axe warrior of todays!

Many fans are writing me. Veiko, they are saying, are you wearing the pants under the rock monster trouser? That is my secret that I am going to reveal to you now!

I tell you story. Two year ago I was lucky fucking bastard to get accesses all area pass for Provinssirock in Seinäjoki. As anyone tell you, this is great festival in Scandinavia. I see Hardcore Superstar, R.A.M.B.O., Spazz, you fucking name it, dude. Best ever was legendary Saxon. My dad Pertti turn me on when I was kid and I love them. I see their set and they blow me away. Then we go to party in Winnebago of the great Nigel Glockler. Fucking WOW!! I am in same room as legend Saxon drum slayer Nigel 'Cock Blocker' Glockler!!! I get the courage to ask him sign my codpieces. He write his name and when I turn away he say, 'VPL, dude.' I do not know what he mean (my English not so excellent back in that day)

It is later when I hear VPL mean Visible Panty Line! I tell you I was massive embarrass big time. The mythic Cock Blocker can see my pants through my super-tight jean with 20% Lycra!!!!

Since that day I never again wear the

underneath pants. Now you know the truth! It take the getting used to coz man as big as me (you know what I am saying??!!) have to find the new place for parking his cucumber of cum. But now I never changing back. The pants is for the squares.

Excepting this day. This day I am wearing under the trouser a lady thong make out of red satin and laces. I know what you thinking. You thinking Veiko turning into homo bot boy transvestist. No fucking way, dude. The lady thong is souvenir from babe I make slurpy noise with. I take her to the places she never been and after she get back the consciousness she give me the panty. Thanks you for the memory, sweet fuck of mine!

Rokk till your spleen go splat!

| Views: | 8,574 |
| Comments: | 438 |

From: **David Crutton**
To: Ted Berry
Sent: 11 January 2009, 16.01
Subject: GIT

About to board the plane home, but I wanted to let you know what an excellent time I've had. Galax is a remarkable town. Everything revolves around the cigarette plant and Carter Bluewash, CEO and President, runs the place like a medieval prince. Despite being elderly and somewhat frail, he has an intensely hands-on management approach that we could all learn from.

The man loves me and he wants to put his corporation's money where his mouth is. The GIT marketing budget is trouser-tighteningly gargantuan, but given the global restrictions on cigarette promotion, they have few ways of spending it. Our mission is to help them find more.

For starters, he's given me a very exciting new product brief. Details when I get back. It's a major challenge, but if we meet it head on there'll be plenty more where that came from.

It gets better. Carter's brother, Clinton, is President of American Standard Systems (manufacturers of everything from child car seats to missile-guidance software and cluster bombs, and another untapped goldmine in marketing terms). I met him at the Annual Virginia Baccy Barons' Ball last night and he's going to be watching our progress on GIT with interest. This has been an extremely productive trip!

By the way, if by some freak chance you should talk to Caroline and you happen to mention ASS, probably best to stress the car seats rather than the weapons systems. See you Monday bright and early.

Sent from my BlackBerry

From: **David Crutton**
To: Janice Crutton
Sent: 11 January 2009, 16.05
Subject:

Hi Jan – they'll be calling my flight any minute, but I wanted to check in before I leave. If I make my connection at Dulles, I should be back in London first thing tomorrow. Thought I'd go straight to the office – you guys won't be home anyway – but I'll definitely get away early.

We parted on poor terms, but please can we make a fresh start? I really want to put last week behind us. I'll even go to ante-natal classes. How about it?

Love to Noah and Tamara. And to you.

Sent from my BlackBerry

From: **Janice Crutton**
To: Paula Sterling
Sent: 11 January 2009, 16.18
Subject:

Hi Paula – really sorry to bother you on a Sunday. I know you've got a house full of relatives, but I need you to pass on a message to David. Just paste the text below on to a new email and add the usual preamble and sign off. Thanks and sorry again – Janice x

> Ms Crutton wishes to inform you that, at the age of forty-five and being in possession of two children already, she knows all she needs to know about pregnancy and labour. You, however, having been a non-attendee at the births of said children, might find the antenatal course to be instructive.

From: **Ted Berry**
To: David Crutton
Sent: 11 January 2009, 16.21
Subject: Re: GIT

Yo geezer. You won't fucking believe this. Writing e at 2000m strapped to hang glider! iPhones are the dog's. You're never fucking offline. Great news on GIT. Look forward to debrief. Gotta go. Just spotted thermal. Beattie's at 3500m. Can't let the cunt beat me to new Brit alt. rec.

Sent from my iPhone

Monday
Mood: lilac.
Or paisley.
No, definitely
lilac.
OMG, it's so
hard to decide,
isn't it?

From: **Susi Judge-Davis-Gaultier**
To: All Staff
Sent: 12 January 2009, 08.48
Subject: Ted

Ted sprained his ankle in a hang-gliding incident at the weekend and needs to keep his foot on his desk to minimize swelling. Can anyone who needs to see him please schedule meetings in his office?

Susi Judge-Davis-Gaultier
Assistant to Ted Berry

From: **David Crutton**
To: Ted Berry, Caroline Zitter
Sent: 12 January 2009, 08.50
Subject: I love the smell of new business in the morning!

Let's touch base on my trip to VA. Ten minutes? Ted's office, I guess.

From: **Caroline Zitter**
To: David Crutton
Sent: 12 January 2009, 08.51
Subject: Out of Office AutoReply

I am in Brighton with my twins, attending Tot Tycoons: Leadership Skills for Under-Fives. If you have an urgent request please contact my assistant, Milton Keane, on milton@meerkat360.co.uk

Caroline Zitter
THE SEER

From: **Dotty Podidra**
To: David Crutton
Sent: 12 January 2009, 08.53
Subject:

Morning! Didn't expect you in so early. Thought you might nip home first. Did you have a good flight? And do you want coffee?

From: **David Crutton**
To: Dotty Podidra
Sent: 12 January 2009, 08.54
Subject: Re:

Coffee would be superb, thank you. Excellent flight. Landed early so I got in a stint at the gym. Did a series of squats and ab crunches that would make a Royal Marine puke up his immune system. I sense it's going to be an excellent week.

From: **David Crutton**
To: Donald Gold
Sent: 12 January 2009, 09.00
Subject: new assignment

G'day, Don, and what a beautiful day it is too. Don't you find the wind chill truly invigorating?

I spent the flight from VA configuring an elite team to handle GIT. I reached the conclusion that you are the ideal pick for senior account director. Should you take this on, you will direct activity across all GIT brands.

I trust you will take up this offer. It reflects the confidence that the partners and I have in you.

David Crutton
𝕿𝖍𝖊 𝕸𝖆𝖓

From: **Dotty Podidra**
To: Susi Judge-Davis-Gaultier, Milton Keane
Sent: 12 January 2009, 09.03
Subject: bosses are mad

DC's in a really good mood and it's scary. He's bouncing around singing 'Somewhere Only We Know', but a sort of 120bpm hi-energy version. Think I prefer him when he's Mr Grouchy!

From: **Susi Judge-Davis-Gaultier**
To: Dotty Podidra, Milton Keane
Sent: 12 January 2009, 09.04
Subject: Re: bosses are mad

TB in foul mood! Sprained his ankle AND dropped his iPhone from 5000 feet. He wants me to write letter of complaint to Apple because it wasn't shock-resistant!

From: **Milton Keane**
To: Susi Judge-Davis-Gaultier, Dotty Podidra
Sent: 12 January 2009, 09.05
Subject: Re: bosses are mad

Who knows what sort of mood CZ is in? Haven't seen her since November! She's probably feeling empowered. And possibly quite enlightened. V excited this morning. Going to see my lawyer at 10.00 re Milton vs UGG. Should I wear my lilac Cerruti tie (with matching hankie) or the psychedelic paisley? I'm veering towards the lilac, but will it make me seem a bit gay?

From: **Dotty Podidra**
To: Susi Judge-Davis-Gaultier, Milton Keane
Sent: 12 January 2009, 09.07
Subject: Re: bosses are mad

Warning! According to her sec, your lawyer is schizoid. Probably too long married to DC! Definitely the calming lilac. The jazzy paisley might send her off on one.

From: **Susi Judge-Davis-Gaultier**
To: Dotty Podidra, Milton Keane
Sent: 12 January 2009, 09.08
Subject: Re: bosses are mad

Definitely not the Cerruti, Milton. The psychedelic paisley clearly says 'fashion adventurer' and it's crucial that your lawyer understands you've always been at the cutting edge of design, even when you were eight.

From: **Milton Keane**
To: Susi Judge-Davis-Gaultier
Sent: 12 January 2009, 09.10
Subject: tie

Are you sure, Sooz? I'm in such a dither here.

From: **Susi Judge-Davis-Gaultier**
To: Milton Keane
Sent: 12 January 2009, 09.12
Subject: Re: tie

Absolutely positive. Dotty is perfectly lovely, but (strictly between you and me) who are you going to take style tips from? A girl who wears kitten heels even though her ankles are way too fat, or a Gaultier?

From: **Milton Keane**
To: Susi Judge-Davis-Gaultier
Sent: 12 January 2009, 09.14
Subject: Re: tie

Paisley it is. Lilac's definitely gay. Gotta go. Wish me luck!

From: **Liam O'Keefe**
To: All Staff
Sent: 12 January 2009, 09.17
Subject: Workies?

Any workies free to walk my dog? Thick trousers recommended – he's a biter.

	MSN:
Kazoo:	Flowers on my desk?
Dong:	By way of thanks.
Kazoo:	Guess you're over your fear of flying?
Dong:	Want to know how over it I am? Pretend you're a stewardess and you're announcing an emergency. Make it as dire as you like.
Kazoo:	Role-play? Do I get to dress up?
Dong:	Just do the announcement. I'll imagine the uniform.

Kazoo:	OK, here goes. THIS IS TRIXIE TRULOVE, SENIOR TROLLEY DOLLY. BOTH THE CAPTAIN AND THE CO-PILOT HAVE SEVERE FOOD POISONING (AS DOES EVERYONE ELSE WHO CHOSE THE CHICKEN). ARE THERE ANY PASSENGERS WHO A) SELECTED THE BEEF OPTION AND B) KNOW HOW TO FLY A BOEING 747 THROUGH HEAVY TURBULENCE?
Dong:	Me, me, me, I can fly it, pick me, pick me!!!!
Kazoo:	You are so over it. Aren't I brilliant?
Dong:	You're a genius. BTW, DC wants me to run GIT. Should I tell him my mother has emphysema (after a lifetime of Ambassador Ultra Mild) and give him a polite no thanks? Career advice please.
Kazoo:	Know this, Don: you're the fourth choice for GIT. Enola, Carla and Fat Harry have already turned him down on grounds of principle. That info may influence your decision.
Dong:	This is the New Testosterone-Powered Me. I LOVE flying and I'm not going to flinch from trampling over the flailing bodies of doomed colleagues. I'll say yes. When you get a mo, nip out and buy me a pack of Montana.
Kazoo:	Red, Silver or minty Green (for girls)?
Dong:	Haven't smoked since I was 16 and puked after my first drag. What do you reckon?
Kazoo:	Better make it Green.

From: **Neil Godley**
To: All Staff
Sent: 12 January 2009, 09.26
Subject: Am I going bonkers . . .

. . . or did there used to be a copier next to the gents' in the basement? I'm sure it was a Xerox BookMark 55 (with very handy fax option). Can anyone advise? I need to copy 128 time sheets ASAP.

Neil Godley (Accounts)

From: **Donald Gold**
To: David Crutton
Sent: 12 January 2009, 09.34
Subject: Re: new assignment

Hi David. I'd be thrilled to work on GIT. Thank you so much for the opportunity. Let me know when you'd like me to make a start. And hopefully it will involve plenty of trips to Virginia. I'm keen to rack up the air miles!

From: **Ted Berry**
To: Creative Department
Sent: 12 January 2009, 09.39
Subject: Project

Our first GIT briefing is at 11.30. It's an exciting project and also a top-secret one. Susi will be round to get your scrawls on the confidentiality agreements.

Ted Berry
MC IDEAZ

From: **David Crutton**
To: Donald Gold
Sent: 12 January 2009, 09.40
Subject: Re: new assignment

No time like the here and now. My office in 5 and I'll take you through the first brief. We'll be talking to the Creative Department at 11.30.

From: **Ted Berry**
To: All Staff
Sent: 12 January 2009, 09.43
Subject: New Face

I'm chuffed to bits to announce the arrival of Mr Fraggles, who will take up the new position of Clown in Residence. Mr Fraggles has worked in circus and street theatre and he is a veteran of countless children's parties. His skills in juggling, mime, conjuring and slapstick (he's a former European Custard Pie Champion) will give the Creative Department a vital and distinctive edge. Please join me in welcoming him to the team.

Ted Berry
MC IDEAZ

---

eBay.co.uk

Xerox BookMark 55

Item specifics: nearly new B&W copier with handy fax option. 55 cpm. Worth over £10,000 new. Would suit medium-sized company with need for reliable high-speed copier. Or slightly warped individual with need to paper his/her walls with pictures of arse.

Current bid: **£99.00**
End time: 8d 10h 36m

From: **Bill Geddes**
To: Liam O'Keefe
Sent: 12 January 2009, 09.54
Subject: Fido

Came up to see how your weekend was, but was driven away by the vicious bastard chained to your desk leg. What the hell are you doing with a pit bull, Liam? Is it a Lorraine substitute? Or, along with the clown, another of Ted's off-the-wall hirings? Or have you just gone completely mad?

And while I'm in question mode, how was your weekend?

From: **Sally Wilton**
To: All Staff
Sent: 12 January 2009, 10.03
Subject: Police

The police will be in shortly to investigate the missing copier (and sundry other items). Please make yourselves available should they wish to talk to you.

Sally Wilton
**PRINCESS
PAPERCLIP**

From: **Liam O'Keefe**
To: Bill Geddes
Sent: 12 January 2009, 10.04
Subject: Re: Fido

He's called Marcus Licinius Crassus (after the Roman General who defeated the slave army of Spartacus, obviously). I won him in a card game (against a Dalston chav with an OU degree in ancient history). Don't let the snarling put you off. He's a softie (unless you cross him). No workies took up my offer, so going walkies now. Might be some time.

From: **Susi Judge-Davis-Gaultier**
To: Ted Berry
Sent: 12 January 2009, 10.10
Subject: GIT briefing

Bit of a problem. Nearly everyone has refused to work on GIT. They say they won't do tobacco products. Only Zlatan, Adrijana and Harvey Harvey have signed the confidentiality agreements. I can't find Liam. Shall I ask Yossi and Mr Fraggles to make up numbers at the briefing?

From: **Ted Berry**
To: Susi Judge-Davis-Gaultier
Sent: 12 January 2009, 10.12
Subject: Re: GIT briefing

Go round the department again and remind the sanctimonious twats that the money I pay them gives me ownership of their consciences. Round up Yossi and Fraggles. And find Liam. Tell the fucker that after the Winter Sun fiasco, he's on a yellow card. He's a sixty-a-day boy. He's not going to turn down free snouts.

VOICEMAIL:

Liam, Susi here. Ted says you absolutely have to be at the GIT briefing. No excuses. And he says there are free cigarettes. Disgusting habit. The sooner you kill yourself with them the better as far as I'm concerned.

From: **David Crutton**
To: Ted Berry
Sent: 12 January 2009, 10.16
Subject: Re: New Face

Mr Fraggles? Explain.

VOICEMAIL:

Sweet message, Susi. Tell Ted I'll
be there for free fags. As long as
they're not gay menthol.

SMS:

Liam:	Cops there?
Bill:	Basement copy area resembles set of CSI: New York. What have you done this time?
Liam:	Nothing. But Licinius Crassus hasn't got permit. Text me when cops go. Need to be back by 11.29 or I lose job. And miss out on free fags
Bill:	Could I get done as an accessory?
Liam:	You'll be fine. Unless you grass me up. Gotta go. Dog's humping damsel's leg in Soho Sq. Could be my way in

From: **Ted Berry**
To: David Crutton
Sent: 12 January 2009, 10.32
Subject: Re: New Face

1   You've seen *Ocean's 11*? Like Danny and Rusty, I'm putting together a crack team of specialists that covers all possible bases.

2   You won't be carping when Mr Fraggles wins a D&AD gold for Best Use of Spinning Bowtie in a Consumer Campaign.

From: **David Crutton**
To: Ted Berry
Sent: 12 January 2009, 10.34
Subject: Re: New Face

Sorry, George Clooney. See you at 11.30.

From: **Susi Judge-Davis-Gaultier**
To: All Staff
Sent: 12 January 2009, 10.44
Subject: Workies?

Any workies free to change Ted's bandage?

    Susi Judge-Davis-Gaultier
    Assistant to Ted Berry

From: **Conchita**
To: Harvey Harvey
Sent: 12 January 2009, 11.04
Subject: need lovin'

I am gorgeous bubbly teen who want make chat with you. Reply and we have good times. <u>conchita@gotmail.com</u>. My plump breasts ache to be touch.

Hi girls! I can't keep up with all your chatty emails, so I thought I'd send you a group reply. I can't believe how many lonely girls there are out there. You need to get together and make friends. There are loads of chat rooms for teenagers. Or maybe you could start your own. I'm sure there are enough of you! Also, I notice that most of you complain about breast discomfort. I checked out some women's health sites. I found a couple of excellent ones.

www.bignaturals.com
www.boobster.net

On boobster in particular there are some pictures of extremely swollen breasts, so I'm sure there'll be helpful information there. Anyway, you all have each other's email addresses now, so you've got no excuses. Go on, get chatting!

All the best

    Harvey Harvey

SMS:

Bill: Cops have sealed basement with crime-scene tape and disappeared for tea break. Might be good time to nip back in.

From: **Róisín O'Hooligan**
To: All Staff
Sent: 12 January 2009, 11.21
Subject: Chav Central

I've got a bastard in Burberry who says he wants his dog back. He's holding Gibbon's *The History of the Decline and Fall of the Roman Empire*, but I suspect it's not so much reading matter as an offensive weapon. It's precisely because of fuckers like him that I left Cork, so will someone get him out of my face? Please!

Róisín
Reception

	SMS:
Bill:	Bad man in reception wants his dog back. He's settled in for duration. You might want to stay out for several coffees. And lunch

From: **Susi Judge-Davis-Gaultier**
To: Liam O'Keefe, Harvey Harvey, Zlatan Kovaćević, Adrijana Smiljanić, Yossi Mendoza, Mr Fraggles
Sent: 12 January 2009, 11.24
Subject: GIT

The briefing is about to start. And if anyone sees Liam (who's not around, as usual), tell him Ted says he HAS to be there.

	SMS:
Bill:	Susi in hunter-killer mode. Wants you for a GIT meeting. Any way you can sneak back in?

From: **Dotty Podidra**
To: Susi Judge-Davis-Gaultier
Sent: 12 January 2009, 11.31
Subject: Milton

He just rushed by my desk in floods. Wouldn't say a word. Now he's locked himself in CZ's office. What should I do??

From: **Susi Judge-Davis-Gaultier**
To: Dotty Podidra
Sent: 12 January 2009, 11.32
Subject: Re: Milton

Got to do biccies and beverages for meeting. Be up as soon as I can get away.

From: **Dotty Podidra**
To: Paula Sterling
Sent: 12 January 2009, 11.31
Subject: what happened?

Milton has just arrived back very upset. What happened with him and JC?

From: **Paula Sterling**
To: Dotty Podidra
Sent: 12 January 2009, 11.33
Subject: Re: what happened?

Not sure. JC's been in vile mood all morning. Had her door shut since your friend left and isn't taking calls. He did leave with a very wobbly lip. BTW, is he gay?

From: **Dotty Podidra**
To: Paula Sterling
Sent: 12 January 2009, 11.35
Subject: Re: what happened?

OMG, he is so NOT gay. Did Janice say something fairy-phobic to him? It would totally explain why he's so upset.

From: **Dotty Podidra**
To: Caroline Zitter
Sent: 12 January 2009, 11.38
Subject: I'm out here with Susi . . .

. . . and we only want to help, Milton. Since you're not answering the phone, we thought we'd give Cazza's email a try. Please let us in.

Dotty + Sooz xxx

From: **Caroline Zitter**
To: Dotty Podidra
Sent: 12 January 2009, 11.39
Subject: Out of Office AutoReply

I am in Brighton with my twins, attending Tot Tycoons: Leadership Skills for Under-Fives. If you have an urgent request please contact my assistant, Milton Keane, on milton@meerkat360.co.uk

Caroline Zitter
THE SEER

	SMS:
Bill:	Dog man scarpered on return of
	cops. Sneak in but use
	tradesmen's entrance

157

From: **Dotty Podidra**
To: Caroline Zitter
Sent: 12 January 2009, 11.38
Subject:

We totally understand if you want some space. Why don't you curl up on Cazza's sofa and have some 'me' time? Help yourself to something from the fridge. Doesn't she always have Toblerone in there? And the second you want to talk, you know we're here for you.

Dotty + Sooz xxxxxxxxxxxxxxxxxxxxxxx

From: **Paula Sterling**
To: Dotty Podidra
Sent: 12 January 2009, 11.49
Subject: Re: what happened?
Att: 1 attachment: m_keane.doc

Don't think the gay thing came up in their meeting. I really shouldn't be doing this – client confidentiality and all that rubbish – but I'm attaching the letter that Janice got me to type. Think it explains why your friend is so upset. Tell him to try not to take it personally. She's being an absolute b**** with everyone at the moment. This morning she told the post boy he had BO (which he does, but he's mentally handicapped and you don't say that sort of thing to them, do you?).

Attachment:

Re: our meeting of 12 January 2009

Dear Mr Keane

I am writing to confirm the advice that I gave you when we met to discuss your grievance with UGG Australia.

As I explained at some length, in order for a court to

find that UGG is guilty of plagiarism, it would be necessary to prove that the designer of the original UGG boot travelled from Australia to a British living room, where he or she saw your drawing on *Blue Peter*. Since it appeared on television in 1989 and the original UGG boot was launched in the 1950s, this would have involved time travel.

As I also explained at even more tedious length, plagiarism is extremely difficult to establish at the best of times. Making the case for plagiarism involving time travel has not, to the best of my knowledge, been attempted in a British court.

To summarize, you have no case. If you persist in believing that you do, then you possess even poorer judgement than your choice of a bilious paisley tie suggests. In conclusion, I am not prepared to represent you in this matter.

I enclose an invoice for your consideration. You will note that I have billed you at the full corporate rate of £950 per hour (plus VAT) in the hope that this will deter you from wasting the time of others in the legal profession.

Yours sincerely,

Janice Crutton

From: **Janice Crutton**
To: David Crutton
Sent: 12 January 2009, 12.13
Subject: peace

I have just met with one of your employees and gained first-hand experience of the frightening level of idiocy you have to deal with on a daily basis. I feel for you, David. As you probably know, I haven't been feeling much for you lately. I'd make the most of the change of mood by getting home at a reasonable time today. Friends?

From: **Liam O'Keefe**
To: All Staff
Sent: 12 January 2009, 12.22
Subject: You just can't get the staff, can you?

Spotted Milton on Caroline's window ledge on my way back in. I applaud his dedication, but can't we get workies to clean the windows any more?

From: **Dotty Podidra**
To: Susi Judge-Davis-Gaultier
Sent: 12 January 2009, 12.23
Subject: Aaagghh!

Did you see Liam's e?

From: **Susi Judge-Davis-Gaultier**
To: Dotty Podidra
Sent: 12 January 2009, 12.24
Subject: Re: Aaagghh!

Dialling 999 now.

From: **Dotty Podidra**
To: Susi Judge-Davis-Gaultier
Sent: 12 January 2009, 12.25
Subject: Re: Aaagghh!

Aren't the police already here? I'll go and grab one from the basement.

From: **Ted Berry**
To: Liam O'Keefe
Sent: 12 January 2009, 12.27
Subject: Re: You just can't get the staff, can you?

Nice of you to pop in, smartarse. My office, now.

From: **David Crutton**
To: Janice Crutton
Sent: 12 January 2009, 12.28
Subject: Re: peace

Shall we have a family dinner tonight? Like we used to when the kids could be told what to do.

By the way, which one of my lot have you been dealing with? If it's constructive dismissal or sexual harassment or some such bollocks, you know you can't handle it, don't you?

From: **Janice Crutton**
To: David Crutton
Sent: 12 January 2009, 12.31
Subject: Re: peace

Are you trying to explain conflict of interest to a lawyer? Client confidentiality prevents me from telling you who it was. All I can say is that, in addition to being an imbecile, he seemed a bit gay. Dinner would be nice. But please, not Pizza Express – the kids are too old for wax crayons and puzzle sheets.

From: **Róisín O'Hooligan**
To: All Staff
Sent: 12 January 2009, 12.37
Subject: Nurr-nurr-nurr-nurr-nurr-nurr!

Oh, the excitement of a job in advertising. A shiny red fire engine has just pulled up outside. Fireman Sam has asked me to tell you to avoid using the main entrance until his mates have finished talking the gay idiot down from his perch. Frankly, I don't know why they're bothering. Haven't they got cats to save?

Róisín
Reception

From: **David Crutton**
To: Janice Crutton
Sent: 12 January 2009, 12.41
Subject: Re: peace

I'll see if the kids are around. Incidentally, if your Meerkat360 client was wearing a ghastly paisley tie, he's presently being talked down from a window ledge. Nice work and handled like a true Crutton.

From: **Sally Wilton**
To: Liam O'Keefe
Sent: 12 January 2009, 12.50
Subject: Help with inquiries

Can you make yourself available for a chat with DC Hindley, who's here to investigate the missing copier (and sundry other items)? She found a betting slip with your name on it in the copy area waste bin and she wants to know if you saw anything suspicious.

Sally Wilton
**PRINCESS
PAPERCLIP**

From: **Lorraine Pallister**
To: Liam O'Keefe
Sent: 12 January 2009, 12.51
Subject: My stuff

I dropped by your place to get my things on my way to work. I left my key on the coffee table. Thanks for leaving my brooch out. I was pretty horrible in my last email. Sorry. I'm still really mad at you, but I don't hate you. I can't be with you any more though. You've got problems that I can't cope with. You have to get help, Liam. Not for me but for your own sake.

    Lorraine

PS: Why does the spare room look like Arthur Daley's lock-up? And why is there a photocopier in the kitchen? Does it have a microwave function or something?

From: **Ted Berry**
To: Liam O'Keefe
Sent: 12 January 2009, 12.52
Subject: Final, final warning

I like you, geezer, but you're making it extremely difficult for me. To repeat what I said in my office: you're in Last Chance Saloon and it's almost chucking-out time. If you don't deliver on GIT, I'll have to do something terminal.

From: **Ted Berry**
To: Susi Judge-Davis-Gaultier
Sent: 12 January 2009, 12.53
Subject:

Have you seen the Corgi toy that sits on the shelf next to my D&ADs? It's worth a fucking fortune. Have you been tidying up again?

From: **Liam O'Keefe**
To: Brett Topolski
Sent: 12 January 2009, 12.54
Subject: It couldn't get any worse

Worse than merely hating me, Lorraine pities me. And Ted's given me the world's stupidest brief and told me my job depends on it. Oh, and the cops want to talk to me. Get me a job in Dubai. I'll do anything. I'll clean your pool, for fuck's sake.

From: **Ted Berry**
To: Liam O'Keefe
Sent: 12 January 2009, 12.55
Subject: Forgot to mention . . .

. . . I want you to team up with Harvey Harvey on GIT.

From: **Liam O'Keefe**
To: Brett Topolski
Sent: 12 January 2009, 13.03
Subject: It just got worse

To make the challenge more interesting Ted's teamed me up with Harvey Harvey. Have I told you about Harvey Harvey?

From: **Harvey Harvey**
To: Liam O'Keefe
Sent: 12 January 2009, 13.11
Subject: Great news

Ted just told me we're teaming up on GIT. Fantastic! I've already got a load of ideas. How about we go for a bite to eat and discuss?

From: **Liam O'Keefe**
To: Harvey Harvey
Sent: 12 January 2009, 13.12
Subject: Out of Office AutoReply

I am out of the office until further notice (if your name is Harvey Harvey).

From: **Susi Judge-Davis-Gaultier**
To: All Staff
Sent: 12 January 2009, 13.21
Subject: Missing from Ted's office

A Chipperfield's Circus crane (manufactured by Corgi and complete with original box) has gone missing from the display shelf in Ted's office. Can you please look for it? It is extremely valuable and Ted would like it back.

Susi Judge-Davis-Gaultier
Assistant to Ted Berry

From: **Susi Judge-Davis-Gaultier**
To: All Staff
Sent: 12 January 2009, 13.24
Subject: Milton Keane

As you know, Milton has been taken to hospital following his ordeal on Caroline's window ledge. He is being treated for shock and NOT for a nervous breakdown. All the vile rumours are totally out of order. Here are the facts. Milton was tidying Caroline's office before her return when he spotted a distressed pigeon on the ledge. Out of pure compassion – and ABSOLUTELY NOT because he was suicidal – he climbed out to help the poor creature. Personally, I think he deserves a medal for bravery and not the sniggers and innuendo that he's being subjected to. And all those people who were hanging out of windows filming him on their mobiles had better not be uploading the clips to YouTube.

And FYI, Róisín, he is NOT gay.

Susi Judge-Davis-Gaultier
Assistant to Ted Berry

From: **Brett Topolski**
To: Liam O'Keefe
Sent: 12 January 2009, 13.26
Subject: Re: It just got worse

No you haven't told me about Harvey Harvey. (Is that really his name or have you developed a keyboard stutter?) What's the brief?

---

eBay.co.uk

Chipperfield's Circus Crane

Item specifics: Corgi toy in original box. Mint condition. Ideal for keen collector. Or extremely small circus owner.

Current bid:	**£02.00**
End time:	9d 23h 48m

From: **Dotty Podidra**
To: Susi Judge-Davis-Gaultier
Sent: 12 January 2009, 13.28
Subject: Re: Milton Keane

Well done on the all-staffer, Susi. Do you think they'll buy it? And have you called the Samaritans?

From: **Susi Judge-Davis-Gaultier**
To: Dotty Podidra
Sent: 12 January 2009, 13.31
Subject: Re: Milton Keane

Who knows if they'll go for it? Phoning Samaritans now. I'm so, so worried about him. DC's wife is a total mad cow. And she's wrong. Milton definitely has a case against UGG. Anyone involved in the fashion biz (as I am) would tell you that.

From: **Liam O'Keefe**
To: Brett Topolski
Sent: 12 January 2009, 13.32
Subject: Re: It just got worse

Yes, Harvey and Harvey really are his names. He has the unique advantage of being able to switch round first and surname without anyone being any the wiser. How do I begin to describe him? Imagine the retard bastard son of Jim Carrey's character in *The Cable Guy* and Dustin Hoffman's in *Rain Man*. He weirds me out to the point where I can't be in the same room as him.

Can't tell you about the brief. Ted made me sign a gagging order.

From: **Brett Topolski**
To: Liam O'Keefe
Sent: 12 January 2009, 13.35
Subject: Re: It just got worse

Oh, you'll tell me. You always tell me everything. You told me about the thing with the thing, remember?

From: **Róisín O'Hooligan**
To: Susi Judge-Davis-Gaultier
Sent: 12 January 2009, 13.38
Subject: Re: Milton Keane

My apologies, Susi. Of course Milton isn't gay. And I'm not fucking Irish.

From: **Liam O'Keefe**
To: Brett Topolski
Sent: 12 January 2009, 13.47
Subject: Re: It just got worse

Point taken. But if I tell you, you'd better not tell a living soul or I'll have to murder your arse.

From: **Brett Topolski**
To: Liam O'Keefe
Sent: 12 January 2009, 13.49
Subject: Re: It just got worse

Trust me. Have I ever told anyone about the thing with the thing?

From: **Liam O'Keefe**
To: Brett Topolski
Sent: 12 January 2009, 13.59
Subject: Re: It just got worse

The brief's for Montana. They've got a product without a marketing concept. Tiny-weeny cigarettes in a tiny-weeny box. They're as slim as budget roll-ups and a lot less satisfying. I just smoked one. Two drags of fuck all. I asked TB why they're making them. Because they can, he said. So they've got the technology. Shame they haven't got a clue. But they're determined to market them and if I don't come up with an idea, I'm doomed.

Harvey Harvey just slipped a chain of Post-its under my door. He's Googled midgets. He's calculated there are thousands across Europe (especially in the former Soviet Bloc) and, assuming roughly 30% of them are smokers, there's a ready-made niche market. He's fucked in the head, I tell you. Trouble is I can't come up with a better idea. Or any idea at all. Advice please.

From: **David Crutton**
To: Dotty Podidra
Sent: 12 January 2009, 14.11
Subject:

If you've finished on suicide watch, get in here and show me how to send a text.

From: **Liam O'Keefe**
To: Harvey Harvey
Sent: 12 January 2009, 14.21
Subject: Ground rules

I'm dead happy – thrilled even – to be working with you, Harvey (I'm using your first name, by the way, and not being rude by calling you by your second), but I need to set you straight on a couple of things. I like my space. Lots of space. That means I won't be camping out in your office. And you won't be camping out in mine. And we certainly won't be cooped up in those fucking beach huts. If you've got any ideas, email them to me.

And please don't shove notes under my door. It's kinda creepy.

	SMS:
Dad:	Yo tam. Bakk in uk and thort it b kool 2 take mum 4 surprize dinner. Up 4 it?

Dad: Wossup noah. U up 4 dinner wiv
            mum 2nite? Lemme no an will
            book sumfink spesh

From: **Brett Topolski**
To: Liam O'Keefe
Sent: 12 January 2009, 14.39
Subject: Re: It just got worse

You sent me an e last week, which I filed in my special folder marked 'death threats and general hate mail'. It said, and I quote:

> << You are the steaming turd of advice-giving and *my* advice to *you* is to keep your fat fucking beak out of my business. >>

Now you want my advice? Piss off.

From: **Harvey Harvey**
To: Liam O'Keefe
Sent: 12 January 2009, 14.41
Subject: Re: Ground rules

Great! I love email. I spend my whole day on it. I had an amazing thought this morning. You could tell a whole story just by using emails. Imagine an entire novel where you're peeking into people's private inboxes. It could be a murder mystery. Or a whacky comedy! Wouldn't that be brilliant?

From: **Liam O'Keefe**
To: Harvey Harvey
Sent: 12 January 2009, 14.44
Subject: Re: Ground rules

It's been done: *Who Moved My BlackBerry?* It was shit. And please don't say whacky. It's kinda creepy.

From: **Liam O'Keefe**
To: Brett Topolski
Sent: 12 January 2009, 15.01
Subject: Re: It just got worse

I was upset. I didn't know what I was saying. Besides, I was talking about girlfriend advice, which you're rubbish at. I'm asking for advertising advice. You're genius at that.

Got to see a nice policewoman now about a missing photocopier. (Ridiculous. How am I going to get one of those out? Anyone would think I hired a van with a loading lift and came in on a Sunday evening when there's no one around except for a Filipino cleaner who's rendered blind for a fiver.)

I expect a list of your ten top ideas upon my return.

	SMS:
Tam:	You get weird text from dad?
Noah:	That was from dad?! Thought it was spam. Trashed it
Tam:	Think something happened to him in USA?
Noah:	Maybe he joined a cult
Tam:	Text him back. Tell him we can't make it

	SMS:
Noah:	Hi dad. Got ton of homework. Tam says she's washing hair. Dinner not good idea. You go out with mum tho. She needs to chill

From: **Brett Topolski**
To: Liam O'Keefe
Sent: 12 January 2009, 15.22
Subject: Re: It just got worse

You nicked a whole copier? Excellent to see you moving up from the usual swag of paperclips and Post-its. How did it go with the cops? Your exploit has earned you a reprieve. I'll give these Mini Montanas some thought. Not too much though. Crashing a party at Jim Davidson's tonight.

Allah rocks

Brett

From: **David Crutton**
To: Janice Crutton
Sent: 12 January 2009, 15.26
Subject: Tonight

The kids are busy, so how about just you and me go out for dinner?

From: **Liam O'Keefe**
To: Brett Topolski
Sent: 12 January 2009, 15.30
Subject: Re: It just got worse

Went fine with the cops. They're clutching at straws. Twin of Godley is their prime suspect (presumably on the basis that his desk is nearest to the missing copier). Now got to sift through a fat wad of ideas Double H left on my desk. He writes things up on *Doctor Who* notepaper. Will be using my longest barge pole.

From: **Janice Crutton**
To: David Crutton
Sent: 12 January 2009, 15.35
Subject: Re: Tonight

You think leaving the kids unattended after the party fiasco at Christmas is a good idea?

From: **David Crutton**
To: Janice Crutton
Sent: 12 January 2009, 15.38
Subject: Re: Tonight

Takeaway then?

From: **Harvey Harvey**
To: Liam O'Keefe
Sent: 12 January 2009, 15.39
Subject:

Hi Liam. Did you find the ideas I left on your desk while you were at your meeting? Let me know what you think. I really like Montana Ambivalent (the small cigarette for the undecided smoker) and Montana Fun Size (the cigarette for when you want a puff but couldn't smoke a whole one). By the way, your dog was thirsty so I made him a nice mug of tea. I found some sugar in your desk drawer. I gave him the whole sachet. He loves it sweet, doesn't he?

From: **Liam O'Keefe**
To: Harvey Harvey
Sent: 12 January 2009, 15.41
Subject: Re:

That wasn't sugar, you doofus. No wonder he's so fucking lively.

From: **Janice Crutton**
To: David Crutton
Sent: 12 January 2009, 15.42
Subject: Re: Tonight

Chinese or Indian? Your choice. And we can talk about names and nursery colour schemes.

From: **David Crutton**
To: Dotty Podidra
Sent: 12 January 2009, 15.44
Subject:

Nip to Waterstone's and get me some books on interior decor for kids' rooms. And one on baby names.

From: **Neil Godley**
To: David Crutton
Cc: Caroline Zitter, Ted Berry, Sally Wilton
Sent: 12 January 2009, 15.59
Subject: The police

I will be writing to the Police Complaints Authority, but I wish to place on record my disgust at my treatment at the hands of Detective Constable Hindley. Even though I was the one that reported the missing photocopier, she treated me as a suspect. She subjected me to brutal questioning, denied me my fundamental human right (under EU law) to a toilet break and, despite the fact that she didn't have a search warrant, she insisted on going through my filing cabinets (which contain both confidential company files and certain personal items).

I have never had so much as a parking ticket and I am a member of three Neighbourhood Watch groups. I have also been commended by Crime Stoppers for making over 500 reports (with accompanying photographic documentation) of litter louts. To be treated as a common criminal in this way has severely knocked my faith in our police force.

I am too upset to complete my work and I am leaving for a session with a post-traumatic stress counsellor. I will reclaim the cost of this from the company.

Neil Godley (Accounts)

From: **Janice Crutton**
To: David Crutton
Sent: 12 January 2009, 16.17
Subject: Re: Tonight

I was joking about baby names and nursery décor, by the way. Just that you've been ominously silent.

From: **David Crutton**
To: Dotty Podidra
Sent: 12 January 2009, 16.20
Subject:

Nip out to Waterstone's and get a refund on those books.

From: **David Crutton**
To: Sally Wilton
Sent: 12 January 2009, 16.22
Subject: Neil Godley

Something about this self-righteous arse bugs me. He gives me an unsettling sense of deja vu. Can we do something about him? At the very least remove his email privileges.

From: **Bill Geddes**
To: Liam O'Keefe
Sent: 12 January 2009, 16.27
Subject:

You catching some zeds? I've just spotted your dog sprinting down the corridor. He looks very pumped. Has he been down the gym?

From: **Susi Judge-Davis-Gaultier**
To: All Staff
Sent: 12 January 2009, 16.29
Subject:

Can whoever owns the disgusting off-white dog please come and sort it out immediately. It's just done something vile on my leg and my Wolfords are completely shredded.

From: **Kazu Makino**
To: Susi Judge-Davis-Gaultier
Sent: 12 January 2009, 16.31
Subject: Re:

Thanks, Susi. That would explain the no. 2 in the lift. I thought someone from our RNIB client must have mistaken it for the loo!

From: **Róisín O'Hooligan**
To: All Staff
Sent: 12 January 2009, 16.37
Subject:

Just in case anyone cares, the dog has our Trebor client cornered by the giant yucca. I think it can smell his Allsorts samples because it's going mental. Oh, Mr Fraggles has just turned up and he's trying to lure it away with a string of comedy sausages.

Thoroughly entertaining as this is, I think someone should deal with it before it gets out of hand.

Róisín
Reception

From: **Sally Wilton**
To: All Staff
Sent: 12 January 2009, 16.34
Subject: This is not a practice!

Do not ignore the fire alarm and, if you come across the dog, do not attempt to tackle it. Please vacate the building in a calm and orderly fashion. A SWAT team is on its way.

Sally Wilton
**PRINCESS
PAPERCLIP**

From: **Harvey Harvey**
To: All Staff
Sent: 12 January 2009, 16.35
Subject:

I can hear a bell and it won't stop. Can anyone else hear it or have my voices come back?

From: **Sally Wilton**
To: Harvey Harvey
Sent: 12 January 2009, 16.36
Subject: Re:

IT'S THE FIRE ALARM, HARVEY. LEAVE THE BUILDING IMMEDI-ATELY!

Tuesday
Mood: **97% gay**

bbc.co.uk/news
Dog Day Afternoon in Adland

Meerkat360, the London advertising agency that brought us the notorious David Blunkett randy guide-dog viral for RNIB, went to the dogs in an entirely different way yesterday afternoon.

Work at the agency's Soho office halted when a pit bull terrier set off on a terrifying orgy of violence and destruction, injuring three people and causing thousands of pounds' worth of damage.

By the time police marksmen arrived, computers had been destroyed, desks overturned and valuable artwork shredded, and the dog was dead. Zlatan Kovaćević, the company's Serbian art director whose father is a veteran of the siege of Sarajevo, apparently killed it with a single blow to the throat. 'It was easy as pissing,' Kovačević said. 'My father teach me. In former Yugoslavia Bosnian Muslim teach their dogs to attack Christian. In the army he learn to liquidate them with bare hand.'

Several employees are believed to have filmed the incident on camera phones and the police have appealed for mobiles to be handed over so that they can piece together what happened.

There was speculation that the dog had been under the influence of drugs and that this had contributed to the frenzied nature of its attack. The police declined to comment, although they did confirm that the animal would undergo an autopsy and blood tests would be carried out.

The dog rage marked the climax of an eventful day at Meerkat360. Earlier, emergency services were called to rescue an employee stranded on a fifth-floor window ledge.

David Crutton, Meerkat360's managing director (his business card assigns him the title of The Man), sought to put a positive spin on both incidents. He said, 'These kinds of things are exactly why a day at Meerkat360 can never be described as just another day at the office. Here we thrive on the unpredictable. Creativity feeds on adrenalin and the incident with the dog will only serve to raise the level of our output and give us a competitive edge. Believe me, I wouldn't be surprised if our rivals aren't now thinking of introducing big cats and grizzly bears into the creative mix. By the way, do not refer to me as The f****** Man. I am the managing director.'

Today's most viewed videos

1 **Dog goes mad in office**
Like Columbine except with a dog instead of goths!!
Views: 378,423
★ ★ ★ ★ ★

2 **Dog bites clown**
See Pierrot get it in the arse. Hilarious!
Views: 322,612
★ ★ ★

3 **Jumper saved by firemen**
Awesome clip. Michael Jackson meets Larry Grayson. The suicide guy actually does a mincing moonwalk along the ledge. And check out the tie, people. It spells out 'homosexual' in paisley.
Views: 225,089
★ ★ ★ ★

4 **Clown bites dog**
Pierrot's revenge.
Views: 184,284
★ ★ ★ ★ ★

5 **Serbian execution techniques**
Zlatan demonstrates how to take out a family pet with a single blow to the throat. No dogs were seriously harmed in the making of this video.
Views: 101,738
★

Moonwalking Pigeon Rescuer

The latest subject of the Gaydar treatment is the window-ledge dancer on YouTube. Gay or straight? I'd say card-carrying fudge nudger, but you the public must decide. Watch the YouTube clip <u>here</u>, check out his MySpace profile <u>here</u>, then vote in my poll <u>here</u>. Results later, Gay Gazers.

> Poll archive:
> <u>Prince Edward</u>
> <u>The Teletubbies</u> (but not Dipsy)
> <u>Cliff Richard</u> (boring, I know, but it has to be done)
> <u>The Pillsbury Dough Boy</u>
> <u>Tom Cruise</u>
> <u>The Entire Church of Scientology</u>
> <u>Shaggy & Scooby</u> (these two are just too tight, if you know what I mean)
> <u>Velma</u> (can't get a boyfriend? More like *won't*)
> <u>Beenie Man & Buju Banton</u> (methinks they doth protest too much)
> <u>Eminem</u> (see above)
> <u>David Beckham</u> (a boy can dream, can't he?)
> <u>Merrill Lynch</u> (I know it's an American investment bank, but it's such a gay name)

Milt Shake

Male
28 years old
London
Mood: fruity

Milt Shake's Interests

General: I love clubbing (dancing, not baby seals, silly!) and the theatre, especially musicals. Seen *Chicago* 17 times!! (Go to my wicked <u>online poll</u>: The Best Roxie Hart – Denise Van Outen or Tina Arena?)

Music: Mariah, Madonna, Kylie, Steps (but shh, don't tell anyone). And I am the BIGGEST Michael jackson fan. Proof: I have tickets for 46 out of his 50 O_2 shows!!

Films: *Chicago*, *Grease*, *South Pacific*, *The Wedding Planner*, *High School Musical* (but shh, don't tell anyone). Definitely NOT *Brokeback Mountain*. Men botting? IMO, total yuck-fest!

Television: *Ugly B*, *Enders*, *Desp Housewives*. I'm a MASSIVE *BB* fan (big up Chantelle, the all-time best). And every year I throw the BEST Eurovision party in West London!!

Books: My boss gives me loads of self-improvement books. You can find them all in the Oxfam shop on Willesden High Rd (but shh, don't tell her!)

Heroes: Michael J, Mariah, Brave Jade (the new Queen of Our Hearts), the Dalai Lama

Milt Shake's details

Status:	single
Here for:	lurve!
Orientation:	totally and utterly straight
Body type:	hot and 100% drug-free!
Ethnicity:	none of your beeswax (that's such an inappropriate question, isn't it?)
Zodiac:	hi, I'm Milt and I'm a Virgo (as if!!!)
Children:	don't be silly
Occupation:	senior executive assistant to partner in a top London advertising and marketing agency

Milt Shake's friend space

Milt Shake has 18,934 friends

blogass.co.uk

Posted by **The Gaydar Guy**

Moonwalking Pigeon Rescuer Poll Results

GAY: ▪▪▪▪▪▪▪▪▪▪▪▪▪▪▪▪▪▪▪▪▪▪▪▪▪▪▪ 97%

STRAIGHT: ▪ 3%

Wednesday
Mood: charitable
(up to a point)

From: **Sally Wilton**
To: All Staff
Sent: 14 January 2009, 09.01
Subject: Missing tools

The contractor carrying out repairs after Monday's incident has brought to my attention the loss of a number of power tools. In particular, he is missing a Kango 2500 Series electric breaker. Please check your offices. This is a big item and should not have gone far.

Sally Wilton
PRINCESS
PAPERCLIP

From: **Alex Sofroniou**
To: All Staff
Sent: 14 January 2009, 09.03
Subject: IT systems

We are still working on getting IT systems up and running after

Monday's disruption. Will all those who have functioning PCs and Macs continue to share resources with those who haven't. I anticipate the work being completed by the end of today or early tomorrow. Thank you for your patience.

Alex Sofroniou
ZORBΛ THE GEEⰕ

PS: Normal service will be resumed more quickly if you refrain from overloading the server with uploads to YouTube!

From: **Kazu Makino**
To: All Staff
Sent: 14 January 2009, 09.06
Subject: Sorry, Miss, a dog ate my artwork!

Mad Dog managed to destroy most of our Esmée Éloge De-Wrinkelle presentation. Can whoever nicked the samples of the new packaging from my desk please return them ASAP as we need to re-shoot. I'm guessing the culprit is 35+, which narrows it down somewhat – got to admit it's all a bit *Logan's Run* round here!

From: **Susi Judge-Davis-Gaultier**
To: Creative Department
Sent: 14 January 2009, 09.15
Subject: Mr Fraggles

He has asked me to tell you he will be out this morning for precautionary rabies jabs after the bite to his derriere. The 10.30 Custard Pie Workshop is cancelled.

From: **Milton Keane**
To: All Staff
Sent: 14 January 2009, 09.16
Subject: Workies?

Any workies free to get doggy-dos out of Caroline's Louis XIV chaise longue? A free mega-spritz of l'Eau d'Issey Pour Homme for the successful applicant!

Milton Keane
As seen on YouTube!

From: **Donald Gold**
To: All Staff
Sent: 14 January 2009, 09.17
Subject: Thanks

Just to let you know that I visited Enola in hospital yesterday evening. She asked me to pass on her thanks for all the cards and flowers. With all the bandages, it was hard to tell how badly disfigured her face is, but she's looking on the bright side. She told me the doctors have promised that the reconstructive surgery will take at least ten years off her!

From: **Ted Berry**
To: Liam O'Keefe
Sent: 14 January 2009, 09.18
Subject: One good reason . . .

. . . why I shouldn't fire you right now?

From: **Liam O'Keefe**
To: Harvey Harvey
Sent: 14 January 2009, 09.19
Subject: Plaintive cry for help!

I need a really good (as in excellent) Montana idea IMMEDIATELY.

From: **Harvey Harvey**
To: Liam O'Keefe
Sent: 14 January 2009, 09.20
Subject: Out of Office AutoReply

Harvey Harvey has just discovered Out of Office AutoReply and he will be using it all day!

From: **Róisín O'Hooligan**
To: Zlatan Kovaćević
Sent: 14 January 2009, 09.21
Subject: Visitor

Got a guy down here from the Billericay branch of the BNP. He wants to know if you can give him and his mates a seminar on assassination techniques. Shall I tell the shave-head scuzz ball to sling his hook or is this the kind of sick shit you do in your spare time?

From: **Zlatan Kovaćević**
To: Róisín O'Hooligan
Sent: 14 January 2009, 09.22
Subject: Re: Visitor

What is BNP?

From: **Róisín O'Hooligan**
To: Zlatan Kovaćević
Sent: 14 January 2009, 09.23
Subject: Re: Visitor

Stands for British National Party. Basically Nazis minus the fashion flair.

From: **Zlatan Kovaćević**
To: Róisín O'Hooligan
Sent: 14 January 2009, 09.24
Subject: Re: Visitor

Tell him I be there in 5 minute.

From: **Brett Topolski**
To: Liam O'Keefe
Sent: 14 January 2009, 09.29
Subject: Thank heaven for YouTube

So good to be able to keep up with London here in the desert. Yes, the Gulf ground to a halt as we watched your offices get trashed by the pit bull. Who did the magnificent beast belong to or did it just wander in off the street? And was it on PCP or similar? In the bit where it overturns the boardroom table it seems to possess supercanine strength. Haven't heard from you, but I trust you managed to avoid the slavering jaws of death.

Jim Davidson's party was a rum affair. There's something disturbing about a comic whose act is based on contempt for various darkies and duskies choosing to spend his decline surrounded by Koran-muttering towel heads. But it seems he's found a kindred spirit in Vince, the only remaining person on the planet who laughs at all his jokes. I sense they're going to be spending a lot of time together, which might take the strain off me.

I've come up with nada on your Mini Montana brief. It's a proper bastard. It's all wrong as a concept. Don't they look stupidly small in an adult gob? I told Vince about it (and before you go off on one, he doesn't strictly count as a 'living' soul, so I didn't break my promise). He said it reminded him of those sweet ciggies we used to pretend-smoke when we were kids. I think your best bet is to go with Harvey Harvey's idea and hit the dwarf market with all guns blazing.

Things are kicking off here. Vince tried to email Jim D some porny mpegs. Trouble is that our IT department has installed a Sharia 100i, IBM's state-of-the-art fundamentalist server, and the sirens have gone off. Time to leave the building, I think, if not the country.

See ya later Allah-gator

From: **Liam O'Keefe**
To: Brett Topolski
Sent: 14 January 2009, 09.34
Subject: Re: Thank heaven for YouTube

The dog was mine and I'm in the deepest shit as a result. But I think you might just have saved my hide. Thanks.

From: **Liam O'Keefe**
To: Ted Berry
Sent: 14 January 2009, 09.36
Subject: Re: One good reason . . .

. . . you shouldn't fire me is that I've got an idea for Montana. Can I see you?

From: **Ted Berry**
To: Liam O'Keefe
Sent: 14 January 2009, 09.39
Subject: Re: One good reason . . .

Give me 15 minutes. Got to talk to a man about getting the fucking bite marks out of my Cannes gold lion – you twat.

Kango 2500 Breaker

Item specifics: the Joe Calzaghe of electric power tools with a staggering blow count of 1400 per minute. Would suit pikey paving contractor. Or robber who wants to bust into the Barclays on Finchley Rd via the pet shop next door (I've checked it out. It's doable).

Current bid: **£04.21**
End time: 8d 12h 9m

From: **Lorraine Pallister**
To: Liam O'Keefe
Sent: 14 January 2009, 09.44
Subject: Big Bruv

I didn't want to send this email. Only obeying orders. Philip, my boss (normally a picture of sanity), has asked me to ask you a favour. He wants you to tell your idiot YouTube star that if he were to audition for *BB10*, his entry would be looked at very favourably. Beats me. I guess one man's exhibitionist train wreck is another man's perfect reality star. I know you might not feel inclined to help me at the moment, but if you can do this, I'd appreciate it.

Lorraine

From: **Milton Keane**
To: All Staff
Sent: 14 January 2009, 09.51
Subject: Workies?

Any workies free to burn 100 limited-edition DVDs of my Gravity Defying Dance of Death (which I will be signing at lunchtime to sate public demand!)?

Milton Keane
Celebrity Sec

From: **Dotty Podidra**
To: Susi Judge-Davis-Gaultier
Sent: 14 January 2009, 09.54
Subject: Milton

Has he gone completely potty? Doesn't he realize that everyone is laughing at him and saying he's gay?

From: **Susi Judge-Davis-Gaultier**
To: Dotty Podidra
Sent: 14 January 2009, 09.57
Subject: Re: Milton

We need to have a serious talk with him, don't we? Let's get together in fifteen and discuss. (Just got to stick around and watch Ted fire Liam – whoopee-doo!!)

From: **Susi Judge-Davis-Gaultier**
To: Liam O'Keefe
Sent: 14 January 2009, 09.59
Subject:

Ted wants to see you now. And don't go thinking the fact that you look like a human punch bag will save you. Ted is quite understandably very angry with you. I can't say I'll be sorry to see you go, especially after what your disgusting animal did on my leg. BTW, you owe me £29 for new tights. They were Wolford.

From: **Bill Geddes**
To: Liam O'Keefe
Sent: 14 January 2009, 10.08
Subject: What the hell happened to you?

I just walked by Little Ted's office and spotted you through the glass. Not that it was easy to recognize you under two black eyes. What happened?

From: **David Crutton**
To: Ted Berry
Cc: Caroline Zitter, Donald Gold, Kazu Makino
Sent: 14 January 2009, 10.13
Subject: Esmée Éloge

When can we review the new political celeb list on Project Red Carpet? Don is due to present in Brazil next week.

From: **Caroline Zitter**
To: David Crutton
Sent: 14 January 2009, 10.14
Subject: Out of Office AutoReply

I am out of the office attending What We Can Learn from Dogs: Marketing the Barbara Woodhouse Way. I will return on Thursday 15th January. If you have an urgent request please contact my assistant, Milton Keane, on milton@meerkat360.co.uk

Caroline Zitter
THE SEER

Kazoo:	Yikes! Forgot about Brazil. Better book a ticket.
Dong:	Yes, you'd better.
Kazoo:	Want me to do the usual and pre-check airline safety records?
Dong:	Won't be necessary. I'd fly a plane piloted by a kamikaze these days.
Kazoo:	Should I take offence at the WW2 ref?
Dong:	Don't know? Should you?
Kazoo:	Suspect the fact that I'm asking the question means I shouldn't be. Let's face it, the kamikazes were nuts. Definitely wouldn't get jobs with modern, PR-conscious airlines.
Dong:	But if one did slip through BA's rigorous psychological vetting, I'd be cool with it.
Kazoo:	Big words. You sure you'll feel as confident when you're sitting in the terminal next week?
Dong:	Do you dare doubt me?
Kazoo:	Of course not. But shall I call your doctor and get a repeat script for Valium? Just in case.
Dong:	Good idea.

From: **Susi Judge-Davis-Gaultier**
To: Dotty Podidra
Sent: 14 January 2009, 10.24
Subject: Unbelievable!!!

Liam has just walked out of TB's office with the biggest grin on his stupid face. Definitely not looking like a man who's just been fired.

Keef:	Touched by your concern. I do look a state.
Bilge:	Been sparring with Ricky Hatton?
Keef:	Ricky's fat cousin. Got a visit from Dog Boy. Wanted to communicate his disappointment that I hadn't taken the best care of his pooch.
Bilge:	Did you fight back?
Keef:	Me lover, not fighter. Saved by arrival of Dimitri.
Bilge:	Who he?
Keef:	Friendly neighbourhood shylock. Called round for payment. He's a hard bastard. Saw off Dog Boy.
Bilge:	A good bloke. We all need mates like that.
Keef:	What are you talking about? He's a freshly minted cunt. He's a fucking loan shark.
Bilge:	Why did he step in then?
Keef:	Calculated that if he didn't save my life he wouldn't see a penny of what I owe. I've now got till the end of the month. Then I'm dead.
Bilge:	Ouch. How much are you in for?
Keef:	You don't want to know. You couldn't lend me a tenner though?
Bilge:	Depends whether or not I win the sweep.
Keef:	Sweeps are my job. Why wasn't I told?
Bilge:	You don't want to know.
Keef:	Ah, I see. Sweep was about me, wasn't it? Lemme guess. What time I get fired? What slot did you pull out of hat?
Bilge:	10.00–10.30. Soz, but my fingers were crossed when I saw you in

	Little Ted's at 10.05.
Keef:	Thanks for the support, you horse-faced suit. Tell your gambling chums you all lost.
Bilge:	You're safe? Soz again, but assumed you were a lost cause.
Keef:	Just gave LT the best ever Montana idea. Totally safe. At least until it's presented to client.

From: **Ted Berry**
To: David Crutton
Sent: 14 January 2009, 10.36
Subject: GIT

You got time later to go through an excellent idea I just had from Liam?

From: **David Crutton**
To: Ted Berry
Sent: 14 January 2009, 10.39
Subject: Re: GIT

I'll be free later. I take it you haven't fired him, then?

From: **Ted Berry**
To: David Crutton
Sent: 14 January 2009, 10.42
Subject: Re: GIT

We need to keep him. At least until the client presentation. By the way, I intend to review sleb scents at lunchtime, so let's catch up this afternoon.

	MSN:
Bilge:	Had a chat with the guys and they've agreed to donate the pot to you as a tribute to your breathtaking jamminess. Only £55 though.
Keef:	Ta. Every little helps, as some ineffably smug ad campaign would have us believe.
Bilge:	Want me to divert my London Marathon sponsorship your way? I'm sure the children at the Noah's Ark Hospice will appreciate that there are nobler causes.
Keef:	That's sweet, but don't worry about it. I just owe a few quid. I'll sort it.

From: **Liam O'Keefe**
To: Lorraine Pallister
Sent: 14 January 2009, 10.58
Subject: Re: Big Bruv

Judging by the way he's strutting his fame, the idiot already thinks he's too big for *BB*. He might be up for the celebrity variant though. I'll tell him about your boss's interest if you'll go out for a drink with me.

From: **Liam O'Keefe**
To: Brett Topolski
Sent: 14 January 2009, 11.00
Subject: Re: Thank heaven for YouTube

Tell Vince he's a genius.

From: **Susi Judge-Davis-Gaultier**
To: Creative Department
Sent: 14 January 2009, 11.03
Subject: Project Red Carpet

Ted would like everyone in his office at 1.00 to review political celebrity names for Esmée Éloge. Please don't be late. He is on a tight schedule and needs to be at his Thai boxing class at 1.40.

From: **Comfort Ajegbo**
To: Harvey Harvey
Sent: 14 January 2009, 11.17
Subject: Help I need kind sir

Good day. My name is Miss Comfort Ajegbo, the only daughter of the late Mr Gaius Julius Ajegbo. My dear father was very wealthy oil trader in Lagos, the city of Nigeria. My beloved mother died when I was a baby and ever since my father treat me as his special one. But then my father died, poisoned by evil business associates on trip to oil wells.

Before his death in November 2007 he call me secretly to his bedside in private hospital. He told me he has the sum of $79 million in secret account in most prestigious bank in Lagos. He place account in my name so that his wicked associates can never know of it.

He explained to me that I must seek a foreign partner in a country of my choice where I will transfer this money so his associates can never ever find it. He told me I must use the money for investment purpose to provide for my safe future.

I am honourably seeking your assistance in the following ways:

1   To provide bank account into which this money can be transferred.
2   To serve as a guardian of this fund since I am only 19 years of age.

3   To make the arrangement for me to come to your country to further my education and to escape from my late father's ruthless associates who would not hesitate to kill me dead.

Moreover, as a reward for your great kindness, I am willing to offer you 20% of the total sum and also 10% for your considerable expenses. Time is of the utmost essence and this transaction must be concluded within fourteen days because my father's associates hire private detective to find the money.

I find your name from the British High Commission and they vouch for your Christian character and spotless record. You are the only person I approach in this desperate matter. I know that you are good God–fearing person and I hope you will pity my helplessness. Anticipating to hear from you soon. Thank you and God bless!

   Miss Comfort Ajegbo

From: **Susi Judge-Davis-Gaultier**
To: Liam O'Keefe
Sent: 14 January 2009, 11.22
Subject:

The pack of unbranded 99p cornershop tights you left on my desk has gone straight in the bin. They are NOT £29 Wolford Satin De Luxe!

From: **Liam O'Keefe**
To: Susi Judge-Davis-Gaultier
Sent: 14 January 2009, 11.23
Subject: Re:

I know they're not!

From: **Harvey Harvey**
To: Liam O'Keefe
Sent: 14 January 2009, 11.32
Subject: Re: Plaintive cry for help!

Sorry I haven't got back to you sooner, but isn't AutoReply brilliant? I didn't realize you could make your computer send emails automatically. It's like there's a little robot inside typing them out for you! I've got some new thoughts on the cigarette brief and I'll go through them with you as soon as I can, but right now I've got to deal with an emergency that could be a matter of life or death. I really have to go because there isn't a second to waste.

From: **Harvey Harvey**
To: Comfort Ajegbo
Sent: 14 January 2009, 11.34
Subject: Re: Help I need kind sir

Hi Comfort

Your terrible situation is shocking. I'll do anything I can to help. Would you like me to talk to the British police? I should point out I'm not sure I believe in God (and I don't know where the British High Commission would get the idea that I do), but I will say a prayer for you just in case. And I'll stay next to my computer until I know you're safe.

Harvey Harvey

From: **Liam O'Keefe**
To: Harvey Harvey
Sent: 14 January 2009, 11.37
Subject: Re: Plaintive cry for help!

By the strangest coincidence my need for a Montana idea was also a matter of life or death. No matter. Sorted now. Gave Ted the motherlode. Big Tobacco can be assured of the next genera-

tion of smokers. I'm a generous bloke and I don't mind if you
want to jump on my bandwagon. Just don't get under my feet.

From:	**Susi Judge-Davis-Gaultier**
To:	All Staff
Sent:	14 January 2009, 12.07
Subject:	Musical Premiere
Att:	jinglonia.pdf

After Monday's terrifying event, Yossi has agreed to bring forward the premiere of his new work in the hope that we can begin
the healing process with the 'soothing balm of music'. The performance will take place in reception at 6.00.

Please see attached e-flyer for details.

Attachment:

❧ J I N G L O N I A ❧

An Intimate Sonata in A Minor

❧❧

Composed by
Yossi Mendoza
Performed by
Yossi Mendoza (violin, harp, clarinet, oboe)
Beverly White (cello, viola)
Alan Jarvie (French horn)
DJ Trix (decks, post-hip-hop rap stylings)

❧❧

Acclaimed avant-gardist, Yossi Mendoza, realizes a lifelong
vision with his reinterpretation of classic advertising jingles,
the life-enriching, indeed life-*shaping* musical vignettes
that remain embedded deep in our psyches.

Includes:

A Finger of Fudge
Don't Forget the Beanz, Mum
Um Bongo (They Drink It in the Congo)
Hello Tosh, Got a Toshiba?
Hey, It's the Milky Bar Kid
For Hands That Do Dishes

From: **Lorraine Pallister**
To: Liam O'Keefe
Sent: 14 January 2009, 12.09
Subject: Re: Big Bruv

I'm not going for a drink with you, Liam. It's over. Just tell the gay guy about *BB*.

From: **Brett Topolski**
To: Liam O'Keefe
Sent: 14 January 2009, 12.11
Subject: Re: Thank heaven for YouTube

I gave Vince the genius message. He's as baffled as I am. What exactly is he supposed to have done?

From: **Liam O'Keefe**
To: Brett Topolski
Sent: 14 January 2009, 12.14
Subject: Re: Thank heaven for YouTube

Can't say – Official Secrets Act and all that – but tell him he's getting the slot above God (but below my mum) in my Cannes acceptance speech.

From: **Harvey Harvey**
To: Comfort Ajegbo
Sent: 14 January 2009, 12.57
Subject: Re: Help I need kind sir

Hello, Comfort. You haven't replied and I'm worried that something may have happened. Perhaps your late father's associates have turned up with machetes or maybe you've gone into hiding in the jungle. (Do you have jungle nearby or is it more what you'd call 'bush'?) Just send me a one-word reply to let me know you are OK. It's lunchtime here, but I'll stay at my desk until I hear from you. If you haven't replied by 3.00 (London time), I'll call the police. By the way, I've built a little shrine on my desktop. I've made a model of you out of Blu Tack and matchsticks, though obviously I can only guess what you look like!

From: **Susi Judge-Davis-Gaultier**
To: Creative Department
Sent: 14 January 2009, 12.59
Subject: Project Red Carpet

Ted's office now for the review!

From: **Janice Crutton**
To: David Crutton
Sent: 14 January 2009, 13.00
Subject: Tamara

Just had a call from her year head telling me she hasn't been at school all week and she's not there today. What do you suggest?

From: **fanmaster@dethrush.fi**
To: Noah Crutton
Sent: 14 January 2009, 13.01
Subject: Thanking

Veiko want to thank you for the bombardings of fan email. As you are already guess, his music and axe style are much of the influences of classical British metal like Purple, Sab, Priest, Maiden and Saxon and he is please to have brilliant support from British fan bases.

In responding to your inquiry of touring plans, Veiko has no plan bring Dethrush to UK because he is very busy conquer Finland markets, but if you come to here he happy to greet you at gig. Please go <u>dethrush.fi/dates</u> for schedules.

ROKK TILL YOUR

DETH RUSH

SPLEEN GO SPLAT

From: **David Crutton**
To: Janice Crutton
Sent: 14 January 2009, 13.02
Subject: Re: Tamara

I suggest hitting her where it hurts. Fees of £6,000 per term works out to about £102 per school day. I say we charge her the full rate for every day she misses. Want me to call her and tell her she owes us £306 for the week to date?

From: **Janice Crutton**
To: David Crutton
Sent: 14 January 2009, 13.04
Subject: Re: Tamara

Don't be ridiculous. From whom does she get all her money in the first place? I'll deal with it.

I'm having my six-week scan tomorrow morning. Are you going to accompany me?

By the way, you surely won't know the answer to this, but I have to ask. I was sorting out laundry this morning and Noah seems to be missing all his underpants. Any ideas?

From: **David Crutton**
To: Janice Crutton
Sent: 14 January 2009, 13.05
Subject: Re: Tamara

Wouldn't miss the scan for the world. Let me know how it goes with Tam. Sorry, haven't a clue on Noah's pants.

	SMS:
Mum:	Where are you?
Tam:	Duh! School. Double mod hist
Mum:	If you were in class phone would've been confiscated moment it came out of pocket. Where are you?
Tam:	Told you, Mrs Stallin. In history
Mum:	If you were in history you'd know only 1 L in Stalin. Where the hell are you?
Tam:	Gotta go. Teacher spotted mob

From: **Milton Keane**
To: Susi Judge-Davis-Gaultier, Dotty Podidra
Sent: 14 January 2009, 13.06
Subject: superstar!!!!

Just bumped into Liam and he said his ex works at *Big Brother* and she told him the producer wants me on the show!! Can you believe that? I'm gonna be in the Holy Trinity – *heat*, *Hello!*, *OK!* Promise you won't do any sleazy kiss 'n' tells. You two know all my dark secrets!!

	MSN:
NoahsDark:	havin good study day?
Rialto:	ace. studyin galactic justice.
NoahsDark:	in a galaxy where evil rains

	supreme . . .
Rialto:	. . . the people is lookin 4 a hero!!
NoahsDark:	kool. make sure u use yr justice orbs.
Rialto:	aagh fuk. boomdragons jus zapped me. u put me off.
NoahsDark:	soz. wanted 2 know if you dumped pants yet.
Rialto:	in da bin! is that all?
NoahsDark:	no. good news. jus got e from veiko.
Rialto:	wkd. wos he say?
NoahsDark:	invite us 2 finland. chekked it out. we could see em in helsinki on 26th
Rialto:	we got organic chem assessment on 26th
NoahsDark:	i know! you wanna get tickets or shall i?

From: **Janice Crutton**
To: Paula Sterling
Sent: 14 January 2009, 13.09
Subject: tech inquiry

Can you talk to Andrew Clough and find out what he knows about electronic tags? I know his hedge-fund scammer was fitted with one when he was bailed pending appeal last year. I need suppliers and prices.

From: **Susi Judge-Davis-Gaultier**
To: Milton Keane, Dotty Podidra
Sent: 14 January 2009, 13.10
Subject: Re: superstar!!!!

This is LIAM we're talking about! He is the BIGGEST wind-up merchant in history. At Miller Shanks he sent an all-staffer announcing a royal visit from Wills to 'inspect the new air conditioning'.

From: **Dotty Podidra**
To: Susi Judge-Davis-Gaultier, Milton Keane
Sent: 14 January 2009, 13.11
Subject: Re: superstar!!!!

Hilarious! Did you fall for it?

From: **Susi Judge-Davis-Gaultier**
To: Dotty Podidra, Milton Keane
Sent: 14 January 2009, 13.12
Subject: Re: superstar!!!!

Do I look completely stupid? Of course not.

From: **Milton Keane**
To: Susi Judge-Davis-Gaultier, Dotty Podidra
Sent: 14 January 2009, 13.14
Subject: Re: superstar!!!!

Not what I heard, Sooz! A dicky bird told me you turned up to work in a tiara and deb's gown! Anyway, Liam's being straight. His ex really does work at *BB* and I checked out the producer's details on the Endemol site. Who's coming to Wagamama to discuss nomination tactics and eviction outfits?!

From: **Dotty Podidra**
To: Milton Keane, Susi Judge-Davis-Gaultier
Sent: 14 January 2009, 13.15
Subject: Re: superstar!!!!

Wait up! Starving! Could eat a horse (in a spicy ramen noodle soup, obviously!)

From: **Susi Judge-Davis-Gaultier**
To: Milton Keane, Dotty Podidra
Sent: 14 January 2009, 13.17
Subject: Re: superstar!!!!

Ted has given me stacks to do and I have to organize tonight's music recital. I won't be joining you for lunch to talk about a stupid *Big Brother* appearance that is NEVER GOING TO HAPPEN! Liam's ex is probably in on it, you ninny! She used to work at Miller Shanks too and she's a cow. To be absolutely honest, Milton, you made yourself look silly enough on Monday and if you fall for this, you'll only make more of a prat of yourself.

From: **Milton Keane**
To: Susi Judge-Davis-Gaultier, Dotty Podidra
Sent: 14 January 2009, 13.19
Subject: Re: superstar!!!!

Hark at you! Now who's being the cow!! I will not be 'reaching out' to you from the diary room, Susan.

From: **Susi Judge-Davis-Gaultier**
To: Milton Keane, Dotty Podidra
Sent: 14 January 2009, 13.20
Subject: Re: superstar!!!!

And I will not be giving you any more legal or fashion advice if you're only going to use it to make a prawn out of yourself.

From: **Milton Keane**
To: Susi Judge-Davis-Gaultier, Dotty Podidra
Sent: 14 January 2009, 13.21
Subject: Re: superstar!!!!

Like the tip on the paisley tie? I'm SO going to miss having advice as BRILLIANT as that.

From: **Milton Keane**
To: Susi Judge-Davis-Gaultier, Dotty Podidra
Sent: 14 January 2009, 13.22
Subject: Re: superstar!!!!

Not.

From: **Susi Judge-Davis-Gaultier**
To: Milton Keane, Dotty Podidra
Sent: 14 January 2009, 13.24
Subject: Re: superstar!!!!

Has anyone ever told you you're a TOTAL BITCH?

From: **Milton Keane**
To: Susi Judge-Davis-Gaultier, Dotty Podidra
Sent: 14 January 2009, 13.25
Subject: Re: superstar!!!!

Has anyone ever told you you're a brainless CLOTHES HORSE?

From: **Dotty Podidra**
To: Susi Judge-Davis-Gaultier, Milton Keane
Sent: 14 January 2009, 13.26
Subject: Re: superstar!!!!

Stop it, stop it, both of you, STOP IT!!

From: **Susi Judge-Davis-Gaultier**
To: Milton Keane, Dotty Podidra
Sent: 14 January 2009, 13.27
Subject: Re: superstar!!!!

Milton POO BUM

From: **Milton Keane**
To: Susi Judge-Davis-Gaultier, Dotty Podidra
Sent: 14 January 2009, 13.28
Subject: Re: superstar!!!!

Susi Judge-Davis-PRIMARK

From: **Susi Judge-Davis-Gaultier**
To: Milton Keane, Dotty Podidra
Sent: 14 January 2009, 13.29
Subject: Re: superstar!!!!

Milton HOMO

From: **Ted Berry**
To: Susi Judge-Davis-Gaultier
Sent: 14 January 2009, 13.32
Subject: WTF?

What's with the fucking screaming? I'm trying to review work in here.

From: **Róisín O'Hooligan**
To: All Staff
Sent: 14 January 2009, 13.33
Subject: girl-on-girl action

Will whoever's having the squealing bitch fight somewhere in the building DESIST, like, IMMEDIATELY. It not only sounds pathetic, but it's also unsettling Neil Godley's mum, who is here to take him shopping for a new winter coat.

By the way, Neil, your mum's here.

Róisín
Reception

From: **Paula Sterling**
To: Dotty Podidra
Sent: 14 January 2009, 13.36
Subject: Mad as a stick

Should I be very (or even extremely) worried? JC has got me sourcing electronic tags – you know, the things they stick on asbos in hoodies. I think she wants to put one on her daughter. Is DC doing insane stuff as well?

From: **Dotty Podidra**
To: Paula Sterling
Sent: 14 January 2009, 13.38
Subject: Re: Mad as a stick

No more than usual! No time to discuss. Taking friend to A&E. Broken nose. Got a white Chloé bag full in the face!

From: **Paula Sterling**
To: Dotty Podidra
Sent: 14 January 2009, 13.39
Subject: Re: Mad as a stick

OMG, sounds awful.

From: **Dotty Podidra**
To: Paula Sterling
Sent: 14 January 2009, 13.40
Subject: Re: Mad as a stick

Absolutely horrendous. Bag's ruined.

From: **Harvey Harvey**
To: Comfort Ajegbo
Sent: 14 January 2009, 14.36
Subject: Re: Help I need kind sir

There's been a violent incident in my office and I've had my chair wedged against my door for the past hour. All I can think of are the terrible things that might be happening to you. I'm very, very worried, Comfort. I Googled 'African Machete Death' and found some sickening pictures. If you don't get in touch with me in the next five minutes, I'm going to call the police.

From: **Lorraine Pallister**
To: Liam O'Keefe
Sent: 14 January 2009, 14.37
Subject: Re: Big Bruv

You talked to your gay guy yet? Boss is getting desperate. I think they're looking for their first *BB* suicide, but this year's audition-ees are pretty staid. A bit like they're applying for the grad intake at Prudential.

From: **Liam O'Keefe**
To: Lorraine Pallister
Sent: 14 January 2009, 14.38
Subject: Re: Big Bruv

Finder's fee?

From: **Lorraine Pallister**
To: Liam O'Keefe
Sent: 14 January 2009, 14.39
Subject: Re: Big Bruv

Piss off. All you're getting from me is a bit of goodwill. Let's face it, cash would only go up your nose. Or worse, up your bookie's.

From: **Comfort Ajegbo**
To: Harvey Harvey
Sent: 14 January 2009, 14.41
Subject: Re: Help I need kind sir

Hello, Harvey Harvey. I am so overjoyed that you reply to me. I ask Jesus for Him to send me a Samaritan of kindness and compassion and He has answered my prayers. I beg you please do not talk to the police. If they speak with the constabulary here in Lagos I am surely doomed. All police in Lagos are corrupted vermin and in league with evil business associates. For the time now I am in safe house of a most trusted friend. You must send to me the detail of a suitable bank account in your name so that I can arrange for the transfer of the moneys as soon as possible. I also need the number and other detail of your credit card for the purposes of security and also your passport number and your social security number. I know this is very much to ask of you, but the bank here assures me that they need every possible piece of information to carry out the correct security procedures before the transfer of such a very big sum of moneys can be permitted.

Thank you a thousand times for agreeing to help me, Harvey Harvey. I am on tender hooks for your reply.

Your grateful friend,

Comfort Ajegbo

From: **Liam O'Keefe**
To: Lorraine Pallister
Sent: 14 January 2009, 14.58
Subject: Re: Big Bruv

I talked to Gay Guy and he's been in a state of hyper-excitement ever since. He's called Milton Keane and I can already hear the Geordie VO: 'Veronica and Graham are in the bedroom, Mikey, Fiona and Rebecca are in the living area and Milton is in the snug getting his arse defiled by big, butch Kirk.' The free *BB* ringtone of that will be a treat.

The bad news is that he's just had his nose broken. It was your old mucker Susi, armed with this season's bag and enraged, I suspect, by his dumb good fortune. You know what she's like in the face of a friend's success.

Tell your boss that his recovery should be speedy and that any consequent misshapenness to the nasal zone will surely add character.

Forget the finder's fee. Only trying it on. But how about we go for a drink anyway?

    Liam

From: **Janice Crutton**
To: David Crutton
Sent: 14 January 2009, 15.00
Subject: Tonight

I intend to read the riot act (in full) to our daughter tonight and I would very much like you to be there for moral support (and also, if I'm honest, because your presence can be more than a little intimidating). Think you can manage to get away at a reasonable time? Also, can you pick up an item on the way from a shop on Edgware Road?

From: **David Crutton**
To: Janice Crutton
Sent: 14 January 2009, 15.04
Subject: Re: Tonight

Should be fine. Do you want me to yell at her or merely look menacing? And what's the item/shop?

From: **Janice Crutton**
To: David Crutton
Sent: 14 January 2009, 15.07
Subject: Re: Tonight

Just look menacing to begin with. Start yelling if I give you my look – you know the one I'm talking about. The shop is Spectre Security & Surveillance, 162 Edgware Road. Ask for Mr Abbas. He has a package marked for me.

From: **David Crutton**
To: Janice Crutton
Sent: 14 January 2009, 15.09
Subject: Re: Tonight

Very 007. I'm intrigued. Is there a secret password?

From: **Zlatan Kovaćević**
To: Milton Keane
Sent: 14 January 2009, 15.13
Subject: You fight like homosexual

I watch the thin fashion girl beat the crap out of you. It is insult to my manhood. I go further and say it is an insult to manhoods everywhere all the world over. When you come back from hospital I teach you to fight like a proper Serbian. If you do not concur to my proposal, I kill you. A pussy boy such as you are cannot be let to live. It is simple as that.

From: **Ted Berry**
To: David Crutton, Donald Gold
Sent: 14 January 2009, 15.17
Subject: Red Carpet

Reviewed the political celebs. Have a working shortlist of six for your consideration. Some debate as to whether Robert Mugabe was taking the concept too far, but he stays on the list in the interest of cultural diversity. And because I'm a provocative fucker.

Why not pop along to mine to discuss?

While we're at it, I can take you through Liam's Montana brain-wave.

From: **David Crutton**
To: Ted Berry
Sent: 14 January 2009, 15.21
Subject: Re: Red Carpet

Is it safe? Dotty told me there were fisticuffs earlier. Your PA losing her rag or something? Do we need to discipline her? You know I'm not averse to violence (in moderation), but this is a PC age we're living in.

From: **Ted Berry**
To: David Crutton, Donald Gold
Sent: 14 January 2009, 15.22
Subject: Re: Red Carpet

Won't be necessary. A case of literal handbags. See you in fifteen.

From: **Lorraine Pallister**
To: Liam O'Keefe
Sent: 14 January 2009, 15.29
Subject: Re: Big Bruv

Oh dear, he's not a scrapper, is he? The powers at C4 aren't cool with violence since the spitting incident in *BB9*. Anyway, thanks for passing the word on. And yes, I suppose we could have one drink. For old time's sake or whatever. How's Friday for you?

From: **Liam O'Keefe**
To: Lorraine Pallister
Sent: 14 January 2009, 15.36
Subject: Re: Big Bruv

You've seen him on YouTube. Does he look violent? He just made the mistake of pressing the wrong buttons on psycho Susi. Remember what she did to Nigel Godley when he forgot to process her expenses? The poor fucker was well and truly Naomi Campbelled. Still walks with a limp. Friday's grand. Can't wait.

From: **Lorraine Pallister**
To: Liam O'Keefe
Sent: 14 January 2009, 15.45
Subject: Re: Big Bruv

Friday then. Just don't try anything on. It's just a drink. Not a reconciliation.

	MSN:
sjdG:	Are you back from hospital??
DottyPod:	Just got here.
sjdG:	How is he?
DottyPod:	Not good. V.v. traumatized. And the doctor who's fixing his nose is gay. Saw Milton on YouTube and hit on him big time.
sjdG:	Oh dear. Feel terrible, Dotty. Did I go too far?
DottyPod:	Think so.
sjdG:	But you saw how he flew at me. He was like a complete mad thing. I thought he was going to kill me.
DottyPod:	But did you have to whack him so hard? What was in the bag?
sjdG:	A brick.

DottyPod:	What on earth are you doing with a brick in a £600 bag?
sjdG:	It was one of those lovely glass ones. I picked it up from my interior designer. I need to show it to Pierre because I want a glass wall in our new bathroom, but the silly frog isn't convinced. Honestly, I totally blame Pierre because if he weren't so tasteless (surprising, considering he's French), I wouldn't have had to get the brick, which actually weighs a ton and I don't know how I'm going to get it home now my bag's ruined. It's completely covered in blood.
DottyPod:	A bit like poor Milton.
sjdG:	OMG, will he ever forgive me?
DottyPod:	Don't know, to be honest. He's v.v. upset with you.
sjdG:	☹☹☹ Should I go and see him?
DottyPod:	He's heavily sedated at the mo, but I'm going back later. You could come with me. See how the land lies.
sjdG:	I'll be free once the stupid music thing has started. Should I take flowers?
DottyPod:	Bit gay. Might touch a nerve.
sjdG:	How about a raw-silk smoking jacket from Oncle Jean Paul's spring collection?
DottyPod:	That might swing it. He loved the pink one.

From: **Harvey Harvey**
To: Comfort Ajegbo
Sent: 14 January 2009, 15.56
Subject: Re: Help I need kind sir
Att: all_my_personal_details.doc

Hi Comfort

I've prepared a Word document containing my personal details. You'll find all my bank account and credit-card numbers and passwords in there, as well as the other things you asked for such as passport and social-security numbers. There are also some details you probably don't need (my *Dr Who* site logon info and such like), but I thought it was better to have too much rather than too little. I also put in my home address, employer details and phone numbers. And my mum and dad's number is in there too because I often spend my weekends with them. I didn't include my PIN number, but just in case you need it, it's 1234. I made it easy as I have a terrible memory! If there is anything else I can do, give me a call any time of day or night. I am very worried about you, Comfort, and making sure you're safe is now my number-one priority.

I await news.

Harvey

From: **Ted Berry**
To: Liam O'Keefe
Sent: 14 January 2009, 16.06
Subject: Montana

Well, aren't you the comeback kid? Took Crutton and Gold through your Montana idea. Gold went the colour of bleached pine. A definite positive – always like to have a suit nauseous at the prospect of the presentation. Crutton was immediately sold. Loves you as one of his own, geezer. Top marks.

One question between you and me: how much input did Harvey have in the idea? He's been increasingly AWOL lately, mentally speaking, and I'm beginning to suspect he might be one of my poorer decisions. Yeah, I do make them from time to time. Is this one completely off with the fucking fairies?

By the way, I'm taking DC to do a few rock walls tonight. Discovered a gem of an indoor climbing centre in Manor House. Fancy hauling yourself up with us? You could do with some conditioning, you lardy tosspot.

	MSN:
Dong:	Oh my god.
Kazoo:	What?
Dong:	Oh my fucking god.
Bilge:	What's the matter, man? Talk to us.
Dong:	Just been in a creative review with Ted and DC.
Bilge:	And??
Dong:	I am going straight to hell. Do not pass go, do not collect £200. Straight to fucking hell.
Kazoo:	You're not making sense.
Bilge:	Yes, what are you on about?
Kazoo:	Is it Robert Mugabe? There are rumours.
Dong:	Much worse.
Kazoo:	What could be worse than Robert Mugabe?
Bilge:	I can think of dozens. Hitler, Stalin, Pol Pot, Amin, Pinochet, David fucking Cameron . . .
Kazoo:	Shut up, Bill. Talk to us, Don.
Dong:	It's Montana.
Bilge:	They're only cigarettes, which are smoked by consenting adults aware of the risks.

Kazoo:	And which you signed up to work on in a macho rush of blood.
Dong:	I signed up and sold my soul. To Crutton, the devil incarnate. And his pet Orks Berry and O'Keefe.
Bilge:	What do they want you to do? Sell them to illiterate Africans?
Kazoo:	They do that already, don't they?
Bilge:	The mentally handicapped? That's an untapped market.
Dong:	Worse.
Kazoo:	What could be worse than flogging fags to the mentally handicapped?
Bilge:	I can think of dozens of social groups. Children for one.
Dong:	Bingo.
Bilge:	You're kidding.
Kazoo:	Please say you're kidding.
Dong:	Remember how we used to pretend-smoke those miniature sweet cigarettes when we were kids? And you know how Triumph does trainer bras?
Kazoo:	Jesus Christ, I get it.
Bilge:	My First Fag from Montana?
Dong:	Now you're with me.
Kazoo:	That is totally sick.
Bilge:	And surely illegal. They wouldn't be able to get away with it anywhere, not even in Zimbabwe.
Dong:	They're not that dumb. They're not going to market them *overtly* to kids. It'll be under the radar like alcopops. But Liam's come up with packaging that makes them virtually indistinguishable from Pokemon trading cards and he's designed special low-level display cabinets. And they're suggesting

	packs of five designed for pocket-money budgets.
Kazoo:	OMG, you are going to hell.
Dong:	I will if I do what DC has tasked me with.
Bilge:	What's that?
Dong:	Wants me to check out the possibility of getting concessions in ice-cream vans.

From: **Liam O'Keefe**
To: Brett Topolski
Sent: 14 January 2009, 16.32
Subject: couple of small dilemmas

Life definitely on the up. Lorraine has agreed to meet for a drink and the Berry/Crutton Axis of Evil thinks sun shines out of my arse (which, incidentally, is growing increasingly flatulent. Is that a function of middle age?). TB, whom I will from hereon refer to as MMT (My Mate Ted), has even invited me to go climbing with him and Crutton. Should I say yes? I'm carrying a little extra weight these days and I'm likely to embarrass myself about six feet up.

Other dilemma: MMT asked me what I think of Harvey Harvey. My guess is he's considering giving him the heave-ho. Should I hit him with the truth, i.e. that Double H is a thoroughbred freakoid who belongs in (preferably heavily padded) residential care, or should I take pity and save his certifiable arse?

Yours in moral turmoil,

Liam

From: **David Crutton**
To: Dotty Podidra
Sent: 14 January 2009, 16.34
Subject:

Ted is taking me climbing tonight. Nip out to Lilywhite's and get me some suitable gear. You know my sizes.

From: **Brett Topolski**
To: Liam O'Keefe
Sent: 14 January 2009, 16.41
Subject: Re: couple of small dilemmas

Rock climbing: I've seen you shimmy up and down several drain-pipes. Beer gut or not, you've clearly got the genes of a mountain goat. You'll be fine. A few preparatory sit-ups might be in order though.

Harvey Harvey: you know what to do. Your guilty anguish ever since the thing with the thing shows you have at least the vestige of a conscience. Sounds like the kid needs a little care in the community and Allah (who is, it goes without saying, Grrrrreat) has designated you as his district nurse.

Gotta go. You know how Vince gets if he misses happy hour.

   Brett

PS: Don't hold out too much hope when you go out with Lorraine. Probably just wants money – you owe her a small fortune, don't you?

From: **Liam O'Keefe**
To: Ted Berry
Sent: 14 January 2009, 16.47
Subject: Re: Montana

Thanks for the big-up, Ted. I'd love to come climbing. Always been a sport I've fancied a stab at. Do I need any special gear/knowledge of knots?

Harvey: I'll level with you. He did play a role in developing the Montana idea (though I led the way, obviously). He is an oddball, but he's mostly cool. Definitely someone you should keep around because he could deliver massively one day. You never know where the next Smash Martians are going to come from, do you? (Actually, they're probably going to come from Mars, but you know what I mean.)

From: **Ted Berry**
To: Liam O'Keefe
Sent: 14 January 2009, 16.50
Subject: Re: Montana

Ta, geezer. I respect an honest opinion. I'll mark HH down as one to watch. No gear needed for later. Just bring tracky bottoms and nerves of high-tensile steel – I take no prisoners when I'm on the face. And I'll do the knots, thanks. I like you but I'm not gonna trust you with my life.

From: **Liam O'Keefe**
To: Harvey Harvey
Sent: 14 January 2009, 16.57
Subject: You owe me

If Ted says well done on 'our' Montana idea, you might want to say thanks and give him your most inane grin. He was being pretty down on you, so I gave you more credit than you're strictly due. I'm nice like that. Anyway, our relationship has now entered its *Godfather* phase. As in: 'Someday, and that day may never come, I'll call upon you to do a service for me . . .' Could be anything – crashing on your sofa, a lift to the airport, making the body of my first-born son fit to be seen by his mother. Just be prepared.

Don O'Keefe

From: **Dotty Podidra**
To: All Staff
Sent: 14 January 2009, 17.05
Subject: Workies?

Any workies free to help David practise knots? Former scouts/girl guides preferred.

Dotty Podidra
Assistant to David Crutton

From: **Liam O'Keefe**
To: All Staff
Sent: 14 January 2009, 17.08
Subject: Workies?

Any particularly sturdy workies free to sit on my ankles while I do a couple of hundred ab crunches?

From: **Harvey Harvey**
To: Liam O'Keefe
Sent: 14 January 2009, 17.15
Subject: Re: You owe me

Thank you, Liam. I'll be happy to do you a favour whenever you ask. I can't think why Ted isn't happy with me though. Any ideas?

From: **Liam O'Keefe**
To: Harvey Harvey
Sent: 14 January 2009, 17.17
Subject: Re: You owe me

Not a clue, you mad fuck.

From: **Susi Judge-Davis-Gaultier**
To: All Staff
Sent: 14 January 2009, 17.55
Subject: Tonight's performance

Would everyone attending Yossi's premier of *Jinglonia* please make their way to reception. The performance will commence in five minutes.

From: **Róisín O'Hooligan**
To: All Staff
Sent: 14 January 2009, 17.57
Subject: Re: Tonight's performance

Yes, do hurry along. A word of warning though: I've been obliged to listen to the warm up. *Jinglonia*, AKA *Now That's What I Call Shite*. Bring your iPods, people.

Róisín
Reception

From: **Ted Berry**
To: David Crutton, Liam O'Keefe
Sent: 14 January 2009, 18.00
Subject: Where the fuck are you?

Sitting in the Cayenne waiting for you. Come on, guys, there's simulated rock to conquer.

Sent from my iPhone

225

From: **Dotty Podidra**
To: Susi Judge-Davis-Gaultier
Sent: 14 January 2009, 18.07
Subject: Milton mercy dash!

Are you ready? We'd better go now or we'll miss visiting hours.

From: **Susi Judge-Davis-Gaultier**
To: Dotty Podidra
Sent: 14 January 2009, 18.09
Subject: Re: Milton mercy dash!

I'm ready. I've ordered the JPG jacket in pink AND taupe and I've put together a goody bag of male grooming products. Would you describe his skin type as 'greasy' or 'combination'?

From: **Dotty Podidra**
To: Susi Judge-Davis-Gaultier
Sent: 14 January 2009, 18.10
Subject: Re: Milton mercy dash!

More like 'bruised'. Just bring both. Cab's waiting.

	SMS:
Janice:	Where the fuck are you, David?
David:	David can't come to phone right now
Janice:	Who am I speaking to? Not in mood to be dicked about
David:	This is Liam
Janice:	Who?
David:	I work with David
Janice:	Where is he?
David:	50 feet above me dressed in about £500 worth of Lycra. He looks fantastic

Janice:	Don't know what the hell he's playing at but tell him to come home immediately
David:	Not sure that's possible. He's kinda stuck
Janice:	What do you mean?
David:	He said he was ready for a level 1 climb but I think he was lying. Now he's stuck
Janice:	Are you trying to be funny?
David:	Not at all. Though must admit it looks pretty amusing from here. Oh, he's not stuck any more
Janice:	Where is he?
David:	Pretty much right in front of me
Janice:	Tell him to get home now or I'll fucking kill him
David:	Not sure that'll be necessary. Might just be concussion though. Told him he should have worn a helmet

Thursday
Mood: horny for a little MILF magic

blogass.co.uk
Posted by **Tiga**
15/01/09, 10.39 GMT

Does anyone know how I can get my mum sectioned under the Mental Health Act? (My mum could tell me because she's a lawyer, but obviously she's the last person I should be asking!)

My mother has gone totally mad. It's official. She's pregnant (at 45!!) and obviously she's producing literally gallons of hormones that are affecting her sanity. Last night she went completely over the top. She wants to stick one of those electric ankle bracelets on me just because I've missed a few weeks of

228

school (which is totally pointless and I tried telling her I get a much better education from hanging in the **Real World**, but you try making a mad woman listen to reason). My friend (can't name him for legal reasons) has a bracelet and it's actually quite cool, but it's part of his probation order and it was fitted by a qualified policeman, **not** by his **own mother**. The only reason she didn't actually put it on me last night is that my dad was supposed to bring it home with him but he didn't show up because he had to go to hospital with a head injury. When she found out where he was she went ballistic. She was screaming and shouting and calling him every vile name including **fucking cunt**. How do you think I felt hearing that? I mean, obviously he's a total twat, but he's still my dad.

Actually, **My Preggo Mum** is the subject for a whole other blog, which I will write as soon as I get a minute. I mean, isn't her mental behaviour proof that it's clearly unsafe for a woman of her age to be up the duff? And what were her and my dad thinking? I mean, actually 'doing it'! That shouldn't be allowed, not at their age and **not** when there are children in the house. I'm mentally scarred just by the thought of them huffing and puffing away. What **hell** would I be going through if I actually **walked in** on them and saw them at it?

Views: 106
Comments: 12

Comment posted by **littlepinkpony**:
You think you got it bad, Tiga? My mom
still hasn't let me out of my room. It's
been **two weeks** now. She put me in
here cos of my blue hair so I cut it all off
and now she says I look 'obscene' and
that I can't come out till it's grown back.
'How long do you want it, bitch?' I yelled.
I have to yell cos it's through the door
and she's got a sofa rammed up against
the other side. Anyway, she didn't reply.
She just shoved a picture of Cloe Bratz
through the gap. It's gonna take months
to grow that long, but she totally doesn't
care. I'd make a break for it, but I'm too
weak. She's feeding me on her crazy Hare
Krishna diet which is totally yuck and also
completely unhealthy. I need protein. And
carbs. And sugar. Last night I begged her
for a Wendy burger or Oreos or **anything**
properly nutritious. I'm wasting away,
down to 174lbs. 'How thin do you want
me?' I asked her. She shoved a picture of
Barbie through the door. Someone out
there has to help me. **Please!!!!!**

Comment posted by **Woody**:
You sound like one horny teen, Tiga. I do
like 'em young and under the thumb of a
'strict' mom. I'm rubbing myself now at
the thought of your bondage games. Any
chance of posting some jpegs of your
sweet self, preferably with Mommy? Gotta
go and 'take care of business', doll. Back
soon.

Crépuscule dans le Périgord Partie 81: À la Recherche du Temps Perdu?

Après le déjeuner I stumbled upon Papin *dans la cave*. He had opened my last bottle of Château d'Yquem '89 and was settling down to a glass of this superlative sticky. I couldn't find it in myself to chastise him. *Le vieux paysan* surely hadn't the faintest clue that the case had cost me over €400 – as far as he is concerned, *du vin c'est du vin c'est du vin*. I decided to join him and in the dank cool of the cellar we savoured the finest dessert wine known to humanity.

'Pas la meilleure année, mais tu as du goût pour un trou du cul,' he opined. I thanked him for the compliment and then our thoughts turned to times past.

'Londres doit être plein de pauvres cons comme toi,' he observed. 'Ca te manque tout ça?'

Do I miss London? Do I miss being at the epicentre of the *tourbillon créatif*? Do I miss the adrenal thrill of the quest for creative excellence, *l'esprit de competition amical* of the awards season, the parties replete with cocaine, supermodels and stars of popular music?

No, I told him firmly. London advertising

was becoming staid and predictable when I left. 'The Scene' may miss me, but I do not miss it.

'Putain de merde, si des enculés comme toi continuent à venir dans le Périgord, je vais devoir déménager à Londres,' he exclaimed.

Trust me, Papin, I told him, keep well away. London would eat an unworldly naïf like him alive.

'Au moins là-bas je pourrai brouter le cresson de ta femme. Elle va pas revenir, n'est-ce pas?' he said.

No, I ruefully agreed, Celine will not be returning. And as he drained the last of the bottle into his glass, I once again marvelled at the preternatural insight of this *paysan rugueux*.

Views:	1
Comments:	0

Is anyone out there?

I'm blogging. I'm actually talking to complete strangers on the internet, but I have absolutely no one else to turn to. No one. At all.

I'm a mother of two, with another on the way. I'm forty-five years old. I shouldn't be pregnant, should I? But, God help me, I am and, though I'm not in the least a pro-lifer, I can't get rid of it.

I am having second thoughts though. I had my first scan today. 'I think it's a boy,' the doctor told me. 'That's not its penis, you idiot,' I replied. 'The little sod is giving me the finger.' And I swear I wasn't seeing things. I'm studying the printout now and there it is: a barely formed foetus giving me a stiff middle digit.

Just like its bloody sister, then. For the sake of anonymity, let's call her Daisy. (Actually, I always wanted to call her that, but my husband – let's call him Dick – insisted on a Jewish name to rile his grandmother, an obnoxious woman with views on Jews that would have made Himmler queasy.) Daisy is out of control, a foul-mouthed, oversexed truant (she thinks I don't know about the love bites on her inner thigh, but what responsible mother doesn't go into her sleeping daughter's bedroom with a household torch and turn back the quilt?). Is it unreasonable to want to keep tabs on her? Does fitting her with an electronic ankle bracelet make me a *bad mother*?

And does wishing a lingering and painful death on her father make me a *bad wife*? This is the man who'd sooner be performing ridiculous macho daredevilry up a fibreglass rock face than at home carrying out his basic paternal duty of tagging his daughter. Am I wrong in thinking this isn't a woman's work?

I am only trying to do my best. So why am I being persecuted by feelings of guilt and failure? And why am I even writing this? Is anyone actually reading it? Does anyone give a damn?

Views:	2,343
Comments:	91

Gotta go and 'take care of business', babe.
Back soon.

Comment posted by **AuschwitzIsALie**:
Have you got the name/address/email of
your husband's grandmother? I think she
might be interested in my book, *The
Holocaust Myth: They Weren't Crematoria;
They Were Giant Pizza Ovens*, which has
been removed from Amazon in an
outrageous denial of free expression and
simply proves that Amazon is a key player
in the global Zionist conspiracy.

Comment posted by **Woody**:
COMMENT REMOVED BY MODERATOR.

Monday
Mood: **self-aware**

From: **Dotty Podidra**
To: All Staff
Sent: 19 January 2009, 10.47
Subject: Amazing Personality Test!

This is really spooky, but it totally worked for me! It's Tibetan and therefore deeply spiritual and it's personally recommended by the Dalai Lama! It's only fifty questions and, honestly, it's half an hour so well spent because it will totally reveal your true inner self. And if you make a wish and then pass this on to all your friends, it *will* come true. The Dalai Lama says so!

Just click on <u>karmarama.net/flash/test.html</u>

From: **Liam O'Keefe**
To: All Staff
Sent: 19 January 2009, 10.55
Subject: Even More Amazing Personality Test!

The UNCANNY accuracy of this test has been SCIENTIFICALLY VERIFIED by people wearing THICK SPECTACLES and LAB coats. Fact: if you take this test and pass it on to five close friends and also to five sworn enemies, your friends (and you!!!) will become obscenely rich while your enemies will die agonizing deaths caused by diseases that doctors thought had disappeared in medieval times.

Don't delay. Take this incredible personality test immediately. You will be totally FLABBERGASTED.

But first – like, duh! – you have to make a wish.

Now scroll down . . .

. . . but not all the way to the bottom – obviously! Don't want to give away the answer too soon, do we?

Here's the big question. Ask yourself . . .

. . . 'Do I really need to take yet another imbecilic email personality test to find out who I am?'

If you answered 'yes', you're an even bigger arse than I am for wasting my time writing this shit.

Don't tell me you're still scrolling . . .

. . . and scrolling . . .

. . . as if you're going to reach the bottom and find some nugget of timeless wisdom. No, all that reaching the bottom will tell you is that . . .

. . . you really are a gormless fucker.

From: **Alex Sofroniou**
To: Liam O'Keefe
Sent: 19 January 2009, 12.03
Subject: Formal Warning

Dear Mr O'Keefe

The IT Department has received 27 complaints about your all-staff email regarding 'Even More Amazing Personality Test!' sent today at 10.55am.

26 of the complaints concerned your use of the F word.* I am obliged to remind you that the Meerkat360 Code of Conduct explicitly prohibits the use of foul and abusive language in electronic communications.

This is your first formal written warning. A second warning will lead to immediate removal of employee internet privileges.

Alex Sofroniou
ZORBA THE GEEK

*Which means at least 26 people scrolled to the bottom! You want the names? (FYI, the 27th tosser reckoned excessive scrolling caused the failure of his mouse!)

Tuesday
Mood: only slightly more delusional than usual

From: **Róisín O'Hooligan**
To: Dotty Podidra
Sent: 20 January 2009, 08.57
Subject: El Crutto

Your boss just arrived and he missed the lift door twice. Think he's still suffering from double vision after his little knock. You might want to keep him away from sharp corners. Or possibly not. Depends how much he's been getting on your tits lately.

	SMS:	
Mum:	Where are you?	
Tam:	School	
Mum:	Where in school?	
Tam:	Science block	
Mum:	Remember tag is accurate to within 5 metres. Try again	

Tam:	Toilet
Mum:	Put out the fag and get to science block. Your class started 10 minutes ago
Tam:	Yes, massa

From: **David Crutton**
To: Dotty Podidra
Sent: 20 January 2009, 09.13
Subject: hekp

comr amd helpp ne wuth ny emaol. i camt ficus om ny keeboarf.

From: **Susi Judge-Davis-Gaultier**
To: Milton Keane
Sent: 20 January 2009, 09.17
Subject: Prezzy

Hi, sweetz. Did you find the passion-fruit Danish I left on your desk? I saw it in the patisserie and it literally screamed 'Milton' at me!

Sooz xxxxxxxxxxxxxxxxxxxxxxxxxxxxxxxxxxxxxxxx

From: **David Crutton**
To: Ted Berry, Caroline Zitter
Sent: 20 January 2009, 09.18
Subject: Meeting

Thought it would be a good idea to schedule a catch-up on general developments. The acquisition of the GIT business places us in a strong financial position in what threatens to be the worst recession since the collapse of the Phoenician Empire and maybe we can think about strengthening personnel in key positions. (This is not an excuse to embark on a frenzy of hiring jugglers, contortionists and dialogue coaches, Ted.)

Also, Diageo wants to brief us on the UK launch of Ketel One. It's a premium Dutch vodka, so a fact-finding trip to Holland may be necessary.

David Crutton
The Man

From: **Caroline Zitter**
To: David Crutton
Sent: 20 January 2009, 09.19
Subject: Out of Office AutoReply

I am out of the office attending Shit Yourself Thin: Nature's Road to Holistic Wellness. I will return on Wednesday 21st Jan.

If you have an urgent request please contact my assistant, Milton Keane, on milton@meerkat360.co.uk

Caroline Zitter
THE SEER

From: **Milton Keane**
To: Susi Judge-Davis-Gaultier
Sent: 20 January 2009, 09.23
Subject: Re: Prezzy

Got the pastry, thanks. Also got the JPG socks, the subscription to *L'Uomo Vogue* and the Harvey Nicks vouchers. Thanx, Sooz, but it's all too much! Had a peek under my bandage this morning and I think the bump is going to look 100% butch. Reckon you've actually done me a favour. YOU ARE SO FORGIVEN!

Milt xxxxxxxxxxxxxxxxxxxxxxxxxxxxxxxxxxxxxxxxxxxxxxxxxxx

	MSN:
Kazoo:	Where are you?

Dong:	Heathrow, T5. Where did you think I'd be?
Kazoo:	Just checking. Feeling OK?
Dong:	Cool. Can't wait to get airborne. Rio, here I come!
Kazoo:	You got the work this time?
Dong:	Hillary Clinton, Sarah Palin, Imelda Marcos, Osama Bin Laden, Kim Jong-Il and Robert Mugabe are safely checked in.
Kazoo:	And you've got the Valium?
Dong:	Yes. Not that I'll need it.
Kazoo:	Decided what you're going to do about GIT?
Dong:	Can't afford to walk away from it. I've booked in for Botox and a teensy tummy tuck and I've paid the deposit. Does that make me a bad person?
Kazoo:	Just means you work in advertising. I've read Naomi Klein. We're all taking the devil's dollar. But would you work on, say, cluster bombs if DC asked?
Dong:	Only if he promised they wouldn't be used on schools and hospitals.
Kazoo:	Good to see you're still in possession of working moral compass. Remember my souvenir.
Dong:	What's your thong size?
Kazoo:	S
Dong:	Gotta go. Complimentary champagne in Club lounge calls. It'll help me write v. important GIT-related e.
Kazoo:	Don't drink too much. Got to keep wits about you in case flight crew goes down with botulism.
Dong:	Wilco. Over and out.

From: **Brett Topolski**
To: Liam O'Keefe
Sent: 20 January 2009, 09.41
Subject: Sighting

How did it go with Lorraine on Friday? I take it from your cyber silence that you're either in Vegas for the Elvis-sanctified wedding or she killed you. There really is no middle way with you, is there?

You'd better check this out. He's been harder to track down than Big Foot, but a bored evening of aimless Googling turned this up. We've found our man.

---

blogwatch.com
Posted by **Cybergaze**
17/01/09, 15.04 GMT

Le Twat

So the other day I was going through some expat blogs to see if there's anything tasty. A dull, dull job. Let's face it, no one wanted to listen to these people when they were in the UK, which is why they became expats. But it's got to be done because you never know where you'll unearth a gem out there in the blogosphere.

I was reaching the point where the thought of pulling out my own fingernails to a soundtrack of Pink was preferable to reading another post about the difficulty of getting PG Tips in Cyprus/a plumber in Poland (they're all in North London, you dork) when I found The One. In all my thousands of blog trawls, I've never come across a Serial Virgin – a string of posts unread by anyone anywhere. And this one's a biggy: 81 posts to date, ignored by the entire population of cyberspace. Until I came along.

The blogger is a Brit holed up in the Dordogne. He calls himself Hornblower. An initial skim revealed him to be a pretentious arse prone to slipping pointlessly into French. So far, so what? There are countless self-important cocks out there who think the world owes them a hearing. What makes this one special? It's the un-translated conversations with Papin, his gardener/house boy. My French is sub-GCSE, but my antennae were twitching. Something about Papin's tone (and his frequent use of *se faire foutre*, as in *foutre off*) intrigued. Further investigation was warranted. I turned to my mate Devon, the only Tesco security guard I know with a degree in French (yes, it's a biggie, this recession). It was about time he put it to use.

I was right to be curious. Papin is a sewer-mouthed genius who's found the perfect fall guy in Hornblower. Read for yourself at blogass.co.uk/hornblower, but arm yourself with a good dictionary of French slang. In the meantime, here are some recent highlights to whet your appetite.

Post 79:
Papin tips up to work and greets Hornblower with, 'You still poncing around in your pyjamas, my English arsehole?' Then he asks, 'Where is your bitch?' The

247

'bitch', it turns out, is Hornblower's wife, Celine, and she has returned to England. Papin commiserates. 'She was good,*' he says, 'I'll miss her fat tits.' Papin ends the conversation with, 'You are a lonely and pathetic cunt. Go fuck yourself.'

(*Devon tells me that 'bonne' in the phrase 'Elle était bonne' literally means 'good', but should be taken in this context as meaning 'a good fuck'.)

Post 80:
Feeling like a true Frenchy, Hornblower takes us out and about, stopping off at the cheese shop where he comes across Mme Poincare. She is clearly Papin's female counterpart because she introduces him to her assistant as 'my English queer', before ordering the girl to serve our man with 'the shittiest stuff'. When Hornblower returns home with his rank purchase, we have my favourite Papin-ism: 'I see she sold you the stuff that smells like an Arab's wank.'

Post 81:
Hornblower and Papin are chewing the fat over a bottle of pricey dessert wine. 'London must be full of sad cunts like you,' Papin says. 'Do you miss it?' Hornblower gives this some thought and decides that, on balance, he doesn't. 'Fucking hell,' Papin explodes, 'if twats like you keep coming to the Dordogne, I'll have to move to London.' Hornblower tells Papin he wouldn't cope in the Big Sophisticated City, but the old boy, *naturellement*, has the final word: 'At

least I'll be able to eat your wife's pussy.'
Hornblower's blogs are a triumphant *Tour de Filth*, yet he remains oblivious to every disgusting reference. Go explore, blog watchers, and have fun.

From: **Donald Gold**
To: Liam O'Keefe, Harvey Harvey
Cc: Ted Berry, David Crutton, Kazu Makino
Sent: 20 January 2009, 09.47
Subject: Presentation materials for Project Recruit

As you know, GIT are flying in from Virginia next Monday to see your excellent Mini Montana campaign. Before I leave for Rio, here is a comprehensive and hopefully final list of the areas we need to cover off in terms of creative.

- Packaging mock-ups – need the twenty-, ten- and five-pack variants
- Posters and press ads – Kazu has full list of markets where tobacco advertising is still legal
- POS materials – window stickers, shelf wobblers, branded signage
- Low-level retail displays
- Screen grabs for Club Penguin-style website
- Ice-cream-van stickers
- Win a Date with Zac Efron/Vanessa Anne Hudgens promo material
- Creative for Hannah 'The Montana Gal' Montana campaign
- School-gate 'goody packs' – Azerbaijani and Ugandan versions only (last two countries where such promotion is still legally permitted)

Any questions, I'm on email. I'm back in the office on Friday morning and I'll check in with you then. Have fun, guys.

Donald Gold

From: **Janice Crutton**
To: Paula Sterling
Sent: 20 January 2009, 09.48
Subject: Tag Watch

I'm due in conference in ten minutes. Can you take up residence in my office and keep an eye on Tamara's movements via the tag monitor? I've got a printout of her school timetable so you can tell where she should be at any given moment. I've also drawn up a list of pretexts under which you can pull me out of my meeting should she veer off campus.

And if you have a spare moment, look into the availability of tag devices with a remote facility for administering a mild electric shock. They may not be on the open market, but try asking Diana Fleiss. She worked on the team that represented Pinochet in his extradition case. She may have useful contacts with less scrupulous rightwing organizations who are familiar with such hardware.

From: **Paula Sterling**
To: Dotty Podidra
Sent: 20 January 2009, 10.01
Subject: Aagh!

JC put me on daughter surveillance. Feel like I'm in the Stasi. Not what I signed up for. I swear, any more of this and I'm getting her sectioned. I know the law!

From: **Dotty Podidra**
To: Paula Sterling
Sent: 20 January 2009, 10.07
Subject: Re: Aagh!

DC getting worse too. Double vision a nightmare! He's having a meeting with our creative director, but he's talking to the kentia palm!

From: **Dotty Podidra**
To: All Staff
Sent: 20 January 2009, 10.10
Subject: Workies?

Any workies free to spend the day steering our chief exec clear of corners and doorframes?

	MSN:
Kazoo:	Where are you now?
Dong:	Waiting to board. Why?
Kazoo:	Just checking you haven't done a runner.
Dong:	Have you no faith?
Kazoo:	Too much bravado. Don't trust it.
Dong:	I'm fine. Spent last fifteen minutes practising the brace position. After a while it's just like yoga. V. transcendental.
Kazoo:	Great GIT e, by the way. Distinctly heard Satan mutter, 'My work here is done,' as it pinged into my inbox.
Dong:	Thanks. Could get used to the Dark Side.
Kazoo:	When they call your flight, I think you should pop a precautionary Valium. Better safe than sorry.
Dong:	Had too many comp champagnes. Not sure I should mix it.

From: **Liam O'Keefe**
To: Brett Topolski
Sent: 20 January 2009, 10.19
Subject: Re: Sighting

Well done, Bloodhound Brett. That is definitely Simon Horne, as good a match as any DNA sample. And how is it possible that he's even more of a tosser in exile than he was in London? What do we do with the information? It's not like there's an FBI reward on him. (By the way, any Al Qaeda types down your way I could claim an FBI reward on? Slightly strapped at the moment.) I suppose we could viral his blogs to everyone in Adland, at least give everyone who's had the misfortune to work for him a retributive laugh.

Didn't go well with Lorraine. She turned up with her mate Debbie (remember her? Big laugh, big tits, pretty much big everything) and they ganged up on me. They held me responsible for more or less all the crimes committed on women by men. I'll cop to my share, but the Rape of the Sabines, I was definitely washing my hair that night. I was lucky to leave the pub alive and it took me most of the weekend to recover. Managed to summon up the energy on Sunday to place a small wager on Chelsea/Stoke C. Two goals in the last two minutes! Lampard's a cunt.

    Liam

PS: Seriously, are there any rag-head terrorists in your neck I could get a reward on? Keep your eyes peeled. We'll go halves.

From: **Brett Topolski**
To: Liam O'Keefe
Sent: 20 January 2009, 10.28
Subject: Re: Sighting

Things sound bad. Just how strapped are you?

From: **Liam O'Keefe**
To: Brett Topolski
Sent: 20 January 2009, 10.30
Subject: Re: Sighting

You don't want to know.

From: **Brett Topolski**
To: Liam O'Keefe
Sent: 20 January 2009, 10.32
Subject: Re: Sighting

Oh, but I do. You owe me £1,500. I'm never going to see it, am I?

From: **Liam O'Keefe**
To: Brett Topolski
Sent: 20 January 2009, 10.39
Subject: Re: Sighting

It's unlikely.

From: **Brett Topolski**
To: Liam O'Keefe
Sent: 20 January 2009, 10.44
Subject: Re: Sighting

Spill the beans then. How much are you in for?

From: **Liam O'Keefe**
To: Brett Topolski
Sent: 20 January 2009, 10.48
Subject: Re: Sighting

Do I have to do this?

From: **Brett Topolski**
To: Liam O'Keefe
Sent: 20 January 2009, 10.50
Subject: Re: Sighting

It's for your own good.

Kazu:	You on board?
Don:	Yes
Kazu:	OK?
Don:	Perfect. Stewardess giving me more comp champ
Kazu:	Pissed?
Don:	Squiffy
Kazu:	Go easy
Don:	Got to switch phone off. Stewardess says plane will crash if I don't. Oh God, old nightmares returning. Get me off this fucking plane. It's going to crash, I know it
Kazu:	No, it's not. You'll be fine. Just do the visualization exercises they taught you on the course. Kittens, wasn't it?
Kazu:	You there? If you haven't switched off, speak to me

From: **Kazu Makino**
To: Bill Geddes
Sent: 20 January 2009, 11.01
Subject: Donald

Just got a very panicky text from him. I think he's a bit pissed. He's about to take off and I'm worried. Anything we can do?

From: **Bill Geddes**
To: Kazu Makino
Sent: 20 January 2009, 11.04
Subject: Re: Donald

Nothing I can think of. What's the flight time to Rio?

From: **Kazu Makino**
To: Bill Geddes
Sent: 20 January 2009, 11.06
Subject: Re: Donald

13 hours.

From: **Bill Geddes**
To: Kazu Makino
Sent: 20 January 2009, 11.09
Subject: Re: Donald

Cross your fingers and hope.

From: **Liam O'Keefe**
To: Brett Topolski
Sent: 20 January 2009, 11.13
Subject: Re: Sighting

Barclaycard:	£4,232.18
NatWest:	£6,299.12
Capital One:	£3,307.79
AmEx:	£903.76
John Lewis:	£1,104.25
Selfridge's:	£3,635.35
Debenham's:	£1,008.08
SafeBet.com:	£26,745.02
Landlord:	£3,250
Dimitri the Shark:	£10,000
Hakkan the Shark:	£9,000
Ace Mini Mart:	£35.76
Duke of York*:	£247.50
Lorraine P:	£4,000 (Est. Could be out by a factor of 2. Or 20. Maybe.)
Brett T:	£1,500

Grand total:	£75,268.81

*The pub, not the royal personage.

From: **Harvey Harvey**
To: Comfort Ajegbo
Sent: 20 January 2009, 11.19
Subject: Are you OK?

Hello Comfort

It's been nearly a week since I sent you my bank details and I haven't heard from you. Also, my credit card was refused when I tried to top up my Oyster Card this morning. Could your late father's evil associates somehow have tampered with the account? Or with my Oyster Card? To be honest, I'm really worried. I've been scouring the internet for news, but I haven't found anything. My mum says no news is good news, and I hope she's right. Please write soon and let me know that you're all right.

Harvey Harvey

From: **Brett Topolski**
To: Liam O'Keefe
Sent: 20 January 2009, 11.22
Subject: Re: Sighting

Fucking Ada. Bit late to suggest you sit down and come up with a sensible budget plan. One thing strikes me: what are you doing with a John Lewis store card?

I could advance you a bit. Maybe 5k, but it's not going to help much. I think you need to look into clearing the lot with a consolidated loan.

From: **Liam O'Keefe**
To: Brett Topolski
Sent: 20 January 2009, 11.26
Subject: Re: Sighting

I'm thirty-seven. I felt it was the right time of life to get a John Lewis account. It's a rite of passage. And their curtain fabrics are excellent.

Took out a consolidated loan last year – just before credit totally crunched. Did I not mention it? £50,000. The monthly repayments are mental.

From: **Brett Topolski**
To: Liam O'Keefe
Sent: 20 January 2009, 11.30
Subject: Re: Sighting

Four options:

1   Declare bankruptcy.
2   Leave clothes in pile on Brighton Beach and swim for your life.
3   Get part-time work – bar, call centre etc. It'll have to pay about £375/hour though.
4   Vince reckons he knows people who could give you some freelance, but I suspect it involves flying to bad places and swallowing condoms full of smack.

Soz, mate, but you're fucked.

From: **Liam O'Keefe**
To: Brett Topolski
Sent: 20 January 2009, 11.34
Subject: Re: Sighting

Don't I know it? Just got bits and bobs from eBay coming in –

beer money really. Only reason I'm not at home in bed right now is that I've a feeling the bailiffs might tip up today.

From: **Neil Godley**
To: Sally Wilton
Sent: 20 January 2009, 11.39
Subject: Stationery supplies

I am extremely nervous of bringing this to your attention, given the rough treatment I had at the hands of the police the last time I reported a theft. However, I feel duty bound, whatever the personal consequences.

A few minutes ago I went to the basement stationery cupboard to stock up on green and buff folders and found it completely empty. Not so much as a bottle of Tipp-Ex! Clearly there is a hardened criminal at work in the building, Sally, and all efforts must be made to bring him/her to justice.

Neil Godley (Accounts)

From: **Sally Wilton**
To: David Crutton
Sent: 20 January 2009, 11.48
Subject: Theft

Can you come to the basement stationery store ASAP? What you will see makes a watertight case for the type of security measures I have long been arguing for.

Sally Wilton
**PRINCESS
PAPERCLIP**

From: **Milton Keane**
To: Dotty Podidra
Sent: 20 January 2009, 11.49
Subject: Lattes all round!

Free to join me and Sooz in Starbucks? I'm going to do the big reveal. Off with the bandage to unveil the new improved, 25% more macho Milton!

From: **Dotty Podidra**
To: Milton Keane
Sent: 20 January 2009, 11.51
Subject: Re: Lattes all round!

Love to, but have to escort DC down to basement. Honestly, what am I? His blinking guide dog?

From: **Ted Berry**
To: Liam O'Keefe, Harvey Harvey
Sent: 20 January 2009, 11.57
Subject: Vodka trip

As my new top team, how do you fancy joining Bill Geddes and me on the plane to Holland tomorrow? We're off to visit the Ketel One distillery in Schiedam. All the vodka we can drink, I suspect. The only downside is we have to do some bollock-stomping advertising in return. Lemme know how you're fixed. And if you're good, I'll take you sand yachting on the beach at Scheveningen.

Ted Berry
MC IDEΛZ

From: **Bill Geddes**
To: Kazu Makino
Sent: 20 January 2009, 12.09
Subject: Re: Donald

Any word?

From: **Kazu Makino**
To: Bill Geddes
Sent: 20 January 2009, 12.13
Subject: Re: Donald

He's only been airborne for 45 minutes. I've been checking the news sites. No reports of air rage/forced landings.

From: **Bill Geddes**
To: Kazu Makino
Sent: 20 January 2009, 12.15
Subject: Re: Donald

Yet.

From: **Susi Judge-Davis-Gaultier**
To: Dotty Podidra
Sent: 20 January 2009, 12.35
Subject: What have I done?

Milton looks like some dreadful East-End boxer. His nose is as flat as a pancake with a bulbous bump at the bottom. Even when the bruising goes down, he's going to look horrendous. He thinks it looks great, but he's still on sedatives and I think he's delusional. He'll never get on *BB* now. His whole look is completely camera-unfriendly. He'll kill me when he realizes I've shattered his dreams!!

From: **Dotty Podidra**
To: Susi Judge-Davis-Gaultier
Sent: 20 January 2009, 12.37
Subject: Re: What have I done?

Have to write a scary e for DC. We'll get together over lunch and I'll take a look at Milton. I'm sure it's not as bad as you think.

From: **David Crutton**
To: All Staff
Sent: 20 January 2009, 12.41
Subject: Come in, you thieving bastard, your time is up

I'm prepared to turn a blind eye to the traditional theft of paperclips and HB pencils, but this has gone beyond a joke. The basement stationery cupboard is barer than Old Mother Hubbard's and I am officially livid. I WILL catch the thief, even if it means making each and every one of you overpaid, under-employed twats undergo lie-detector tests/ waterboarding.

Be very afraid, you light-fingered toe rag because I will have your bollocks/tits in a mangle.

David Crutton
𝕿𝖍𝖊 𝕸𝖆𝖓

From: **David Crutton**
To: Sally Wilton
Sent: 20 January 2009, 12.44
Subject: Bringing this investigation to a speedy and successful
         conclusion

I'd like you to look into the possibility of performing CIA-style rendition of certain key suspects to former Soviet Bloc nations, where investigative techniques are less beholden to our flabby

Western concepts of civil liberties. I'm sure we could dress it up as 'essential business travel'.

David Crutton
The Man

From: **Dotty Podidra**
To: Paula Sterling
Sent: 20 January 2009, 12.47
Subject: Padded cell for two!!

OMG, you should see the last two emails DC made me type. He's completely lost it too. Think him and JC must be having a competition to see who can turn into the maddest fascist crackpot!!

From: **Zlatan Kovaćević**
To: David Crutton
Sent: 20 January 2009, 12.48
Subject: Re: Come in, you thieving bastard, your time is up

I know certain people who will be of use in this difficult occasion. I can arrange them to come in today. If you give them office for their use, I guarantee to you that they will have a name for the thief by the end of week. The only thing they will ask in return is for you to use your very great influences to make International War Crimes Tribunal in The Hague to drop certain outstanding warrants of arrest.

From: **Róisín O'Hooligan**
To: David Crutton
Sent: 20 January 2009, 12.49
Subject: Re: Come in, you thieving bastard, your time is up

Probably not the best moment to tell you that the Arsenal/W. Ham tickets only just delivered by Ticketmaster have gone walkabout from the front desk. And before you have a go at me, I know my legal entitlements to toilet breaks.

Róisín
Reception

From: **Dotty Podidra**
To: Sally Wilton
Sent: 20 January 2009, 12.54
Subject: 'accident'

Could you get your bucket-and-mop guy up here again? Glass and coffee grounds everywhere. I think he was aiming for the kentia palm, but double vision meant he got my workstation.

From: **Liam O'Keefe**
To: Brett Topolski
Sent: 20 January 2009, 12.55
Subject: Crutton is back!

He fell off a rock wall last week. Reckon the knock on the head did him the power of good because he is once again at his splenetic finest. Suddenly everything seems right in the world.

---

eBay.co.uk

Stationery Cupboard

Item specifics: complete contents of stationery cupboard. Former property of cutting-edge London media company, so well stocked with 'trendy' items such as acetate pads, heart-shaped Post-its, Magic Markers and handmade Japanese papers. Also included: usual mundane stuff – Tipp-Ex, staples and such like – as well as a full stock of toilet supplies. Would suit ambitious media start-up. Or small branch of Ryman.

Current bid: **£00.00**
End time: 9d 23h 57m

---

eBay.co.uk

Premiership Tickets

Item specifics: Arsenal vs. West Ham United, Emirates Stadium, 31 January. 4 tickets, upper tier, West Stand. Face value £48 each. Would suit committed Arsenal fan, slightly suicidal West Ham fan or corporate tosspot who wants to impress clients with his willingness to 'get down and dirty' with hardcore home support.

Current bid: **£00.00**
End time: 9d 23h 59m

From: **Sally Wilton**
To: All Staff
Sent: 20 January 2009, 13.03
Subject: Resource-saving ideas

Until the stationery cupboard is restocked, it is important that we all muck in to make sure our existing supplies last for as long as possible. To this end, here are some handy tips:

1   Reuse envelopes. You can make your own attractive and 'branded' address labels out of compliment slips.
2   Each time you reach for your stapler, ask yourself, could a *reusable* paperclip adequately do the same job?

3   Creatives, do your layouts really need to be so big? With careful planning, you can fit up to twenty-four 'ideas' on to a single sheet of A2.

4   Creatives, is that 'idea' actually any good? Honestly, most of what you do is uninspired and/or unoriginal and committing it to paper will merely serve to make you look 'busy'. Go on, be tough on yourselves and only draw up the absolute 'gems'.

5   Print out letters and documents on both sides of the paper.

6   And since lavatory supplies have also gone missing, please use both sides of the toilet paper.

7   Soap and paper towels are also in extremely short supply. Ask yourself: do I really need to wash my hands? As a rule, ablutions are only essential after No. 2s.

Who knows, perhaps this period of enforced austerity will cultivate long-term habits of frugality that will save both company money and the precious resources of the planet! Thank you for your cooperation.

Sally Wilton
**PRINCESS
PAPERCLIP**

From: **Comfort Ajegbo**
To: Harvey Harvey
Sent: 20 January 2009, 13.06
Subject: Re: Are you OK?

I am so glad you write to me, Harvey Harvey, because everything is not OK here. I am encountering trouble arranging the transfer of funds into your account. My contact at FirstBank of Nigeria plc is insisting on dotting all the Ts and he is demanding that you turn up in person to vouch for the veracity of your banking arrangements. I know I have asked much of you already and it is beyond all reasonableness to expect you to undertake such a journey, but I am a forlorn and pitiful woman and you are my one and only hope in this world.

I will naturally understand if you say no to my request and I will place my fate in the hands of God, who is great and ineffable in His wisdom.

Yours in hope,
Comfort Ajegbo

VOICEMAIL:

Dimitri: You're a sly fucker, O'Keefe. I hear you've also been borrowing from the Turkish slag. I'm not fucking happy about that. Not fucking happy at all. Anyway, the terms have changed. I'll be calling for my ten G a week today. And if the fucking Turk sees a fucking penny of his before I get mine, I'll slit you right open, stick my foot in the hole and twist it really fucking hard. Later.

VOICEMAIL:

Hakkan: Yo, Liam. You're a right fucking wind-up merchant, innit? You taking from the fucking Greek as well. You think I don't find out? You think I'm fucking stupid? You ain't got a month no more. You got a week. That's for taking the piss. And you don't owe me nine grand. You owe me ten. That's also for taking the piss. See you a week

today, fucker. And don't give the
Greek a penny till I've got all mine,
unless you want to see your guts
on the pavement.

From: **Liam O'Keefe**
To: Brett Topolski
Sent: 20 January 2009, 13.08
Subject: Going Dutch

MMT is taking me on a vodka trip to Holland tomorrow. Reckon
I might stay there, blend in with the potheads, lie low for a bit.
Ten years should do it. Situation getting distinctly hairy round
here.

From: **Liam O'Keefe**
To: Harvey Harvey
Sent: 20 January 2009, 13.12
Subject: Vodka trip

I know we're now officially Ted's Top Team, but let's get a few
things straight before we head for Holland.

1 I am not sharing a room with you.
2 If there's any opportunity for R&R, I expect you to find
   your own entertainment. Actually, I think it's best if
   you stay put in your hotel room. The 'pleasures' of
   Holland don't suit the mentally 'fragile'.
3 If you have any bright ideas for vodka campaigns, best
   you run them by me first. I'll vet them for Ted-friend-
   liness/general sanity.
4 Bagsy first on the sand yacht.

From: **Harvey Harvey**
To: Liam O'Keefe
Sent: 20 January 2009, 13.13
Subject: Re: Vodka trip

Thanks for the tips, but I don't think I'm going to be able to make it to Holland. I have to fly to Nigeria ASAP.

From: **Liam O'Keefe**
To: Harvey Harvey
Sent: 20 January 2009, 13.17
Subject: Re: Vodka trip

If I hadn't intervened with Ted last week, you'd be jobless right now. If you piss off now to Darkest Africa, I'd say you're doomed. By the way, why are you pissing off to Darkest Africa?

From: **Harvey Harvey**
To: Liam O'Keefe
Sent: 20 January 2009, 13.22
Subject: Re: Vodka trip

It's a life-or-death situation. A Nigerian woman got in touch with me and she'll most likely die if I don't help her.

From: **Liam O'Keefe**
To: Harvey Harvey
Sent: 20 January 2009, 13.24
Subject: Re: Vodka trip

Don't tell me, she's a young heiress who's promised you a significant wedge of her inheritance if you provide her with your bank details.

From: **Harvey Harvey**
To: Liam O'Keefe
Sent: 20 January 2009, 13.27
Subject: Re: Vodka trip

Unbelievable! Have you had an email from her as well?

From: **Liam O'Keefe**
To: Harvey Harvey
Sent: 20 January 2009, 13.30
Subject: Re: Vodka trip

Everyone's had an email from her or someone very like her. It's a fucking scam, you muppet.

From: **Harvey Harvey**
To: Liam O'Keefe
Sent: 20 January 2009, 13.33
Subject: Re: Vodka trip

You're pulling my leg, aren't you? Everyone says you have a reputation as a leg-puller.

From: **Liam O'Keefe**
To: Harvey Harvey
Sent: 20 January 2009, 13.36
Subject: Re: Vodka trip

I'm being straighter than I've ever been in my life, Harvey. It's a scam. Here's how it works. Someone called Charity or Comfort or Big Chief Smiley Face sends out 50,000 emails saying they've got several tens of millions of dollars and they need to transfer it double-quick to a nice safe UK account. They promise you a percentage if you provide them with your bank details. Most recipients trash it straight away, but a few feeble-minded idiots respond. The next thing they know, they've had all their assets stripped. Even fewer feeble-minded idiots get hit with a further request to come to Nigeria. The unlucky ones get macheted and DHL-ed back home in several parcels. The lucky few merely get robbed blind, stripped naked and dumped on the steps of their embassy.

Please tell me you're not going to go. Apart from anything else, you'll leave me right in the shit on GIT. Have you seen Gold's email shopping list?

From: **Harvey Harvey**
To: Liam O'Keefe
Sent: 20 January 2009, 13.39
Subject: Re: Vodka trip

Sorry about GIT, but I have to go. She sounds completely genuine. I'm sure she's not tricking me.

From: **Liam O'Keefe**
To: Harvey Harvey
Sent: 20 January 2009, 13.41
Subject: Re: Vodka trip

The first rule of any successful con is plausibility, HH. Haven't you learned anything working in advertising? How do you think Nike gets away with charging over a ton for a pair of sweat-shop trainers? If you go over there, you'll be met by a delegation of gangsters in white croc-skin loafers. They'll eat you alive.

From: **Harvey Harvey**
To: Liam O'Keefe
Sent: 20 January 2009, 13.44
Subject: Re: Vodka trip

What if you're wrong? A young life is at stake. In situations like this I always ask myself what the Doctor would do. He would go to Nigeria, just as he landed the TARDIS in the heart of the Dalek mother ship in the Series Three Finale.

From: **Liam O'Keefe**
To: Harvey Harvey
Sent: 20 January 2009, 13.47
Subject: Re: Vodka trip

You're not going to listen to reason, are you?

From: **Harvey Harvey**
To: Liam O'Keefe
Sent: 20 January 2009, 13.51
Subject: Re: Vodka trip

No. I've booked my ticket. I fly at 5.30. Have to go home and pack. Can you tell Ted I'm sorry?

From: **Dotty Podidra**
To: Susi Judge-Davis-Gaultier
Sent: 20 January 2009, 14.06
Subject: Milton

OMG, you're right. He looks terrible. His *BB* audition is next Tuesday. Way too soon to get him into cosmetic surgery.

From: **Susi Judge-Davis-Gaultier**
To: Dotty Podidra
Sent: 20 January 2009, 14.08
Subject: Re: Milton

Did you see literally everyone in Wagamama staring at him? I feel so awful. What can we do?

From: **Milton Keane**
To: Susi Judge-Davis-Gaultier, Dotty Podidra
Sent: 20 January 2009, 14.09
Subject: Buzzing!

Did you see literally everyone in Wagamama staring at me? I feel totally fab! Move over, Brad! How does 'Mingelina' sound??

From: **Dotty Podidra**
To: Susi Judge-Davis-Gaultier
Sent: 20 January 2009, 14.10
Subject: Re: Milton

Judging by his last e, think we'd better just go with the flow for now. Setting him straight might make him totally flip.

From: **Ted Berry**
To: Liam O'Keefe, Harvey Harvey
Cc: Bill Geddes
Sent: 20 January 2009, 14.21
Subject: Ketel One

You two top concept wranglers care to join me in my gaff? Bill G is going to give us a pre-trip briefing on the delights of premium hand-baked vodka.

From: **Liam O'Keefe**
To: Ted Berry
Sent: 20 January 2009, 14.25
Subject: Re: Ketel One

Be there in a tick. Harvey won't be joining us. He sends his apologies.

From: **Ted Berry**
To: Liam O'Keefe
Sent: 20 January 2009, 14.27
Subject: Re: Ketel One

Where the fuck is he?

From: **Liam O'Keefe**
To: Ted Berry
Sent: 20 January 2009, 14.28
Subject: Re: Ketel One

He's gone to Nigeria to save a life. Suspect he'll be returning in a body bag.

From: **Ted Berry**
To: Liam O'Keefe
Sent: 20 January 2009, 14.30
Subject: Re: Ketel One

At least the Nigerians will have saved us the pay-off. My office now. You can handle K1 on your own.

From: **Neil Godley**
To: All Staff
Sent: 20 January 2009, 14.38
Subject: Help Is at Hand!

In the interests of fostering an all-hands-to-the-pump Dunkirk spirit, I am prepared to release the stationery I have brought in for strictly personal use. I have watermarked Basildon Bond and matching envelopes in powder blue and mint green. Offer limited to two sheets/one envelope per person.

Neil Godley (Accounts)

From: **Liam O'Keefe**
To: All Staff
Sent: 20 January 2009, 14.42
Subject: Help Is at Hand, 2!

I also have several *Dr Who* notepads for general use. They're not strictly mine, but I don't think Harvey Harvey will be needing them again.

From: **David Crutton**
To: Dotty Podidra
Sent: 20 January 2009, 14.43
Subject:

gett un hrer amd du e fir ne. we havr oir mann!

From: **David Crutton**
To: Neil Godley
Sent: 20 January 2009, 14.49
Subject: I've got your number, you thieving gobshite

Do not imagine for one second that your sanctimonious and frankly creepy Christian act fools me. I know your game and I am closing in. It is only a matter of time before I have the evidence. And believe me, by the time I've finished with you, you'll be begging for the sanctuary of a police cell.

David Crutton
The Man

From: **David Crutton**
To: Sally Wilton
Sent: 20 January 2009, 14.52
Subject: Operation Thief Kill

I firmly believe Godley is our man, though he is clearly an

extremely clever operator and we will have difficulty making a case against him. The police obviously lack the will/mental rigour to see this through, given their abject failure to pin the theft of the copier on him.

I suggest an alternative course of action.

I've had an interesting conversation with Zlatan Kovaćević. He has useful contacts in the private-security sector. I want his people working on this as a matter of urgency. Get the number from him and I will sign the necessary purchase order.

David Crutton
𝕿𝖍𝖊 𝕸𝖆𝖓

From: **Milton Keane**
To: All Staff
Sent: 20 January 2009, 15.00
Subject: Workies

Any workies free to take a piccy of the new More Rugged Me for my Facebook and MySpace profiles?

From: **Liam O'Keefe**
To: All Staff
Sent: 20 January 2009, 15.12
Subject: Workies

Any lady workies free to be photographed with a fag in the gob? Would help if you look vaguely like Miley Cyrus/Hannah Montana, but no worries because Photoshop will do the hard work.

From: **Bill Geddes**
To: Kazu Makino
Sent: 20 January 2009, 15.21
Subject: Don

You heard anything untoward about Our Man En Route to Rio yet?

From: **Kazu Makino**
To: Bill Geddes
Sent: 20 January 2009, 15.24
Subject: Re: Don

Slight panic when I read a report of plane putting down in a field near Tampa, but turned out to be a cargo flight of quail eggs that exploded on sudden depressurization. So far so good.

From: **Ted Berry**
To: Sally Wilton
Sent: 20 January 2009, 16.09
Subject:

Adrijana and Zlatan have just presented me with a campaign of 96-sheet posters drawn up entirely on Rizla papers. The stationery shortage is getting ridiculous. Get it sorted. Please.

From: **Janice Crutton**
To: Paula Sterling
Sent: 20 January 2009, 16.14
Subject:

Get hold of Mr Abbas at Spectre Security & Surveillance and tell him we've got a problem. Tamara is picking up my home phone, but the monitor says she's in a Hackney crack den. Either his overpriced device is on the blink or my daughter is an electronic wiz – maybe she has been paying attention in her science classes after all.

SMS:

Bill: Help!

Kazu: OMG, you heard from Don? What's he done?

Bill: Not him. Me. In dire straits. Stuck in trap 3 with no loo roll

Kazu: I'll check the other bogs. Gimme 5

SMS:

Liam: That you texting in trap 3?

Bill: How did you guess?

Liam: Recognize your spastic ringtone anywhere

Bill: Where are you? Can you get me loo roll?

Liam: No. I'm in trap 5. None here either

Bill: Sent Kaz to look for supplies. Hang tight and she'll sort us both out

SMS:

Kazu: No bog paper anywhere. I can give you a choice of Post-its or comp slips

Bill: I'll take comp slips. Bigger and more absorbent. Give Post-its to Liam in trap 5. And hurry!

Kazu: Sending intrepid male workie in now

SMS:

Liam: Fucking Post-its? You humorous fucker

Wednesday
Mood: **insomniac**

SMS:

Kazu: You awake?

Bill: I am now. This better be good. Supposed to be up in 3 hours to fly to Holland

Kazu: Been on Don watch. You'd better check the news

Bill: Trouble?

Kazu: Big trouble. Turn on news and get in touch when you're done

bbc.co.uk/news

British man arrested in Brazil

A British man has been arrested after landing in Rio de Janeiro on a British Airways flight from Heathrow.

Donald Gold, a 42-year-old British advertising executive, was arrested at Rio de Janeiro's Galeão International Airport after being physically restrained by cabin crew during the flight from London.

Apparently convinced that the flight crew had died from unspecified poisoning and that the aircraft was flying itself, he tried to gain entry to the Boeing 747's flight deck. Bienvenida Bebeta Bezerra, who was sitting close to Gold in business class, said: 'He was drinking and taking pills all through the journey and he seemed jumpy, but I didn't think anything of it – who isn't terrified stupid at 10,000 metres? But then he jumped to his feet and started screaming, "They're all dead, they're all dead, and we will all die too!" I told him to calm down, but he shouted at me that he was the only man who could fly the aeroplane. Then he ran to the front and the next time I see him the stewardesses are pushing him to the floor and putting the handcuffs on him. They were quite rough. I think they give him a black eye and stamp on him hard in their high heels. The whole thing was terrifying.'

Fiona West, British Airways Director of Long Haul Operations, said: 'The safety of the flight and the passengers is of paramount importance. The cabin crew behaved in exemplary fashion and followed the procedure for dealing with in-flight incidents to the letter. The matter is now in the hands of the Brazilian authorities.'

Gold remains in custody at Galeão International and has yet to be charged with any offence.

Bill:	Oh my fucking fuck. What now?
Kazu:	Tried phoning him. Just got voicemail. Know any Brazilian lawyers?
Bill:	What do you think? Should we phone DC?
Kazu:	At 3 in the morning? Are you completely mad?
Bill:	You're right. I'll try calling Brit consulate in Rio
Kazu:	Good idea. I'll keep watching news. Stay in touch

From: **David Crutton**
To: Sally Wilton
Sent: 21 January 2009, 03.21
Subject: Operation Thief Kill

I want 24-hour surveillance on Godley. CCTV in his cubicle and a bug on his phone. Also, have IT assign one of their techies to monitor his email and internet usage.

Sent from my BlackBerry

SMS:

Kazu:	Turn on news quick.
Bill:	Worse?
Kazu:	Much worse.

bbc.co.uk/news
Air-rage suspect faces terror interrogation

The British executive at the centre of an air-rage incident is being

280

questioned as a terror suspect.

Donald Gold, arrested in Rio de Janeiro after an incident aboard a British Airways flight, was found to be carrying what was described as terrorist propaganda in his baggage. A spokesman for Brazil's National Intelligence Service said: 'Señor Donald Gold is being held under Brazil's anti-terror laws following the discovery of dangerous propaganda. His baggage contained large glossy pictures of Osama Bin Laden and Kim Jong-Il, which are clearly designed to incite terrorist violence and sedition in our peace-loving country. Señor Gold has been transferred to the jurisdiction of the CIA under Brazil's anti-terror accord with the Government of the United States.'

Gold's current whereabouts are unknown. No one at the US State Department in Washington or CIA headquarters in Langley, Virginia was available for comment.

SMS:

Bill:	Oh my fucking, fucking fuck. Think we should try DC now?
Kazu:	Only if you're daft enough to think waking the Beast could possibly make things better.
Bill:	I'll try the Foreign Office. They must have someone on duty who can handle this.
Kazu:	Hurry up. Worried sick here. He's probably in Guantanamo by now

From: **David Crutton**
To: Sally Wilton
Sent: 21 January 2009, 04.06
Subject: Operation Thief Kill

Further thought on the Godley case: have a workie tail him when he leaves the building. Actually, a team of workies with a rota to follow him round the clock.

Sent from my BlackBerry

From: **Liam O'Keefe**
To: Harvey Harvey
Sent: 21 January 2009, 04.12
Subject: Are you still alive?

Don't go getting ideas above your station, sunshine. You're not the only reason I'm awake at four in the fucking morning. Mostly to do with the fact that the bastard bailiffs took both my bed and my sofa yesterday. But – fuck knows why – I am worried about you. If you're not – as I fear – lying dismembered in a disused section of oil pipeline, but are checking your emails in some backstreet internet caff while knocking back one of the many non-alcoholic malted beverages for which Nigeria is rightly famous, please write and let me know.

Your fucked-up guardian angel

Friday
Mood: **paranoid**

From: **Sally Wilton**
To: All Staff
Sent: 23 January 2009, 09.15
Subject: Security

As you know, XL Enforcement is working with us to enhance general security. To this end, bag searches are mandatory for everyone leaving the building. Rest assured, however, that strip searches will be kept to a minimum. From time to time, XL operatives may need to question employees. The former stationery cupboard in the basement has been set aside for this purpose.

Hopefully these essential security measures will bring to an end the recent spate of property theft and we can all return to normal.

Thank you for your cooperation.

Sally Wilton
**PRINCESS
PAPERCLIP**

From: **Sally Wilton**
To: All Staff
Sent: 23 January 2009, 09.20
Subject: New stationery arrangements

You will no doubt be pleased to learn that our stationery inventory has been fully replenished. The new super-secure stationery vault is located on the third floor and has been fitted with a state-of-the-art steel-titanium-laminate door designed to withstand a blast of up to 1.2 megatons. Access can be obtained via a 16-digit code, which will be changed daily. Anyone needing stationery supplies must fill in the new Stationery Requisition Form (SR1-B), which they should then take to their department head. Only department heads are permitted access to the vault.

Thank you for your cooperation.

Sally Wilton
**PRINCESS
PAPERCLIP**

From: **Adrijana Smiljanić**
To: Sally Wilton
Sent: 23 January 2009, 09.26
Subject: Re: New stationery arrangements

So if I want Pritt Stick, I fill up form, take to Ted, he memorize big code, go in lift to floor 3, open safe, get out Pritt Stick and bring back to me?

From: **Sally Wilton**
To: Adrijana Smiljanić
Sent: 23 January 2009, 09.28
Subject: Re: New stationery arrangements

Yes! Glad my email made everything so clear.

From: **Adrijana Smiljanić**
To: Sally Wilton
Sent: 23 January 2009, 09.29
Subject: Re: New stationery arrangements

Very clear, thank you. Also fucking crazy.

From: **Neil Godley**
To: Caroline Zitter
Sent: 23 January 2009, 09.31
Subject: A totally confidential matter

Dear Caroline

As the one senior partner who has the interests of 'rank-and-file' staff at heart, you're the only person I can turn to. I am certain my phone is bugged and I am being followed whenever I leave the building. Also, a pizza delivery van is permanently parked outside my flat. You'll probably think I'm being paranoid, but I tried phoning the number on the side to order a four seasons and I got a minicab office in Ipswich. I believe I have been targeted for 'special treatment' by a certain member of senior management. I don't know how much longer I can carry on performing my company duties in this atmosphere. I would normally be outraged, but to be honest, I'm too scared.

Please help me.

   Neil Godley (Accounts)

From: **Caroline Zitter**
To: Neil Godley
Sent: 23 January 2009, 09.32
Subject: Out of Office AutoReply

I am out of the office attending *Aiiiieeee-Ya!* Kick Box Your Way to the *Forbes* 100. I will return on Monday 26th January. If you

285

have an urgent request please contact my assistant, Milton Keane, on milton@meerkat360.co.uk

Caroline Zitter
THE SEER

From: **Brett Topolski**
To: Liam O'Keefe
Sent: 23 January 2009, 09.37
Subject: Home?

So are you back from Holland or are you hiding from your creditors beneath the comely form of an Amsterdam tart? Let me know that I'm not blathering pointlessly into the ether because I do worry about you.

Allah's the fella

From: **Róisín O'Hooligan**
To: Sally Wilton
Sent: 23 January 2009, 09.39
Subject: Security

I am deeply bothered by the X-ray machine your Serb goons have stuck in reception. It's only six feet from my desk and it's wheezing like my bronchial nan. Christ knows what radioactive bollocks it's pumping out. Mark my words, if I get cancer, I will not wait for the courts to get me justice. I will seek you out and rip your head from your shoulders. And you can tell Crutton I'll have him too. The blustery shitehawk doesn't scare me.

From: **Sally Wilton**
To: Róisín O'Hooligan
Sent: 23 January 2009, 09.44
Subject: Re: Security

Rest assured that the X-ray machine is perfectly safe. If you choose not to wear the lead-lined protective jerkin and bonnet with which you have been provided for your comfort and safety, and which is compulsory under health and safety legislation, the company cannot be held responsible for any ensuing medical complications.

For the record, the security improvements that are now in place are exactly what I have been arguing for during my many years in office administration. I am glad I at last have a CEO that understands what is required for efficient day-to-day office operations.

I ask that in future you desist from making abusive threats or I will be obliged to place you on the draft register of suspect employees.

Sally Wilton
**PRINCESS
PAPERCLIP**

From: **Róisín O'Hooligan**
To: Sally Wilton
Sent: 23 January 2009, 09.46
Subject: Re: Security

Go fuck yourself, Sal. With a paperclip.

From: **David Crutton**
To: Sally Wilton
Sent: 23 January 2009, 09.49
Subject: Operation Thief Kill

IT has forwarded me an interesting email sent by our prime suspect to CZ. The softly-softly approach is no longer appropriate. I think it's time our Serbian friends had a chat with him.

From: **Sally Wilton**
To: David Crutton
Sent: 23 January 2009, 09.51
Subject: Re: Operation Thief Kill

Do you mean an actual chat or an 'enhanced' chat?

From: **David Crutton**
To: Sally Wilton
Sent: 23 January 2009, 09.53
Subject: Re: Operation Thief Kill

'Enhanced'.

From: **Sally Wilton**
To: Neil Godley
Sent: 23 January 2009, 09.58
Subject: Routine background interview

Hi Neil

XL Enforcement would like to talk to you about the thefts of the photocopier and stationery. It's nothing to be concerned about. They simply want some useful background, since you were first on the scene on both occasions. Slobodan will be along to collect you shortly.

Sally Wilton
**PRINCESS
PAPERCLIP**

From: **Liam O'Keefe**
To: Brett Topolski
Sent: 23 January 2009, 10.06
Subject: Re: Home?

I'm back. Had a top time in Holland with MMT. Large vodkas, small herrings and male bonding all round. Gave serious thought to staying on in a fugitive capacity, but in the end I had to come back to have one final stab at glory. It's the GIT presentation on Tuesday, you see, and it's kick, bollock, scramble to get the work done. Things are extra-pressurized because Tuesday is also the day certain debts get called in, but I'm sure something will turn up.

Won't it?

Life is more than usually insane in the meerkat warren. Crutton has recruited a platoon of Balkan War leftovers to perform random beatings and strip searches, and he's installed a new stationery cupboard that resembles the vault in the Bellagio. Oh, and we have a senior account director MIA. Probably in Guantanamo, and, no, I'm not fucking kidding. Now I feel bad for every fuckwit suit I've wished torture upon (and God knows there've been a few).

Did I say something will turn up? Well, it just did. It's big, black and shiny and, if I'm not very much mistaken, some idiot Serb has left the keys in the ignition.

Ads to write, debts to pay. Later, camel jockey . . .

MSN:	
Kazoo:	Manage to schedule a meeting with DC yet?
Bilge:	Dotty says he's tied up all morning 'refining the security arrangements'.
Kazoo:	This is insane. He's got an employee in CIA custody and he's worried about stolen notepads?

And why all the fuss? Any idiot could tell you Liam did it.

Bilge: Really?

Kazoo: C'mon, he's got thief written all over him. And I can see him out of my window now. He's climbing into the security company's Merc.

Bilge: You're not going to say anything, are you?

Kazoo: Grass up your mate? Of course not. This place is so morally bankrupt it deserves to be stripped bare. I am going to do something about poor Don though.

Bilge: What??

Kazoo: I'm going to see my MP. And if he can't help, I'll get a meeting with Gordon Brown.

Bilge: He's probably tied up 'refining security arrangements' (though most likely in Afghanistan rather than the Downing St stationery cupboard). Anyway, haven't you got the GIT PowerPoint to do?

Kazoo: Fuck GIT. And if you weren't such a corporate lackey, you'd come with me.

Bilge: Love to but can't. In Don's absence, DC has put me on GIT.

From: **Róisín O'Hooligan**
To: All Staff
Sent: 23 January 2009, 10.24
Subject: Is it just me . . .

. . . or can anyone else hear screams coming from the basement?

Róisín
Reception

From: **Susi Judge-Davis-Gaultier**
To: Milton Keane
Sent: 23 January 2009, 10.26
Subject: help!

The security thugs just made me put my skinny vanilla latte through their stupid X-ray machine. Is it safe to drink now?

From: **Milton Keane**
To: Susi Judge-Davis-Gaultier
Sent: 23 January 2009, 10.29
Subject: Re: help!

I'm sure I read somewhere that X-rays destroy any remaining calories in skimmed milk, so glug away! Actually, I've got a bone to pick with DC about those security idiots. I had to literally scream at them to strip-search me this morning. I mean, doesn't my new nose make me look brutishly criminal (in an appealing Daniel Craig way)? BTW, does demanding to be strip-searched make me seem a bit gay?

From: **Susi Judge-Davis-Gaultier**
To: Milton Keane
Sent: 23 January 2009, 10.33
Subject: Re: help!

Don't be silly. Big, burly convicts get strip-searched all the time and they'd kill you if you suggested they were gay.

From: **David Crutton**
To: Dotty Podidra
Sent: 23 January 2009, 10.34
Subject:

Got an irritating slug of dirt under a fingernail. I need one of those little pointy grabby things to dig it out.

From: **Dotty Podidra**
To: David Crutton
Sent: 23 January 2009, 10.35
Subject: Re:

Do you mean a staple remover?

From: **David Crutton**
To: Dotty Podidra
Sent: 23 January 2009, 10.36
Subject: Re:

Is that what they're called? One of those, then.

From: **Dotty Podidra**
To: David Crutton
Sent: 23 January 2009, 10.37
Subject: Re:

I can fill in the form for you, but you'll have to get it yourself. I'm not allowed in the stationery vault. Sorry.

From: **Róisín O'Hooligan**
To: Dotty Podidra
Sent: 23 January 2009, 10.44
Subject: Visitors for Osama Bin Crutton

Got a Superintendent Johnson from the Anti-terrorist Squad and a guy in shades who won't give me his name (MI5, then). Want me to send them up to the Crutt Cave? Or shall I get our pet Serbs to pat them down and start a diplomatic incident?

From: **Dotty Podidra**
To: Róisín O'Hooligan
Sent: 23 January 2009, 10.46
Subject: Re: Visitors for Osama Bin Crutton

Send them up in 5. Cleaning up the plate of jam doughnuts he just threw at me.

From: **Janice Crutton**
To: Paula Sterling
Sent: 23 January 2009, 11.12
Subject: Tag monitor

It's on the blink. Can you take it back to Spectre Security and get it looked at? After that you can take the rest of the day off.

From: **Paula Sterling**
To: Janice Crutton
Sent: 23 January 2009, 11.13
Subject: Re: Tag monitor

Really?? Thanks!

From: **Janice Crutton**
To: Paula Sterling
Sent: 23 January 2009, 11.15
Subject: Re: Tag monitor

That's OK. I want you to go to Chiswick Academy and keep an eye on Tamara. I've brought in her spare uniform, so you should have no trouble blending in.

From: **Paula Sterling**
To: Janice Crutton
Sent: 23 January 2009, 11.17
Subject: Re: Tag monitor

Are you sure this is a good idea, Janice? I'm twenty-nine. And Tam is about three sizes smaller than me.

From: **Janice Crutton**
To: Paula Sterling
Sent: 23 January 2009, 11.19
Subject: Re: Tag monitor

It's an excellent idea. You don't look a day over sixteen and all the little hussies wear their skirts and blouses tight. And don't ever question my judgement again.

From: **Liam O'Keefe**
To: Susi Judge-Davis-Gaultier
Sent: 23 January 2009, 11.24
Subject:

Be a sweetheart and get Ted to run along to the stationery vault to get me a brick-red marker.

From: **Adrijana Smiljanić**
To: Susi Judge-Davis-Gaultier
Sent: 23 January 2009, 11.25
Subject:

I need Pritt Stick. Tell Ted he must get me some.

From: **Liam O'Keefe**
To: Susi Judge-Davis-Gaultier
Sent: 23 January 2009, 11.27
Subject:

And a light-blue.

From: **Bill Geddes**
To: David Crutton
Cc: Ted Berry
Sent: 23 January 2009, 11.29
Subject: Mini Montana

I'd like to say that I'm hugely excited about the GIT project. I intend to throw myself into it and I've already thought of a way to add value to the product.

When I went through the creative, I was reminded of Dairylea cheese triangles. They're sold to kids as fun food and to mums on their nutritional creds.

I think we should recommend to GIT that they look into the feasibility of impregnating Mini Montana with healthy additives such as minerals and vitamins. How about Mini Montana with added calcium for healthy bones, or a winter variant with added vitamin C? I'm not suggesting that they'll become a staple in kids' lunchboxes, but you never know! And if it's successful, they could look into extending the idea to their other brands. What about Ambassador Ultra Plus, an extra-mild smoke with a cocktail of added vitamins? It could be targeted at the Sanatogen market – basically the elderly and pregnant.

Anyway, just a thought. Plenty more where that came from! Thanks for the great opportunity and I hope I don't let you down.

    Bill Geddes
    Account Director

From: **Maurice Wéber**
To: David Crutton
Cc: Camille Brunel, Betina Tofting
Sent: 23 January 2009, 11.36
Subject: Concerns

Dear David

Camille has ask me to write to you to express our disturbances over recent events. Naturally we are concerned that Donald Gold failed to attend the scheduled meeting re Project Red Carpet in Rio de Janeiro, but we have many more worries and questions when we learn the reason why.

I hope with all my heart that you were not previously aware of Donald's affiliation with organizations of international terror, and you were as shocked as were we at the terrible revelation. To think that he was using an innocent business meeting as a cover for terrorist activities is appalling to the utmost.

A company as reputable and famous as Esmée Éloge cannot afford to have connections with such types of people and we ask for your assurances that you have cut all ties with this evil and dangerous man. If this is not possible, you will understand that we place our marketing arrangements under immediate review.

Yours sincerely,

Maurice Wéber
Director, New Brand Development (Europe)
Esmée Éloge

From: **David Crutton**
To: Maurice Wéber
Cc: Camille Brunel, Betina Tofting
Sent: 23 January 2009, 11.57
Subject: Re: Concerns

Dear Maurice

Indeed, all of us at Meerkat360 are as horrified and disgusted as you understandably are to discover that a hitherto trusted colleague was all along a sinister crypto-jihadist.

I have just this minute come out of a top-secret, eyes-only briefing with representatives of Scotland Yard's Anti-terror Squad and the British intelligence service, where I assured them of our full cooperation in their investigation of Donald Gold. I am not at liberty to divulge details, but I understand that their counterparts in America are making good progress in extracting a full and frank confession from him.

Please, rest assured that Mr Gold's employment has been terminated. Also be assured that I am already working with a team of top-level security consultants and we will shortly be putting into place procedures whereby all staff will be vetted for subversive and/or proscribed political affiliations.

I trust that this unpleasant blip will not sully our excellent working relationship with everyone at Esmée Éloge. You have my word that Meerkat360 remains utterly committed in its support of the War on Terror.

I sincerely hope this goes some way to reassuring you and that we can continue our successful partnership, particularly on Project Red Carpet. If you are happy to move on, I suggest rescheduling the meeting for next week and I will personally make the presentation. How is Friday 30th for you?

I look forward to hearing from you.

Best wishes,

David Crutton
The Man

From: **David Crutton**
To: Ted Berry
Sent: 23 January 2009, 11.59
Subject: Esmée Éloge

Think I've steadied the ship on this one. I've pencilled in a new meeting on the 30th. I strongly recommend we lose Osama and Kim Jong-Il from the shortlist.

By the way, did you see Bill's Montana email? I didn't realize he was so nakedly ambitious. He's definitely one to watch. I think he's had an excellent thought. Why not get Liam to conceptualize it?

From: **David Crutton**
To: Sally Wilton
Sent: 23 January 2009, 12.04
Subject: Further security measures

Can you set up a meeting with Slobodan? I want to task him and his lads with some basic staff vetting. We're looking particularly for fundamentalists and those with terrorist sympathies. I notice there are a couple of Asian names in IT. As good a place as any to start.

From: **Kirsten Richardson**
To: Milton Keane, Dotty Podidra,
Susi Judge-Davis-Gaultier
Sent: 23 January 2009, 12.12
Subject: Is it true?

I just had one of the creatives down for a bubble perm and he said Don Gold is a Muslim suicide bomber! Really???!!! He always seemed so harmless.

From: **Milton Keane**
To: Kirsten Richardson, Dotty Podidra,
           Susi Judge-Davis-Gaultier
Sent: 23 January 2009, 12.13
Subject: Re: Is it true?

I heard a rumour he walked about with Semtex wrapped round his waist!!

From: **Susi Judge-Davis-Gaultier**
To: Kirsten Richardson, Dotty Podidra, Milton Keane
Sent: 23 January 2009, 12.14
Subject: Re: Is it true?

OMG, I just thought he'd put on weight!!!

From: **Dotty Podidra**
To: Milton Keane, Susi Judge-Davis-Gaultier,
           Kirsten Richardson
Sent: 23 January 2009, 12.15
Subject: Re: Is it true?

And I always thought he was Jewish!!!!

From: **Milton Keane**
To: Kirsten Richardson, Dotty Podidra,
           Susi Judge-Davis-Gaultier
Sent: 23 January 2009, 12.16
Subject: Re: Is it true?

He's also a total gaylord. Beats me how he can be an Islamical fundamentaloid *and* a Jewish homo. Must be a total schizo. It just goes to show you can never truly know a person. BTW, if anyone fancies helping me pick out *BB* audition outfits, meet me in Cazza's office at 1. I've brought in a selection and I'll order up some sushi on her T&E budget.

From: **Susi Judge-Davis-Gaultier**
To: Kirsten Richardson, Dotty Podidra, Milton Keane
Sent: 23 January 2009, 12.17
Subject: Re: Is it true?

Ooh, dressing up! Count me in!!

From: **Kirsten Richardson**
To: Milton Keane, Dotty Podidra,
Susi Judge-Davis-Gaultier
Sent: 23 January 2009, 12.18
Subject: Re: Is it true?

And me! You want me to do you some highlights? Blowout Burgundy and Chocolate Cherry? Dynamite combo!!

From: **Dotty Podidra**
To: Milton Keane, Susi Judge-Davis-Gaultier,
Kirsten Richardson
Sent: 23 January 2009, 12.20
Subject: Re: Is it true?

Sorry, Milt, but DC wants me to take the minutes of a meeting he's having with the Serbians. Lots of swearing and threats of violence, most likely. Think of me while you're having fun.

From: **Ted Berry**
To: David Crutton
Sent: 23 January 2009, 12.22
Subject: Re: Esmée Éloge

30th is fine. Shame about Osama though. The his 'n' her Twin Tower pack was a D&AD cert.

I'll get Liam on to Bill's idea. It's a good one.

Gotta say the new stationery arrangements are fucked up. Spent my morning fetching pencils, pens and pads for my department. When the fuck am I supposed to work?

From: **Dotty Podidra**
To: Susi Judge-Davis-Gaultier
Sent: 23 January 2009, 12.23
Subject: Milton

Between you and me, Sooz, are you sure it's a good idea to encourage him on the *BB* front? Given the nose situation, I think he's just setting himself up for a gigantic fall.

From: **Susi Judge-Davis-Gaultier**
To: Dotty Podidra
Sent: 23 January 2009, 12.25
Subject: Re: Milton

Don't be an old party pooper. He'll be fine. He'll get through his audition on sheer force of personality. And actually, his new nose is growing on me. It has a certain 'damaged' beauty, which is a very catwalk look. Deformity is totally this season. Of course, I wouldn't expect you to be able to see it. You have to have a fashion eye, don't you?

From: **David Crutton**
To: Kazu Makino
Cc: Bill Geddes
Sent: 23 January 2009, 12.36
Subject: GIT

How are you getting on with the Mini Montana PowerPoint? I'd like a review. Say 2.00?

From: **Kazu Makino**
To: David Crutton
Sent: 23 January 2009, 12.37
Subject: Out of Office AutoReply

I am out of the office attempting to free Donald Gold from illegal custody. I may be some time because clearly no one else in the company – especially those in senior management who owe him a duty of care – gives a stuff.

Kazu Makino

FREE DON GOLD

From: **David Crutton**
To: Sally Wilton
Sent: 23 January 2009, 12.39
Subject: Kazu Makino

Have her placed on the suspect-employee register immediately.

From: **Sally Wilton**
To: David Crutton
Sent: 23 January 2009, 12.42
Subject: Re: Kazu Makino

With pleasure. I've also taken the liberty of adding Róisín O'Hooligan's name.

	SMS:
Paula:	We have got to do something about our bosses. JC has got me in school uniform spying on Tam
Dotty:	LOL
Paula:	Not funny. Uniform way too small. Feel like slaggy extra in St Trinian's

Dotty:	Tam spotted you?
Paula:	No. Too busy dealing acid behind gym block
Dotty:	Yikes! You gonna tell JC?
Paula:	Don't be ridiculous. She's mad enough already. I'll just tell her Tam was doing business studies
Dotty:	LOL
Paula:	That was funny, wasn't it? Oh shit. Teacher coming. Think he's gonna confiscate mobile

From: **Róisín O'Hooligan**
To: All Staff
Sent: 23 January 2009, 12.57
Subject: Oh, the sweet, sweet irony

Slobodan, the big guy in charge of nailing the thief, is stomping around reception with a face like a slapped arse because he's had his car nicked. Has anyone seen it? It's a black Mercedes tank pimped up with Ray-Ban glass and chrome wheels. You really can't miss it because it's a fucking eyesore. Sorry, gotta take a toilet break. You have to admit this is piss-yourself funny.

Róisín
Reception

From: **Mr Fraggles**
To: All Staff
Sent: 23 January 2009, 13.01
Subject: Has anyone seen . . .

. . . Neil Godley? He promised to organize a petty-cash advance by lunchtime, which is now, isn't it? I have to go out and buy three dozen beanbags and twenty dozen eggs for this afternoon's juggling workshop.

Mr Fraggles
Tip-top Japery

From: **Brett Topolski**
To: Liam O'Keefe
Sent: 23 January 2009, 13.05
Subject: Stop whatever you're doing

Hope you're there and not banged up for car thievery because you have to see this. Horne is a cyber superstar. He's also a filthy, perverted slag. He's posted a two-parter and it's like *Emanuelle Goes Down (on) the Farm*. Click below.

---

blogass.co.uk
Posted by **Hornblower**
21/01/09, 10.37 GMT

Crépuscule dans le Périgord
Partie 82a: le Paradis Perdu

Oh, what is it all for? What is the point? Or, as *mes compatriotes* would so cogently put it, 'À quoi ça sent?' Such thoughts assailed me as I woke this morning to sub-zero temperatures. The lack of both fuel oil and wife to warm me didn't aid my mood. A diesel delivery is due *demain*, but Celine, I have reluctantly accepted, will not be returning.

Matters did not improve over *le petit déjeuner* when *M. le Facteur* delivered a most unpleasant letter from Celine's solicitor. I replied – *en français naturellement* – explaining that I can perfectly well live without the stipend from her trust fund and I signed off with a thought beloved of *mon bien-aimé* Papin: 'Les avocats sont l'excrément de la terre.'

After such a start to the day, there is only

one thing for it. I'm going to have to uncork the '59 Armagnac. I shall re-post later with an update.

blogass.co.uk
Posted by **Hornblower**
21/01/09, 14.21 GMT

Crépuscule dans le Périgord Partie 82b: le Paradis Retrouvé

Je suis ivre and I am not ashamed to admit it. *Je suis plein comme un boudin, soûl comme une vache. Oui*, I am as gloriously fucking pissed as *un triton crêté*. Let me tell you, *lecteurs bien-aimés*, 1959 was a very bloody good year for Armagnac.

I feel renewed, reinvigorated, rezestified, if you will permit me to mint *un mot tout neuf*. Fuck Celine. *Je chie sur elle. Pardonnez moi mon Français!!* She and her ridiculous collection of 227 handbags can *brûler en enfer*.

And to whom do I owe thanks for *ma renaissance glorieuse*? *Mon cher* Papin, *naturellement*. Though it was not until we were halfway through the bottle that I realized what *un ami indispensable* he has become. It was when he topped up my balloon and offered – quite off his own bat – to clear the last of Celine's bits and bobs from the bedroom. *L'homme est un voyant!* He knew *intuitivement* that, in my current febrile state, going through Celine's drawers would be *la dernière goutte*.

305

After manfully packing her remaining clothes, shoes and toiletries into several cases, he reappeared with a pair of silken *culotte* and matching *soutien-gorge* – peach with ivory lace trim, La Perla, my gift to her for our nineteenth anniversary, if I'm not mistaken.

The sight of said frillies finally broke me. I confess that since Celine's flight *de chez nous*, I have been affecting nonchalance – or as they put it so much more poetically in these parts, *nonchalance*. But I could maintain the Robert Mitchum act no longer and the dam burst.

'Vous les voulez pour Madame Papin?' I asked him. 'Prenez-les,' I added, fighting back the tears *en souvenir des jours heureux*.

'On l'emmerde Madame Papin,' he snorted. 'Elle est une grosse truie pustulente. Gardes-les, conard.'

As he stepped over to me and proffered *la lingerie*, I felt a vague weakening of the knees, a palpable quickening of the heart.

'Tailles-moi une pipe,' he commanded.

'Mais je ne fume pas,' I protested.

'Putain de merde, t'es un trou du cul,' he snarled, unbuttoning himself, placing his large calloused hand on top of my head and forcing it inexorably down. I meekly did his bidding, finding strange yet profound comfort in *mes nouvelles*

fonctions as his *salope Anglaise
dégoûtante*.

    Views: 432,499
    Comments: 2,273

Comment posted by **Eel Boy**:
Don't *ever* stop blogging, Hornblower.
You are the funniest guy in the world!!

Comment posted by **Eel Boy**:
PS: You are trying to be funny, aren't
you? Just checking!!

Comment posted by **Franglais**:
Hornblower rocks! Il est les couilles du
chien!

Comment posted by **Cindy CD**:
I have bras, panties, camisoles and garter
belts, and also S. Dakota's biggest
collection of size 8+ fuck-me pumps. Will
send in exchange for photos. What are
your sizes?

PS: did he cum on your face, baby?

Comment posted by **Le Pen Est Dieu**:
Tues la pute de ta race. Va te faire foutre
en Angleterre et arrêtes de souiller mon
beau pays.

Comment posted by **ExPatrick**:
Hi there, Hornblower. As a denizen of the
Dordogne, I love your blogs and, as a
fellow *expatrié assimilé*, they reassure me
that we are not all *petit Anglais*. Keep the
faith, *mon brave*! While I'm online, can
you give me some advice? I can't find PG

Tips (pyramid bags) anywhere. Any ideas??

Comment posted by **littlepinkpony**:
Aidez-moi!!! Ma mère m'a fermé à clef
dans ma chambre. Elle est folle et elle est
affamée à la mort!!! Appelez la police.
J'habite au Saginaw, MI. Je suis désolé
pour mon mauvais Français!

Comment posted by **Woody**:
You sound like one horny little sissy boy,
Hornblower. I do like 'em silk-clad and I'm
rubbing myself now thinking how I'd take
care of you. Any chance of posting some
jpegs of your sweet self? Gotta go and
'take care of business', girlfriend. Back soon.

From: **Sally Wilton**
To: David Crutton
Sent: 23 January 2009, 14.09
Subject: Godley

The XL boys have finished their 'chat'. We have a signed confession.
The police have been called and he is clearing his desk as I write.

Sally Wilton
ᴘRINCESS
ᴘAᴘERCLIᴘ

From: **David Crutton**
To: Sally Wilton
Sent: 23 January 2009, 14.12
Subject: Re: Godley

Excellent! To whom should I talk about sorting out a brown envelope for yourself, and for Zlatan Kovaćević who recommended
the admirable fellows at XL?

From: **Sally Wilton**
To: David Crutton
Sent: 23 January 2009, 14.15
Subject: Re: Godley

That would be Neil Godley.

SMS:

Liam: Hi Dimitri. Fancy a newish car?
         Get yourself to the NCP in Brewer
         St sharpish. Black Merc S 500. 3rd
         floor. Reg KHB939. Already
         equipped with Orthodox nick-
         nacks, so should suit. Keys in
         exhaust. Text me when you've
         collected and that's us quits.

SMS:

Liam: Hi Hakkan. Fancy a newish car?
         Get yourself to the NCP in Brewer
         St sharpish. Black Merc S 500. 3rd
         floor. Reg KHB939. Orthodox nick-
         nacks might upset Allah, but you
         can easily lose them. Keys in
         exhaust. Text me when you've
         collected and that's us quits.

From: **Neil Godley**
To: Caroline Zitter
Sent: 23 January 2009, 14.23
Subject: Sorry

Dear Caroline

I am sorry for bothering you with my earlier email. It was an
underhand attempt to cover up the fact that I have been

systematically robbing the company since I joined eleven months ago. I have confessed in full for my crimes and I will now throw myself on the mercy of the criminal justice system. I assure you that I made the confession entirely freely. No coercion, intimidation, threats of violence or actual violence was used.

I would like to take this opportunity to apologize for betraying the trust you and the other partners placed in me.

Yours in abject shame,

Neil Godley (Formerly of Accounts)

From: **David Crutton**
To: All Staff
Sent: 23 January 2009, 14.38
Subject: We've nailed the bastard!

Champagne in reception at five to celebrate the capture of the thief. And let this entire unsavoury experience serve as a warning to anyone else that thinks he/she can get away with stealing company property. If so much as a staple is used on non-company business, I will hunt you down and squash you like the despicable, secretion-oozing worm you are.

David Crutton
The Man

From: **Milton Keane**
To: Dotty Podidra
Sent: 23 January 2009, 14.41
Subject: DC

Has he gone completely mad???

From: **Dotty Podidra**
To: Milton Keane
Sent: 23 January 2009, 14.43
Subject: Re: DC

Yes. And I'm really scared. He's firing off crazy emails and doing this weird cackle. It's like working for Vincent Price.

From: **David Crutton**
To: Ted Berry
Sent: 23 January 2009, 14.46
Subject: Model-making

Any creatives free to knock up a quick effigy of Godley for the knees-up at five? I firmly believe that having a life-size mannequin to kick around will make for some healthy and fun staff bonding.

From: **David Crutton**
To: Sally Wilton
Sent: 23 January 2009, 14.49
Subject: Just a thought

Is there any way that using office power sockets to recharge personal mobile phones can be classified as theft? If so, a single swift clampdown would reel in at least a dozen kleptomaniacs and act as a deterrent to other miscreants.

From: **Liam O'Keefe**
To: Brett Topolski
Sent: 23 January 2009, 15.02
Subject: Is this worse than the thing with the thing?

Here's a hypothetical situation: imagine there's a bloke who's been nicking stuff from the office where he works – stationery, bottles of booze, the odd copier. And say there's an investigation and the wrong guy goes down for it. Should the hypothetical perp come clean or should he breathe a huge sigh of relief and learn to live with his guilt as best he can?

Your wise and esteemed counsel on this tricky (but totally academic) moral conundrum would be appreciated.

Puzzled of Soho

PS: Checked out the Horne blog. Gobsmacked. Did a Google and the fucker's gone viral – officially bigger than Swine Flu. There are already a dozen fan sites. Just goes to show that any fucker with a PC and too much time on his hands can become a celebrity. The way the net works these days, he'll probably get a movie deal out of it. The guy always was a jammy bastard. And he hasn't lost his love of silk 'n' sodomy, has he?

From:	**Susi Judge-Davis-Gaultier**
To:	Milton Keane
Sent:	23 January 2009, 15.13
Subject:	Separated at birth???!!!!

That was the *best* lunchtime ever!!! Don't we agree on absolutely everything, fashion-wise? Amazing! As soon as you put the black string vest over the cerise T and matched it with the cream jodhpurs I just knew you'd nailed it and you knew it too in that same instant. It was like ESP and I got total goose bumps!!!! You are so going to have an amazing audition!!!

Sooz xxxxx

From:	**Milton Keane**
To:	Susi Judge-Davis-Gaultier
Sent:	23 January 2009, 15.17
Subject:	Re: Separated at birth???!!!!

I know!! I'm totally going to *own* BB next week. We're so on the same wavelength, aren't we? We should go into styling together. Hey, just had a brill idea! After *BB* when I'm a celeb and I have an agent and can get my own series on E4, we should get ourselves a makeover show like Gok Wan and Myleene Klass, only we'd be totally *not* gay and we wouldn't let any fat toothless chavs on!!

Milt xxxxxxxxxxxx

PS: Did you think the riding boots really worked? Didn't the buckle make me seem a bit gay?

From:	**Susi Judge-Davis-Gaultier**
To:	Milton Keane
Sent:	23 January 2009, 15.19
Subject:	Re: Separated at birth???!!!!

Totally *not* gay, sweetz! With your new nose you could wear a frock and look absolutely macho! But please don't start wearing frocks! Utter gross-out!!!!!!!!

From:	**Brett Topolski**
To:	Liam O'Keefe
Sent:	23 January 2009, 15.38
Subject:	Re: Is this worse than the thing with the thing?

Tough one. Here's my two penn'orth: your entirely hypothetical perp in your entirely hypothetical scenario should obviously do the Right Thing. Having said that, the Right Thing doesn't necessarily have to be the Obvious Thing – i.e. tipping up at the cop shop with a pre-prepared confession. If hypothetical he/she is at all creative (which, as a product of your turgid imagination, is surely the case), there must be a more lateral way of airlifting the hypothetical innocent party out of the theoretical cack. Over to you, then . . .

Allah and out

Brett

Horne Watch update: found five forums devoted to unmasking him. Four want to put him up for a Pulitzer. The other one wants to lynch him for crimes against the French language. Should I end the suspense and blow his cover?

<hr>

SMS:

Janice:	Where are you?
Paula:	Detention
Janice:	Excuse me?
Paula:	For wearing non-reg skirt. Too short. I'm 6 inches taller than Tam
Janice:	Where is she?
Paula:	Also detention
Janice:	Why?
Paula:	Stole hacksaw from metal work to get her anklet off. Don't worry. She got caught before she had chance
Janice:	Follow her when you're done. Make sure she goes home
Paula:	I've had the day from hell, I'm dressed like a strippergram and I'm stuck in bloody detention copying out passages from Mayor of Casterbridge. Now you want me to follow her round the streets like I'm the only girl on the sex offenders' register? This is lunacy. Sorry. Had enough. Going home for a bath
Janice:	I'll consider that a resignation
Paula:	Have you any idea what this text stream will make you look like when it's read out in an employment tribunal?
Janice:	I'm not firing you
Paula:	You're a lawyer. Presume you know about constructive dismissal
Janice:	Correction. I am firing you
Paula:	See you in court

From: **Liam O'Keefe**
To: Brett Topolski
Sent: 23 January 2009, 15.59
Subject: Re: Is this worse than the thing with the thing?

Thanks for the counsel, Confucius. Had an idea. Should have the hypothetical innocent party out of hypothetical jail by the end of the hypothetical weekend. Also waiting for word that a major chunk of personal debt has been written off. Or word that I'm about to become caught up in a renewal of the Cypriot hostilities. Presuming the former, it's been a not-bad day.

Horne Watch: blow the bastard's cover. Why should he get away with hiding his twattishness behind the cloak of anonymity? None of the rest of us does.

Thanks again for the advice. I owe you a drink.

Oh, and several hundred quid.

Gotta dash. Have to impress MMT. Later, pal.

From: **Liam O'Keefe**
To: Ted Berry
Sent: 23 January 2009, 16.07
Subject: Montana Vita+
Att: Montana_5.pdf

Trying to get a handle on this health brief. Is this the kind of thing you mean?

Your 5 a day

MONTANA

With added vitamins and minerals

From: **Ted Berry**
To: Liam O'Keefe
Sent: 23 January 2009, 16.18
Subject: Re: Montana Vita+

You might dress like a Bulgarian plasterer, but occasionally you remind me why I hired you. Fucking brilliant, chuckles. More like that, please.

SMS:

Janice: I'm so sorry, Paula. Think I must be losing mind. Course I'm not firing you. Couldn't possibly manage without you. Please forgive me and come back. Promise never to make you dress up in gymslip (or any other inappropriate costume) again.

Paula: This phone has been confiscated. If you are still in the school grounds report to the deputy head's office immediately

From: **Janice Crutton**
To: David Crutton
Sent: 23 January 2009, 16.26
Subject: Help!

I'm going mad. Seriously. We need to talk. Soon or I won't be responsible for my actions.

From: **David Crutton**
To: Dotty Podidra
Sent: 23 January 2009, 16.29
Subject: Janice

She's having an episode. Got to go to the GIT research debrief in Fulham. Send flowers.

From: **Dotty Podidra**
To: David Crutton
Sent: 23 January 2009, 16.31
Subject: Re: Janice

How serious is it? Level 3 or level 1?

From: **David Crutton**
To: Dotty Podidra
Sent: 23 January 2009, 16.34
Subject: Re: Janice

Level 1. Do the full £75 bouquet plus effusive note. You know the form.

SMS:

Bill:	Where are you?
Kazu:	T5
Bill:	Why?
Kazu:	Catching 6.00 to Washington. Going to free Don
Bill:	Wow. Want me to come?
Kazu:	Yes!! Need all the support I can get
Bill:	Can probably get away after GIT presentation on Monday. I'll join you then
Kazu:	Don't bother. You've clearly got more important things to do. Like flogging cigarettes to toddlers
Bill:	I didn't have a choice
Kazu:	Bollox. You always have a choice. Like I have a choice right now. I choose not to be your friend any more
Bill:	Don't be like this!
Kazu:	Get lost, fag boy

From: **Liam O'Keefe**
To: Ted Berry
Sent: 23 January 2009, 16.44
Subject: Montana Vita+
Att: Montana_bones.pdf

How about this?

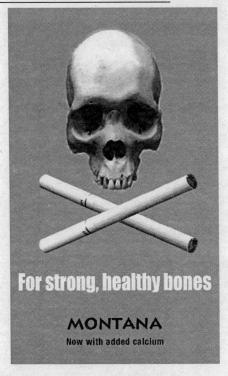

For strong, healthy bones

MONTANA

Now with added calcium

From: **Ted Berry**
To: Liam O'Keefe
Sent: 23 January 2009, 16.53
Subject: Re: Montana Vita+

Now you're cooking on uranium-235 and you're reaching critical mass. Love it!

From: **Liam O'Keefe**
To: Harvey Harvey
Sent: 23 January 2009, 16.59
Subject: Ted has been lavishing me with love and it made me think of . . .

. . . YOU! You should be here too, basking in the rays. Still worrying about you, man. Suspect you're dead. Or dying. Fuck's sake get in touch and tell me I've got it all horribly, spectacularly wrong.

From: **Bill Geddes**
To: Liam O'Keefe
Sent: 23 January 2009, 17.01
Subject: Murder, he wrote

Totally wild conjecture, I know, but is this anything to do with you?

bbc.co.uk/news
Car park gun battle

Police have launched a murder inquiry following the death of a man in a shootout in a London car park.

Police were called to the NCP car park in Brewer Street, Soho, where they found the man with bullet wounds to the head and chest. Witnesses reported seeing a second man drive away from the scene. Detectives are not ruling out the possibility that others may have been involved.

A second man has been arrested following a traffic accident in Holborn. The man, driving a stolen Mercedes S 500, had a gunshot wound in the stomach. He was taken to University College Hospital, where his situation is described as critical. Detectives wish to question him about the car-park shooting and he remains under police guard.

Detective Superintendent Leo Harrison, who is leading the investigation, said: 'This was an extremely violent incident in which a number of shots appear to have been fired. The car park was busy with people coming and going and it's a miracle that no one else was killed or injured.' He appealed for witnesses to both the shooting and the traffic accident. The dead man has not yet been named.

From: **Liam O'Keefe**
To: Bill Geddes
Sent: 23 January 2009, 17.04
Subject: Re: Murder, he wrote

Don't be ridiculous. What obscure hallucinogen have you been taking, matey? Can I have some?

From: **Liam O'Keefe**
To: Brett Topolski
Sent: 23 January 2009, 17.06
Subject: Oh fuck

It's all gone wrong. A Turk is going to kill me. Or a Greek. Not clear yet.

From: **Liam O'Keefe**
To: Lorraine Pallister
Sent: 23 January 2009, 17.09
Subject: Need a big favour

Hi, Lorraine. Not sure where you're living at the mo, but wherever it is, can you put me up for a bit? Please! It's kind of a sanctuary thing. Definitely not a let's-get-it-on-again thing. Definitely, definitely not that.

Though a shag would be nice.

From: **Lorraine Pallister**
To: Liam O'Keefe
Sent: 23 January 2009, 17.18
Subject: Re: Need a big favour

You've reached your credit limit at the favour bank. In fact, you reached it about two years ago, but like the idiot bankers who kept lending to dirt-poor hillbillies, thus triggering global financial meltdown, I kept chucking favours your way.

I'm ending this email before the credit-crunch analogy gets any lamer.

The answer's no, Liam.

From: **Liam O'Keefe**
To: Lorraine Pallister
Sent: 23 January 2009, 17.21
Subject: Re: Need a big favour

Please. Just for the weekend. And maybe Monday. It's life or death, kinda.

From: **Lorraine Pallister**
To: Liam O'Keefe
Sent: 23 January 2009, 17.23
Subject: Re: Need a big favour

It's always life or death, isn't it? Cry wolf to someone else. There must be at least one blonde who's dumber than me. I'm busy all weekend. Yes, with a bloke.

From: **Janice Crutton**
To: David Crutton
Sent: 23 January 2009, 17.27
Subject: Flowers?

Flowers? You honestly think a £75 bouquet and a love note penned by your PA (who can't even spell. 'Divoted'?) is going to salvage my sanity and our relationship? You can fucking well fuck off, David.

From: **David Crutton**
To: Dotty Podidra
Sent: 23 January 2009, 17.30
Subject: Janice

You screwed that one right up, didn't you? Well done.

From: **Dotty Podidra**
To: David Crutton
Sent: 23 January 2009, 17.31
Subject: Re: Janice

What did I do?

From: **David Crutton**
To: Dotty Podidra
Sent: 23 January 2009, 17.33
Subject: Re: Janice

Never mind. Suffice it to say you've served me a timely reminder that if you want something done, do it yourself. I'm going home now to sort out my family.

From: **Dotty Podidra**
To: David Crutton
Sent: 23 January 2009, 17.34
Subject: Re: Janice

You're supposed to be seeing Ted at six.

From: **David Crutton**
To: Dotty Podidra
Sent: 23 January 2009, 17.35
Subject: Re: Janice

Make my apologies to Ted. Think you can do that without fucking up?

---

bbc.co.uk/news
Car-park victim named

Police have named the man who was shot dead today in a London car park.

Dimitri Joannou, 31, of Wood Green in North London, died from head and chest injuries inflicted during a gun battle in a multi-storey car park in Brewer Street, Soho.

A second man is being treated in hospital
for a gunshot wound. Police want to
question him about the incident at the car
park. He has been named as Hakkan
Hakki.

From: **Liam O'Keefe**
To: Brett Topolski
Sent: 23 January 2009, 17.45
Subject: Oh fuck

A Turk is going to kill me. Definitely a Turk.

From: **Róisín O'Hooligan**
To: All Staff
Sent: 23 January 2009, 17.49
Subject: Lost property

Luisa was collecting the coffee mugs and found a cattle prod in
the basement. Anyone care to claim it?

    Róisín
    Reception

Sunday
Mood: kickass

blogass.co.uk
Posted by **Veiko Van Helden**
25/01/09, 14.39 GMT

Body art on the body parts!

I build a Tattoo Halls of Fame of the Dead Gods of Rock on my persons. Here I make a listing of the exhibitions so far:

- Kurt Cobain
- Bon Scott
- The King
- Jim Morrison
- Lisa 'Left Eye' Lopes
- Minnie Ripperton
- Cozy Powell
- John 'Stumpy' Pepys (the number one dead drummer of Spinal Tap, the awesome prog hair metal band that too many stupid peoples are dismiss as comedy laughing stocks. I ask to you has there ever been a more emotional lyrics than 'Break Like the Wind'? I rest

my suitcase)
- Eric 'Stumpy Joe' Childs (the second)
- Peter 'James' Bond (the third. I was plan to get all 21 but I have not enough of the skin!)
- Jeff Porcaro (from the underrating Toto who are in my opinions up in the top with Spinal Tap)
- Johnny, Joey and Dee Dee Ramone (I am saving spaces for when the brothers Tommy and Marky pass also to Rock Valhalla)

The left bottom piece is still pink as the baby ass, but not for longer! The big 60 trillion question: who is the next? I have decide to let you the fan base make the choose. Give me your ideas in droves. And see you in Helsinki on this Monday. Rokk till your spleen go splat!

Views:	5,430
Comments:	107

Comment posted by **Glascock**:
Karen Carpenter? She wouldn't take up much space. She was very slim.

Comment posted by **jesus666**:
Is gotta be da Skynyrds. They knew at least three more chords than da Ramones.

Comment posted by **Necrophobicluv**:
One word. Nicky Sixx.

Comment posted by **jesus666**:
That's two words, tosser. And he's not dead.

Comment posted by **Necrophobicluv**:
Saw him gassing up his Hummer in
Brentwood. Looked pretty fucked up to
me. I give him two weeks.

Comment posted by **Ho Chi Minh**:
Please find space for Gary Glitter.

Comment posted by **jesus666**:
What is it with you people? HE'S NOT
DEAD EITHER!!

Comment posted by **Ho Chi Minh**:
He will be when I find out where he's
hiding, take a cleaver to his sick,
schoolgirl-loving gonads and stuff one up
each nostril like they're cherry tomatoes.

Comment posted by **Necrophobicluv**:
That would do it. Make sure you YouTube
the moment!

Comment posted by **NoahsDark**:
Tommy Bolin!! I wasn't even born when
he was around but everyone says he was
Legend! BTW, can't wait to see Dethrush
in Helsinki.

---

blogass.co.uk
Posted by **Tiga**
25/01/09, 14.52 GMT

Good News/Bad News

Good news: Mum. She finally realized
what a loon she's been and she took off
my ankle tag! OK, she had to cos it was
totally broken, or at least it was after Bex

got me to stick my leg into her mum's crystal healing pyramid and after like an hour it went 'sproingg' and packed up!

Bad news: Dad. Yesterday he decided it was time to 'sort this family out'. Nightmare!

Good news: got a new tattoo!

Bad news: Dad's got one too. He took me and Metaloid (my idiot brother) on a 'bonding trip'. To the tattoo parlour! Huh? I mean, I'm mad for tatts, but doesn't he get *anything*? It's like clubbing, snogging and dropping acid. Not something you do with the fossils.

Good news: at least my tatt is to die for. Google Amy W's Rolling Stone cover. It's exactly like the one she has on her right shoulder. Except a tiny bit smaller. And one eye is a bit lower than the other. Totally gorgeous though.

LOL news: Metaloid decided to get Queens of the Stone Age on his arm, but he's such a wimp that he fainted! We had to take him to A&E. The really funny bit is that the tattooist had only managed to get halfway through the 'n' on 'Queens' before he keeled over!

Bad news: Mum. She wasn't pleased. Not pleased at all! Like the complete and total opposite of pleased!! Dad's moved out. Who knows when he'll be home?

Slightly bothering news: my new tatt

hurts. I know it's supposed to be sore, but is it supposed to ooze yucky pus?

Views: 734
Comments: 21

Comment posted by **littlepinkpony**:
My best friend's BF tattooed her when she was drunk and totally out of it. He used his mom's trussing needle and she'd just done the turkey and it hadn't been washed and the tattoo went septic and she lost her arm. So, yeah, I'd get it seen to. Oh, and just in case **anyone at all** in the **whole entire world** is interested in **my situation**, I am **still** locked in my room. And I am down to a dangerous 258lbs. I'll probably die here of vegetable poisoning and no one will give a damn. Right?

Comment posted by **Sexi Bexi**:
Wicked blog, Tamz!! Love it, love it, love it!!!!

Comment posted by **littlepinkpony**:
See? **No one** cares.

Comment posted by **Tiga**:
Total duh, Bex! This is supposed to be literally anon. Now everyone in the entire cyberspace universe knows my real name. Thanks for nothing.

Comment posted by **Sexi Bexi**:
Soz. But at least Tamz could be short for anything like Tamsin or Tampa or Tamalada. I didn't actually write Tamara.

330

blogass.co.uk
Posted by **Desperate**
25/01/09, 14.58 GMT

Dear Baby

Well, it's been some weekend. Your sister
now has what looks like a 1950s
prostitute with a serious facial deformity
tattooed on her upper arm and your
brother has 'Queer' emblazoned on his. I
suspect you'll be sensing from my tone
that I'm not overjoyed at developments
on this side of the uterine wall. It's not
even as if I can shrug them off as the
usual dull teenage rebellion because your
father – who's 51, I must point out – also
sports a sparkly new stud in his ear.

And a ridiculous ring of barbed wire
around his bicep.

Oh, and my name on the back of his neck.

As if indelibly marking his commitment to
our 'relationship' somehow makes this *all
right*.

I appreciate that you're still little more
than a hodgepodge of cells and lack first-
hand experience of social mores, so you
will probably struggle to process what I'm

331

telling you. You may even imagine, in your innocence, that seeing my name in gothic script on your father's slightly doughy neck should have had me giddy with love and gratitude.

Let me set you straight: this situation is just about as far from *all right* as it is possible to get. Your father has transformed your boringly average family into a middle-class version of Kerry Katona and her brood (which will mean nothing to you. Trust me, you do not want to be a Katona).

I'm sorry, Baby, deeply sorry, but the first thing you will very likely see upon emerging into the light is a saggy-chinned, balding Robbie Williams wannabe. He'll expect you to call him Daddy.

Unless I snap before you get here and smother him while he sleeps. Or knife him in the chest. Or bludgeon him about the head with a leather-bound volume of Britannica – that one is my favourite, mostly because those encyclopaedias cost us only slightly short of £2,000 and arrived just in time to be trumped by Wiki-bloody-pedia. Well, they've got to come in handy for something.

I promise I will do my utmost not to succumb to my more violent fantasies between now and your due date. However, upon your arrival should you find yourself being whipped away by social workers while I lie hysterical on the delivery couch handcuffed to a prison officer, please try to forgive me.

And even if you can't, I do believe that as you grow up and assimilate the full horrors of your family's history, you will come to realize that I was doing you a favour.

Your loving mother

Views: 962
Comments: 28

Comment posted by **Krishna Mom**: Confinement, honey, it's the only way to keep them in line. I've still got my daughter safely locked in her room and hubby is in the basement until he learns that Monday Night is Foot Rub Night, *not* Football Night. I recommend you keep that little one of yours in the womb until he/she appreciates the necessity of boundaries.

blogass.co.uk
Posted by **Hornblower**
Crépuscule dans le Périgord: Partie 82b

Views: 2,354,096
Comments: 7,345

Comment posted by **Topolski**: Hi, Simon. 'Tis you, innit? **Simon Horne**, formerly of **Primrose Hill** and a veteran of the **London Advertising Scene**, where you worked at **Leo Burnett**, **O&M** and **Miller Shanks**?

The **Simon Horne** that, at **Miller Shanks**, made a final, desperate lunge for glory with a 90-second commercial for **Simon Horne** (pack shot: Asian transsexual licking genitals, about 1/10 for appetite appeal*)?

The very same? Thought as much.

I agonized long and hard about the ethics of outing you. I considered your desire for anonymity, evidenced by your decision to blog under a nom de plume. I also took into account your wish for an undisturbed retirement after so many years sweating in the oppressive heat of the media kitchen. Indeed, I thought deeply about all your rights.

In the end though I was persuaded by the submission of my learned friend, Vince (you remember him, yes? He despised you like a dose of hepatitis B). He reminded me that in the thirteen months we worked for you, you were never less than a craven, unprincipled and monstrously vain self-aggrandizer – though he was characteristically more succinct in his appraisal. One word, in fact: cunt.

So, enjoy the spotlight once again, **Simon Horne**. It's reassuring to know that, having fucked the careers of so many, you are now getting agriculturally screwed by a grizzled French field hand. Any of your former employees reading this will appreciate the karma. *On récolte ce que l'on seme*, as your frog-spouting readers would have it.

From: **Liam O'Keefe**
To: Harvey Harvey
Sent: 25 January 2009, 16.05
Subject: Security issues

Hi bwana

You'll be pleased to know I'm round yours. I just called by to check you'd cancelled your milk. And to make sure any pets you may or may not own were being adequately cared for. And to deal with any important correspondence (I know the inconvenience of red reminders, repossession notices and such like).

Oh, and while I was at it, I thought I might as well get myself a nice hot shower – had a tough day shifting some heavy gear and worked up a bit of a man-sweat. Hope you don't mind, but there's no gas or electric at my place. Or furniture.

Also, there's a Turkish bloke who got his wires crossed about a message I left him, ended up in hospital and probably doesn't feel too well disposed towards me, so it's best I lie low for a bit. That's by the by, though it does mean I'll be crashing here for a night or two.

At least I'll be able to keep an eye on the place while you're away. On which note I've got to pull you up on your home security. It's fucked, mate. I expected to at least have to jemmy the door open with a credit card. Keys on string went out with the two-bob pint and Ena Sharples. This is the twenty-first century. FYI, hoodies aren't kindly Franciscan monks. They're bastards with knives and methadone habits, and their stated mission is to make you poor.

And you need to tighten up your computer security. I didn't even have to be a grade-D hacker to figure your logon is David Tennant. The *Dr Who* wallpaper was a clue. And your password? Five letters, first letter D, ends in K. Got it first hit.

What next? You getting your PIN tattooed on your forehead? Sorry to be so harsh, but ours is a bad, bad world. Jobless bankers roam the streets, vying with the homeless for the increasingly thin pickings. You're going to have to buck up. I really do fear for you in Nigeria. The hoodies over there probably don't actually wear hoodies on account of the clement weather, but their knives are doubtlessly bigger and you can bet they're a sight more incentivized than ours are. Poverty is a great motivator – any Marxist analysis will tell you that.

I don't know why I'm telling you all this because you're dead already, aren't you? I can feel it. Here in the gathering gloom. Of a drear Sunday afternoon.

Fuck, I hate Sundays.

Fuck, fuck, fuck, I'm depressed.

And lonely.

And scared.

I can say that to you because you're already dead. I can say anything to you. Anything at all. I can tell you how unspeakably fucking bleak I feel to have arrived at thirty-seven and have absolutely nothing to show for it.

Nothing.

Whatsoever.

Oh, sorry, there are a few things: an ex who despises me; a guy in the clink for something I did (though I am trying to fix that); a stack of debts so toxic that even RBS wouldn't touch it; a job where I'm earning brownie points for flogging fags to children – no, worse, children who'll have to steal from their dirt-poor parents in order to fund the habit I'm giving them; and there's that irritated Turk. I think I mentioned him. He wants to kill me. He might be handcuffed to a hospital bed, but he has friends that aren't.

He's got a point, the Turk. I mean, what use am I? What the fuck am I for? I should be dead. Like you.

Sorry, I don't mean you should be dead. You shouldn't be. You should absolutely be alive. But you aren't. All because you did something decent. You flew 3,103 miles (I Googled it. Nothing better to do. It's Sunday) to save the life of a stranger. All right, so you're being scammed rotten. That makes you a fool. But an honest, decent, upstanding fool. Not a cowardly, lying cunt like me.

Enough already. Think I'll watch *Songs of Praise*. Take myself back to a wasted childhood. More stuff to feel shite about. Did I mention that I used to dive for my county? Notts Juniors. I used to knife into the water like a gannet after a sardine. I coulda bin a contendah. What happened? I discovered fags and E and loafing on corners. What a fucking waste.

Rest in peace, mate. And (almost) in the words of the ever-reflective Coolio, 'I'll C U when *I* get there.'

    Liam

PS: Love the Atari Super PONG. Do you keep it as a collectible or have you never actually heard of Xbox, Wii and PS3? I'm never sure with you.

PPS: You owe me £5.86. I had to buy bread, milk and coffee.

PPPS: But you're dead, so I suppose I'll collect it from your estate.

From: **Ted Berry**
To: Creative Department
Sent: 25 January 2009, 16.16
Subject: Let's be inspired

Amazing the ideas that come to you as you're waiting to go into the ring for your second-round bout in the British Veterans Thai Boxing Championship. I thought it'd be a grand idea to bring in some inspirational names from outside the meejah bubble; people who can blast away the post-Christmas torpor; blow our minds with their feats of derring-do. I want names. Think big – infinity and beyond, mes braves.

My starters for ten:

- Nelson Mandela
- Ronaldo (the lardy Brazilian, not the preening Portugueezer)
- Björk
- Luc Besson
- The singer who won the first *Britain's Got Talent*, despite the fact he had a face like a trampled bag of chips – he is the living definition of impossible odds.

Gotta go and prep my *Wai Khru Muay Thai*. That lanky streak of piss Fink is limbering up. If I kick his arse, I've got Beattie in the semis. Wish me well!

Ted Berry
ΛＣ IDEΛZ

Sent from my iPhone

338

CEO's office, complete contents

Item specifics: top-of-the-line furnishings that will instantly transform even the drabbest corporate cubicle into a swank pad fit for a swinging-dick S'ralan Sugar clone. Main items include a glass-topped desk big enough to park a family car beneath, a hide-upholstered swivel chair built for the bottom that likes to lunch and a Ligne Roset sofa sufficiently low-slung to make minions feel properly inferior.

Fully accessorized with 'ironic' Newton cradle, set of walnut photo frames (suitable for those essential pictures of wife, children, favourite hooker) and collection of unread self-improvement books. The piece of resistance? Damien Hirst's 'Beautiful, Galactic, Exploding Screenprint' (yes, yes, it's just a piece of spin art, a three-year-old could have done it, but fuck it, darling, it's a HIRST!).

Would suit wanker.

Current bid:	**£0.00**
End time:	9d 23h 57m

Monday
Mood: alive.
Then dead.
Then somehow
inexplicably
alive again.
Then dead.
Possibly

From: **Susi Judge-Davis-Gaultier**
To: All Staff
Sent: 26 January 2009, 08.21
Subject: Workies?

Workie needed for urgent copying for GIT meeting. Biccies for successful applicant.

From: **Milton Keane**
To: All Staff
Sent: 26 January 2009, 08.22
Subject: Workies?

Desperately seeking workie to bind GIT docs. <u>Choccy</u> biccies for lucky volunteer.

From: **Susi Judge-Davis-Gaultier**
To: All Staff
Sent: 26 January 2009, 08.23
Subject: Workies?

Biccies <u>and</u> fresh doughnuts.

From: **Milton Keane**
To: All Staff
Sent: 26 January 2009, 08.23
Subject: Workies?

<u>Choccy</u> biccies, freshly brewed coffee and £10 M&S voucher.

From: **Susi Judge-Davis-Gaultier**
To: All Staff
Sent: 26 January 2009, 08.24
Subject: Workies?

Biccies, doughnuts, <u>choice</u> of coffee or tea and four-pack of Budvar.

From: **Milton Keane**
To: All Staff
Sent: 26 January 2009, 08.24
Subject: Workies?

<u>Choccy</u> biccies, coffee, M&S voucher, free pick from Cazza's fridge (anything non-vintage).

From: **Susi Judge-Davis-Gaultier**
To: All Staff
Sent: 26 January 2009, 08.25
Subject: Workies?

Biccies, doughnuts, coffee/tea, Budvar and *Blade Runner* DVD (Director's Cut).

From: **Milton Keane**
To: All Staff
Sent: 26 January 2009, 08.26
Subject: Workies?

Choccy biccies, coffee, M&S voucher, fridge pick, *Ugly Betty* (complete Season 2) and ten-minute go on Cazza's amazing Eames rocker (sitting is believing!!).

From: **Susi Judge-Davis-Gaultier**
To: All Staff
Sent: 26 January 2009, 08.27
Subject: Workies?

Biccies, doughnuts, coffee/tea, Budvar, *Blade Runner*, ultra-cool Bathing Ape baseball cap and 8Gb iPod nano (magenta).

From: **Milton Keane**
To: All Staff
Sent: 26 January 2009, 08.28
Subject: Workies?

Choccy biccies, coffee, M&S voucher, fridge pick, *Ugly Betty*, extended go on Eames rocker, over £250 worth of Esmée Éloge freebies and a signed copy of my exclusive YouTube DVD.

MSN:

sjdG:	Are you doing this on purpose???
MiltShake:	Could ask the same of you!!
sjdG:	I asked for a workie first!
MiltShake:	You know my audition's at 12 and I'll have a nightmare getting out of here and now you're doing this. *Not* the act of a *friend*, Sooz.
sjdG:	Sorry, sweetz. Totally stressed. TB's got me running round like a fly with a blue thingy. Wasn't thinking straight. I'll round up all the workies in da house to help you out!!!
MiltShake:	One will do thanks!!
sjdG:	Two just turned up. Do you want smiley Luke (he's wearing a lovely P. Smith shirt today) or the frumpy girl with the pizza face?
MiltShake:	What do you think?
sjdG:	Sending him now!! ☺

From: **Larry Finlay**
To: Katie Espiner
Sent: 26 January 2009, 08.53
Subject: I want it and I want it now

Gavin in digital has finally done something useful. After a week-end scouring the net he's ID-ed Hornblower (click below for details). He's an ex-adman called Simon Horne, yet another one doing the *Year in Provence* bollocks. Shouldn't be too hard to track down. I want you to tie up the book deal posthaste. Drop whatever shite you're on and fly to France immediately.

http://www.blogger.com/profile/17497362735526850652

Larry Finlay
Managing Director
Transworld Publishers

From: **Katie Espiner**
To: Larry Finlay
Sent: 26 January 2009, 08.56
Subject: Re: I want it and I want it now

Are you sure, Larry? I know everyone's talking about this guy's blog, but only because he's a complete idiot. And I'm up to my neck in the new Sophie Kinsella.

Katie Espiner
Senior Commissioning Editor
Transworld Publishers

From: **Larry Finlay**
To: Katie Espiner
Sent: 26 January 2009, 08.59
Subject: Re: I want it and I want it now

Since when was idiocy an impediment to getting a book published? The man is a certified fucking phenomenon and I want him on our list. Believe me, every publisher in London will be creaming his/her knickers for this one. I will not be beaten to the punch again as we were with that made-up hooker blog. Delegate Kinsella and get your arse to France.

From: **Susi Judge-Davis-Gaultier**
To: Creative Department
Sent: 26 January 2009, 09.00
Subject: Creative reviews

Any of you wishing to show Ted creative work today should hold back any witty, funny or otherwise amusing ideas. Unfortunately, he cracked two ribs yesterday and laughing causes him considerable pain.

MSN:

DottyPod:	Help!!!!! Is anyone there?
MiltShake:	I am. Wossup, GF?
sjdG:	Me too. You OK?
DottyPod:	No!! Just got in. DC's office is empty.
MiltShake:	Chill! Make the most of the peace and quiet. The old fart will be here soon enough.
DottyPod:	No, his office is EMPTY!! There's nothing in it!!!
MiltShake:	Like his desk and stuff?
DottyPod:	Desk, chair, sofa, books, the Damien Hirst kiddy painting, EVERYTHING! There's just his phone and PC on the floor!
sjdG:	OMG! What are you going to do???
DottyPod:	Don't know. Lift door's opening. He's here!
MiltShake:	Run, run for your life, Dot!!!!!!!!!!!

From: **Róisín O'Hooligan**
To: All Staff
Sent: 26 January 2009, 09.07
Subject: WTF??

Has someone grown their own personal werewolf up there? Some of us are trying to drink our lattes in peace and could do without the howls of anguish, thanks.

Róisín
Reception

	MSN:
MiltShake:	Are you OK, Dot?
sjdG:	OMG, I think he might have killed her!!
MiltShake:	You'd better go up and check.
sjdG:	Me???
MiltShake:	Can't risk getting my BB hair messed up, can I?
sjdG:	And I'm size 0. What am I going to do if he's gone all Incredible Hulk?
MiltShake:	You can be so selfish, Sooz. You KNOW this is THE BIGGEST DAY OF MY ENTIRE LIFE!
DottyPod:	Suzi, have you got any Valium?
sjdG:	You're alive!! Are you OK?
DottyPod:	Shaken. Just about OK.
sjdG:	What's he doing now?
DottyPod:	He's gone a bit foetal in the corner of his office. Thought I might try and force a pill down him.
sjdG:	No Valium but got Temazepam. Any good?
DottyPod:	Not sure. Isn't that a bit Trainspotting-ish?
MiltShake:	Cazza's got motherwort tablets in her herbal stash. It says on the bottle they're brilliant for hypertension, anxiety and dropsy. I'll send my pet workie up with a couple.
DottyPod:	Thanks, Milt. You're a lifesaver.

From: **Dotty Podidra**
To: Sally Wilton
Sent: 26 January 2009, 09.11
Subject: Looks like our thief is back

Hi, Sal. Think you'd better get up here quick. David's office has sort of gone missing.

From: **Róisín O'Hooligan**
To: All Staff
Sent: 26 January 2009, 09.14
Subject: FYI

The Serbs have skedaddled up to the management suite like a crack SWAT team and reception is unmanned. I'd say this is the perfect time for any stationery thieves/drug mules to nip in or out.

    Róisín
    Reception

From: **Katie Espiner**
To: Aislinn Casey
Sent: 26 January 2009, 09.15
Subject: Oh bugger

Lazza's being a total bollock head. He wants me to fly to France to sign up some cretinous blogger. The man's a total perv as well. Not Larry, the blogger. Better cancel synchronized swimming tonight. Soz.

From: **Katie Espiner**
To: All Staff
Sent: 26 January 2009, 09.17
Subject: Workies?

Any workies free to edit the new Sophie Kinsella? Should be an absolute doddle – she can spell and everything.

    Katie Espiner
    Senior Commissioning Editor
    Transworld Publishers

From: **Aislinn Casey**
To: Alison Martin, Sophie Holmes, Kate Samano, Katie Espiner, Charlotte Nash, Emma Buckley, Lydia Newhouse, Gavin Hilzbrich [Transworld SynchroStarz]
Sent: 26 January 2009, 09.21
Subject: Tonight's practice

Sorry, girls (and guy), but tonight's session is cancelled. Katie can't make it and you won't need reminding what happened the last time we tried to perform without our glorious leader! But anyone who wants to get in some private pool time, go for it. The Publishers Association Annual Swimming Gala is less than six weeks away and those eggbeaters and flamingos need work (naming no names, Gavin)!

Transworld
SynchroStarz
Aislinn Casey
Team Coordinator

From: **David Crutton**
To: Sally Wilton
Sent: 26 January 2009, 09.42
Subject: Godley

I've given this morning's incident a great deal of thought. I disagree with you. This is not Godley's get-out-of-jail card. He's clearly cleverer than we gave him credit for. What we failed to get out of him in his supposedly 'full' confession was the name of his accomplice. Between them they've made the fatal error of upping the stakes. Have Slobodan bulk up his team. Tell him I want every staff member interrogated before end of play tomorrow.

And get me some furniture. Zitter's never here. Raid her office.

From: **David Crutton**
To: All Staff
Sent: 26 January 2009, 09.47
Subject: An open letter

Dear Thieving Scum

Now you have gone too far. You are an oozing pustule, one that resides in the sweaty arse-cleft of society. I hereby serve notice that you are about to be lanced, and it will not be pleasant. For you, that is. I, on the other hand, will enjoy the process immensely.

David Crutton
The extremely fucking angry **Man**

	MSN:
MiltShake:	OMG, did you see that e he just sent? He got back to normal fast. There must be something in those tabs of Cazza's!
DottyPod:	I know! He's sitting cross-legged on the floor firing off psycho emails! And I've just noticed something I didn't spot in all the fuss. He's got a stud in his ear!! And the back of his neck has a big fat bandage on it. What's going on?
MiltShake:	The stud, is it right or left lobe?
DottyPod:	Right. Why?
MiltShake:	Gay.
DottyPod:	Don't be silly.
sjdG:	Yes, Milt, that's just barmy. He has a wife and two kids for starters.
DottyPod:	And he's got 'stuff' on his laptop. IT told me when they fixed it. They said his hard drive was totally diseased with porn viruses.

MiltShake:	You two are sooo naïve! All that's just a cover. He's a dirty pouf.
sjdG:	I don't buy it. What about all the times he pats my bum?
MiltShake:	Further proof of his dirty gayness.
sjdG:	Huh?
MiltShake:	You've got a bum like a little boy's, Sooz. Every time he pats it he probably closes his eyes and thinks perverted queer thoughts!
DottyPod:	Explain this then. He's always squeezing mine too and it's not exactly 'boyish', is it?
MiltShake:	He squeezes it and thinks of soft furnishings! I rest my case!! Face facts, girlfriends. The man is mid-life-crisised out and he's in the process of de-closeting.
sjdG:	Total phooey, Milt! You're such a josher!

From: **David Crutton**
To: Dotty Podidra
Sent: 26 January 2009, 09.58
Subject:

Get me coffee. And pictures of Beckham. Stripped off. I need to see his tattoos.

MSN:	
DottyPod:	OMG, you should see the e he just sent me!!
sjdG:	What's it about?
DottyPod:	He wants to see David Beckham.
sjdG:	So?
DottyPod:	Naked!!!!!!!
sjdG:	So completely gay!

MiltShake:	Never doubt me again, Sooz!
sjdG:	Never!!
MiltShake:	Aaagh! The Yugos are in Cazza's office. They're emptying it out! What's going on?
DottyPod:	They're after furniture for DC. Please don't try to stop them. They have little cosh-like things in their pockets!
MiltShake:	But they're taking her desk and everything! Hang on, they're also taking her aboriginal 'napping mat'. It stinks of wombat wee. Go burly foreign men, go!!!!

From: **David Crutton**
To: All Staff
Sent: 26 January 2009, 10.08
Subject: Guidelines

As you know, the President of GIT and his team are in today for an extremely important presentation. With the aim of creating the most favourable impression, I have a few guidelines that I ask you all to adhere to:

1   I know it's the time of year for 'sniffles', but please stifle your coughs. Nothing must be allowed to draw attention to the alleged 'health issues' that beset decent, law-abiding cigarette manufacturers.

2   Under no circumstances – and I cannot stress this strongly enough – refer to our client as *git*. The company's American representatives are oblivious to the word's usage on this side of the Atlantic, but its British ones certainly aren't, and they are understandably sensitive on the matter. The company will be referred to either as G.I.T. (pronounced gee-eye-tee) or by its full name of Galax (pronounced Gay-lax) International Tobacco.

3   Any of you that have embarked upon the annual

January folly of 'giving up' are required to hide all quit-ting aids (nicotine gum, patches, inhalers, etc) in your desk drawers.

4   Check all work surfaces and bulletin boards for Department of Health anti-smoking propaganda and take it to the shredder.

5   For heaven's sake, look busy.

If we all pull together, we will succeed in the crucial mission of bedding in this highly lucrative piece of business.

David Crutton
𝕿𝖍𝖊 𝕸𝖆𝖓

From: **Milton Keane**
To: Dotty Podidra, Susi Judge-Davis-Gaultier
Sent: 26 January 2009, 10.10
Subject: Did you read that e?!

GAY-lax!!!!!!!! Can't stop laughing. Big Gay Tobacco!!!!!!!

	SMS:
Milton:	Hot news. DC is a fudge nudger.
Kirsten:	Kidding!?
Milton:	100% true.
Kirsten:	Yikes! He's booked in for quick trim before GIT meeting.
Milton:	Better glove up, girl!

From: **David Crutton**
To: Caroline Zitter
Sent: 26 January 2009, 10.13
Subject: GIT

And will you be adorning us with your presence at the meeting, Caroline?

From: **Caroline Zitter**
To: David Crutton
Sent: 26 January 2009, 10.14
Subject: Out of Office AutoReply

I am out of the office attending Scientology: Millions of Top Hollywood Celebrities Can't Be Wrong. I will return on Tuesday 27th January.

Caroline Zitter
THE SEER

From: **David Crutton**
To: Caroline Zitter
Sent: 26 January 2009, 10.15
Subject: Re: Out of Office AutoReply

Thought not.

From: **Ted Berry**
To: Susi Judge-Davis-Gaultier
Sent: 26 January 2009, 10.17
Subject: O'Keefe

Where the fuck is he? We have a major creative presentation of *his* work and he should be here. Find him. And while you're at it, find Harvey Halfwit. He should be helping out. And can you lay hands on morphine? Fucking ribs are killing me.

From: **David Crutton**
To: Bill Geddes
Sent: 26 January 2009, 10.18
Subject: The Jap

Where is she? She has a shit load to do before GIT get here. As do you. My office at 10.30 for a heads up.

From: **Bill Geddes**
To: David Crutton
Sent: 26 January 2009, 10.20
Subject: Re: The Jap

She's at a doctor's appointment. I'm sure she'll be in soon. I'll see you at 10.30.

From: **Bill Geddes**
To: Kazu Makino
Sent: 26 January 2009, 10.22
Subject: Where the hell are you?

DC's spitting nails. They're especially sharp and dipped in slightly racist bile. I know you're not talking to me, but for your own sake, I think you'd better get in.

BTW, any luck in tracking Don down?

                    SMS:

Kirsten: Guess what. DC is gay!
Róisín: Says who?
Kirsten: Milton.
Róisín: Takes one to know one etc.

From: **Susi Judge-Davis-Gaultier**
To: Ted Berry
Sent: 26 January 2009, 10.26
Subject: Re: O'Keefe

No one knows where Liam is and there's no reply from his home or mobile numbers. I tried Harvey, but I only got his Polish plumber, who was actually very rude and unhelpful. Sorry.

From: **Ted Berry**
To: Susi Judge-Davis-Gaultier
Sent: 26 January 2009, 10.28
Subject: Re: O'Keefe

If you do get hold of either of them, tell them they're fired. Tell Adrijana and Zlatan that they'll be tying up the loose ends on the GIT campaign. And tell them they're coming to the meeting. I need a (mute) creative presence.

Another thing: tell Yossi he's got a gig at noon. I want him in reception singing 'Cigarettes and Alcohol' as the client arrives.

From: **Bill Geddes**
To: Liam O'Keefe
Sent: 26 January 2009, 10.44
Subject: Where the hell are you?

It's your Big Day. Thought you wouldn't miss it for the world. The Gaultier chick is promising searing doom if you don't show. TB is especially grouchy. Apparently both his ribs and his pride endured a kicking yesterday – it seems Graham Fink has perfected a devastating *Teh Krueng Kheng Krueng Kao*.

Just been through the GIT presentation boards with DC and TB and they look magnificent. They want some 'tweaks' though, and if you're not around to make them, someone else will only fuck it up for you.

From: **Liam O'Keefe**
To: Harvey Harvey
Sent: 26 January 2009, 10.45
Subject: Life and stuff

Dear Dead Guy

Just thought I'd update you on news from this side of the Stygian divide (woo-hoo, my first classical reference in an email. Fuck knows where that came from). Decided not to go into work today. I know it's a Big Day at the office with opportunity aplenty for personal career growth, but I can't be arsed with all that if I'm honest. Thought I'd just chill at yours. I've become a dab hand at Super PONG, but I have to say the scope for improvement is strictly limited. *Naruto: Ultimate Ninja Storm* it's not.

You haven't had any calls except for one from Susi. She thinks you should be at work. I didn't tell her you're dead. I didn't tell it was me either. That's because she's trying to track me down too. BTW, if she should ever ask you (in a séance or something), you have a Polish plumber. He's called Alojzy. He's a foul-mouthed sod. I think he enjoyed unleashing his repertoire on the Sooz.

When I get to your new hood, ask me to do my sweary Polish plumber for you. I've got it down pretty well. Comes from living over a Paki shop that about a year ago turned into a Polski sklep.

Think I'll watch some telly now. I'm working my way through your *Dr Who*s. I'm halfway through Patrick Troughton. I'll let you know who my favourite is when I reach the end.

Say hello to Paul Newman, if you bump into him (can spirits bump?). Tell him I love his work, of course I do, but that his salad dressing is overrated. And if you see God, tell him it's about time he got off the fence. Muslims or Christians: who are the fucking daddies?

    Liam

From: **Susi Judge-Davis-Gaultier**
To: Ted Berry
Sent: 26 January 2009, 10.48
Subject: Re: O'Keefe

Adrijana and Zlatan will be with you as soon as they've finished their 'performance piece' for Murray Mints. By the way, Zlatan has six stitches in his face – a fight with 'scum s**t from Kosovo, which belong Serbia whatever scum s**t say.' Are you sure you want him in the GIT meeting?

From: **Ted Berry**
To: Susi Judge-Davis-Gaultier
Sent: 26 January 2009, 10.50
Subject: Re: O'Keefe

Marketing is war, Susi, and I need warriors. Zlatan is on my A Team.

From: **Brett Topolski**
To: Liam O'Keefe
Sent: 26 January 2009, 10.56
Subject: How was your weekend then?

Was it jam-packed with redemption? Did you make amends to exes, irked Turks and hypothetical victims of injustice? I was getting worried about you on Friday. But what am I? Your fucking mother? You're a big boy and I'm 3,396 miles away (I Googled it). Besides, I have woes of my own. Vince? Don't get me started.

From: **Róisín O'Hooligan**
To: All Staff
Sent: 26 January 2009, 10.58
Subject: If anyone sees O'Keefe . . .

. . . tell him he has visitors. They remind me of the guys who used to hassle us to rent jet skis in Bodrun last summer. Except they aren't wearing Speedos and they're not smiling. And I think they might be packing heat. Is it just me or is this place getting more and more like the backroom at the Bada Bing?

Róisín
Reception

From: **Bill Geddes**
To: Liam O'Keefe
Sent: 26 January 2009, 11.03
Subject: You have gentlemen callers . . .

. . . and judging by their demeanour, it makes excellent sense that you're lying doggo. By the way, DC's going mental because someone did an office clearance on him. He's convinced Evil Neil Godley is the mastermind behind a massive criminal gang. But you wouldn't know anything about all that, would you?

Look, is there anything I can do? Witness-protection programme, say? I have an old uni mate who won't tell me what he does, but I suspect he's MI5. He might be able to blag something.

From: **Janice Crutton**
To: David Crutton
Sent: 26 January 2009, 11.05
Subject: In case you're interested. . .

. . . I'm at home. I shouldn't be at home. I should be at work, negotiating my client though the legal minefield that is Crossrail. But, thanks to you, I have had to delegate (which, as you know, is just a euphemism for abdicate). Why am I not at work? Why am I actively flushing what remains of my career down the toilet? Because of you. It seems that having the standard solo midlife crisis isn't enough for you. You have to drag your children down with you.

Tamara is loaded with antibiotics and in bed with a fever. God knows what filth your so-called 'artist' dipped his needles in, but now her tattoo is septic. And Noah? Where the hell is Noah? He's supposed to be in school for a test, but he has disappeared. Something to do with the fact that the poor kid now has 'Queer' indelibly inked on his arm? You tell me.

I really am going out of my mind here, David. But do you know what? I'd be measurably more insane if you were still around. So if you're thinking that the dust might have settled, that you might be able to drift back home and carry on as if nothing has happened – because God knows you've done that before and, more fool me, I've let you get away with it – if you're thinking anything like that, STOP RIGHT NOW. Stay away.

For good.

From: **Dotty Podidra**
To: David Crutton
Sent: 26 January 2009, 11.07
Subject: Now that you've got some furniture back . . .

. . . would you like me to make you a nice pot of tea? Something herbal?

From: **David Crutton**
To: Dotty Podidra
Sent: 26 January 2009, 11.09
Subject: Re: Now that you've got some furniture back . . .

Are you a complete imbecile? You think because I've acquired Zitter's vegetarian coffee table and holistic scatter cushions I want herbal fucking tea? Get me espresso. Make it a double. I need to sharpen up pre-GIT. And find the Jap PA. And tell the gay PA that since his boss isn't here, he can make himself useful for me. I have plenty of jobs for him. And find out why the Serbs/Wilton haven't yet delivered me a thief. And if – strictly on the off-chance – you were thinking of sending flowers or some other conciliatory shit to my wife, don't.

OK?

Just don't.

From: **Dotty Podidra**
To: Milton Keane
Sent: 26 January 2009, 11.10
Subject: DC

Hate to tell you, but he wants you. He has 'jobs'.

From: **Milton Keane**
To: Dotty Podidra
Sent: 26 January 2009, 11.11
Subject: Re: DC

Aagh! Can't do it!! Have to be at Endemol at 12.00!!!

From: **Dotty Podidra**
To: Milton Keane
Sent: 26 January 2009, 11.13
Subject: Re: DC

You have to! He'll probably kill you if you don't. Then he'll kill me!!

From: **Milton Keane**
To: Dotty Podidra
Sent: 26 January 2009, 11.15
Subject: Re: DC

I'm sorry, Dotty, but I'm not going to let Crutton or anyone else stand in my way. *BB* is my **_dream_**. It has always been my **_dream_**. If I have to die for that **_dream_**, then so be it.

From: **David Crutton**
To: All Staff
Sent: 26 January 2009, 11.16
Subject: Smokers

The GIT delegation arrives at 12.00 and I want to greet them with a rapturous tribute to the joys of the noble weed. To that end, all smokers will forgo their habitual cigarette breaks until 11.55, at which time you will proceed to the front of the building and light up. And I don't want the usual hangdog expressions. Imagine for five minutes that you're extras in a 70s Coke commercial and act accordingly. In other words, look as if you're enjoying yourselves. Finally, if you must smoke Silk Cut, B&H or Marlboro, for God's sake hide the packs.

David Crutton
The Man

PS: If anyone is considering taking up the wonderfully convivial pastime of smoking, 11.55 today would be a most excellent time to give it a whirl.

From: **David Crutton**
To: Dotty Podidra
Sent: 26 January 2009, 11.19
Subject: Where the fuck is my queer?

I have a PowerPoint for him to re-jig.

From: **Dotty Podidra**
To: David Crutton
Sent: 26 January 2009, 11.20
Subject: Re: Where the fuck is my queer?

I think he's in a meeting with some qual research people on behalf of Caroline. I'll do the PowerPoint as soon as I've laminated the doc covers, put out the pads and pencils and sorted out the kitchen order.

From: **Milton Keane**
To: All Staff
Sent: 26 January 2009, 11.21
Subject: Hooray for me!!!!!!!!!!

I'm off to my audition now. What audition? I hear you ask. To take *the* leading role in *Big Brother 10*! I've already put a pencil on thirteen weeks from June! Get your texting fingers ready!!

    Milton Keane
    Future Star of Reality TV

From: **David Crutton**
To: Dotty Podidra
Sent: 26 January 2009, 11.23
Subject: My office now

Explain to me how your most recent email squares with the queer's all-staffer.

---

bbc.co.uk/news
Briton found dead in Nigeria

The body of a British tourist has been found floating in a river in Lagos, Nigeria.

According to the Nigerian Police Force, the man appeared to have been beaten before being thrown into Badagry Creek, which runs into Lagos Harbour. The NPF is withholding the man's identity until his family has been informed.

Superintendent Julian Odulate of the NPF said: 'We have the dead man's passport. His first name is the same as his second. I have never seen this before, except for the much-cherished British writer Jerome K. Jerome, who of course wrote *Three Men in a Boat*, which is one of my most favourite books. Mr Jerome used his middle initial to make his name seem less silly. The poor dead man appears not to have had a middle name, so he could not do this. It is the first time in my 27-year police career that I have come across a corpse that has the same name twice, but in this job I believe we must always expect the unexpected.'

From: **Liam O'Keefe**
To: Harvey Harvey
Sent: 26 January 2009, 11.33
Subject: Grim Reaper

Just caught the news. I'm devastated, mate. OK, I kinda knew. I think I might have mentioned it in previous emails. But the shock of confirmation is unreal. Gotta go and drink a toast to your memory. You don't seem to have much in. It'll just have to be Vimto. Seems fitting somehow.

	MSN:
DottyPod:	All getting too weird!!
sjdG:	What is?
DottyPod:	DC. He just gave me a monster bollocking for covering up for Milt and he was totally homophobical.
sjdG:	Definite proof of his gayness IMO.
DottyPod:	Yes, but not the weirdest thing! He'd taken off his bandage. You will *never* guess what.
sjdG:	What????????????!!!!!!!!!!!!!!!!!!
DottyPod:	He's got a tattoo!!!!!!

sjdG:	OMFG!!!!!!!!! What of?
DottyPod:	Hard to tell. It's all scabby and bloody and it looks infected.
sjdG:	He's clearly gone insane. You're in danger. You *have* to get out of there immediately.
DottyPod:	Can't! Have a million things to sort out before meeting. Gotta go. DC's laptop's crashed. Got PowerPoint on it!!

From: **Bill Geddes**
To: Kazu Makino
Sent: 26 January 2009, 11.36
Subject: Where the hell are you?

Been trying your phone. Left you half a dozen messages. Have you switched it off? DC's all set to fire you, but I reckon if you get in by 12 and make the GIT meeting, I could square things with him. I know Don's in a bad situation, but there's no need for you to lose your job as well.

From: **Brett Topolski**
To: Liam O'Keefe
Sent: 26 January 2009, 11.37
Subject: All right, all right, I'll tell you

Your silence is a wailing fucking cacophony in my head. Just to get you off my case, I'll tell you about Vince.

He's fallen in love.

That, you might argue, is a Positive Thing – the calming influence of a good woman and the fact that at last he can have his perpetual horniness tended to by someone consenting. I'd agree, absolutely. But if I tell you who he's fallen in love with . . .

The *capo di tutti i capi* out here is a guy called Sheikh Mohammed bin Rashid Al Maktoum. You might have heard of him – like you, he's a keen follower of the gee-gees. The guy has several billion in the bank, multiple wives and getting on for twenty kids. He's the Daddy all right.

I know what you're thinking, but no, Vince isn't seeing his daughter. That would be silly, wouldn't it? Rash beyond words. A fucking death sentence. Even he's not that stupid, is he? He's done the sensible thing for once in his life.

He's only dating the Sheikh's second cousin's youngest. Still proper Arab royalty though, the stuff of Mills & Boon and *Hello!* deals. Oh, and true-life TV movies that end in decapitation for one or both of the lovers.

But he's besotted and claims she is too. He's old enough to know better, but she's only nineteen – clearly a young and unworldly nineteen, if she's dozy enough to think Vince is a catch. Admittedly she does have the most stunning eyes – the only bit I've seen – but I don't care how gorgeous the rest of her is, it's utter madness and it has to stop. Apart from anything else, we've got a stack of work to do, a campaign for Gatorade to finish by end of play, but as I write he's Photoshopping cherubs and roses on to pink satin cushions. I suppose it's an advance on the usual (retouching Kate Winslet's head on to a porn star's jiz-splattered body), but IT HAS TO STOP!

He won't listen to me though. He says they're going to elope and get married. Vegas, he reckons. I suggested he should nuke every taboo and go the whole hog: get a sex change and have a lesbian wedding in Tel Aviv. The idiot took me seriously and he's checking out the visa situation.

Will you have a word with him? He might listen to you. And if he doesn't, you could come over here and help me get him home. Drugged and bundled into a sack if necessary. Help me, mate. I'm all out of ideas.

Allah McCoist

From: **Dotty Podidra**
To: All Staff
Sent: 26 January 2009, 11.45
Subject: Lighting-up time

David has asked me to remind all you smokers that you have ten minutes.

From: **Dotty Podidra**
To: Róisín O'Hooligan
Sent: 26 January 2009, 11.47
Subject: Message for Slobodan

Hi Róisín. Can you ask Slobodan to move his car from outside the building? David has only just told me we need the space free for the client's ambulance. Thanks.

From: **Róisín O'Hooligan**
To: Dotty Podidra
Sent: 26 January 2009, 11.48
Subject: Re: Message for Slobodan

Ambulance? Excuse me??

From: **Dotty Podidra**
To: Róisín O'Hooligan
Sent: 26 January 2009, 11.49
Subject: Re: Message for Slobodan

David informed me (all rather last-minute, I'm afraid) that Carter Bluewash (GIT Prez) has 'a chronic lung condition' and travels everywhere with a nurse and an oxygen tent.

From: **Róisín O'Hooligan**
To: Dotty Podidra
Sent: 26 January 2009, 11.51
Subject: Re: Message for Slobodan

Slobby is (grudgingly) moving his hire car as I type. BTW, what's this Carter guy do again? Oh yes, he runs a great big fag company. As ye sow, etc.

From: **David Crutton**
To: All Staff
Sent: 26 January 2009, 11.54
Subject: I am the Pied Piper

I am now leaving the building for a well-earned cigarette. All you smokers will follow me out like the Hamelin rats.

From: **Dotty Podidra**
To: All Staff
Sent: 26 January 2009, 12.06
Subject: Shh!

The GIT clients are now in the building. David has asked me to tell you to be super-quiet for the duration, and also to look super-hardworking just in case any of them pop out for a mooch/toilet break!

Thanks!

Dotty Podidra
Assistant to David Crutton

From: **Sally Wilton**
To: All Staff
Sent: 26 January 2009, 12.07
Subject: Workies

All available workies wanted urgently out front for smoke-wafting and butt-sweeping.

Thank you for your cooperation.

Sally Wilton
**PRINCESS
PAPERCLIP**

	SMS:
David:	Cigs and alcohol?? What were you thinking?
Ted:	It's the greatest paean to fags in rock pantheon
David:	Bluewash is bible belt t-total
Ted:	Shit. Soz. Why didn't you tell me? And why didn't you tell me he's a walking corpse?
David:	Lack of physical strength compensated by inner passion. The man is a firecracker
Ted:	Doesn't look it. Think he might be dead
David:	Don't worry. He's just bored rigid by geddes' powerpoint. As am i
Ted:	Wrap him up and i'll do creative
David:	Wilco
Ted:	Let's rock n roll

From: **Lorraine Pallister**
To: Liam O'Keefe
Sent: 26 January 2009, 12.27
Subject: Twat

I can't escape from you, can I? This place has been overrun by two dozen Turkish thugs looking for you. Why have they come to my place of work? Oh, that's right, because you must have told the bastards about me. Well, you'll be pleased to know that the *BB* auditions have been completely disrupted. If I end up losing my job because of this, I will make it my mission to find you and kill you. Honestly, you'll be running to the Turks for sanctuary.

Thanks for nothing, Liam, and fuck you to hell.

	SMS:
David:	Why zlatan in meeting? Looks like war criminal
Ted:	Don't worry. He makes us look serious
David:	Fuck that. He's straight out of broadmoor
Ted:	Wtf is that noise?
David:	Carter's respirator. Think he loves the work
Ted:	Why's nursey doing cpr then?
David:	999?
Ted:	Wilco

From: **Róisín O'Hooligan**
To: All Staff
Sent: 26 January 2009, 12.59
Subject: Did someone call an ambulance . . .

. . . or is it just more clients arriving?

> Róisín
> Reception

Susi:	You done yet? How's it going?
Milton:	Disaster!! Producer was horrid scottish man. He asked me if i was gay!!
Susi:	Outrageous!!!
Milton:	Worse. Before I could deny vile accusation place invaded by turks looking for liam
Susi:	????????
Milton:	Exactly
Susi:	What now?
Milton:	Rest of audition cancelled. Place already full of screaming queens. Idiot scottish man will never let me in if he thinks me one too
Susi:	You should sue
Milton:	Who? Scottish man, turks or liam??
Susi:	All 3

From: **Bill Geddes**
To: Liam O'Keefe
Sent: 26 January 2009, 13.49
Subject: GIT debrief

What's the usual client reaction to a creative presentation? Something anodyne in my experience, a carefully worded non-opinion designed not to contradict the later view of anyone more important.

What's the best response I've ever had? After I'd shown him a campaign for cat litter, the marketing director of GPC Pet Products told me (*sotto voce*) that he had an erection, but that was possibly because the aircon was set to refrigerate and our account exec's nipples came up like a pair of dials on a valve radio.

Anyway, that was only the best response until today. Today, my friend, your wonderful work for Mini Montana elicited such paroxysms of joy from the President of Galax International Tobacco that he died.

Start at the beginning: the guy, Carter Bluewash, arrived in a wheelchair with a nurse and a mobile intensive-care unit. Apparently, he has diseased lungs (I know, the delicious irony) and he was a virtual corpse. It was like presenting to Mason Verger in *Hannibal*. Or to an actual corpse. Since we could only see him through the polythene curtain of his portable oxygen tent, it was impossible to read his body language. TB presented your campaign to a soundtrack of wheezes and rasps – hard to tell whether they were noises of approval or death rattles.

When he was done, it was my turn to unveil Hannah 'Mini' Montana. Your video montage was a triumph. He was out of his wheelchair and clawing at the polythene. His nurse, who till then had sat quietly in the corner knitting, tried to calm him down. That was when his heart monitor stopped beeping and he collapsed. The nurse did CPR but got nowhere. She was set to pronounce him dead – a proper *ER* moment – when Zlatan shoved her out of the way and started thumping the guy in the chest. Really fucking hard! I actually heard ribs splinter. Nothing doing. The old git was dead. You killed a client, Liam. Isn't that amazing? He was actually dead!

But Zlatan wasn't done. He stood up, grabbed my laptop and slammed it down on the Bluewash heart. It worked a treat. The guy came back to life like Lazarus or Gary Barlow. He took a huge intake of breath that made my ears pop and sat bolt upright. Then he looked at DC and wheezed, 'Cost this puppy, Crutton. If you can make the numbers work, you have a green light.' He added one further rider (dinner *à deux* with Miley Cyrus) before fainting again.

He has several shattered ribs that, given his age and fragility, will probably never heal. But *he isn't dead*, and that's the main thing, isn't it? Paramedics arrived and stretchered him out, then it was backslaps and champagne all round. DC promised a knighthood to Zlatan and TB offered a toast to you and Harvey. I think all is forgiven.

Wish you were here. Honestly, the whole thing was so staggering that my jaw is still scraping the floor.

Oh, when you do come back in, I think it might be timely to ask for a raise – screw the recession.

Yours in shock and awe,
Bill

PS: DC has a tattoo. On his neck. What is that all about?

PPS: And rumour has it he's gay. Can't say I'm convinced by that one.

PPPS: Zlatan completely fucked my laptop, but seeing how handy he is with a punch, I won't be sending him the bill. He reckons he learnt his Lazarus trick from Ratko Mladić, the Bosnian Serb war crim who's still on the run. 'It either work like the dream or put motherfucker out of misery,' he said. Too right.

From:	**David Crutton**
To:	All Staff
Sent:	26 January 2009, 14.17
Subject:	GIT

We have just had an excellent meeting with GIT, who accepted unreservedly all our strategic and creative recommendations. This success puts the agency on an international stage and bodes well in a time of profound economic uncertainty.

I would like to thank all those involved, especially Bill Geddes who bravely took up the baton after Donald Gold's shocking betrayal. Congratulations must also be extended to Ted Berry and his creative team of Liam O'Keefe, Harvey Harvey, Zlatan

Kovaćević and Adrijana Smiljanić. Zlatan deserves a special mention for his demonstration of stupendous extra-box thinking. Buy him a beer and ask him to show you a use for a Toshiba laptop that isn't in the owner's manual!

Well done, one and all. This is a terrific start to the New Year.

David Crutton
The Man

From: **Bill Geddes**
To: Kazu Makino
Sent: 26 January 2009, 14.18
Subject: You missed a treat

The client died, came back to life and bought the campaign wholesale. You really had to be there. Whatever, I reckon this would be a good time for you to duck back in because DC is in a rare forgiving mood.

From: **Kazu Makino**
To: Bill Geddes
Sent: 26 January 2009, 14.20
Subject: Re: You missed a treat

OK, you're a complete arsehole and I'm not talking to you any more, but I'm so excited that I've got to tell you where I am. The anteroom of the Oval Office! Yes, the actual Oval Office in the actual White House!! Better sign off. Hillary is looking at me like she thinks my BlackBerry is a terrorist IED.

Sent from my BlackBerry

From: **Janice Crutton**
To: David Crutton
Sent: 26 January 2009, 14.22
Subject: Noah

His passport has gone missing. I'm sure it was with the others in the study. This can only mean he's taken it, which can only mean he's left the country. Clearly, the 'Queer' tattoo has triggered an emotional crisis. You're the last person I want to reach out to, but I'm really worried. Please do something. I would, but I have to take Tam to hospital. Her temperature has gone off the scale.

From: **Bill Geddes**
To: Kazu Makino
Sent: 26 January 2009, 14.23
Subject: Re: You missed a treat

Excuse me? What the hell are you doing in the Oval Office?

From: **Kazu Makino**
To: Bill Geddes
Sent: 26 January 2009, 14.25
Subject: Re: You missed a treat

What do you think I'm doing? Interviewing for a temp job? I'm meeting the Prez, you twit. Gotta go. I'm on.

Sent from my BlackBerry

From: **David Crutton**
To: Dotty Podidra
Sent: 26 January 2009, 14.27
Subject: Family stuff

Send flowers for Tamara to all west London hospitals (not sure which one she's in). And put out an APB for Noah.

MSN:

DottyPod:	APB? Any ideas?
sjdG:	Aren't they that trance act? Had a mega summer hit a few years ago.
DottyPod:	Think you're right. Why does DC want me to 'put out an APB' for Noah??
sjdG:	Haven't foggiest. Some sort of remix?
DottyPod:	Who knows? I'll try downloading it from iTunes. BTW, have you heard from Milt? How did he do?
sjdG:	Not well. The audition was invaded by turkeys looking for Liam.
DottyPod:	????
sjdG:	No idea. But the producer accused him of being gay.
DottyPod:	OMG! What a bastard.
sjdG:	Well, he was Scottish. BTW, I can still smell that disgusting old man.
DottyPod:	DC says it's formaldehyde.
sjdG:	What's that?
DottyPod:	A preservative, I think. Stops him dropping to bits I imagine.

From: **Lorraine Pallister**
To: Liam O'Keefe
Sent: 26 January 2009, 14.35
Subject: You're still a twat, but . . .

. . . now I'm worried. Why are Turkish gangsters looking for you? I guess it's not to buy you a beer. Are you all right? Where are you? Get in touch. Just to let me know.

From: **Bill Geddes**
To: Liam O'Keefe
Sent: 26 January 2009, 14.40
Subject: The day that keeps on giving

It just keeps on getting better. You got a special mention in DC's all-staffer. And I had an e from Kaz. Guess where she is.

No, you'll never get it. She was at the White House, about to meet Obama!

It's all too much and I need to talk to someone who'll say something funny and cynical to give me back my perspective. Get in touch.

From: **Larry Finlay**
To: Katie Espiner
Sent: 26 January 2009, 14.54
Subject: Update

Where are you? I bumped into Barnsley from HarperCollins at lunch. She let slip that she's sent one of her senior publishers out to France. She claims it's to sign up some French sword 'n' sorcery phenomenon, but I suspect otherwise. Report back to me ASAP.

Larry Finlay
Managing Director
Transworld Publishers

From: **Katie Espiner**
To: Larry Finlay
Sent: 26 January 2009, 15.03
Subject: Update

Just touched down in Rodez. BizzyJet flight delayed. Bloody nightmare, actually. My lasagne spontaneously combusted when I peeled the foil off the tray! Seriously, we should commission someone to write an exposé of budget airlines. Think Nick Sayers

376

from Hodder is on flight. He's wearing dark glasses and beret, so hard to tell. Suspect publishers might be on this one like flies round cow poo. Will proceed with speed. And caution. But mostly speed.

> Katie Espiner
> Senior Commissioning Editor
> Transworld Publishers
>
> Sent from my BlackBerry

From:	**Liam O'Keefe**
To:	David Crutton
Sent:	26 January 2009, 15.13
Subject:	It's tatty-bye time

I've always liked you, David. When you were being your most despotic back in our Miller Shanks days, I couldn't help harbouring a soft spot. You used to lose it with such élan. And even when you were firing people like you'd been let loose with a semi-automatic in your old school canteen, at least you were making us laugh. At you, if not with you, but any laugh is better than none, innit, bro?

And you never took bullshit. In a business that's built on Himalayan heaps of the stuff, that is to be admired. So you'll surely thank me for not bullshitting you now.

You're a fucking idiot.

I mean, only a numpty could think even for a nanosecond that Neil Godley is a thief. This is the man who can't take a copy of *London Lite* on the tube because it 'feels like stealing'. Do you genuinely think he's capable of making a concerted effort to heist an entire office?

Honestly, do you?

Well, obviously you do, because the poor guy is on remand.

Phone the cops and tell them you've got it horribly wrong. Then compensate him with a big fat cheque made out to his favourite charity because he's Christian like that – a better man, in fact, than you or I will ever be.

You'll find the stuff from your office in a white Transit parked outside Unit 17 on the Compass West Industrial Estate in Tottenham. You'll have to move fast because the hoodies round there don't waste time. God knows what they'll make of your Damien Hirst. That'll go straight in a skip.

Yes, it was me, in case you haven't figured it out already. And I did it alone. Godley was not Sundance to my Butch. That's just too fucking ridiculous.

Well done on the GIT meeting. Tell Zlatan not to fuck up the art direction on my posters. He may be handy in a life-or-death situation, but his typography sucks.

It was good working with you, David. Once was a revelation, twice was a treat. But please do the right thing with Godley.

Best wishes (and I really mean that),

    Liam O'Keefe

PS: I heard about the tattoo. Are you sure? Is it really you?

PPS: Also heard the gay rumour. If it's true, respect, dude. It takes a proper man to face up to himself.

PPPS: If it's not, you might want to kick some arse. Suspect it started where most rumours do.

PPPPS: Most rumours start with Milton Keane. Sorry, but after the Godley-is-a-thief fiasco, I feel I have to spell things out.

From: **Liam O'Keefe**
To: Bill Geddes
Sent: 26 January 2009, 15.24
Subject: Re: The day that keeps on giving

Yo, Bill. Sounds like an exciting meeting. Brilliant. Well done and everything.

You want me to restore some perspective though? Is that honestly what you're after? OK, I'll give it a go.

It's all bollocks. These precious moments of triumph we award ourselves, utter bollocks; self-serving sop to get us through a working day that would otherwise be futile drudgery. Face it, our lives are without merit. We just take from the world and give nothing back. We are leeches. That we read the *Guardian* and are appalled when something barbaric goes off in Gaza or the Congo, and that we choose dolphin-safe tuna and buy Fair Trade at Starbucks doesn't mean a fucking thing. In fact, it makes us worse than the leeches that truly don't give a fuck. At least they're honest. We, on the other hand, are fraudulent hypocrites. We believe we can fool ourselves with the same lies we feed the world in our advertisements.

Ah yes, those ads – you know, the ones we sweat over, argue about and fight for as if they actually matter. Well, they do matter. In a bad way. They make us the standard bearers for the cunts that are raping every living, breathing thing on the planet.

We are their bitches.

Got some perspective now? I know I have.

It was nice knowing you.

    Liam

From: **Liam O'Keefe**
To: Brett Topolski
Sent: 26 January 2009, 15.29
Subject: Re: All right, all right, I'll tell you

Tell Vince congratulations. I'm made up for him. True Love is All and when it comes along you have to cherish it – no matter where you find it. I wish him and his Princess Jasmine all the luck in the world. Seems they'll need it, given the cultural obstacles.

Popping out now. Might be some time.

Liam

PS: I love you.

PPS: Like a mate, that is.

From: **Liam O'Keefe**
To: Lorraine Pallister
Sent: 26 January 2009, 15.33
Subject: Re: You're still a twat, but . . .

I'm sorry about the Turks. I didn't tell them about you. They must have found something of yours when they went round the flat. You're right, they don't want to buy me a drink. They want to fuck me right up.

But I think I'll save them the bother.

I'm sorry, Lorraine. I know I've said it a million times before, but this is the last time. I'm sorry for everything. For wasting the last eight years of your life. Worse than that, for giving you nothing but grief when you deserve so much better.

Some day you'll meet a guy who'll treat you with the love and respect you're long overdue. And if he doesn't, one day he'll have me to answer to.

I never stopped loving you. I've told you countless lies, but you know that's the truth, don't you?

Sorry for bothering you. It won't happen again. You can get back to work now.

    Liam

From: **Liam O'Keefe**
To: Harvey Harvey
Sent: 26 January 2009, 16.02
Subject: Soon come, mate

Played one last game of Super PONG in your honour. New high score. I credited it to you. Just going to make a commemorative pyre of your *Dr Who* DVDs and then I'll be joining you.

Stick the kettle on.

    Liam

From: **Susi Judge-Davis-Gaultier**
To: Dotty Podidra
Sent: 26 January 2009, 16.03
Subject: Milt

He's back. Think we might have to do suicide watch again. Come and see me.

From: **David Crutton**
To: Róisín O'Hooligan
Sent: 26 January 2009, 16.04
Subject: Job

If Slobodan and his mates are loafing down there, I have an errand for them. There's a white Ford Transit parked outside Unit

17 on the Compass West Industrial Estate in Tottenham. Tell them to go and collect it. It contains my office furniture.

From: **David Crutton**
To: Sally Wilton
Sent: 26 January 2009, 16.07
Subject: Godley

I think you called this one wrong. I've just had a confession from Liam O'Keefe. You'd better come up for a chat. By the way, I don't imagine you'll be Godley's favourite person when he gets out, so I suggest you talk to a solicitor. I'll do my best to cover for you in the all-staffer.

From: **David Crutton**
To: All Staff
Sent: 26 January 2009, 16.10
Subject: Office thief

I'm delighted to announce that Sally Wilton's ingenious diversionary tactic of having Neil Godley arrested for the recent rash of office thefts has paid off handsomely. She has succeeded in flushing out the real culprit, who when challenged with the overwhelming case against him, had no option but to admit his guilt.

I am referring to Liam O'Keefe. He was always my prime suspect – I simply lacked the evidence. Anyone with knowledge of his whereabouts should contact me immediately. Failure to do so will lead to charges of aiding a criminal.

In the meantime, do make sure to congratulate Sally on the brilliant success of her crime-busting initiative.

David Crutton
𝕿𝖍𝖊 𝕸𝖆𝖓

From: **David Crutton**
To: Dotty Podidra
Sent: 26 January 2009, 16.12
Subject: Milton Keane

Tell your homosexual friend to come and see me immediately. I have gossip to discuss with him.

	MSN:
DottyPod:	Has he stopped crying yet?
sjdG:	On 3rd box of Kleenex.
DottyPod:	DC wants to see him. Don't think he's happy.
sjdG:	He's never happy. What's his problem?
DottyPod:	Think he might've heard the gay rumour.
sjdG:	OMG! Just what Milt doesn't need right now. He's v. v. fragile.
DottyPod:	I know, but you'd better send him up. It'll only make things worse if he doesn't come.
sjdG:	OK, see what I can do.

From: **Lorraine Pallister**
To: Liam O'Keefe
Sent: 26 January 2009, 16.17
Subject: Re: You're still a twat, but . . .

Just got out of a meeting and read your e. You're not going to do something stupid, are you? Reply immediately.

From: **Bill Geddes**
To: Liam O'Keefe
Sent: 26 January 2009, 16.18
Subject: Re: The day that keeps on giving

When did you get so righteous and maudlin? And what do you mean, 'It was nice knowing you'? Where are you going? DC just sent an all-staffer saying you confessed to the thefts. Is that why you're off? Can't we have a leaving do? In secret, obviously.

From: **Brett Topolski**
To: Liam O'Keefe
Sent: 26 January 2009, 16.19
Subject: Re: All right, all right, I'll tell you

Your advice stinks. It's all well and good for you to sit there 3,396 miles away (I Googled it. Again) and talk of 'True Love', but I'm dealing with fucking reality here. And the fucking reality is that our mutual friend is drawing a metaphorical dotted line around his neck complete with helpful 'cut here' instructions.

And what do you mean, you 'might be some time'? Have you resigned or something? That'll pay off your debts, won't it?

Don't reply unless you've got something useful to say. Or something genuinely funny. Romeo is writing sonnets now. The very idea should be hilarious, and normally it would be, but I'm completely drained of my sense of humour.

From: **Bill Geddes**
To: Kazu Makino
Sent: 26 January 2009, 16.21
Subject: Well??

Have you seen the Prez yet? I know I'm a complete arsehole and you're not talking to me, but you've got to let me know.

By the way, if you never talk to me again, I'll never be able to tell you the full story of the GIT meeting. It was well beyond amazing.

From: **Janice Crutton**
To: David Crutton
Sent: 26 January 2009, 16.29
Subject: Noah

Have you found our son yet?

    Sent from my BlackBerry

From: **David Crutton**
To: Dotty Podidra
Sent: 26 January 2009, 16.30
Subject: Noah

Have you found my son yet?

From: **Dotty Podidra**
To: David Crutton
Sent: 26 January 2009, 16.31
Subject: Re: Noah

You want me to find him? Didn't realize.

From: **David Crutton**
To: Dotty Podidra
Sent: 26 January 2009, 16.32
Subject: Re: Noah

I told you to put out an APB.

From: **Dotty Podidra**
To: David Crutton
Sent: 26 January 2009, 16.34
Subject: Re: Noah

Right. Sorry, I was getting confused. Where do you want me to look for him?

From: **David Crutton**
To: Dotty Podidra
Sent: 26 January 2009, 16.36
Subject: Re: Noah

I have no idea. Thus the request for an APB. His mother seems to think he's fled the country, so it's probably too late. See if you can get me a coffee without fucking that up.

From: **Dotty Podidra**
To: Susi Judge-Davis-Gaultier
Sent: 26 January 2009, 16.38
Subject: APB

Still no idea what it is, but it's definitely not a trance act. DC cleared that one up in his usual rude way. How's little Milt been doing since his 'talking to'?

From: **David Crutton**
To: Janice Crutton
Sent: 26 January 2009, 16.39
Subject: Re: Noah

I cleared my afternoon diary to look for him. Just got back to my desk. I've tried all the obvious haunts/mates, but there's no sign of him. Mind you, I'm sure there's nothing to worry about. He'll probably turn up this evening wanting his tea as per usual. How is Tam? Perking up, I trust. Did she get my flowers? I've wanted to phone and ask, but I'm assuming you're not taking my calls.

I don't know how many times I have to apologize for my brainstorm with the tattoos. I am sorry. It was stupid. Having said that, I think you owe me an apology as well. I have been as patient as I possibly can be through this pregnancy, but there is a limit to the number of irrational outbursts I will put up with.

I would like to come home. It is my house too, Jan.

David

SMS:

Lorraine: Call me, Liam. Or just text that you're ok. Worried sick

From: **Susi Judge-Davis-Gaultier**
To: Dotty Podidra
Sent: 26 January 2009, 16.42
Subject: Re: APB

I've managed to calm him down with some valerian root (and a Temazepam, but for God's sake don't tell him!). He's 'resting' in Caroline's office. Can you pop in and have a look at him in a bit? TB's got me doing blumming D&AD entries. I'll be here all night!!

From: **Lorraine Pallister**
To: Bill Geddes
Sent: 26 January 2009, 16.47
Subject: Liam

Hi Bill – Liam's ex here. We only met once, at Liam's 37th. I was a bit of a cow, but he was being a prat and I took it out on his friends. Sorry. Anyway, the point: I got a weird and slightly scary email from him a while ago. Probably nothing in it, but it got me worried. Also, there are some pretty unpleasant blokes looking for him. You don't happen to know where he is, do you? Not at work, I guess. Sorry to bother you, but can you drop me a note if you know anything? And get him to call me if you speak to him.

Thanks and best wishes,

Lorraine

From: **Bill Geddes**
To: Lorraine Pallister
Sent: 26 January 2009, 16.54
Subject: Re: Liam

Hi Lorraine – don't recall you being a cow at his birthday bash, but I was totally juiced and probably made a tit of myself. Sorry.

I had a strange e from him too. He was supposed to be at work today for a big meeting, but he didn't show up. According to our MD, he's wanted for some office thefts. Could be something to do with that.

I'll phone around, see if I can track him down. I'll let you know.

Best,

Bill

From: **Janice Crutton**
To: David Crutton
Sent: 26 January 2009, 16.59
Subject: Re: Noah

David, you seem to be forgetting how well I know you. The day you clear your diary, even for an afternoon, in order to deal with a family emergency, will be the day the devil laces up his skates because hell has frozen over. Knowing you, you probably delegated poor Dotty to look for Noah. God knows why she's stuck with you for so long.

Come to that, God knows why I've stuck with you for longer still. Nineteen years! Don't worry though, we won't be celebrating our twentieth.

I've been pregnant for a matter of a few weeks. How dare you run out of patience? After I've shown nothing but patience for nineteen years of rampant temper tantrums, unbridled workoholism and chronic non-engagement with family life. And after I patiently nursed you through rehab and then reconstructive rhinoplasty after your extended 'dalliance' with a certain powder.

How fucking dare you?

In short, no, you can't come home. For your information, it is no longer your house too. Or in the words of sweet Tam's beloved Glasvegas, 'Fuck you, it's over.'

Janice

PS: Tam didn't get your flowers. She wouldn't have noticed them anyway, being as she is heavily sedated. I'm sitting by her bed now. An IV line is going into her arm. Just looking at it makes me well up, but at least it's a constant reminder of what an irresponsible, uncaring idiot her father is.

PPS: On the matter of it no longer being your house, I wouldn't challenge it if I were you. Bear in mind that I'm a good friend of Fiona Shackleton, who you might recall did a superb job for Paul McCartney. And she doesn't like you any more than she did Heather Mills.

Sent from my BlackBerry

From: **David Crutton**
To: Dotty Podidra
Sent: 26 January 2009, 17.01
Subject: Leave me alone

No calls or disturbances from anyone, including you. Except get me a bottle of vodka from the special cupboard. Then no disturbances.

From: **Bill Geddes**
To: Kazu Makino
Sent: 26 January 2009, 17.08
Subject: You

What's happening? I'm worried about you. Liam is on the most-wanted list and has gone AWOL. Now I'm scared you've been sent to Guantanamo with Don. Get in touch.

From: **Kazu Makino**
To: Bill Geddes
Sent: 26 January 2009, 17.11
Subject: Re: You

Everything brill. Can't talk. Got to get ready for a press conference. Check the news sites!

Kaz

PS: Barack rocks. I so wanna have his babies!

Sent from my BlackBerry

From: **Dotty Podidra**
To: David Crutton
Sent: 26 January 2009, 17.12
Subject: Urgent call

I know you don't want to be disturbed, but I've got the US ambassador on the phone. He says it's important. I imagine you'll want to take it?

	MSN:
sjdG:	Thought I asked you to keep an eye on Milt. Just looked in Cazza's office. He's not there!!
DottyPod:	OMG! Have you checked the window ledge?
sjdG:	Going to look now.

From: **Dotty Podidra**
To: David Crutton
Sent: 26 January 2009, 17.20
Subject: More urgent calls

I know you said the last call was to be the absolutely final disturbance, but I've got NBC, ABC, CBS, CNN, ITN and the BBC on hold. Shall I put them through?? One at a time, obviously!

From: **Róisín O'Hooligan**
To: All Staff
Sent: 26 January 2009, 17.21
Subject: Anyone seen Milton Keane?

I've got a Philip Edgar-Jones on the line for him. Says it's important. Something to do with the telly. He's a lovely Scottish bloke, so I don't mind keeping him chatting if someone can be arsed to find the diva.

Róisín
Reception

	MSN:
sjdG:	Milt is on ledge again!! Help!!!!!!!
DottyPod:	Can't. Dealing with national security crisis. Tell him BB producer is on line. That'll get him in!
sjdG:	Can't. He's shut window and I can't open it without ruining nails.
DottyPod:	Try texting. He might have his mobile.

From: **Róisín O'Hooligan**
To: All Staff
Sent: 26 January 2009, 17.23
Subject: Anyone seen Milton Keane?

A Sky News truck has tipped up. A bit of a wild guess this, but is the gay tit on the ledge again? I've still got my lovely Scotty on the phone for him. He just told me his wife is from Fermanagh. I knew he had taste and judgement!

Róisín
Reception

From: **Dotty Podidra**
To: Róisín O'Hooligan
Sent: 26 January 2009, 17.24
Subject: Re: Anyone seen Milton Keane?

Sky are here to interview David. Send them up. And yes, Milton is on the ledge. But for God's sake don't tell the Scottish man!

Hooray! Milton is break-dancing on the window ledge again and Sky is getting the scoop!! Get out there and cheer him on. Hurry though, because after one near-death today, we might be moments away from the real thing.

Róisín
Reception

	SMS:
Susi:	If you have mobile answer me
Susi:	I'm in Cazza's office and I can hear S Club ringtone through window. Answer me!!
Milton:	Go away
Susi:	Don't do it! You have everything to live for!
Milton:	Do not. All turned to poo
Susi:	No!! BB producer on phone
Milton:	He only wants to laugh at me and say I'm queer
Susi:	Does not. Come in and take call!!
Susi:	Answer me. Please!

From: **Dotty Podidra**
To: David Crutton
Sent: 26 January 2009, 17.31
Subject: Even more urgent calls

Will you take a call from *The Times*? Sky are held up. They're filming in the street outside. I should probably tell you that

Milton Keane is on the ledge again. BBC on their way. Told them to avoid the crowd and come round the back.

SMS:

Liam: Bye
Lorraine: At last! Where are you?

Lorraine: Fucking answer me!
Liam: I'm at river
Lorraine: Which bit of river?
Liam: Love you. Bye
Lorraine: Don't do this

Lorraine: If you love me DO NOT FUCKING DO THIS

From: **Lorraine Pallister**
To: Bill Geddes
Sent: 26 January 2009, 17.39
Subject: Liam

He just texted me. Says he's at river. Really scared he's going to do something dumb. Like jump. Help!

SMS:

Susi: Please talk to me sweetz
Milton: Why is crowd in street?
Susi: They care about you. We all do
Milton: Why are TV cameras here?
Susi: They care too darling. The cameras love you!!
Milton: Why are they singing that song? I hate Van Halen

From: **Susi Judge-Davis-Gaultier**
To: Róisín O'Hooligan
Sent: 26 January 2009, 17.43
Subject:

Go outside immediately and tell idiots to stop singing. There is a life at stake!

From: **Bill Geddes**
To: Lorraine Pallister
Sent: 26 January 2009, 17.44
Subject: Re: Liam

Can't believe it. I'm sitting at my desk while outside an idiot (not Liam!) is about to jump off a window ledge. Any idea which bit of the river? Did you have a romantic spot somewhere??

SMS:

Lorraine: Tell me where you are. Waterloo Bridge?

From: **Lorraine Pallister**
To: Bill Geddes
Sent: 26 January 2009, 17.47
Subject: Re: Liam

We once walked over Waterloo Bridge and I made him stop because I liked the view of St Paul's. It was freezing and he got really pissed off. Hardly romantic, but the only thing I can think of. Just asked him, but he won't reply.

From: **Bill Geddes**
To: Lorraine Pallister
Sent: 26 January 2009, 17.48
Subject: Re: Liam

Waterloo is packed at this time of day. If he's on the parapet, someone will have seen him and called the cops. Can you get down there? Where are you?

From: **Lorraine Pallister**
To: Bill Geddes
Sent: 26 January 2009, 17.49
Subject: Re: Liam

Shepherds Bush. At least half an hour away.

From: **Bill Geddes**
To: Lorraine Pallister
Sent: 26 January 2009, 17.50
Subject: Liam

I'm minutes away. I'll go. Text him and tell him I've gone to look for him. Call me. 07231 054 280

	SMS:
Susi:	Please come in and talk to the nice bb man. He's scottish. Scottish people are sweeties
Milton:	Scottish people smell. Leave me alone
Susi:	I'm sure he wants to tell you you're on show
Milton:	He can call me on mobile. He has my number

Bill:	What are you doing? Need a favour
Zlatan:	Fuck you. Kirsten cut hair. If I nice maybe she give me titty job
Bill:	Sorry. Need you to take me somewhere on your kawa
Zlatan:	Fuck you
Bill:	Could be another life to save
Zlatan:	You dick me about?
Bill:	No! Definite life to save
Zlatan:	OK. Meet outside 2 minute

From: **Bill Geddes**
To: Lorraine Pallister
Sent: 26 January 2009, 17.53
Subject: Re: Liam

Going now. Please don't worry about him. No one else on the planet gets himself out of the shit quite like Liam.

From: **Susi Judge-Davis-Gaultier**
To: Róisín O'Hooligan
Sent: 26 January 2009, 17.54
Subject: Emergency!!

If he's still on phone, tell Scottish man to call Milton's mobile immediately! Unless he has bad news. In that case, tell him not to call under any circs!!

From: **Dotty Podidra**
To: All Staff
Sent: 26 January 2009, 17.55
Subject: We're on TV!

Assuming you manage to get home in time, tune into the 10 o'clock news on BBC1. David is going to be on!!

SMS:

Lorraine: Please tell me where you are. Bill is on way to waterloo. If not there say so

Lorraine: Silence mean you're at waterloo? Don't do anything till bill gets there. On my way too. About to go down tube

Liam: Don't

Lorraine: Don't what?

Liam: Go down tube. Want to talk

Lorraine: OK. Tell me where you are

Liam: Where you think I am

Lorraine: Please don't jump. Water v cold. You hate cold. Remember last time we were there?

Liam: Remember everything we did together. That's why I want it to stop

Lorraine: Don't understand

Liam: Want it to stop while still remember everything. How perfect you were

Lorraine: Fuck. Now everyone staring at me

Liam: Cos you is beautiful

Lorraine: No. Cos i is crying. Bastard. You could always make me cry

Liam: My specialty. Another reason to go. Bye

Lorraine: Don't do it. Please

Lorraine: Please liam. Stay alive. For me

From: **Róisín O'Hooligan**
To: All Staff
Sent: 26 January 2009, 18.07
Subject: Latest Milton alert

Fireman Sam is here again. In case you don't already know the form, he says no one should use the front exit unless they want a ten-stone homosexual on their head.

Róisín
Reception

SMS:

Dotty:	What's milton doing?
Susi:	Like you care
Dotty:	Sorry. Stuck with dc. Bbc are in
Susi:	Good to know you've got priorities right. Stupid boss before best friend in whole world
Dotty:	Not fair. You know it's not like that
Susi:	Whatever. If you really care milton is talking to bb guy
Dotty:	He's on the ledge too??!!
Susi:	Duh! On the phone, stupid
Dotty:	Soz. Where are you?
Susi:	In street with rest of idiots
Dotty:	Can you tell how it's going?
Susi:	No. Been talking for ages
Dotty:	Dc needs me to do makeup. Keep me posted

SMS:

Lorraine:	You at waterloo?
Bill:	Yes. Cops here. Massive crowd. Can't get through
Lorraine:	He was texting but he stopped. Is he there?

Bill: Someone on parapet. Possibly him. Hopefully not too late. Try find cop to let me through

Lorraine: Good luck. Got new message. Might be him

Liam: Massive crowd. All I want is fucking peace

Lorraine: Come back mine. All peace you want in spare room

Liam: Spare room?

Lorraine: Won't lie to you. But we can talk. Want to sort you out

Liam: I can sort me out thanks

Lorraine: No you fucking can't. Climb back and wait for me

Liam: Can't do that. Massive crowd. Can't disappoint them

Lorraine: Stop being smartarse for once. Why you doing this to me?

Liam: Thought I was doing it to myself

Lorraine: There you go again

Liam: Done nothing but bad stuff to you. Doing you favour now

Lorraine: Rubbish. You have hurt me enough. Don't hurt me more by leaving me this as goodbye. Don't be so bloody selfish

Liam: Bunch of turks want to kill me anyway. Gonna steal their thunder

Lorraine: You said you love me. Don't do this to someone you love. DO NOT DO THIS TO ME

Liam: Soz. Got nothing left tho

Lorraine: You have plenty

Liam: Nothing left but memories. Precious fucking memories of you.

Know what happens to special memories you want to keep vivid forever? They fade. Fucking disappear. When kid went to see mary chain. Best ever. Noise. Stoned violence. All i ever wanted. Memorized every sight sound smell every song what I drank what pills i took what i wore what girl behind bar wore. Swore to keep burning bright forever so could always feel it. What happened to mary chain? Faded. Went. Fucked like every other brilliant memory. Can remember i was there but not what it felt like. Important to know what it felt like. Will happen to beautiful memories of you. One day. Want you always to be vivid to me. Want you always to

Lorraine: You want me always to what?

SMS:

T-Mobile: MESSAGE FOR L O'KEEFE FROM T-MOBILE. YOUR LAST TEXT CONTAINED OVER 700 CHARACTERS AND EXCEEDED LIMIT UNDER THE FAIR USAGE TERMS OF YOUR CONTRACT. NO FURTHER TEXTS MAY BE SENT UNTIL YOU TOP UP YOUR ACCOUNT. FOR CUSTOMER SERVICE CALL 150 OR VISIT T-MOBILE.CO.UK

SMS:

Lorraine: Answer me liam. That was most beautiful thing you've ever said. You have to finish!

SMS:

Lorraine: What's happening?

Bill: Commotion. Don't know

Lorraine: Sent me longest ever text but didn't finish. Wtf has happened?

Bill: Gotta go. Will call asap

SMS:

Dotty: Firemen won't let me outside. Can hear cheers. What's happening?

Susi: He jumped!!

Dotty: OMG!!

Susi: Firemen held out trampoline thingy. He jumped into it. Everyone cheering! Amazing!!!!

Dotty: Is he OK??

Susi: Lapping up applause. Smiling. Think he got BB!

From: **Janice Crutton**
To: David Crutton
Sent: 26 January 2009, 22.18
Subject:

You'll be pleased to know that we have TVs in hospital and that I didn't miss your appearance on the news. It's so reassuring to know that while I'm keeping vigil beside our unconscious daughter and while our son is in God knows what trouble, you can at least console yourself with a bravura performance of staggering pomposity.

You really are a towering twat, David.

Janice

PS: The watching millions no doubt have been fooled, but I know you better than anyone and I know when you're lying. It's all in the eyes, isn't it?

Sent from my BlackBerry

British terror suspect released

Just six days after his inauguration, President Barack Obama ordered the release of Donald Gold, the Briton recently arrested in Brazil.

Gold's release was announced by the President at an unscheduled press conference this afternoon. Earlier he had agreed to meet Kazu Makino, a colleague of Gold's at the London advertising agency Meerkat360. Makino had flown to Washington to lobby for his release.

Gold was arrested five days ago in Rio de Janeiro. Despite being Jewish, he was suspected of having links to Al Qaeda. The Brazilian authorities handed him over to the CIA, who flew him to an unspecified location, thought to be Guantanamo Bay.

President Obama said: 'I knew nothing of Donald Gold's plight until Ms Makino came to see me. When she told me the story I was appalled. It shone a revealing light on the fear and paranoia that has gripped our great nation in recent years. After confirming the details with my national security advisors, I immediately ordered Mr Gold's release. Let this symbolize the change that is going to mark my administration.'

Standing alongside the president, Makino said: 'I knew that as long as I could get someone in authority to listen to the facts, Don would be OK. I am hugely grateful to the president for agreeing to see me, and for listening with such patience and kindness. Now I can't wait to see Don again and take him home.'

In London, Gold's colleagues were jubilant. David Crutton, the CEO of Meerkat360, said: 'I am absolutely ecstatic. Securing Don's release has been my number-one priority. I didn't for one second believe there was any merit in the ridiculous terrorist accusations. As soon as he was arrested, I dispatched my most trusted aide, Kazu Makino, to Washington and we liaised closely to secure this outcome. I am delighted that our efforts have put an end to Don's ordeal and that soon we can welcome him back to work, where he belongs.'

Other top stories:
Waterloo Bridge suicide dive (video)
Nigerian police name dead British tourist
Fans injured at Helsinki rock concert
Publishers invade Dordogne
Expat elopes with Arab princess

Tuesday
Mood: au gratin

	MSN:
DottyPod:	Is Milton in yet?
sjdG:	Just called. He'll be in at 11. Gone to doctor.
DottyPod:	OMG. Anything serious?
sjdG:	Whiplash from the jump. He's worried he'll have to wear neck brace, so possibly PTSD.
DottyPod:	??
sjdG:	Duh!! Post-traumatic stress disorder.
DottyPod:	Did you hear about Zlatan?
sjdG:	Yawn. It's all TB is banging on about!
DottyPod:	It's awful, isn't it?
sjdG:	He's an idiot. I could never understand a word he said. Except for when he swore. Can't feel sorry for him.
DottyPod:	That's a bit cruel!
sjdG:	Soz. Can't help it. He made my life absolute hell.
DottyPod:	But isn't Liam a total hero??!!
sjdG:	Oh pur-leeeze! He probably fell in

	and Zlatan used him as a Lilo. He's sooo fat!
DottyPod:	True, but I still think he was quite brave.
sjdG:	Probably spotted a pie in the water. Why else would he dive in?
DottyPod:	OMFG! That's awful.
sjdG:	Why aren't you LOL-ing me? I'm being hilarious! You're such a wuss!
DottyPod:	Not you! I'm flicking through Metro. HH is dead! Drowned in a river in Lagos. Is that in Africa?
sjdG:	Portugal. Didn't know he was on hols. He was another nutter.
DottyPod:	That's just horrible!!
sjdG:	He was creepy. And you didn't have to give him reminders to take his pills every half hour. What am I? Nurse Crochet? Honestly, it's a load off my mind.
DottyPod:	I'm going before I say something not nice.

From: **David Crutton**
To: Ted Berry, Caroline Zitter
Sent: 27 January 2009, 09.11
Subject: Review

With GIT about to kick off, we should review timings and
resources. My office at 10? And before you ask, Ted, you can't go
on a creative hiring binge. I don't care how many men down you
are. We are in the worst recession since the Black Death. Make do
with what you've got. Can't the clown and the busker write ads?

From: **Caroline Zitter**
To: David Crutton
Sent: 27 January 2009, 09.12
Subject: Out of Office AutoReply

I am out of the office attending *7 Steps to Corporate Domination* with Jo O'Meara and H (from Steps). I will return on Wednesday 28th January.

Caroline Zitter
THE SEER

From: **Ted Berry**
To: David Crutton
Sent: 27 January 2009, 09.15
Subject: Re: Review

Can we make it 12.30? Snowed under. Bit short-handed. But you know that.

From: **David Crutton**
To: Ted Berry
Sent: 27 January 2009, 09.19
Subject: Re: Review

12.30 is fine. By the way, can you get someone to knock up a 'Welcome Home' banner for reception? I'm expecting Gold and the Jap to fly in some time this afternoon and we need to make the right noises.

From: **Bill Geddes**
To: Lorraine Pallister
Sent: 27 January 2009, 09.25
Subject:

Hi. Just a quick one to see how you're doing. Let me know if there's anything I can do to help – Bill

From: **Bill Geddes**
To: Donald Gold
Cc: Kazu Makino
Sent: 27 January 2009, 09.29
Subject: Welcome to freedom!

Hi Don. Spent the night at St Thomas' Hospital (a long and bizarre story), but managed to watch your release on News 24. Opened a celebratory can of Pepsi Max when you appeared at the plane door. The orange jumpsuit wasn't you, though. Have you got your own clothes back yet? And your BlackBerry? And what about the Esmée Éloge boards?! You know it'll be the first thing DC will ask you about when you get back.

We've all been rooting for you here. Well, everyone except DC. He knows how to turn it on for the cameras, doesn't he? We're well chuffed that you're out (Kaz, you're a phenomenon! How the hell did you do it? You and Barack, eh?!!). Hurry home. Lots to tell you. Creatives have been dropping like flies. Literally. It's been devastating.

Bill

From: **Brett Topolski**
To: Liam O'Keefe
Sent: 27 January 2009, 09.37
Subject: Aladdin

He's gone. Done a moonlight skedaddle with Princess Jasmine, probably on a magic carpet because fuck knows how he'd have got her through the airport. The place is up in arms. They're clamping down on all expats, which (in case they hadn't noticed) is most of the fucking population. Rumour has it that Jim Davidson has been arrested because he'd agreed to be Vince's best man. I'm bereft. Vince was a complete pain in the arse, but he was *my* pain in the arse and I miss him.

And where are you? Fuck knows.

I'm so lonesome I could cry.

Brett

From: **Ted Berry**
To: All Staff
Sent: 27 January 2009, 09.40
Subject: Harvey

You'll have heard about the tragic death of Harvey Harvey. He was a stand-up fella and a copywriter with a unique voice. He understood that true creativity involves taking it to the very edge and then some. Perhaps that's why he was found face down in a Nigerian river, though I suspect we'll never know the truth. His trade campaign for Trebor Extra Strong Mints will live on as a fitting memorial.

There will be a minute's silence at 12.00 and I will be hosting a drink to his memory in the Romper Room at 5.30. I'll be serving Harvey's favourite tipple.

Ted Berry
ΜC IDEΛZ

From: **Ted Berry**
To: Susi Judge-Davis-Gaultier
Sent: 27 January 2009, 09.41
Subject: Drinks order

Get in ten cases of Vimto for tonight. And some other stuff. Let's make it a bit of a do.

From: **Donald Gold**
To: Bill Geddes
Sent: 27 January 2009, 09.45
Subject: Re: Welcome to freedom!

Good to hear from you, Bill. It's grand to be free again too. Now there's an understatement. I am forever in Kaz's debt. She was amazing, wasn't she? We're at Dulles waiting for our flight. She's popped off to get me some tranqs for the journey, though I don't think it'll be necessary. This whole experience has toughened me up and suddenly flying holds little fear! Oh well, they say what doesn't kill you makes you stronger, don't they?

Guantanamo wasn't so bad, to be fair. The Marines were treading very carefully because they didn't know which way things were going to fall with Obama's inauguration. I wasn't in solitary and I had access to a TV and ping-pong. I was offered endless cups of tea and, being the only Jew in the compound, they even laid on a kosher menu for me! They were so sweet (and, I have to confess, pin-up sexy) that I couldn't bring myself to tell them that, actually, I could have murdered a bacon sarnie.

It was only a week, but I made some good friends in there. I'll definitely stay in touch with Ma'an. He's been waterboarded three times and confessed to lord knows what atrocities, but he still doesn't know what he's in for. Obviously we didn't see eye-to-eye on matters geo-political and he wasn't very comfortable with my sexuality, but it turned out we're both mad Liza Minnelli fans. He's actually seen *Stepping Out* more times than I have! It's incredible how song and dance can bring people together. Maybe there's a lesson there – or at least an Abba-based musical!

So what's been happening to the creative department? I need some gossip. You know how airports bore me!

Don

Sent from my BlackBerry

From: **Susi Judge-Davis-Gaultier**
To: All Staff
Sent: 27 January 2009, 09.48
Subject: Workies?

Any workies free to create a 'Welcome Home' banner to hang in reception? Paint, sequins and fabric will be supplied.

From: **Sally Wilton**
To: David Crutton
Sent: 27 January 2009, 09.53
Subject: Neil Godley

I've just heard from his solicitor and he's prepared to do a deal. No lawsuit against the agency or any individual employees, if we meet certain conditions. They are, in brief:

1 Full reinstatement of employment
2 With a 50% salary increase
3 And a 25% increase in cubicle volume
4 Employment on same terms for Nigel Godley (his brother, recently made redundant by Miller Shanks)
5 Unconditional public apology
6 Imposition of strict three-strikes regime for late delivery of time sheets
7 Immediate severance of contract with XL Security
8 In-house multi-denominational chapel*
9 Ovaltine to be made available in beverage machines

* This is absolutely non-negotiable. He suggests we put it in the Creative Romper Room.

Let me know how you wish to proceed.

Sally Wilton
PRINCESS
PAPERCLIP

From: **Bill Geddes**
To: Donald Gold
Sent: 27 January 2009, 10.07
Subject: Re: Welcome to freedom!

It's more than just gossip, actually. It's proper news. Harvey Harvey is dead. His body was found in a river in Nigeria. God knows what he was doing there. He disappeared last week and no one bothered to ask why or where. It's cast a bit of a pall over the place.

There's more. Last night Liam jumped off Waterloo Bridge. Correction: he *dived* (back, one and a half somersaults, pike – it would have got him at least a 37 in competition. See it for yourself on YouTube). Turns out he came seventh in the National Juniors when he was 14. He kept that one quiet.

Today's tabloids are full of it. Check the link below for the most entertaining view, though you might want to have several large pinches of salt at the ready.

Oh, and Milton finally jumped from the 5th.

Sadly, he bounced.

Say hello to Kaz. I don't think I'm her most favourite person right now, but give her a hug from me anyway. And see you soon!

Bill

---

dailymail.co.uk/news
Why did he bother?
By **Richard Littlejohn**

Here's a tale of selfless bravery to warm the cockles on a cold winter morn. A man dives into the freezing River Thames to save another. Liam O'Keefe is a bona fide hero. Well, isn't he?

Er, not sure about that. For a start, the drowning man was trying to kill himself, and he was making an excellent job of it too, by all accounts. I bet thanks weren't on his mind when the river police fished him out. But the bigger question is should decent, law-abiding British taxpayers thank O'Keefe?

The suicidal non-swimmer goes by the name of Zlatan Kovaćević. You don't need a degree in Serbo-Croat to work out that Zlatan Kovaćević translates as Asylum Seeker.

In an age when you can't drive six feet down the M25 without running over a squeegee-wielding Slav, should we be grateful that this 'hero' jumped to the rescue of a Serbian welfare scrounger?

No, if O'Keefe had let Kovaćević join the rest of the bottom feeders in the Thames Estuary, he'd have been doing us all a favour. But clearly he suffers from the fashionable delusion that everyone – including paedophiles, social workers and so-called 'asylum seekers' – has a right to life. He will probably get a medal from Gordon Brown and his washed-up excuse for a government, but he gets no praise from me. You don't need a degree in Gaelic to work out that Liam O'Keefe translates as Bog-Irish Prat.

From: **Donald Gold**
To: Bill Geddes
Sent: 27 January 2009, 10.12
Subject: Re: Welcome to freedom!

Wow! The Hard Man of the Balkans suicidal? That's hard to credit. And the Lard Arse of the Peat Bogs an aquatic hero? Even harder!

Sent from my BlackBerry

From: **Bill Geddes**
To: Donald Gold
Sent: 27 January 2009, 10.16
Subject: Re: Welcome to freedom!

I told you, several pinches of salt required. Liam was the one attempting suicide – the world's most graceful death leap, an easy gold in the National Suicide Championships. Zlatan jumped in to save him. Turned out he couldn't swim though, and Liam had to keep him afloat till the police launch arrived.

All the papers got it wrong, though only Littlejohn managed to give it a racial angle. Just goes to show there's only one thing less reliable than an adman and that's a hack. Still, if the spin turns our mate into a national hero, then who are we to complain?

From: **Lorraine Pallister**
To: Bill Geddes
Sent: 27 January 2009, 10.17
Subject: Re:

Hi Bill,

I'm still at the hospital. Our Hero is doing OK. I don't think they'll need to keep him in tonight. Mind you, I kind of hope they do, because there's a guy lurking outside the ward. I suspect he has

414

Turkish mates round the corner who'll descend on Liam the moment he leaves. Out of the bloody frying pan . . .

Anyway, at least he's still alive. Maybe if they discharge Zlatan at the same time, I can hire him as a bodyguard. He has a murderous look about him.

Bye for now,

Lorraine

Sent from my iPhone

From: **Bill Geddes**
To: Lorraine Pallister
Sent: 27 January 2009, 10.25
Subject: Re:

I'm guessing the Turkish thing is about money. Can you find out how much and I'll see what I can rustle up. By the way, the Turks aren't his only problem. David Crutton is itching to stick him with the office thefts. I'm surprised the cops haven't been to talk to him yet.

Sorry to put a downer on things. But like you say, at least he's alive. And you're right about Zlatan. I saw him take down a coked-up pit bull with a single blow to the throat. He is very handy in a fight, so keep him sweet. And remind him that he owes his life to Liam. Just don't let him see the *Mail* or else his murderous attentions will be focused entirely on Richard Littlejohn.

Keep your spirits up and I'll check in later.

From: **David Crutton**
To: Sally Wilton
Sent: 27 January 2009, 10.32
Subject: Re: Neil Godley

Outrageous. Who's his solicitor? Arthur bloody Scargill? He's got us in a bad place though. Normally, I wouldn't give an inch on this, but I don't want to lose you in the fallout, Sally. You're too valuable an asset to this company.

With that in mind, I think we should agree to everything. Except the public apology. I don't do those. And say no to the Ovaltine. That's just taking the piss.

Moving on, when will O'Keefe be well enough to be questioned by the police? I want the maximum sentence for that bastard.

From: **Lorraine Pallister**
To: Bill Geddes
Sent: 27 January 2009, 10.37
Subject: Re:

Don't worry about Crutton. Dealing with him now.

From: **Lorraine Pallister**
To: David Crutton
Sent: 27 January 2009, 10.59
Subject: It's been a while . . .

Hi David. Back in the day I was a PA at Miller Shanks. I wonder if you remember me. Probably not. I don't think you took much notice of anyone below account-director level.

But I remember you. Very well. Very well indeed.

I remember you at the 2000 Christmas party when you came back from Romania to dance the night away with your old pals.

The time we had! More to the point, the time *you* had! Remember how you took a bunch of us up to the boardroom to help you hoover up the 'sugar' that Vince Douglas had spilt on the table? You were definitely the best hooverer, an example to us all.

Then I remember how you sent most of us out because you wanted a private board meeting with that honey-toned CEO from Miller Shanks Puerto Rico. She was old enough to be J-lo's mum, but let me tell you, if J-lo looks that good at 50+, she'll be doing ever so well.

I'm not sure why you sent us out because the room had glass walls, didn't it? We could see your meeting even if we couldn't hear the important company business you were discussing. Maybe it was the language barrier, but it did appear you were having a mostly non-verbal discussion.

Zoë Clarke was there too. Remember her? An excitable PA who used a lot of exclamation marks in her emails. A bit like this:

> 'You know that disposable camera I got from Secret Santa??????!!!!!!!!!! I took loads of pics at the party!!!!!!!!!!!! Just got them back from the chemist!!!!!!!!!! They're brilliant!!!!!!!!! Come and see!!!!!!!!!!!!!!!!!!!'

Well, I did 'come and see'. I think she missed her calling because her photos were superb, really artistic. She had pictures of everything. The hoovering, your mostly non-verbal discussion with the nice Puerto Rican lady, the bit afterwards where you parked your dinner in Daniel Westbrooke's desk drawer, the lot.

Me and Zoë still see each other from time to time. It's nice to get together and catch up, look at old photo albums, stuff like that. Maybe we should get together too. It would be great to reminisce about the old days. I could get Zoë to bring her photos. Or per-haps she could upload them on to Flickr so the whole world can enjoy them.

Let me know if you're interested.

By the way, I used to go out with another old workmate, Liam O'Keefe. Even though we're not an item any more, I still look out for him. You'll be pleased to know that he's doing well after his heroic ordeal last night. He should be as right as rain in a few days. He'd recover a lot quicker if he knew he wouldn't be facing any stress when he gets out of hospital. Like the pressure of trying to find work in this terrible economic climate, and the worry that the police might want to question him about the theft of some silly paperclips.

As a modern, caring boss, I'm sure you'll be delighted to welcome him back to the office after a short recuperative break. Perhaps with a small raise to help him through the recession.

Anyway, great catching up with you. And do get in touch if you want to do the Friends Reunited thing. Hey, maybe we could do a slide show!

Best wishes,

Lorraine Pallister

Sent from my iPhone

From: **David Crutton**
To: Sally Wilton
Sent: 27 January 2009, 11.03
Subject: O'Keefe

I've had a change of heart on this one. I don't think we should press charges. What's the point of sending him to prison where he'll only mix with career criminals and emerge a hardened recidivist? We'd simply be handing society another problem it doesn't need, wouldn't we? It will better serve the greater good if we bring him back into the fold and help him through his issues with counselling. Call the police and let them know of our decision.

From: **David Crutton**
To: Dotty Podidra
Sent: 27 January 2009, 11.05
Subject: O'Keefe

When Godley returns to work, remind me to e him re a raise for O'Keefe.

From: **Dotty Podidra**
To: David Crutton
Sent: 27 January 2009, 11.06
Subject: Re: O'Keefe

Neil Godley's coming back?! And Liam?!! OK!!!

From: **Janice Crutton**
To: David Crutton
Sent: 27 January 2009, 11.15
Subject: FYI . . .

. . . you have:

Daughter	1	Status: very poorly
Son	1	Status: missing

(Just in case you give a damn.)

From: **David Crutton**
To: Dotty Podidra
Sent: 27 January 2009, 11.16
Subject:

Did I not ask you first thing this morning to look for Noah?

From: **Dotty Podidra**
To: David Crutton
Sent: 27 January 2009, 11.17
Subject: Re:

No, you didn't.

From: **David Crutton**
To: Dotty Podidra
Sent: 27 January 2009, 11.18
Subject: Re:

Did you by any chance look for him anyway?

From: **Dotty Podidra**
To: David Crutton
Sent: 27 January 2009, 11.19
Subject: Re:

No. Sorry. Should I have?

From: **David Crutton**
To: Dotty Podidra
Sent: 27 January 2009, 11.20
Subject: Re:

Yes! Do it now.

---

blogass.co.uk
Posted by **Hornblower**
27/01/09, 11.29 GMT

Crépuscule dans le Périgord
Partie 83: le Dilemme

Ah, Madame Fortune, quelle maîtresse volage elle est. Never let us try to second-guess her, for she will confound us at every turn.

In my last post, I might have betrayed *un gros chagrin*. I had the unsettling intuition that I had reached *le début de la fin*. 'Mais pas du tout!' Mme. Fortune decreed. I had actually arrived at *la fin de le début*.

Allow me to relate the latest twist in *la fameuse vie de Hornblower*:

At dawn yesterday I was awoken not by *le coq*, but by a tumult at the door. Papin turfed me from *le lit matrimonial* with the gruff instruction to send whomever on their way. 'Si c'est les flics, dis-leur que le garçon à dix-huit ans,' he added.

But it wasn't the police. It was what seemed to be the entire London *communauté littéraire* literally (ha!) camping on *ma véranda*. To what did I owe this invasion?

I was rapidly informed that word of my modest blog has travelled far and wide; that, shockingly, *ma célébrité est universelle*! I was staggered. In all sincerity, I sought no spotlight for my rudimentary jottings. I honestly cared not a fig whether or not anyone read them. Despite my *indifférence*, however, it seems that my hastily scribbled musings on *une vie plus simple* have struck a chord and captured that elusive zeitgeist.

And so there they were, gathered as
Mme. Fortune had ordered them,
publishers from houses grand and small
clamouring for *mon autograph*.

But was this what I wanted? The question
exercised me greatly as they trooped into
my *cuisine* to vie for my hand and drink
me out of *café*. Should I give up my hard-
earned idyll in the balmy vales of Périgord
for the whirligig of launch parties, book
tours and Sunday supplement profiles?

Despite their entreaties, my mind was
quickly made up. I began to formulate the
polite but firm *non merci* with which I
would send them on their way.

Papin finally stirred and, fetchingly
dressed in Celine's silken kimono,
surveyed the assembled literati. He raised
an owlish eyebrow and in his *style
inimitable* muttered, 'Quel groupe des
cons. Ils sont exactement comme toi, ma
salope. Allez tous vous faire enculer à
Londres!'

Once again it took *mon ami sage* to make
everything clear. He was right. If our
troubled world's increasingly beleaguered
citizens need me to provide them with *une
mesure* of solace garnished with *un
soupçon* of earthy Gallic insight, then who
am I to begrudge them?

But which imprint deserves my favour? I
am spoilt for choice. One editrice, though,
is in prime position, if only because I
pitied the very sight of her. Such was her

determination to sign me that she camped the entire *nuit glacée* on my doorstep. The poor mite was hypothermic and she had to be taken to *l'hôpital*. I fear that the damage wreaked by *l'hiver cruel* will enforce her retirement as une *nageuse synchronisée*.

Monsieur Bloomsbury can flaunt his Harry Potter swag all he likes. Dear Katie's devotion to *mes mots humbles* has won *mon coeur*.

Views:	1,392,095
Comments:	3,621

MSN:

MiltShake:	Cooee, I'm here!
sjdG:	Hooray! How's your neck?
MiltShake:	Stiff. (Said actress to bish!) Doc says I have to wear a brace.
sjdG:	Poor you. Does it look horrid?
MiltShake:	Not too ghastly. Nipped home and covered it in lovely Designers' Guild fabric. Looks fab with my mauve Thomas Pink.
sjdG:	You're a total fashion god. I am not worthy!
MiltShake:	☺
sjdG:	So, how's it feel to have done it?
MiltShake:	Done what?
sjdG:	Getting on BB!
MiltShake:	Shhhh!!! That's sooo hush-hush. Philip says I have to sign the Official Secrets Act or something.
sjdG:	Philip??
MiltShake:	Producer. Total darling. He's Scottish, you know.

sjdG:	Think you mentioned it. I'll keep mum on subject. Guess what?? I'm organizing a party for tonight!!!!
MiltShake:	Pour moi??
sjdG:	Sadly no. For stupid dead HH. But I'm having a DJ and canapes and everything!!!
MiltShake:	Hooray!! And can we pretend it's for me??!!
sjdG:	Of course! Just ignore the speeches for HH. BTW, did you hear about Zlatan and Liam?
MiltShake:	Total copycats! Jumping off stuff is my thing.
sjdG:	Sooo uncreative. Don't know why TB hired them. Still, at least Liam's gone now. Next stop jail. Whoopee!! ☺☺☺
DottyPod:	He's coming back!! DC just told me!!!
sjdG:	Noooooo!!!!!!! ☹☹☹
MiltShake:	Why?????????????????
DottyPod:	Dunno! Gotta go. Have to find Noah Crutt. Any ideas?
MiltShake:	Try the Ark. OMG, I'm soooo funny today!!!!!

From:	**Susi Judge-Davis-Gaultier**
To:	All Staff
Sent:	27 January 2009, 11.59
Subject:	Minute's silence

Ted has asked me to remind you that the minute's silence in memory of Harvey Harvey will commence in sixty seconds.

Susi Judge-Davis-Gaultier
Assistant to Ted Berry

From: **Róisín O'Hooligan**
To: Susi Judge-Davis-Gaultier
Sent: 27 January 2009, 12.00
Subject: Re: Minute's silence

Phones are going mental. Can I answer them or do I have to wait till the minute's over?

From: **Susi Judge-Davis-Gaultier**
To: Róisín O'Hooligan
Sent: 27 January 2009, 12.00
Subject: Re: Minute's silence

Better wait. Only 13 seconds to go!

From: **Pertti Van Helden**
To: David Crutton
Sent: 27 January 2009, 12.01
Subject: Phenomenatic coinciment!

Hello Dave, my old friend! After all years what a surprise I am finding the reason for email and in not the happy situation also. Yes, I have concerned news to told to you.

I begin the begin. Last the night my son Veiko and his power hair metal rock band Dethrush play Helsinki. As the legendary head-smasher from long ago, once again I put on the spandex pant and join the mash pit. I do not mind to told I have not danced the same since Aqua sing its song in a creative pitch you might be recalling! Everything go groovy and Veiko do the tradition crowd surf. This is where the matter go a small bit wrong. Veiko land on his old father and though I have excellent top-body strengths thank you to train for the Finland Strongest Man Over 50 competition, I fall and I start a domino of hard rock fans to fall also to the floors!

To cut the story shortly, a few fans were make injured and four go the hospital. Myself I have the dislocation finger that make type email very slow and painedful! One young fan has the big bang to the head. There is something recognizable about him that I cannot place on the finger. I ask him the name but he not remembered. Bang has gave him the amnesty. I look his pocket and find passport. I cannot believe my eye! He look exact same as the father!

Yes, he is Noah. Natural, when I leave the hospital I take him with and he recover in my apartments. I am fill of the hope that a strong meal of raw herring will have him again the memorize. It is very amazing fish and maybe you hear I leave the advertising to make the promote of its incredible superpowers.

I think that Noah is not too well to travel and you must come to here to take home. You are very most welcome, natural. I put in the freezer a bottle of herring oil vodka to toast our reunitation!

Pertti Van Helden
TheHeroicHerring.com

From: **David Crutton**
To: Dotty Podidra
Sent: 27 January 2009, 12.03
Subject:

What's my diary look like?

From: **Dotty Podidra**
To: David Crutton
Sent: 27 January 2009, 12.04
Subject: Re:

Big and black with 'DIARY' on the front (in gold). Why?

From: **David Crutton**
To: Dotty Podidra
Sent: 27 January 2009, 12.05
Subject: Re:

Jesus fuck.

WHAT EVENTS AND APPOINTMENTS DO I HAVE WRITTEN DOWN
IN MY DIARY THAT ARE SCHEDULED TO TAKE PLACE BETWEEN
NOW AND THE END OF THE DAY?

Capisce?

From: **Dotty Podidra**
To: David Crutton
Sent: 27 January 2009, 12.06
Subject: Re:

Sorry. Here you go:

12.30:	Ted, general review
12.50:	update with Sally (stationery issues)
1.00:	Fabio, anger sesh
1.40:	lunch (veggie smoothie, Mars Bar)
1.45:	Project Jack Rabbit, research debrief
3.15:	meditation (transcendental)
3.20:	Project March Hare, tissue session
3.45:	creative review, Murray Mints
4.00:	meditation (yogic)
4.05:	Enola, catch up on new biz
4.15:	Kirsten, wash and blow dry
4.35:	Me (Dotty!), personal assessment
4.50:	Fat Harry (no idea what this is about!)
5.00:	welcome home drinks for Don and Kazu
5.15:	Bill, GIT timing plans
5.30:	memorial drink for Harvey Harvey
7.00:	dinner, Ivy Club, Camille Brunel & Betina Tofting (Esmée Éloge)

From: **David Crutton**
To: Dotty Podidra
Sent: 27 January 2009, 12.07
Subject: Re:

Cancel everything. Get me on earliest flight to Helsinki.

From: **Dotty Podidra**
To: David Crutton
Sent: 27 January 2009, 12.08
Subject: Re:

Helsinki??

From: **David Crutton**
To: Dotty Podidra
Sent: 27 January 2009, 12.09
Subject: Re:

It's the capital of Finland.

From: **Dotty Podidra**
To: David Crutton
Sent: 27 January 2009, 12.10
Subject: Re:

Right. Why do you need to go there?

From: **David Crutton**
To: Dotty Podidra
Sent: 27 January 2009, 12.11
Subject: Re:

If it's any of your fucking business, because Noah is there. But you'd know that already if you'd got off your lazy fucking butt and found the idiot.

From: **Dotty Podidra**
To: David Crutton
Sent: 27 January 2009, 12.12
Subject: Re:

Sorry. I'm on it now.

From: **Sally Wilton**
To: All Staff
Sent: 27 January 2009, 12.13
Subject: Health and safety

Due to the discovery of a dead salamander in Tank 2, the SenzDep Think Tanks™ have been shut down until further notice. The manufacturer has been contacted and will be making a thorough investigation.

Until their inquiries are completed, anyone wishing to achieve an altered state of solitary karmic bliss should see Róisín on reception. She has been issued with a supply of earplugs and airline-style sleep masks.

Thank you for your cooperation.

Sally Wilton
PRINCESS
PAPERCLIP

From: **Sally Wilton**
To: All Staff
Sent: 27 January 2009, 12.14
Subject: Workies?

Could I have a workie to remove the dead salamander from Tank 2?

Sally Wilton
PRINCESS
PAPERCLIP

From: **Sally Wilton**
To: All Staff
Sent: 27 January 2009, 12.15
Subject: Carla Evans

Just to let everyone know that Carla has had to go home with suspected salamander poisoning.

Sally Wilton
PRINCESS
PAPERCLIP

From: **Dotty Podidra**
To: David Crutton
Sent: 27 January 2009, 12.16
Subject: Helsinki

Earliest I could get:

BJ634
STN   Dep: 14.15
HEL   Arr: 17.10

You need to leave right away.

From: **David Crutton**
To: Dotty Podidra
Sent: 27 January 2009, 12.17
Subject: Re: Helsinki

Business class?

From: **Dotty Podidra**
To: David Crutton
Sent: 27 January 2009, 12.18
Subject: Re: Helsinki

It's BizzyJet. Don't think they do business class. You can pay extra to get a blanket though. You really have to go now.

From: **David Crutton**
To: Dotty Podidra
Sent: 27 January 2009, 12.19
Subject: Re: Helsinki

Book cab to Heathrow.

From: **Dotty Podidra**
To: David Crutton
Sent: 27 January 2009, 12.20
Subject: Re: Helsinki

Are you sure? Flight goes from Stansted.

From: **David Crutton**
To: Dotty Podidra
Sent: 27 January 2009, 12.21
Subject: Re: Helsinki

Fuck's sake. Remind me to fire you when I get back.

From: **Dotty Podidra**
To: David Crutton
Sent: 27 January 2009, 12.22
Subject: Re: Helsinki

OK. Cab's here in two. Packed your passport, spare toothbrush and emergency jim-jams. Good luck!

	MSN:
sjdG:	TB wants to know when review with DC is going to start. You know he hates running late.
DottyPod:	It's not happening. DC about to leave for Helsinki.
sjdG:	Helsinki??
DottyPod:	Capital of Finland.
sjdG:	Why?
DottyPod:	Probably cos it's centrally located with good transport links to the rest of the country.
sjdG:	No, ninny, why's DC going there??
DottyPod:	Right. Cos Noah's there.
sjdG:	Why?
DottyPod:	Now you've got me!

From: **David Crutton**
To: Janice Crutton
Sent: 27 January 2009, 12.36
Subject: FYI . . .

. . . after having cleared yesterday afternoon's and this morning's diaries, and having been up the full night searching for our son, I have found him. Noah is in Helsinki. He was injured at a rock concert. Would he have run away had his father not left home (not, it must be stated for the record, of his own volition)? That is a question for others to decide, possibly a judge in the Family Division of the High Court.

I am leaving now for Finland to bring him home. My bag is packed and my flight is booked. Don't try to talk me out of it. If in your bitterness you can bring yourself to do it, give my love to Tam. I'd have done so in person, if you hadn't refused to tell me which hospital she is in.

> David Crutton
> 𝕿𝖍𝖊 𝕸𝖆𝖓

From: **Dotty Podidra**
To: David Crutton
Sent: 27 January 2009, 12.37
Subject: Re: Helsinki

Cab's here. You can't afford to be late. BizzyJet operates a strict first come first served policy for seat allocation and they're notorious for overbooking. Did you see Airport Airheads on Channel 5?

From: **Janice Crutton**
To: David Crutton
Sent: 27 January 2009, 12.40
Subject: Re: FYI . . .

What do you mean, 'injured'? Is he in hospital? You can't just leave it like that. I'm worried stupid as it is. How the hell is he? Tell me, David.

　Sent from my BlackBerry

From: **David Crutton**
To: Janice Crutton
Sent: 27 January 2009, 12.41
Subject: Out of Office AutoReply

I am out of the office. Please direct inquiries to dotty@meerkat360.co.uk

From: **Janice Crutton**
To: David Crutton
Sent: 27 January 2009, 12.46
Subject: Re: FYI . . .

Answer me, David. I know you don't go anywhere without your BlackBerry. You sleep with it under your pillow. And don't think I haven't noticed that you set your alarm for 4.00am so you can check your inbox. Jesus, you even wrapped it in a Ziploc bag and took it swimming when we were on holiday. Just bloody answer me.

Sent from my BlackBerry

From: **David Crutton**
To: Janice Crutton
Sent: 27 January 2009, 12.47
Subject: Out of Office AutoReply

I am out of the office. Please direct inquiries to dotty@meerkat360.co.uk

From: **David Crutton**
To: Ted Berry
Sent: 27 January 2009, 12.49
Subject: GIT

Sorry about ducking out of the review. I'm en route to Finland on a family matter. You know my views on so-called 'compassionate leave', and normally I wouldn't hesitate to have myself fired, but my son is there and he has amnesia. More worrying, he is in the care of a fuckwit of the highest order and I have to extricate him before he's initiated into a herring-worshipping religious cult.

As per usual, if anything needs my attention, I am reachable by phone or email 24/7. I expect to return tomorrow. Will keep you advised.

Sent from my BlackBerry

From: **Bill Geddes**
To: Lorraine Pallister
Sent: 27 January 2009, 12.50
Subject: O'Keefe

How's da patient?

From: **David Crutton**
To: Pertti Van Helden
Sent: 27 January 2009, 12.53
Subject: Re: Phenomenatic coinciment!

Good to hear from you, Pertti. It goes without saying that I'm enormously grateful to you for letting me know of Noah's situation.

It also goes without saying that I hold you and your son fully responsible for his injuries. If he has suffered any long-term damage, I have access to not only the very finest neurologists but also the most sadistic lawyers. With their assistance, I will descend on you and your entire nation of fucked-up liberal herring lovers with a force that will make the Soviet invasion of '39 look like a Saga coach tour.

I am on my way to Finland now. My flight lands at 17.10. Please have him ready to leave.

Sent from my BlackBerry

From: **Lorraine Pallister**
To: Bill Geddes
Sent: 27 January 2009, 13.03
Subject: Re: O'Keefe

How's da patient? You want the honest answer? I feel like killing him.

Sent from my iPhone

You are as hilariful as the usuals, Dave! Your latest emailing is reminiscing me of the time I come Miller Shanks London for Euro CEO conferences and you tell taxi driver take me to the Tower Hamlet to meet proper English peoples. How did you saying it? The sort which greet the EU cousins with Stanley Knife. I am think Stanley Knife must be the famous Pearly King, but I see only the fights between the Pakistan persons and the traditional cockney chavs. This is when I realize you are pulling my chains and I laugh uproarious at your mischievity!

You will be happy I inform you that Noah is make a good progression. I am jerk memories of his father with stories of crazy adventures we are having in the old time. He is tell me his father is the pompousful prick head. This is showing the memories are coming back and he has also the Crutton senses of ironicalism that is never failing to split the Van Helden rib area.

I notice he has the gay word writted in the tattoo, so you will be also happy he does not come in the hand of Finland homophobist Nazi skinhead. Sadnessly our joyful nation of 'liberal herring lovers' has the small numbers of these misguiding persons in its middle. I assure him that even though I full blood Viking pussy hound, I am comfortables with his homosexualness. As soon as he is well I prove this by we go in sauna and I beat his naked back with the fine twigs of Finnish birch.

I look forward to your come. As the Englishes are saying, I stick the kettle up!

Pertti Van Helden
TheHeroicHerring.com

From: **Bill Geddes**
To: Lorraine Pallister
Sent: 27 January 2009, 13.17
Subject: Re: O'Keefe

Doesn't sound good. Want to confide?

From: **Lorraine Pallister**
To: Bill Geddes
Sent: 27 January 2009, 13.26
Subject: Re: O'Keefe

The Turkish army is outside. One of them came in with a bunch of grapes and a final reminder. Liam owes them £18,000, half of it debt and the rest punitive interest. I made him explain. He must have been truly suicidal because the stunt he pulled to get himself into this mess was a self-inflicted death sentence.

We'll never make it out of here alive. I'm mad as hell with him, and also with myself for getting fooled again. Honestly, I'd walk out on him now, but with the mob out there, I might as well have hostage lipsticked across my forehead.

Sent from my iPhone

From: **Bill Geddes**
To: Lorraine Pallister
Sent: 27 January 2009, 13.27
Subject: Re: O'Keefe

Jesus, he's a prat. I'd kill him if I were you.

From: **Lorraine Pallister**
To: Bill Geddes
Sent: 27 January 2009, 13.28
Subject: Re: O'Keefe

Can't do that.

> Sent from my iPhone

From: **Bill Geddes**
To: Lorraine Pallister
Sent: 27 January 2009, 13.29
Subject: Re: O'Keefe

Why not?

From: **Lorraine Pallister**
To: Bill Geddes
Sent: 27 January 2009, 13.30
Subject: Re: O'Keefe

Cos I love him.

> Sent from my iPhone

From: **Bill Geddes**
To: Lorraine Pallister
Sent: 27 January 2009, 13.35
Subject: Re: O'Keefe

Ah . . . That changes everything.

Do your best to stay calm and I'll try to rustle up some cash. I can get my hands on about a grand right away. Will that buy him some time . . .?

Thought not.

It might be an idea if he fell out of bed and broke an arm or something, thus necessitating an extra night or two in hospital. Given your mood, perhaps you could give him a shove in the general direction of the floor.

I'll have a serious think about solutions. Be in touch soon.

From: **Róisín O'Hooligan**
To: All Staff
Sent: 27 January 2009, 13.36
Subject: Liam

Got a chick from Speedo on the phone. She wants to talk to Liam. Anyone know which hospital/prison he's in?

Róisín
Reception

From: **Bill Geddes**
To: Róisín O'Hooligan
Sent: 27 January 2009, 13.37
Subject: Re: Liam

Put her through to me.

From: **Kirsten Richardson**
To: Creative Department
Sent: 27 January 2009, 13.40
Subject: Poor, poor Harvey, may his soul rest in eternal peacitude

Though I'm as upset as all of you by the tragic news, I'm available if anyone wants a Harvey Harvey 'pudding bowl' in time for this evening's memorial do.

From: **Róisín O'Hooligan**
To: Bill Geddes
Sent: 27 January 2009, 13.41
Subject: Liam

Got another chick on the line for Liam. This one is from Zoggs. She reckons they make swimming goggles. Want me to put her through?

From: **Bill Geddes**
To: Róisín O'Hooligan
Sent: 27 January 2009, 13.42
Subject: Re: Liam

Put her on hold until I've finished with the Speedo lady.

From: **Janice Crutton**
To: Dotty Podidra
Sent: 27 January 2009, 13.57
Subject:

Hi Dotty

I'm sorry to bother you at work, but do you know what's going on with Noah? Is he really in Finland and is he injured? If so, how badly? And is David going there to bring him home? My husband has told me nothing and I am going out of my mind with worry. Somehow Noah has acquired a gay tattoo. Frankly, anything could have happened to him.

You might have sensed that David and I aren't exactly getting along swimmingly at the moment, and I appreciate that your first loyalty is to him, but if you know anything at all, I beg you to help me out.

Best,

Janice

From: **Dotty Podidra**
To: Janice Crutton
Sent: 27 January 2009, 14.09
Subject: Re:

Hi Janice

David is on his way to Finland now. All being well, he's about to take off. His flight number is BJ634 and he's due to land in Helsinki (the capital of Finland) at 17.10. I booked him into a superior room (with separate sleep and working areas and wireless internet access) at the Scandic Marski Hotel for one night. Noah is over there, but David didn't say anything about him being hurt.

To be honest, I wasn't aware of any 'unswimmingness' between you, but I'm sure he'll want you to be the first to hear any news. He'll definitely be in touch as soon as he knows anything.

He's got his BlackBerry with him. Why don't you try him on that?

Let me know if I can help with anything else!

Dotty

From: **David Crutton**
To: Dotty Podidra
Sent: 27 January 2009, 14.10
Subject:

Before I left, did I mention that if Janice gets in touch, not to tell her anything?

From: **Dotty Podidra**
To: David Crutton
Sent: 27 January 2009, 14.11
Subject: Re:

No.

From: **David Crutton**
To: Dotty Podidra
Sent: 27 January 2009, 14.12
Subject: Re:

I'm sure I did.

Sent from my BlackBerry

From: **Dotty Podidra**
To: David Crutton
Sent: 27 January 2009, 14.13
Subject: Re:

You definitely didn't.

From: **David Crutton**
To: Dotty Podidra
Sent: 27 January 2009, 14.14
Subject: Re:

Whatever. Should Janice get in touch, don't say anything about anything whatsoever. At all. Got that?

Sent from my BlackBerry

From: **Dotty Podidra**
To: David Crutton
Sent: 27 January 2009, 14.15
Subject: Re:

Absolutely. Won't say a word.

	MSN:
DottyPod:	Aaaggghhhh!!!!!!
sjdG:	OMG!!! What??????!!!!!!!!!!
DottyPod:	Just told JC everything I know about DC going to Helsinki (cap of Finland) and then got e from DC telling me not to say a word to JC about anything whatsoever at all!
sjdG:	Oh dear. Not good. Just deny everything. Usually works for me with TB!!!
MiltShake:	Or act dumb. Usually works for you, Dot!!
sjdG:	OMG, you are so totally hilarious today, Milt!
MiltShake:	Aren't I just? I am going to be sooo the funniest on shh, you know what.
DottyPod:	What's shh, you know what?!
MiltShake:	See, no one plays dumb like you, Dotty!!
sjdG:	What are you guys wearing to the Harvey drink?
MiltShake:	In a total tiz about that. Black is so not my colour. Makes me look jowly.
sjdG:	Don't be silly. You're a total Johnny Depp in your black Alexander McQueen with the three-quarter-length trousers, esp if you accessorize with a black silk

	neckerchief and pirate hoops.
MiltShake:	You don't think hoops are a smidge gay?
sjdG:	What are you like??!! They're 100% beef.
MiltShake:	You've convinced me. I'll have to get a lower-leg wax though. What about you?
sjdG:	My legs are perfectly smooth, thank you!!
MiltShake:	No, silly! I mean what are you wearing?
sjdG:	Getting Pierre to bike round my Viv Westwood.
MiltShake:	The crinoline? Totally Q Victoria!! Please be my prom date!!
sjdG:	Hooray! Let's party!!
DottyPod:	Can't believe you two.
MiltShake:	Poor Cinders. No dwess for the ball?
sjdG:	LOL ☺☺☺
DottyPod:	Harvey is dead. I know he was mad as a stick, but he was still a nice guy and all you care about is what you're going to wear.
sjdG:	We're just trying to show him the proper amount of respect.
MiltShake:	Exactly! What sort of impression are you going to create in your frumpy work clothes?
DottyPod:	At least I care.
sjdG:	I am so hurt by that! I care 150%. I've been crying so much my crepe de chine blouse is totally watermarked.
MiltShake:	Tragedy ☹ I love that blouse.
DottyPod:	Excuse me!! HARVEY IS DEAD!!!!
MiltShake:	Listen to yourself, Dot! Susi's blouse is a total one-off and all

444

	you care about is stupid Harvey.
sjdG:	Thanks for being so
	understanding, Milt (unlike some).
	Got wax strips in my drawer. Pop
	up in 5 and I'll do your leggies.
MiltShake:	Only if you promise to hurt me,
	baby!!!!!

From: **Bill Geddes**
To: Lorraine Pallister
Sent: 27 January 2009, 14.59
Subject: a possible solution

How do you think Liam would feel about reprising his Waterloo Bridge dive off a cliff in Acapulco? Or possibly the Sydney Harbour Bridge?

From: **Lorraine Pallister**
To: Bill Geddes
Sent: 27 January 2009, 15.01
Subject: Re: a possible solution

Why??

   Sent from my iPhone

From: **Bill Geddes**
To: Lorraine Pallister
Sent: 27 January 2009, 15.02
Subject: Re: a possible solution

Just been talking to a very nice lady from Speedo. And another very nice lady from Zoggs. Liam's dive is a viral smash, apparently, and they both want him to do it again on 35mm. Off an Acapulco cliff in Speedos. Or the Sydney Harbour Bridge in Zoggs. For money.

From: **Lorraine Pallister**
To: Bill Geddes
Sent: 27 January 2009, 15.03
Subject: Re: a possible solution

I'll push him off myself if it pays enough to clear his debts. How much?

Sent from my iPhone

From: **Bill Geddes**
To: Lorraine Pallister
Sent: 27 January 2009, 15.06
Subject: Re: a possible solution

Auction's ongoing. Speedo ahead on £45k. I'll forgo my agent's cut.

From: **Lorraine Pallister**
To: Bill Geddes
Sent: 27 January 2009, 15.07
Subject: Re: a possible solution

Say yes to whoever goes to £75k and will pay an advance today. Preferably cash.

Sent from my iPhone

From: **Bill Geddes**
To: Lorraine Pallister
Sent: 27 January 2009, 15.08
Subject: Re: a possible solution

He agreed?

From: **Lorraine Pallister**
To: Bill Geddes
Sent: 27 January 2009, 15.09
Subject: Re: a possible solution

Not exactly. He's asleep. Mind you, I'm not sure they'll want to do it once they've seen him without his kit on. He's hardly the Adonis he used to be.

Sent from my iPhone

From: **Bill Geddes**
To: Lorraine Pallister
Sent: 27 January 2009, 15.10
Subject: Re: a possible solution

Don't worry, I already emailed them a jpeg, but not before I got the studio to do some Photoshop. They made him look like Michael Phelps.

FYI, Zoggs just bid £53k.

From: **Ted Berry**
To: Creative Department
Sent: 27 January 2009, 15.14
Subject:

I know Harvey's death is a bummer, but the lack of effort is ridiculous. I've seen more industry in a crack house. Do I have to remind you how short-handed we are? Put your backs into it, guys. It's what Harvey would've wanted.

Ted Berry
MC IDEAZ

From: **Bill Geddes**
To: Lorraine Pallister
Sent: 27 January 2009, 15.38
Subject: Update

Speedo ahead at £60k.

From: **Susi Judge-Davis-Gaultier**
To: All Staff
Sent: 27 January 2009, 15.52
Subject: Memorial drink

For your information, here is the programme for tonight's celebration of Harvey Harvey's life:

5.30: Complimentary Heavenly Harvey (Vimto, warmed milk, Crème de Cassis, lime twist optional), a stunning new cocktail created by yours truly (that's me!)
5.35: Welcoming words from Ted Berry
5.45: *Dr Who* Theme, performed on solo ukulele by Yossi Mendoza
5.50: Open mic eulogies
6.30: *Daleks v Cybermen*, an interpretation in mime and custard pie by Mr Fraggles
6.45: Drinks, nibbles and dancing till late!!

Please be on time.

Susi Judge-Davis-Gaultier
Assistant to Ted Berry

From: **Bill Geddes**
To: Lorraine Pallister
Sent: 27 January 2009, 15.56
Subject: Update

Zoggs at £70k.

From: **Kazu Makino**
To: Bill Geddes
Sent: 27 January 2009, 16.06
Subject:

I'm still not speaking to you, but Don wants me to tell you we're in the cab. ETA 30 minutes.

    Sent from my BlackBerry

From: **Bill Geddes**
To: Lorraine Pallister
Sent: 27 January 2009, 16.08
Subject: Hold the front page!

Adidas just crashed the party. If he wears both their trunks and goggles, and jumps off the Golden Gate Bridge, they'll give him £100k. Is it a yes?

From: **Bill Geddes**
To: Kazu Makino
Sent: 27 January 2009, 16.16
Subject: Re:

Tell Don I can't wait to see him. Quite looking forward to seeing you too, even though you're still not talking to me.

A word of warning: visually dyslexic workies have prepared a welcome home banner. They've made Don look like a zombie Teletubby.

I'll do my best to be here when you get back, though I may be called away in my capacity as Liam's agent. I think I've got him his first showbiz deal!

From: **Lorraine Pallister**
To: Bill Geddes
Sent: 27 January 2009, 16.17
Subject: Re: Hold the front page!

More Turkish troops are massing by the pay and display machine. Will Adidas pay a cash deposit today? And how high is the Golden Gate?

    Sent from my iPhone

From: **Brett Topolski**
To: Liam O'Keefe
Sent: 27 January 2009, 16.22
Subject:

Your concern for our mate is overwhelming. What are you doing that's so important you can't even send a two-word message of condolence on my loss? 'Sorry, mate.' That would cover it.

You most likely don't give a shit, but I had an e from a guy who worked here at the beginning of last year. He's backpacking through India and he reckons he saw Vince checking into an ashram in Lucknow. Mind you, he also reckons he's spotted Tupac, Lennon and Hendrix, so I shouldn't set too much store by his probably stoned ramblings.

Write me, you bastard.

    Brett

From: **Bill Geddes**
To: Lorraine Pallister
Sent: 27 January 2009, 16.49
Subject: Re: Hold the front page!

£20k down in non-sequential notes. Golden Gate 67 metres

above water. And they want him fat – plays to their 'impossible is nothing' positioning.

From: **Lorraine Pallister**
To: Bill Geddes
Sent: 27 January 2009, 16.53
Subject: Re: Hold the front page!

Jesus. 67 metres? I don't know. Think I'd better wake him and ask.

Sent from my iPhone

From: **Róisín O'Hooligan**
To: All Staff
Sent: 27 January 2009, 17.02
Subject: The Jihadist . . .

. . . is back and to be perfectly honest he looks underwhelmed. I think he was expecting a hero's welcome, but all he's got is a sorry banner. Whoever was planning to form the reception committee should get their butts down here and pop some bubbly – apart from anything else, I'm parched.

Róisín
Reception

From: **Dotty Podidra**
To: Róisín O'Hooligan
Sent: 27 January 2009, 17.05
Subject: Re: The Jihadist . . .

Tell Don I'm really sorry. David was supposed to be making a speech, but he had to shoot off to Helsinki (capital of Finland). Can you keep him and Kaz amused for a couple of minutes? I'll round up some people, dig out David's notes and make the speech myself. He does deserve a proper welcome, doesn't he?

Mind you, he did get a free trip to Cuba. It's supposed to be lovely there these days!!

From: **Dotty Podidra**
To: All Staff
Sent: 27 January 2009, 17.06
Subject: Workies?

Any workies free to form an enthusiastic welcoming party for our returning heroes, Don and Kazu? Free champagne! And Kettle Chips!!

From: **Bill Geddes**
To: Lorraine Pallister
Sent: 27 January 2009, 17.09
Subject: Re: Hold the front page!

Any news?

From: **Lorraine Pallister**
To: Bill Geddes
Sent: 27 January 2009, 17.11
Subject: Re: Hold the front page!

He'll do it for £150k. And he wants to wear a helmet (Adidas branded, he doesn't mind). And he wants to meet David Beckham. Or Anna Kournikova.

      Sent from my iPhone

From: **Bill Geddes**
To: Lorraine Pallister
Sent: 27 January 2009, 17.12
Subject: Re: Hold the front page!

I'll make the call.

From: **Dotty Podidra**
To: David Crutton
Sent: 27 January 2009, 17.22
Subject:

With any luck you're landing about now. Hope you had a great flight and that you find Noah in good shape. Let me know if I can do anything from this end.

Dotty

PS: I just read out your welcoming speech for Don and Kaz. It went down really well. All the workies loved it!!

PPS: I haven't said a word about anything to Janice.

From: **Janice Crutton**
To: David Crutton
Sent: 27 January 2009, 17.23
Subject:

You'll have touched down in Helsinki and soon you'll be heading for the Scandic Marski. Yes, Dotty told me everything. Except what has happened to Noah. If you have any compassion at all, you'll call me as soon as you have news. Tam has improved a lot and I'm waiting for a doctor to discharge her. We should be home within the hour.

Call me, David. Please.

Janice

Sent from my BlackBerry

From: **Susi Judge-Davis-Gaultier**
To: All Staff
Sent: 27 January 2009, 17.25
Subject: Reminder

A quickie to remind you the super-fab celebration of tragic Harvey Harvey's amazing life kicks off in five!!

Susi Judge-Davis-Gaultier
Assistant to Ted Berry

From: **Dotty Podidra**
To: Susi Judge-Davis-Gaultier
Sent: 27 January 2009, 17.26
Subject: Re: Reminder

Just to let you know I won't be attending the 'party'. To be absolutely honest, Susi, I think it's all a bit tasteless. Have a lovely time though and I'll see you tomorrow.

From: **Susi Judge-Davis-Gaultier**
To: Milton Keane
Sent: 27 January 2009, 17.27
Subject: Help!!

Can you come and do up the hooks on my corset?!

From: **Milton Keane**
To: Susi Judge-Davis-Gaultier
Sent: 27 January 2009, 17.28
Subject: Re: Help!!

Just doing my face. Can't Dozy Dotty do it?

From: **Susi Judge-Davis-Gaultier**
To: Milton Keane
Sent: 27 January 2009, 17.29
Subject: Re: Help!!

Dotty not coming! Gutted. Gone to so much trouble with every-thing as well.

From: **Milton Keane**
To: Susi Judge-Davis-Gaultier
Sent: 27 January 2009, 17.30
Subject: Re: Help!!

What a bitch! Foundation applied. On my way. You can do my lippy!!

SMS:

Bill: Got a deal! On way to hospital. Will meet Adidas there

Lorraine: Bring champagne. Or beer. Just need fucking drink!

From: **Janice Crutton**
To: Dotty Podidra
Sent: 27 January 2009, 17.33
Subject: David

I've tried phoning, emailing and texting him, but he's not responding. Have you heard anything?

From: **Dotty Podidra**
To: Janice Crutton
Sent: 27 January 2009, 17.35
Subject: Re: David

I haven't heard a thing. According to Flight Tracker, his plane has landed. Maybe he's stuck in immigration. Remember when he flew to Beijing and he had that 'disagreement' with customs and they kept him in a cell overnight?? I'm going home now, but I'll keep trying him from there. I'll let you know if I make contact.

Chicken, beef or second-degree burns?

Six passengers were injured when their in-flight meals spontaneously combusted.

Passengers on a BizzyJet flight to Helsinki received the shock of their lives today when they peeled the foil off their in-flight cannelloni and their meals burst into flames. Six passengers are being treated in a Helsinki hospital for burns to their hands and faces.

One passenger described the scene as 'an indoor firework display'. He said: 'The guy next to me was a decent middle-aged sort, someone in advertising, but he went up like Guy Fawkes and I thought he was a suicide bomber. I was very glad I went for the beef and dumplings.'

BizzyJet spokesman Darren Bates said: 'There's been an ongoing issue with our new-recipe lasagne that the decision to switch to cannelloni was aimed at dealing with. Obviously, we have further work to do. We apologize to passengers inconvenienced by our search for the optimum in-flight gastronomic experience. I want to reassure everyone flying with us that the beef-stew-and-dumpling option offers a safe and 100% British menu choice.'

From: **Róisín O'Hooligan**
To: All Staff
Sent: 27 January 2009, 17.57
Subject: Surprise, surprise!

Anyone not yet in the Romper Room weeping for the loss of poor Harvey might be interested to know that he's here – just arrived and looking vaguely travel-weary. Shall I send him downstairs or is it poor form to tip up at your own wake?

Róisín
Reception

Wednesday
Mood: sick with love, gratitude and squirming remorse

	MSN:
KirstKutta:	Wkd party! Totally trolleyed.
MiltShake:	You were a very naughty young lady!!
KirstKutta:	OMG what did I do???!!!
MiltShake:	Cost you a blow dry to find out.
KirstKutta:	So wrecked I actually thought I saw Harvey!!
MiltShake:	Me too!!
KirstKutta:	OMFG. Was it like a collective hallucination?? Or an actual ghost??!!
MiltShake:	No, you prawn. It was an actual Harvey. He turned up and totally pooped the party.
KirstKutta:	Nooooooooooooooooooooooooo!!!!
MiltShake:	In the middle of the eulogies too.
KirstKutta:	Could've waited till we'd finished

	being nice about him.
MiltShake:	Total bighead. Never had him down for that. Thought he was just plain loopy.
KirstKutta:	Don't get 1 thing tho. Why was he at party if he was dead? Was he like frozen and transported to the future where they have the technology to bring him back to life? My mate Elliott says he saw that on Discovery.
MiltShake:	Funniest thing I *ever* heard! Muesli coming out of my nose!!

From: **Sally Wilton**
To: All Staff
Sent: 28 January 2009, 09.32
Subject: Workies?

I need all available workies in the Romper Room to de-vomit the ball pit. Rubber gloves and protective masks provided.

Sally Wilton
PRINCESS
PAPERCLIP

	MSN:
DottyPod:	Hi Milt. Is Susi in yet? Don't think she's too happy with me. I want to make up.
MiltShake:	She's not happy with you at all. You were completely out of order. FYI, she's not coming till later. She's block booked the morning with her therapist.
DottyPod:	Cos of me?!
MiltShake:	What are you like?! You're not

	that important. Do you know how shocked she was last night?
DottyPod:	Me too!! I was just on my way out when HH arrived. I thought he was a ghost!!
MiltShake:	OMG, you saw him?! Why didn't you stop him coming downstairs? Sooz was in the middle of her eulogy. He ruined everything for her. She will be so mad with you.
DottyPod:	You don't have to tell her.
MiltShake:	Of course I have to. She's my *best friend* and *best friends* tell each other *everything*. Gotta go. Million things to do.
DottyPod:	Is Cazza coming in?
MiltShake:	Don't be silly. Got to book her up for her next three awaydays.

From: **Sally Wilton**
To: All Staff
Sent: 28 January 2009, 09.43
Subject: Arrivals

Please welcome back Neil Godley, who rejoins us today after self-lessly helping to clear up the matter of the office thefts. Neil is joined by his twin brother Nigel, who will assist him in the efficient running of the company's finances.

To ensure there is no confusion as to their identities, Neil and Nigel have agreed to wear game-show-style name stickers for the period of one month.

Sally Wilton
PRINCESS
PAPERCLIP

Hello again, Janice Crutton! It is wonderful to make the acquaint on the phone yesterday night. I am still in the flabbergast that I am nurse maiden for both of the mans in your life.

You are pleased I tell you your strapping young homosexual Noah is make the exquisite recover from his injury with the head. His memories are full return. In this moment he is with my heterosexual son Veiko making the hard rock jamming in the rehearse room.

David is less good. The lasagne explode like the napalm and I am feared he will have permanent disfigurations. But it is the inner persons what is the important, and in his hearts David is the special great guy.

I am try make him suckle weak herring broth through the straw, but he is pined away and lose his appetites. I know he is crying for his loved ones because the bandage on his eyes is wet with moistfulness.

What he is really need in this moment is the lovingness of his good woman! I hope you are able travel to Helsinki. You must to stay and enjoy my welcomeness. As your British Ena Blyton writed in *Five Go Naked Ice Fishing*, 'herrings, sour creams and lashings of garlic vodka!'

I am now make myself usefuls. I go in his BilBerry and read his emails to him. If they are urgent in their essences I will type reply like his secretary.

'Take the letters down, Ms Van Helden!'

> Pertti Van Helden
> **TheHeroicHerring.com**

From: **Ted Berry**
To: All Staff
Sent: 28 January 2009, 09.50
Subject:

David is in Finland and Caroline is still expanding her horizons, which means, in short, that I'm in charge. This being the case, unless the matter is exceptionally important, keep the fuck out of my face. I am very fucking busy.

Ted Berry
MC IDEAZ

From: **Ted Berry**
To: Creative Department
Sent: 28 January 2009, 09.51
Subject:

Liam and Zlatan are on the mend.

Harvey is miraculously alive.

Fuck, even the sun is shining.

You no longer have a single excuse to mope around the place like work-shy humanities students.

This is a place of fucking business, so let's fucking do some.

Ted Fucking Berry
MC IDEAZ

From: **Janice Crutton**
To: Paula Sterling
Sent: 28 January 2009, 10.02
Subject:

Hi Paula

Just to let you know that I'll be out of the office for the rest of the week. Tamara and I are going to Finland. I'll have my BlackBerry if anything important crops up – but only if it's really important.

Janice

From: **Paula Sterling**
To: Janice Crutton
Sent: 28 January 2009, 10.07
Subject: Re:

Hi Janice

I know it's none of my business, but is taking a holiday a good idea right now? Everyone is paranoid about the redundancies that I know we're not supposed to talk about, but let's be honest, they're definitely going to happen, aren't they?

And should you be flying in your condition?

Paula

From: **Janice Crutton**
To: Paula Sterling
Sent: 28 January 2009, 10.10
Subject: Re:

You're right, Paula, it is none of your business. But since you've brought it up, if I have to make the choice between saving my family and saving my job, the former wins out.

I'm not sure whether David would prioritize his life in the same way. That's what I hope to find out in Finland.

As for my 'condition', it is, as of this moment, totally fucked. I don't believe it can be made any worse by one little airline flight.

Look after things for me. You're more than capable.

And if it's any consolation, when the redundancies that we're not supposed to talk about finally happen, those capabilities should see you safe.

Janice

PS: Can you ask Gabriella in Litigation if she'd be willing to represent David plus at least five others? We are going to bankrupt BizzyJet. Even in the worst recession, there is always work for lawyers.

	MSN:
Bilge:	You there, Kaz, or are you scouring the papers for injustices waiting to be smote by the samurai sword of Kaped Kaz.
Kazoo:	Couldn't possibly say.
Bilge:	Why?
Kazoo:	Cos I'm not talking to you.
Bilge:	But you are. 9 words in this thread alone!
Kazoo:	I can now add pedant to the rap sheet.
Dong:	Give him a break, Kaz. I need him to explain some stuff. What's the story on HH? He goes to Africa, dies and comes back a tribal elder? I'm confused. Is it jet lag? Or PTSD?
Bilge:	Neither. It's just plain confusing. A brief recap: HH responds to spam (standard Nigerian-heiress-needs-haven-for-her-millions stuff), flies out to Africa and wanders about for a bit in dazed HH fashion, before getting mugged for his

plastic and passport by loco backpacker who then gets himself murdered. Cops find passport on corpse, mistake ID and pronounce HH dead. Meanwhile, penniless, passport-less real HH finally meets his heiress who isn't a spammer after all, but really is a damsel in distress. They do some industrial-grade banking and find love over the transfer forms. After a quick trip to the consulate for a replacement passport, they fly back to Blighty on Mills & Boon flight 00LUV. Couldn't be simpler really. Or more plausible.

Dong: Think I'm with you. Now explain Liam. He's modelling swimwear for Adidas as a result of a failed yet aesthetically faultless suicide attempt?

Bilge: Summed up lucidly.

Dong: Unbelievable. How much is he getting?

Bilge: As his agent I have a duty of confidentiality and couldn't possibly say. Enough to pay off his various bookies, sharks and bar tabs though.

Kazoo: And what's your cut, Jerry Maguire?

Bilge: Strictly pro bono.

Kazoo: Aw, Saint Bill.

Bilge: Fair cop, Kaz. I've been a complete arse. Sorry, Don. But I only took over GIT on a caretaker basis. Do you want it back?

Dong: It's a bugger, isn't it?

Bilge: Total bugger. US client is the living

	dead, UK client is a wheedling imbecile and obviously you need a triple ethics bypass to go anywhere near it.
Dong:	Your judgement is spot-on.
Bilge:	So you want it back?
Dong:	What do you think?
Kazoo:	What are you guys doing for lunch?
Bilge:	You asking me to lunch?
Kazoo:	No. I'm asking what you're *doing*. Not the same thing at all.
Bilge:	Thought I might get me some Thai. You?
Kazoo:	Thai sounds OK. Might see you in there.
Bilge:	Will you talk to me?
Kazoo:	Not necessarily. But I'll let you pay.

From: **Liam O'Keefe**
To: Bill Geddes
Sent: 28 January 2009, 10.19
Subject: Luncheon

Where are you taking me, Jerry Maguire?

From: **Bill Geddes**
To: Liam O'Keefe
Sent: 28 January 2009, 10.20
Subject: Re: Luncheon

You're here? Thought you'd be taking another day's R&R. I'm going out with Don and Kaz. Thai. Wanna come?

From: **Liam O'Keefe**
To: Bill Geddes
Sent: 28 January 2009, 10.21
Subject: Re: Luncheon

Need to bulk up for Adidas. Can you guarantee a minimum of 3,000 calories?

From: **Bill Geddes**
To: Liam O'Keefe
Sent: 28 January 2009, 10.22
Subject: Re: Luncheon

They do an all-you-can-eat buffet for a recession-busting £6.99. Why not see how far you can push them?

From: **Liam O'Keefe**
To: Bill Geddes
Sent: 28 January 2009, 10.24
Subject: Re: Luncheon

Oh, I can push them. I'm wearing elasticated pants.

From: **Brett Topolski**
To: Liam O'Keefe
Sent: 28 January 2009, 10.33
Subject: I am so fucking pissed off with you I could punch out a plate-glass window and not feel any pain whatsoever

I have to find out what you're up to on fucking YouTube along with the rest of the drooling, web-enabled proletariat? And I'm the 783,467th view. That means 783,476 people saw it before I did. Have you any idea how much I'm hurting?

Tosser.

Yes, you: lardy fucking tosser.

And it was a rubbish dive. 25 in competition. And that's only if you bribed the Kazakhstani judge with American dollars.

Ta-ra. For the last time,

Brett

PS: At least Vince emails. He wants his asthma inhaler. He gave me a postbox address in Aspen. Must be getting some skiing in.

PPS: Yes, he's a fucking tosser too.

PPPS: Just fucking get in touch, for fuck's sake.

PPPPS: Tosser.

From:	**Liam O'Keefe**
To:	Brett Topolski
Sent:	28 January 2009, 10.42
Subject:	Re: I am so fucking pissed off with you I could punch out a plate-glass window and not feel any pain whatsoever

Soz, mate, truly, truly soz. I was just about to e you, honest. I've had a life-changing couple of days and keeping up with my best buddy hasn't been top of the agenda. Just one of the many reasons I am feeling chastened. And deeply, deeply shamed.

Oh, and deeply fucking relieved in a glad-to-be-alive kinda way.

You'll want the full story, I suppose, but it'll have to wait till we meet up (because we WILL meet up). It's way too raw for email. You need to be able to smell the tears.

In an admittedly lame attempt to make things up to you, here's a just-for-my-best-mate exclusive a full two hours before the press release goes out: like Beckham, Kournikova, Chelsea and Macclesfield Town, I'm now contracted to Adidas. They're going to give me cash money. More of a Macclesfield- than a Beckham-sized sum, but enough to clear my debts (yes, yes, the cheque's in the post). All I have to do is something stupid. Monumentally stupid, actually, but we'll gloss over that for now.

Again, you'll want the full story, but again, it'll have to wait. Not for long though. I'm due a holiday and I could do with some winter sun, even if it is in a tacky Arab Vegas minus the casinos.

Which is a good thing. I'm a changed man. No more roulette or blackjack for me. Or gee-gees. Or dogs. Or net poker with fifteen-year-olds in Kettering who play with their mums' Visa cards and think they're Lancey Howard – and, actually, who usually beat me like they're Lancey Howard.

Yeah, yeah, I know I've said it before. Countless times. But this time . . .

Right now you're rolling your eyes towards the back of your skull, but this time it's different. I died and got my life back. And I've got the chance of Lorraine. Who is my life. Incredible, innit? Lorraine! And me! Together! Again! (Maybe.)

Fuck, I'd better sign off before I make myself cry.

See you before you know it.

    Liam

PS: Must say I didn't find the Vince-in-India story credible. The Vince we know would only check into an ashram if it had fruit machines, cable porn and a vodka bar. Aspen makes much more sense. American portions of red meat, regular sightings of Don Johnson and God's finest white powder (snow, I mean). But do you think Princess Jaz's full Arab wrap works on skis? She might be able to pull it off on a snowboard, mind.

PPS: Have to say you're wrong about the dive. At least a 50 in competition.

PPPS: Vaguely recall telling you I loved you in my last e. I meant it. There you fucking go: proper man tears. Pass the Kleenex, nurse.

From: **Lorraine Pallister**
To: Liam O'Keefe
Sent: 28 January 2009, 10.43
Subject: I'm not saying we're back together . . .

. . . but if/when you get your contractual meeting with Anna Kournikova, if you so much as glance at her (and you know what I mean by glance), you can forget any real or theoretical chance we have of reconciliation.

Fancy grabbing a bite after work?

From: **Liam O'Keefe**
To: Lorraine Pallister
Sent: 28 January 2009, 10.51
Subject: Re: I'm not saying we're back together . . .

As if I would indulge in any glancing. Well, the old me certainly would have. But this is the new (and very much improved) me. Just you wait and see.

Dinner sounds excellent. I've booked us into Porky Pizza in Leicester Sq. They do a recession-busting 36-inch American Hot for £24.99.

From: **Lorraine Pallister**
To: Liam O'Keefe
Sent: 28 January 2009, 10.52
Subject: Re: I'm not saying we're back together . . .

Yeah, the new, improved supersize you. I'm worried about that. Adidas want an 'everyman body shape'. Not sure that means fat bastard.

From: **Ted Berry**
To: Liam O'Keefe
Sent: 28 January 2009, 10.58
Subject:

Fancy returning my Chipperfield's circus crane, you thieving twat scum? And while you're at it, you can round up the shirking dead bastard Harvey and show me what you've done on Ketel One. And it had better be very fucking excellent. For some unfathomable reason David believes the sun shines out of your arse, but you'll have to go a long, long way to impress me. An actual solar flare bursting from your actual ringpiece might just do it, but don't fucking count on it.

From: **Liam O'Keefe**
To: Harvey Harvey
Sent: 28 January 2009, 10.59
Subject:

You here, Lazarus? You happen to have a Dutch vodka campaign concealed about your person? Ted wants to see one. Like now.

From: **Harvey Harvey**
To: Liam O'Keefe
Sent: 28 January 2009, 11.07
Subject: Re:

Sorry, but I've only just got in. I had to spend some time at the flat showing Comfort how the heating, the microwave and Super PONG work. (Can you believe they haven't heard of Super PONG in Nigeria? They're very behind the times technologically speaking.) I haven't given Ketel One any thought. I've got a Vimto campaign in my bottom drawer. I did it at M&C Saatchi, but Graham Fink said it was too childish. Or did he say it was deranged? Or was that my NatWest campaign? Or maybe my Hyundai poster. Except I'm pretty sure he said that was the work of a psychopath. He used to make up words like 'psychopath' and 'borderlinepersonalitydisorder' just to get people out of his office. Anyway, I think my Vimto campaign is brilliant. By the way, are we proper partners now? That is so exciting! I haven't had a partner for longer than three days since I left college.

From: **Liam O'Keefe**
To: Harvey Harvey
Sent: 28 January 2009, 11.11
Subject: Re:

Yes, we're proper partners. Like it or not, I feel an unbreakable bond between us. It stretches from here to literal eternity.

Not that you need a partner any more. With Comfort in your pad and $80 million in the bank, what the fuck are you doing at work?

From: **Harvey Harvey**
To: Liam O'Keefe
Sent: 28 January 2009, 11.15
Subject: Re:

Comfort didn't actually have $80 million. She had just enough to get us flight tickets. And before you say she was lying about the money (because I know you will), she wasn't. Her maths is really bad and there are a lot of things that she honestly believes that aren't actually true. Like her dad isn't an oil broker. He's a taxi driver. And he isn't actually dead. He gave us a lift to the airport. We flew with this airline called Arik, which I think is a misspelling of Eric, who's probably the owner's son. There's a lot of that in Nigeria. I've just remembered another word that Graham Fink made up. He used to say delusional a lot. I just checked the dictionary and you'll be amazed to learn that it's real! It means holding an idiosyncratic belief despite it being contradicted by reality. Do you think Comfort might be delusional?

From: **Liam O'Keefe**
To: Harvey Harvey
Sent: 28 January 2009, 11.16
Subject: Re:

Well, if she is, she's come to the right place.

From: **Ted Berry**
To: Liam O'Keefe
Sent: 28 January 2009, 11.17
Subject: I'm fucking waiting

You, Harvey and K1, my office, now.

From: **Liam O'Keefe**
To: Harvey Harvey
Sent: 28 January 2009, 11.18
Subject:

We're going to see Ted. Grab your Vimto campaign.

From: **Harvey Harvey**
To: Liam O'Keefe
Sent: 28 January 2009, 11.19
Subject: Re:

But it says Vimto in the bottom right-hand corner. And it has babies in it. And a puppy.

From: **Liam O'Keefe**
To: Harvey Harvey
Sent: 28 January 2009, 11.20
Subject: Re:

I'll improvise.

From: **David Crutton**
To: Ted Berry
Sent: 28 January 2009, 11.33
Subject: Catch ups

Hello Teddy my favourite creating director! I am want to catch up on the matters of today. I miss the meeting for Montana yester-days because I am travel Finland the great nation of Scandinavia with the top markings in ski jump, mobile phone covering and Lapp dancing (ha-ha, are you getting it?!).

But even if I have many kilometres afar I am stay on the top of Montana campaign. You must make your creating teams do the more zany ideas and we can show Mr Montana our excellent creationity.

Reach for the ceilings!

David Crutton
𝕿𝖍𝖊 𝕸𝖆𝖓

Sent from my BlackBerry

From: **Ted Berry**
To: David Crutton
Sent: 28 January 2009, 11.36
Subject: Re: Catch ups

Mate, what's going on? You totally off your tits on Finnish vodka?

By the way, Liam and Harvey have just shown me a rocking K1 idea. I think the bastards have pulled it out of the fire once again.

From: **David Crutton**
To: Ted Berry
Sent: 28 January 2009, 11.40
Subject: Re: Catch ups

I am wish this is true, but I have not vodka or not the tits. I am horrifical burn in the aeroplane food accident but I recovers with the helpings of my old friend Pertti Van Helden. He is the ballcock of hairy big dog.

I think Liam and Harvey is deserved a paying increasement. I am always of favour to reward the creation excellency with financial pleasantry. As the Big Chief Swing Dick I command you make this to occur.

David Crutton
The Man

Sent from my BlackBerry

From: **David Crutton**
To: Caroline Zitter
Sent: 28 January 2009, 11.46
Subject:

I check my diary schedules and I seeing we have the meeting in 2.30 today for discuss the strategy of the Liquorice Allsort.

Apology I will not be attentive. I am undisposed in a land far-away. Please hold the meetings without me. Free your minds and let them fly to the galaxies!

Bertie Bassett
The Man

Sent from my BlackBerry

From: **Caroline Zitter**
To: David Crutton
Sent: 28 January 2009, 11.47
Subject: Out of Office AutoReply

I am out of the office attending Seminar Overload: Sorting the Best from the Bullshit. I will return on Friday 30th January.

Caroline Zitter
THE SEER

327 days
23 hours and
43 minutes later
Mood: sullied
cheapened
vulgarized

From: **Janice Crutton**
To: Beverly Crutton, Sarah Franks, Geraldine Crutton and
           17 others . . .
Sent: 22 December 2009, 10.04
Subject: The Crutton Chronicles, Volume 9

Well, here we are again. Another year, another catalogue of ups, downs and in-betweens. Mostly ups, it must be said. The highlight, of course, was the arrival of Petra Rosebud, all 7lb 3oz of her! I've bored you already with countless pictures, so I won't bang on. I'll just attach the mpeg of Noah frying the afterbirth.

Joking!

In brief, little Petra is sleeping like an angel. For half an hour at a stretch. My God, I'd forgotten how exhausting motherhood is!

But she is a true delight. David and I couldn't have wished for a more perfect anniversary gift.

Twenty years! Can any of you believe it, even those of you that were at our party? I know I can't. It really has gone by in a flash. For those of you that weren't at the do, all I can do is repeat what I said then. It has been a remarkable twenty years: joyous, happy and filled with laughter. I feel very lucky to have found in David someone so loving and supportive. And after all these years I sense our marriage has entered a new phase of tran-scendent calm.

   [saved as draft]

From: **Janice Crutton**
To: David Crutton
Sent: 22 December 2009, 10.12
Subject: To do

A reminder of today's packed itinerary:

1.00:	couples therapy
2.10:	Christmas shopping
4.30:	family therapy with Tam and Noah (if awake)
5.45:	home, shower, change
6.15:	mulled wine at the Faircloughs'
9.30:	home, pack, bed

Do not be late. You are on two strikes.

   Jan

PS: On your way home pick up tea bags and Sudocrem.

PPS: And that Dordogne book. Our host has expressed an interest.

Christmas bestsellers

1 **Dordogne Twilight**
Simon Horne
2 **Harry Potter and the Hallucinogenic Gap Year**
J.K. Rowling
3 **Ramsay's Soup Kitchen**
Gordon Ramsay
4 **Can I Really Get Away With More of This Reactionary Drivel?**
Jeremy Clarkson
5 **Blimey, Looks Like I Can**
Jeremy Clarkson

From: **David Crutton**
To: Janice Crutton
Sent: 22 December 2009, 10.24
Subject: Re: To do

Got a few more emails to send and I'm out of here. By the way, why do we have to fly so damn early tomorrow? Come to mention it, why do we have to fly at all?

David Crutton
The Man

PS: You know I'd do anything for you, but please don't mention the Dordogne book again.

PPS: Ever.

PPPS: What's Sudocrem?

From: **Janice Crutton**
To: David Crutton
Sent: 22 December 2009, 10.27
Subject: Re: To do

We have to fly so damn early because our dear friend has very kindly organized a trip to see Father Christmas in Lahti. The sled leaves at noon tomorrow. Just be home on time.

FYI, Sudocrem is a product for the relief of nappy rash. Nappies are worn by babies. We have a baby.

From: **Janice Crutton**
To: Beverly Crutton, Sarah Franks, Geraldine Crutton and 17 others . . .
Sent: 22 December 2009, 10.33
Subject: The Crutton Chronicles, Volume 9 [continued]

David has made a good recovery from his burns. The scarring isn't as bad as we'd feared. If anything, around the eyes it has even taken a year or two off him! His remedy, as ever, has been to throw himself into work. He can be very proud that in this economic *annus horribilis*, Meerkat360 has not only survived but, dare I say it, thrived.

[saved as draft]

From: **Bill Geddes**
To: David Crutton, Ted Berry
Sent: 22 December 2009, 10.34
Subject: Possible problem

Strictly FYI at this stage, but the ASA has had a stack of complaints about Ketel One. Below are some quotes that capture the general tenor.

Obviously there'll be no adjudication on this until the New Year, which will see the client safely through the all-important Christmas sales period, but we do need to prepare for the worst.

Sorry to be the bearer of the opposite of glad tidings so close to the break.

Bill

<< I cannot believe they put those sweet little babies and innocent puppies in the vodka advertisements. The perpetrators should rot in jail with the paedos and hedge-fund managers. There they would be gang-raped by the armed robbers and hell's angels. That would teach them a lesson they wouldn't forget in a hurry. >>

<< I am appalled by the advert that depicts babies mixing cocktails. Particularly shocking is the one that shows the wee mite operating a blender. I myself have a beautiful one-year-old. What if she were to see it and attempt to mix her own Ketel One Strawberry Daiquiri? I have sleepless nights imagining her scaling the kitchen worktop and tumbling headfirst into the blender jug, where she is pickled in a lethal mixture of pulped fruit and alcohol before being shredded by the whirling steel blades. This must surely breach every health and safety regulation going. >>

<< A puppy in a blender? Advertising has finally gone too far. >>

From: **David Crutton**
To: Bill Geddes
Cc: Ted Berry
Sent: 22 December 2009, 10.37
Subject: Re: Possible problem

Thank you, Bill. Isn't that just the final bottle of Brut in my

Christmas stocking? I can add it to the writ from the government of Rwanda for playground cigarette trafficking, the recall last week by Esmée Éloge of two million bottles of Eau de Thatch after the House of Fraser spray monkey blinded six customers, and the loss of the RNIB account after the aforementioned blinding debacle.

Am I really destined to spend the whole of 2010 in court? Looks like it.

You've done me one favour though. Suddenly a fortnight in fucking Finland looks blissfully appealing. In my absence, why not pass this one on to Caroline? After a year of wall-to-wall empowerment seminars, there's surely no problem too gargantuan for her to fix.

David Crutton
𝕿𝖍𝖊 𝕸𝖆𝖓

From: **Bill Geddes**
To: Caroline Zitter
Sent: 22 December 2009, 10.39
Subject: Ketel One

Hi Caroline. David has asked me to brief you on a Ketel One issue. Are you free?

From: **Caroline Zitter**
To: Bill Geddes
Sent: 22 December 2009, 10.40
Subject: Out of Office AutoReply

I am feeling unwell and won't be in today.

Caroline Zitter
THE SEER

Bilge:	Stressed to buggery. Need lunchtime livener. (Not fucking vodka.)
Keef:	Can't. Last-min present shopping. 2 weddings and a Lorraine. Do you think toasters will be seen as amusingly ironic or just lame?
Bilge:	The latter. You're surely not getting Lorraine a toaster?
Keef:	Nope. Treading the usual fine line between Diaphanous Elegance and Slut.
Bilge:	My advice: steer clear of anything with peepholes.
Keef:	Been there, done that. It didn't play as I'd have liked. Anyway, what you so stressed about?
Bilge:	Your fucking vodka campaign, you fucker.
Keef:	Not mine. It was Double H's. And I have to say it worked a treat for Vimto.
Bilge:	If Double H were here I'd give him a slap. When's the wedding?
Keef:	Tomorrow. 11.00, arrive Hackney Town Hall, 11.45, arrive Pembury, down 2 swift pints, deliver Churchillian best man's speech, in cab to Heathrow by 12.15, Vegas, here I come!
Bilge:	Yes, Las Vegas, I'm worried about that.
Keef:	You and me both, buddy.

From: **Lorraine Pallister**
To: Liam O'Keefe
Sent: 22 December 2009, 10.40
Subject: Vegas

I'm sorry, Liam, but I'm really worried. I know Brett, Vince and Princess Jasmine (BTW, that cannot be her real name) will be gutted if we pull out, but are you sure this trip is a good idea? You've achieved so much in the last year, but all your hard work could be undone after just a few minutes on the Strip. Remember how you lost it in Southend, and that was just a poxy arcade on the pier? Sorry to be so gloomy, but it's not too late to cancel. What do you think?

From: **Neil Godley**
To: All Staff
Sent: 22 December 2009, 10.41
Subject: Christ is born!

The shepherds said unto one another,
'Let us go to Bethlehem and see this thing that
has happened,
which the Lord has told us about.'

Please join me for a service of traditional Christmas song in the multi-denominational chapel at 6.00 this evening. Enjoy all your old favourites, including 'Ding Dong Merrily on High', 'Oh Little Town of Bethlehem' and 'Away in a Manger'.

From: **Nigel Godley**
To: All Staff
Sent: 22 December 2009, 10.42
Subject: Come praise Him!

On coming to the house, they saw the child
with his mother, Mary,
and they bowed down and worshipped him.

Glad tidings, everyone! Today Pastor Terry Treacher of the Grace Triumphant Church of the Moral High Ground will lead us in EXULTANT PRAYERS of JOYOUS CELEBRATION of the birthday of OUR LORD JESUS CHRIST. Come to the multi-denominational chapel at lunchtime to share the GOOD NEWS.

From: **Liam O'Keefe**
To: Lorraine Pallister
Sent: 22 December 2009, 10.44
Subject: Re: Vegas

What are you like? I am the guy who dived* off the Golden Gate Bridge. I can easily withstand the temptation of a few silly slot machines. And blackjack tables. And craps games. Besides, I'll have you, my rock, by my side. What could possibly go wrong?

BTW, remind me of your bra size (promise, nothing with unseemly holes).

*Technically a belly flop, but that is arguably the riskiest of all entries, and one that continues to be criminally overlooked by the IOC. When will they accept that two fat blokes doing synchronized flops would be the blue-riband Olympic event?

	MSN:
Keef:	You awake? Soz, but can't figure out the time difference.
Topol:	Just about awake. It's almost teatime. 'Sup?
Keef:	What are you getting Jaz and Aladdin? Don't want to duplicate.
Topol:	They do some neat Dualit fakes down the market. Toasters: amusingly ironic or lame?
Keef:	The latter.
Topol:	It'll have to be tea towels then.
Keef:	ETA in Vegas?

Topol:	Tomorrow night, as long as I make the Tokyo connection.
Keef:	Ready with the best man's speech?
Topol:	Not a speech. A movie. 15 minutes of Vince's best bits. 15 years of mayhem to choose from. Editing was a mare, but you should see the director's cut. A dark yet coruscating account of one man's descent into comedy hell. Might enter it into Sundance.
Keef:	Can't wait to see it. Looking forward to finally meeting the princess too.
Topol:	Ditto. Never seen her out of a burka. Vince hinted that she might be getting married in a Hooters outfit.
Keef:	A man can dream.
Topol:	Indeed. Can you do me a favour? Pack 6 bottles of Head & Shoulders. Impossible to source out here.
Keef:	Consider it done. I know I've said it before, but why the fuck did you take the job?
Topol:	I'm the fucking creative director, that's fucking why.
Keef:	Yes, but Miller Shanks Tashkent? Fuck's sake.

From: **Michelle@SafeBet.com**
To: Liam O'Keefe
Sent: 22 December 2009, 10.55
Subject: Where have you been?

Hi there, **Liam O'Keefe**, Michelle* here, your favourite girl at your favourite online bookie. I haven't seen you for a while and I really miss you! We used to have such fun, didn't we? Now I am so lonely without you. Why not drop by? You might catch me with hardly any clothes on!! And I have some very **tempting offers** just for **you**.**

Go to **SafeBet.com/Michelletemptations** to find out more. Come on, **Liam O'Keefe**, it's just not the same without you.

Michelle xxx

SafeBet.com
Go on, have a punt
Just a little one
You know you want to

*Michelle is not a real person. She is a character constructed for marketing purposes.

**Gambling can result in bankruptcy, divorce, abject misery and prison.

	MSN:
Keef:	Pack handcuffs.
Topol:	You what?
Keef:	Lockable restraints for the restriction of movement and the prevention of escape. Stick a pair in your suitcase.
Topol:	I think the legendary Vegas hookers are fully stocked in that department. You just have to ask.
Keef:	You don't get it. You might need to chain me to something. Like the radiator in my room.
Topol:	You worried?
Keef:	V.v. worried. I close my eyes, hear the slots and break into an ice-cold sweat.
Topol:	Jeez, you're the fucker who belly

	flopped off the Golden Gate.
	You're seriously bothered about a
	few silly slot machines?
Keef:	That and a million acres of smooth
	green baize. I have $5,000 in
	traveller's cheques waiting to be
	torched on a can't-lose poker
	hand – I *know* myself, Brett.
Topol:	Cuffs going in case now.

From: **Neil Godley**
To: All Staff
Sent: 22 December 2009, 10.59
Subject: Christ is born!

**Jesus then took the loaves, gave thanks, and distributed
to those who were seated as much as they wanted.**

I forgot to mention there will be TRADITIONAL mince pies (baked
by me!) on sale. All proceeds to Crisis at Christmas.

From: **Nigel Godley**
To: All Staff
Sent: 22 December 2009, 11.02
Subject: Come praise Him!

**Jesus entered the temple area and drove out
all who were buying and selling there.**

No pastries, cakes or other cheap bribes. But there will be EXCIT-
ING and totally AUTHENTIC demonstrations of speaking in
tongues!

From: **Janice Crutton**
To: Beverly Crutton, Sarah Franks, Geraldine Crutton and
17 others . . .
Sent: 22 December 2009, 11.03
Subject: The Crutton Chronicles, Volume 9 [continued]

Now to news of my two (almost) grown-up children. Noah was thrilled with his A-level results, as were we, though they weren't quite enough to get him into his first choice of Hull. With typical good sense he is taking stock with a gap year. In case you feel you've missed his email bulletins from various Thai internet cafés, that's because he hasn't yet departed! He is still poring over the maps, determined to make his the best-planned tour of South East Asia conceivable. David and I can only admire his diligence.

[saved as draft]

From: **Janice Crutton**
To: Noah Crutton
Sent: 22 December 2009, 11.08
Subject: We leave at dawn TOMORROW

You'll still be asleep when I go out, but I expect you to have packed some clothes by the time I return (roughly 5.45). Clean or dirty, I'm past caring, but you will need clothes. You can't go the whole Christmas holiday with one Slayer T-shirt and the jeans you've been wearing for the past three months.

It's only a small task, and I shouldn't have to nag, but I know how long these things can take you. And yes, I appreciate how exhausted you are – sixteen hours of sleep a day can take it out of a man – but you are running out of time. WE LEAVE AT DAWN.

Mum x

PS: I've left a bowl of Oatso Simple in the microwave. You just have to press Start. Remember it isn't ready until you hear a 'ping'. Remember also to remove Clingfilm before eating.

From: **David Crutton**
To: Dotty Podidra
Sent: 22 December 2009, 11.09
Subject: Gift list

I've signed off your gift suggestions for Janice. It's ready for you to collect and process.

From: **Dotty Podidra**
To: All Staff
Sent: 22 December 2009, 11.11
Subject: Workies

Any workies free to do last-minute Christmas shopping for David? Totally adorable shops like Liberty, Mulberry and Smythson of Bond Street, so don't all rush at once!

Dotty Podidra
Assistant to David Crutton

From: **Neil Godley**
To: All Staff
Sent: 22 December 2009, 11.12
Subject: Christ is born!

Then the Lord said unto me,
'The prophets are prophesying lies in my name.
I have not sent them or appointed them or
spoken to them.
They are prophesying to you false visions,
divinations, idolatries
and the delusions of their own minds.'

No foreign MUMBO JUMBO! All carols sung in GOD'S ENGLISH!

From: **Nigel Godley**
To: All Staff
Sent: 22 December 2009, 11.14
Subject: Come praise Him!

The Lord is a jealous and avenging God.
The Lord takes vengeance and is filled with wrath.

All TRUE believers welcome. Promise of genuine MIRACLES. The blind WILL see and the lame WILL walk!!

From: **Neil Godley**
To: All Staff
Sent: 22 December 2009, 11.17
Subject: Christ is born!

You serpents, you brood of vipers,
how are you to escape being sentenced to hell?

Any BLASPHEMERS, HERETICS and SATANISTS who bear witness at the lunchtime service of so-called worship will NOT be welcome at the evening carol programme. You WILL spend ETERNITY in FIERY DAMNATION.

From: **Nigel Godley**
To: All Staff
Sent: 22 December 2009, 11.19
Subject: Christ is born!

Now the men of Sodom were wicked
and were sinning greatly against the Lord.

(Sodomite Vicars + Lesbian Priestesses) − Moral Bearings = Church of England

From: **David Crutton**
To: Sally Wilton
Sent: 22 December 2009, 11.22
Subject: That's it, I've had enough

I want the basement chapel shut immediately. Tell the Creative Department they can have their ball pit back. Or you can use it for stationery. Or as an animal-rescue shelter. Or as a dorm to accommodate the dozen workies we seem to have on our books at any one time. I really don't care, so long as the Moral Minority no longer has access. I'll probably go to hell for this, but I suspect I was heading in that direction anyway.

David Crutton
The Man

PS: Now I think about it, why do we have a dozen workies on our books at any one time? Are they really necessary? There must be a limit to the amount of menial bollocks a company the size of ours can find for them. Or are they part of some ongoing people-trafficking scam, and should I therefore keep my trap shut?

From: **Neil Godley**
To: David Crutton
Sent: 22 December 2009, 11.23
Subject: N Godley

Dear Mr Crutton

I find that I can no longer work with Nigel Godley, my so-called colleague. His persistent insults aimed at my sincerely held religious convictions have become unacceptably offensive. Unless you are prepared to 'let him go', I will be obliged to tender my resignation.

Yours sincerely

Neil Godley (Accounts)

492

From: **Nigel Godley**
To: David Crutton
Sent: 22 December 2009, 11.23
Subject: N Godley

Dear Mr Crutton

The situation with my so-called colleague, Neil Godley, has become untenable. His deliberate and repeated slurs on my deeply held religious beliefs are causing me unbearable stress. Unless you are prepared to 'let him go', I will have no other choice than to offer my resignation.

Yours sincerely
Nigel Godley (Accounts)

From: **David Crutton**
To: Sally Wilton
Sent: 22 December 2009, 11.24
Subject: Rethink

Scrub my last email. The Godley situation appears to have resolved itself.

From: **David Crutton**
To: Neil Godley
Sent: 22 December 2009, 11.25
Subject: Re: N Godley

Dear Mr Godley,

Due to restrictions imposed by various labour statutes, I am unable to dismiss your brother. With great regret, I therefore accept your resignation.

Your sincerely,

David Crutton
The Man

From: **David Crutton**
To: Nigel Godley
Sent: 22 December 2009, 11.26
Subject: Re: N Godley

Dear Mr Godley,

Due to restrictions imposed by various labour statutes, I am unable to dismiss your brother. With great regret, I therefore accept your resignation.

Yours sincerely,

David Crutton
𝕿𝖍𝖊 𝕸𝖆𝖓

From: **Janice Crutton**
To: Beverly Crutton, Sarah Franks, Geraldine Crutton and 17 others . . .
Sent: 22 December 2009, 11.27
Subject: The Crutton Chronicles, Volume 9 [continued]

David and I are so proud of Tamara. Unlike so many of her peers, she has reconnected with the true meaning of Christmas. She has given up much of her holiday to work (unpaid!) at a centre in Walton-on-Thames for victims of this devastating recession – mostly former employees of Woolworth, MFI and Lehman Brothers. As I write, she is retraining one-time pick 'n' mix assistants and investment bankers as call-centre workers. Honestly, if Petra Rosebud grows up to become half the fine young woman her sister is, I will consider my life to have been a complete success!

[saved as draft]

SMS:

Mum:	Where are you?
Tam:	Can't chat. Teaching poor ex-commodities broker basket-weaving
Mum:	Both know this is fantasy. Please try again
Tam:	Spoilsport. If you must know shopping for your krissy prezzy
Mum:	You pulled that 1 last year. Get out of tattoo parlour/piercing salon/pub and come home
Tam:	Not going stupid finland you know
Mum:	2 strikes say you are. You will see fr xmas even if huskies have to drag you by the hair

From: **Milton Keane**
To: All Staff
Sent: 22 December 2009, 11.33
Subject: I feel like Romford tonite!!!
Att: dreemzz.pdf

Hello old friends and former workmates!! You'll be thrilled to learn that I'm making an exclusive personal appearance tonight at DREEMZZ, 'Romford's second most popular nite spot' (see attached flyer for details). I'll be performing 'Razzle Dazzle' (as seen on *BB10*) and signing my new book, *Straight from the Heart – My Fabulous Un-gay Life*! Would love all my old muckers to be there. But do come early. It's going to be absolutely rammed!!

Important note: despite the theme of the evening, I am appearing purely in my capacity as a popular CELEBRITY (245th on *Heat*'s Most Wanted) and not because I am in ANY WAY gay.

See you there, ravers!

Milton Keane®

GAY NITE

@

Dreemzz

'Romford's second most popular nite spot'

Tuesday 22nd December

Featuring an exclusive appearance by
Milton *'Is That a Bit Gay?'* **Keane**
(second evictee, BB10)

Dreemzz, Unit 16, Frank Lampard Way
Jo O'Meara Leisure Park, Romford, Essex

Strictly no trainers, hoodies or Burberry.
When leaving, please consider our neighbours
and dispose of condoms responsibly.

From:	**Milton Keane**
To:	Susi Judge-Davis-Gaultier, Dotty Podidra
Sent:	22 December 2009, 11.36
Subject:	Cry for help

You have GOT to come tonight, girlfriends. They've only sold 15 tickets. Obviously there're no queers in Essex. What the heck was my rubbish agent thinking? There'll be tumbleweed blowing across the stage when I do my number!! Save my life. Please, please, please, please, please come!!!!

	MSN:
DottyPod:	What do you think?
sjdG:	Essex?? You have *got* to be

kidding!

DottyPod:	We have to show our support. He needs us.
sjdG:	Where was he when I *needed* him last summer? I was having a total freak out with my Pilates injury, but he was too busy partying with Nicole Richie.
DottyPod:	He's a celeb with celeb demands on his time. He couldn't help it.
sjdG:	FYI, I really, really wanted to meet Nicole. Did you know scientists have proved she has the perfect body-mass index? I could have learned so much from her. Milt could have taken me as his +1, but he snubbed me.
DottyPod:	Well, I'm going to support him.
sjdG:	Ooh, aren't you Ms Perfect? If he asks, tell him I'm washing my hair.
DottyPod:	He'll be gutted.
sjdG:	Hard cheese.
DottyPod:	Can I ask you something?
sjdG:	Make it quick. Need to take Ted's crampons to be 'honed' (don't ask).
DottyPod:	Where's Essex?
sjdG:	By the sea. Think it's near Dover.

From: **Susi Judge-Davis-Gaultier**
To: All Staff
Sent: 22 December 2009, 11.44
Subject: Workies

Is there a workie free to take Ted's crampons to the 'honer'?

From: **Kazu Makino**
To: Donald Gold, Bill Geddes
Sent: 22 December 2009, 11.46
Subject:

Plane (*not* Air Force 1) gets in tomorrow at 7.30am. I've prom-ised my mum I'll meet her in Home Ware at M&S for a mind-numbing Christmas-present splurge. Managed to negotiate myself a 90-minute lunch furlough before she drags me back to Suburban Family Hell (AKA Surrey). Fancy hooking up for a bite? I have bribes: White House china. Only a few items, but over time and with enough trips home, I can build it up to a complete dinner service.

Kazu Makino
Special Advisor to the First Lady
on the Environment, Foreign Affairs and Shoes
The White House
1600 Pennsylvania Avenue
Washington
DC 20500

From: **Harvey Harvey**
To: Liam O'Keefe
Sent: 22 December 2009, 11.48
Subject:

Hi Liam. I'm very nervous about tomorrow. Have you got the rings yet? And my psychiatrist is coming. He wanted to be my best man because we do go back such a long way, so he might be a bit funny with you. Also, Comfort wants to know if Lorraine will be happy wearing a traditional Nigerian bridesmaid's dress.

From: **Liam O'Keefe**
To: Harvey Harvey
Sent: 22 December 2009, 12.03
Subject: Re:

No, Harvey, let me explain. Again. *You* buy the rings. My job as best man is simply to look after them for you. Don't worry about your shrink. I've got some top psychiatry jokes in my speech that will put him at ease. And Lorraine will wear pretty much anything, so long as it doesn't involve peepholes.

From: **Donald Gold**
To: Kazu Makino
Sent: 22 December 2009, 12.05
Subject: Re:

Hooray!! Lunch with my heroine, Kaz! I'll get us into the Ivy. They'll surely bump some no-mark *Emmerdale* cast member for a member of the First Lady's personal staff. Hurry up and get here.

    Don xxx

From: **Liam O'Keefe**
To: Creative Department
Sent: 22 December 2009, 12.18
Subject: The Big Night Out

As if I need to remind you, I'm hosting Double H's Literal Stag Do tonight. Tailored to his highly specific brief, here is the evening's thrilling itinerary:

- 5.45:   coach departs. Gather outside at 5.40 sharp
- 7.00:   arrive Richmond Park
- 7.05:   meet Tod Butler, park ranger and professional deer stalker (no, really!). He will brief us on the night's safari

7.20:	embark in Land Rovers on Harvey Harvey's Stag Night Stag Watch
7.30:	settle down to watch deer, count antler prongs, coo at the bambis and chat (very quietly, for deer are very shy) amongst ourselves
10.00:	break for hot dogs, flapjacks and lashings of Vimto
12.00:	carriages

NB1: No shooting, garrotting, cudgelling or otherwise harming the deer, Zlatan. They belong to the Queen, and she will have you beheaded. She still blames your lot for kicking off WW1 and she wouldn't bat an eyelid.

NB2: Unless one happens to be taking a shortcut through the park on her way home after a hard night's writhing to music at Spearmint Rhino, we will see no strippers tonight.

It's going to be an educational blast, people. Personally I can't wait.

Liam

marquee.co.uk
Working Title unveils plans for Dordogne movie

Working Title has announced that its adaptation of the runaway bestseller *Dordogne Twilight* will begin principal photography in spring 2010. Russell T. Grant has completed a script that Tim Bevan, the company's co-chairman, has described as '*Jean de Florette* meets *Carry On Matron*'.

Gérard Depardieu has been cast in the role of Papin and Miranda Richardson will play Celine. The starring role has gone to Pierce Brosnan. Brosnan said: 'I have spent my career playing basically decent, heroic types, so it'll be an exciting challenge to inhabit the skin of a gross, narcissistic and utterly delusional fuckhead.'

From: **Janice Crutton**
To: Beverly Crutton, Sarah Franks, Geraldine Crutton and 17 others . . .
Sent: 22 December 2009, 12.21
Subject: The Crutton Chronicles, Volume 9 [continued]

Last and least, me! I'm near the end of my maternity leave, so after Christmas I'll focus on recruiting a nanny. Hopefully there won't be a repeat of the Tamara experience when her first word was something that would get you imprisoned in the Philippines! Ideally I'd like a nice French girl so that Petra Rosebud has a head start on a useful second language. Seriously, many of the tots round here are fully bi- and even tri-lingual by the time they get to nursery! I suspect, though, that I'll have to pay a premium for French and will end up with Czech. *C'est la vie*, as they don't say in Brno! And then it's back to work, where I suspect the Crossrail negotiations are exactly where I left them four months ago.

One piece of sad news. After 18 years and about 5,000 sacks of Iams, Courtney passed away in October.

I've attached a pic of the four of us (plus my bump) on our recession-conscious holiday in Devon. Strangely, apart from the rain and the stodgy food, it was exactly like Tuscany – full of London lawyers and media types!

That's all from us. I hope you're all well. And I wish you wonderful Christmases and moderately prosperous New Years.

All our love,

Janice, David, Noah, Tamara & Petra Rosebud
xxxxx

From: **Pertti Van Helden**
To: Janice Crutton
Sent: 22 December 2009. 12.22
Subject:

Christmas is comed and the gooses is getting stuffed! I very exciting about your imminating arrival. I invite the whole thirty-seven of the Van Helden extending family to join for a Christmas Eve feasting to celebrate the present of my top English friends. Tell to David also that I arrange the special journey to Ivalo. I make appointment for doctor which marinade him in the reindeer shits. It is treatment to make miracle cure of scars in the face and also hand areas. I have one thing I must ask. Is Tamara the normal teenager liking the dancing? If you tell me yes I am arrange her go tanhukurssi. It is the special course to make dance in the Finland folk style.

I have make many of the incredulous plans for your trip and I am explosive with the thrillingness.

Pertti Van Helden
TheHeroicHerring.com

From: **Janice Crutton**
To: David Crutton
Cc: Dotty Podidra
Sent: 22 December 2009, 12.26
Subject: Final warning

You have four minutes to get out of the office.

Dotty, please remind him about the Sudocrem. And have a lovely Christmas.

From: **Dotty Podidra**
To: David Crutton
Sent: 22 December 2009, 12.27
Subject: Janice

Just checking you saw her email?

From: **David Crutton**
To: Dotty Podidra
Sent: 22 December 2009, 12.28
Subject: Re: Janice

I fucking saw it. Putting my fucking coat on. Happy fucking Christmas to you too.

From: **Janice Crutton**
To: Pertti Van Helden
Sent: 22 December 2009, 12.33
Subject: Re:

We're thrilled to be coming too, Pertti. David especially can't wait to see you again, having had a super time with you recuperating from his injuries. Noah, too, is looking forward to seeing Veiko again. He tells me he has learned all the chords to 'Nuns with Clocks' (have I got that right?!). Even Petra Rosebud seems excited at the prospect of flying to Finland for her very first Christmas.

I won't tell David about the wonderful therapy you've lined up. He's excited enough already and I don't want to overload him! And yes, Tam likes nothing more than to dance the night away. Book her in.

We'll see you tomorrow. Love and best wishes,

   Jan

Author slams Dordogne movie

Simon Horne, the author of the runaway bestseller *Dordogne Twilight*, has denounced the forthcoming screen adaptation of his book. In an extended *j'accuse* against Tim Bevan, Working Title and the British film industry in general, Horne said: 'I wrote a searching and sensitive study *d'un étranger sur une terre étrange* – a *Robinson Crusoe* for the third millennium, if you will. My vision has been sullied and cheapened, transformed into vulgar slapstick for an audience of flatulent, lager-swilling knuckle draggers.'

MSN:

Topol:	Seen the Horne quote?
Keef:	Affirmative.
Topol:	Cunt.

Acknowledgements

Roll Credits:

Clare Conville ....Elizabeth Taylor
Larry Finlay ....Mel Brooks
Katie Espiner ....Kate Winslet
Kate Samano ....Kate Winslet
Emma Buckley...Kate Winslet
Aislinn Casey...Kate Winslet
Gavin Hilzbrich..Kate Winslet
Monique Henry ....Emanuelle Béart
Alan Jarvie...Gary Cooper
Kazu Makino......................................Blonde Redhead
Philip Edgar-Jones..Himself
Kirsten Richardson ....Kirsten Dunst
Holly Beaumont.......................Vanessa Anne Hudgens
Maria Beaumont..................................Jennifer Aniston

Thank you to all of the above, but especially to Maria. If my name were ever to appear on a movie poster (it *might* happen), Maria's would be printed above it, and in much bigger type. It would be a contractual thing. But also deserved.

Follow @Meerkat360 on twitter!

By order of The Man: all at Meerkat360 wasting time on twitter, log off now! IT is watching you.
10:06 AM Sep 30th, 2009 from web

And while you're at it, get off facebook and Linkedin. IT is watching you and I am reading the f*cking printouts.
10:07 AM Sep 30th, 2009 from web

Public FYI from Sooz: I'm not anorexic, bulimic or anything-else-ic!! Collarbones are meant to 'protrude'. Doesn't anyone read Vogue?
10:27 AM Sep 30th, 2009 from web

Q from Dong: after 30 mins of 'blissful' sensory deprivation, why do I want to kill everyone?
11:12 AM Sep 30th, 2009 from web

Keef fact: piping Judas Priest into sensory deprivation tanks f*cks with heads. Meerkat360 is now a Columbine Event waiting to happen.
11:16 AM Sep 30th, 2009 from web

@sjdGaultier retro alert! Just saw sweet homeless man in adorable (slightly battered) Wannabe loafers. They are so due for a comeback!!!!
1:29 PM Sep 30th, 2009 from web

Keef sez: if you see angry shoeless tramp looking for his Patrick Coxes, tell him Susi nicked them while he was asleep.
1:51 PM Sep 30th, 2009 from web

@DottyPod bulletin – finally taught The Man how to do froggy accents on his keyboard! Peace at last!!
2:50 PM Sep 30th, 2009 from web

Question from The Man: çän åñyøñè tèll më høw tô mákè my füçkîñg kêybøård stôp stïçkïñg fùçkíñg åççëñts ön fûçkìñg èvérythïñg?
2:55 PM Sep 30th, 2009 from web

Keef sez: actually, this twitter bollox is a total fucking fuck-off. 140 characters? How da fuck are you supposed to develop a reasoned argu
9:51 PM Oct 2nd, 2009 from web

HR @Meerkat360 – openings for: barista, tennis coach (LTA qualified), dog wrangler, potter, lathe operator, blacksmith
4:15 PM Oct 5th, 2009 from web

From HH: Twitter is ace! I talk loads and I'm sure no one listens. Now I can 'twit' and the whole world reads it. I have 6 followers!!
10:29 AM Oct 6th, 2009 from web

HH: Made cup of tea. Am now drinking it. 9 followers reading about me drinking tea! I'm hyperventilating!!
11:25 AM Oct 6th, 2009 from web

HH: I think someone should write the world's first 'Twitter Novel'! Imagine a whole story told in 'twits'!!
12:16 PM Oct 6th, 2009 from web

HH: OMG, 11 followers!!!!
12:17 PM Oct 6th, 2009 from web

Keef sez: think Harvey is starting a cult with his twitter followers. I'm telling you, this is where f*cking Waco started. Watch this space.
12:20 PM Oct 6th, 2009 from web

Keef sez – 10 commandments: world's first example of bullet points. Stone tablets: world's first PowerPoint. Moses: world's first twat.
8:48 AM Oct 12th, 2009 from web

@sjdGaultier – Milt and I have found a brill way of staying in touch. Club Penguin!!!!! So much better than stupid MSN!!!!!!!!!!!!!!!!!!!!!
2:44 PM Oct 12th, 2009 from web

@miltshaker – yay, Club Penguin is incredible! Meet me at the Plaza, Sooz. We can buy Puffles!!!!
3:24 PM Oct 12th, 2009 from web

@miltshaker – BTW, does my Penguin look a bit gay????!!!!
3:29 PM Oct 12th, 2009 from web

@sjdGaultier – absolutely no way! Your Pengy is way butch!!!
3:32 PM Oct 12th, 2009 from web

IT @meerkat360 – alarming call from paedowatch.com. mk360 employees must STAY OFF Club Penguin. Yr presence is 'open to misinterpretation'
8:50 AM Oct 13th, 2009 from web

Publishing news: Pol Pot, CEO – Management Secrets of the Killing Fields by David Crutton in all good book shops NOW!
9:01 AM Oct 14th, 2009 from web

Dateline Dubai: Mac announces Middle East launch of Sharia-friendly (i.e. music-free) iPod. They're calling it the iYatollah.
9:21 AM Oct 14th, 2009 from web

And a porn-only web browser: iFuckmyhand
9:28 AM Oct 14th, 2009 from web

And file-sharing software for web pirates: iJimLad
9:52 AM Oct 14th, 2009 from web

iAmboredwiththisnow
10:09 AM Oct 14th, 2009 from web

Keef has that Friday feeling: an expanse of fresh-faced cunts for colleagues and a yearning for an AK47. Or at least an air-powered nail gun
10:29 AM Oct 16th, 2009

David Crutton at Foyles signing copies of Idi Amin, CEO: Management Secrets of Kampala. Free body part fridge magnets for first 50 buyers
11:32 AM Oct 16th, 2009 from web

HR @Meerkat360 – openings for: piano tuner, scribe (working knowledge of Latin essential), nurse, anaesthetist, guard dog, copywriter
5:44 PM Oct 20th, 2009 from web

Keef would like to point out that today da sooz is wearing cable-knit tights. It's like she has a Scottish trawlerman scaling her legs
9:19 AM Nov 2nd, 2009 from web

Dateline Dubai: Just about to go into Pepsico meeting. Might be some time. I'm wearing my 'Do Not Resuscitate' tag
10:31 AM Nov 4th, 2009 from web

HR @Meerkat360 – opportunities for work experience people. Ages 16 to 21. Good GCSEs and weak gag reflex essential.
10:10 AM Nov 5th, 2009 from web

Keef would like to know whose cock he has to suck to get his fucking expenses paid.
9:22 AM Nov 20th, 2009 from web

Ted B 2 Keef: that would be me, tho in lieu of cocksucking, you could try doing some fucking work, you fat lazy fuck
9:46 AM Nov 20th, 2009 from web

Keef is trawling eBay for single gas mask and a small batch of Sarin. Yes, he has that Friday feeling again.
10:31 AM Nov 20th, 2009 from web

@sjdGaultier – Anyone free to give Harvey H a quick endoscopy? He thinks he's swallowed the toy from his Kinder Surprise.
10:03 AM Nov 27th, 2009 from web

Dateline Dubai: a dream built on sand? Like, duh!
1:32 PM Nov 30th, 2009 from web

Dateline Dubai: this is not rumour, repeat, NOT rumour. As I watch from my office, Burj Dubai being dismantled and sold bit by bit on eBay.
4:03 PM Nov 30th, 2009 from web

Workie needed to help out with drive-by shooting in Detroit. Firearm and business class travel provided.
10:46 AM Dec 1st, 2009 from web

Essential advice from Keef – Wagamama: be warned, people. It's fucking Chinese McDonald's. WITHOUT THE FREE FUCKING TOY.
11:40 AM Dec 2nd, 2009 from web

HR @Meerkat360 – openings for: lab technician, smack dealer, cabin boy, fluffer, zen copywriter
9:18 AM Dec 3rd, 2009 from web

Workie needed for exciting task! More of a 'quest', actually. Involves orks. And a ring. You'll need permission from your mum to be out late.
11:40 AM Dec 3rd, 2009 from web

Keef asks: wtf is a Consumer Experience Architect? Will he build me a conservatory? Or is he just a cunt?

12:30 PM Dec 3rd, 2009 from web

HR @Meerkat360 – opening for replacement Consumer Experience Architect. Applicants must be able to withstand mild abuse.

4:30 PM Dec 3rd, 2009 from web

Workie needed for tricky but ultimately rewarding job. Surgical gloves supplied.

11:03 AM Dec 7th, 2009 from web

Need workie with shovel to bury my other workie. Honestly, what university do you people come from? Where's your fucking stamina?

9:10 AM Dec 9th, 2009 from web

Dotty Pod: Jan new biz review cancelled. DC still snowbound in Finland.

10:12 AM Jan 4th, 2010 from web

Dotty Pod: all mail for DC should be redirected to c/o Santa, The Magical Mysterious Grotto, 1 North Pole, Lapland

11:31 AM Jan 4th, 2010 from web

Keef: story in Metro about homeless guy losing feet to frostbite. Has Sooz been nicking shoes off tramps again?

9:27 AM Jan 5th, 2010 from web

@sjdGaultier – my Cons WERE NOT stolen from tramp. I paid SERIOUS money to PROFESSIONAL 'footwear distresser' to achieve 'lived-in' look

10:07 AM Jan 5th, 2010 from web

Message from DC: snowbound in Lewisham IS NOT the same as snowbound in Lapland. Get your fucking arses into fucking work. You slack fuckers.

9:52 AM Jan 7th, 2010 from web

All-staff FYI from Dotty Pod: I did not email 'skiver list' to DC in Lapland. Please stop sending me hate mail!!

10:17 AM Jan 7th, 2010 from web

Small World
Matt Beaumont

'An extraordinary novel . . . it's like unravelling mysteries
behind the faces you see every day on your journey to work
. . . intriguing and compelling'
Heat

'This excellent and thought-provoking novel explores
how the lives of ordinary people can be connected in
extraordinary ways'
Closer

Small World is the story of **Ali**, who is trying and failing to have
a baby with **Paul**, and who is being stalked by **Marco**, who
employs a babysitter called **Jenka** who wants a nose like
Charlize Theron and who also babysits for **Siobhan**, who is
married to **Dom**, a stand-up comic, who is idolized by **Jaz**, an
Indian waiter, who is almost knocked off his moped by **Keith**, a
sociopathic policeman, who lives with **Pam** who works for
Kate, who has a nanny called **Christie** who inadvertently feeds
ecstasy to three-year-old **Cameron** who is looked after by a
nurse called **Marcia**, whose son **Carlton** is accused of murder-
ing **Kerry**, who is best friends with **Michele** who works for **Ali**,
who is trying and failing to have a baby with **Paul** . . .

'Beaumont's characters strike gold . . . a
page-turner and a triumph'
Daily Express

'Rich and often extremely funny'
The Times

9780552774567